CONVERSATIONS WITH AN
OCTOPUS

REBECCA SMITH

Legend Press Ltd, 51 Gower Street, London, WC1E 6HJ
info@legendtimesgroup.co.uk | www.legendpress.co.uk

Print ISBN 9781915643742
Ebook ISBN 9781915643759
Set in Times.
Cover by Rose Cooper | www.rosecooper.com

Rebecca Smith was born in London and grew up in rural Surrey. She studied History at the University of Southampton and is now a principal teaching fellow in English and Creative Writing there. She is the author of four previous novels for adults, a novel for children, two works of nonfiction and the text for a picture book.

Rebecca is one of Jane Austen's five times great nieces, and *Conversations With An Octopus* takes inspiration from *Sanditon*. She has Indian, English and Scottish heritage and often draws on this in her work.

Follow Rebecca on X
@RMSmithAuthor

and Instagram
@rebeccamarysmith7

For Elsa and Les

Ottersea, South Devon

Things You Might Find in a Rock Pool

In the perpetual battle between gulls and crows, an uneasy truce had been declared. The tide had left something huge and strange on the rocks. Its head lay in a rock pool. Its limbs were cushioned by bladderwrack. Its skin was grazed and swollen, and areas that had been above the water when it floated were now burnt and cracked by the sun and salt. The birds crowded around it, harsh cries signalling their find.

Six o'clock. A middle-aged man in lime Lycra ran along the promenade. He'd hoped to avoid the July heat, but it was already building, despite the early hour. He saw the commotion of birds and the prone figure, jumped down onto the beach and jogged across the sand, shouting and waving his arms to scare away the scavengers. As he got close, he saw that it was much, much too late. He took out his phone and checked how far he'd already run (not wanting to skimp on the morning's session) before he dialled 999.

DI Jim Paddon, whose case this would be, was still asleep in an ordinary terraced house a few streets back from the shore. The wing of steely grey hair that flopped across his forehead gave him the look of an ageing corvid, though his face was kind. The sleigh bed his former girlfriend had chosen was too short, and Jim, at six foot two, couldn't stretch out properly unless he lay diagonally. Now that he always slept alone, this was no longer a problem. Jim was dreaming that Johnny Cash was cooking him eggs for breakfast. They were both wearing long black coats.

'Jim, you have to walk the line,' Johnny Cash said. Dream Jim was hoping that Johnny Cash would start singing, but his phone woke him and the dream evaporated.

Mint Choc Chip

A couple of weeks before that body washed up, Lottie Heywood arrived in Ottersea. It was a sweltering Saturday afternoon. She got off the bus from Exeter St David's at the centre of the town by the floral clock. There was a crowd and the sound of a drum and bells and melodic thwacks of wood striking wood. Uh oh, thought Lottie, Morris dancers. The path ahead was completely blocked with crowds of day-trippers, holidaymakers, and locals watching them. Lottie had a rucksack *and* a large wheelie case. The only way to get past would be to venture to the front of the audience and cross the square where the Morris people were cavorting. Lottie didn't want to risk getting bonked on the head by their appointed Fool with his pig's bladder balloon or be exhorted to dance by a sinister hobbyhorse figure. She decided to sit on the seawall for a while. She'd managed to catch an earlier-than-expected train so wasn't worried about inconveniencing her Aunt Cass, who was very chilled anyway.

Lottie sat with her back to the hideous bronze sculpture, *The Wild Swimmers*, a work by Ottersea's most famous son, Si Jacks, the least celebrated of the YBAs. *The Wild Swimmers* cast their shadows over the sea pool where Lottie's aunt and her WI friends swam every day. The largest of the bronze figures was a female, bending over with a huge, dimpled bottom in the air; next to her was one who was not only pregnant, but breastfeeding what looked like a very newborn baby; the only male got to hold a surfboard to maintain his dignity, and there were two children who just looked cold. The sculpture was on generous loan from the artist, intended, he said to "really put Ottersea on the map", Ottersea's Domesday Book listing and long history being insufficient. People had written to the local paper asking for a nicer sculpture, perhaps of a Tommy from the First World War, or something like a dolphin. One letter writer wished for a nice shell like the Maggi Hambling one at Aldeburgh. During storms, waves crashed onto *The Wild Swimmers*. Anyone who had ever looked after a baby pitied the figure who never got to put her baby down. To be out there in all weathers, pregnant, breastfeeding, naked, would be enough to make anyone turn to murder.

Although she had her back to it, Lottie was still aware of the sculpture's presence. She watched the Morris troupe for a while – as much as she could through the crowd – and then swung around and looked out to sea instead. She was here for the whole summer to do an internship at the Oceanworld Centre, but also, she hoped, to walk on the beach, hang out with her favourite aunt, and swim every day.

Just when she thought the Morris troupe were done, another drum started, and the cries of the gulls were joined by male voices. The Ottersea Shanty Crew began to sing. It was a song about Ottersea in the time of Covid and had rhymes of mask and hipflask, virus and bus, and loo paper and caper.

After a few more songs, the crowd was still thick but the entrance to Flakies Ice Cream Parlour became visible on the other side of the square. Lottie glanced at her watch, a sea-green Swatch with a thin silicone strap that looped twice around her wrist: 4pm. Her aunt wasn't expecting her for a little while yet. Ice cream beckoned.

There were two girls behind the counter. Lottie saw at once that they were sisters. They had identical long black plaits reaching down their backs and the same bright brown eyes and high cheekbones. Lottie joined the queue – relieved that there was one as it would give her time to choose from the dozens of flavours and many types of cone. There were also sundaes and waffles and pancakes – all served with cream, ice cream or both. Lottie still hadn't decided by the time her turn came, but found herself saying, 'A scoop of mint choc chip and one of chocolate brownie in a chocolate cone.'

'I could tell you were a mint-choc-chip girl,' said the older of the two sisters. 'Eat in or take away? Flakie?'

'Eat in, with a flake,' said Lottie. If she worked here, she would be constantly making jokes to herself about being a bit flaky. She took her cone in one hand and pulled her wheelie case with the other. There were empty booths at the back of the café. She stashed her case under a table and slid onto a red vinyl banquette. A picture of "Jail House Rock" era Elvis hung above her table in a cheap black plastic frame. Dionne Warwick was singing "I'll Never Fall In Love Again". Too right, thought Lottie. She was glad to be away from university in Southampton and a fellow oceanography student who she'd thought she had a thing with. It had turned out that the thing wasn't a thing at all, and now he was moving in with some girl who played ice hockey. Other images of stars from the fifties and sixties and mirrors in gold frames filled the walls. She resolved to sit below Doris Day in her rolled-up jeans next time. The ice cream was delicious.

Lottie got up to go. The little girl was now clearing and wiping tables, while a teenage boy moving in a miasma of weed started to half-heartedly push a broom around. Lottie left a pound coin as a tip, hoping that the little girl would be the one to find it. As she passed the counter a woman who must be the girls' mother came in through the café door.

'Nice walk, Mum? Any cooler up on the cliffs? You know when Dad's back?' the older girl asked her.

'It was nice up there. I don't know when he's back,' the mother replied. 'I think he's gone to Reading'. "Gone to Reading" sounded like a euphemism.

Back outside, the crowds had thinned and Lottie could

pull her case to Teapot Paradise without incident, although by the time she arrived the cooling benefits of the ice cream had completely evaporated.

'Lottie! You're here! God, isn't it hot? Would you like some iced tea?' cried Aunt Cass, coming out from behind the counter and giving her niece a hug. People could easily tell that Cass and Lottie were related and would have guessed they were mother and daughter before aunt and niece, even if they weren't both wearing stripy tops. Cass's once blonde curls were now silvery white. Today they were piled high on her head and she was wearing baggy blue linen dungarees over her stripes. Lottie's own curls and skin were darker than her maternal aunt's thanks to her Indian grandmother on her father's side.

Dusting the teapots was the only rent Lottie would have to pay, that and working in the café when she wasn't at her internship. She had a few days before that started; it would be nice to hang out with Cass. There were hundreds of teapots on dressers and pine shelves around the café. They took many forms – animals, famous buildings, members of the royal family, film stars, cottages, cupcakes. Lottie was sad to see that the most hideous one of all, a Nigel Farage, was still there, lurking between a corgi whose snout was the spout and a Sherlock Holmes. She knew Cass would never have bought Nigel Farage. Her friends in the WI gave her their charity shop finds or brought them back from holidays for her.

Lottie took her bags through the 'staff only' door and lugged them up to the attic bedroom which would be hers for the summer. Cass had left the skylight window open and there was a bit of a breeze, but it was still sweltering. Back in the café, she saw that Cass had let her staff go home already. She sat behind the counter with her aunt and drank her iced tea. There was just one couple left, and some women in their early thirties who were all wearing dungaree shorts. One whose were patterned with sunflowers came up to the counter to pay.

'That was lovely,' said the woman. She paid with her

contactless card but still put a two-pound coin in the tips jar. Cass smiled and said thanks. 'Actually, I wondered, I saw you have a noticeboard and a leaflets rack – could you take some of ours?' The woman pulled a brown envelope out of her rucksack and put a wad of shiny black and red leaflets down on the counter.

'Rage Room,' said Cass. 'Oh, I read about these. I didn't know there was one in Exeter.'

'We're new,' said the woman. 'Ten per cent off with the leaflet.'

'Your WI could go on a trip,' said Lottie.

'Oh, you're in the WI – we'd be perfect for you. Women have so much rage, suppressed rage. We do group bookings and parties,' said the woman. 'People do their smashing by themselves – we just block out as many sessions as you need.'

'Hmm,' said Cass, who didn't look full of rage, though she must be keen for her last customers to leave.

'Scratch the surface of any woman, and you'll find rage,' said the woman.

'You're welcome to leave some leaflets,' said Cass, 'and I'll put one on the noticeboard.'

'Cheers,' said the woman, 'And I'll give you five stars on TripAdvisor – those were great scones.'

'Do you have much rage?' Lottie asked, after the women had gone.

'Do you?' asked Cass.

'Anger,' said Lottie. 'Fury – about pollution, plastics, war – you know…' she trailed off, thinking "I'll Never Fall in Love Again".

'Most of mine has probably turned to quiet despair, though that's not good.'

'You always seem like a very Zen aunty,' said Lottie.

'Some of the other WI members, though,' said Cass, 'I think there's a lot of rage locked up there. They could do with letting some of it out.'

Innovative Treatment for Hair Loss

Diana Parks, Chair of Ottersea WI and owner of Marine Heaven Health and Beauty, was waiting for her last client of the day. The string of Indian bells and shells tinkled as he came in: Raj Sumal, local landlord and owner of Flakies. He had been in a couple of days before to have a patch test for hair restoration treatment. She was glad to see he had returned – if he signed up for the whole course it would be lucrative.

'Ah, Mr Sumal, how are you?'

'Fine,' he said, looking around. 'I thought you'd have some younger girls working here too. Just you, is it?'

'I'm the proprietor,' said Diana, wanting to add that she was hardly old and definitely younger than him. 'My assistant is on holiday. So, Mr Sumal, any reaction to the patch test?'

'Nah.' He showed her his forearm. Some reddish dots were visible, but no inflammation.

'That looks absolutely fine,' said Diana, though the dots looked redder and more stubborn than usual. 'Come on through to the treatment room. I'll give you a minute. You can put your clothes on the chair, just keep your boxers on – you're having a massage too, aren't you? When you're ready, lie down on the couch and you can cover yourself up with this towel. I'll be back in a moment.' She indicated the treatment couch where a pristine blue and white striped towel was waiting. When she went back in he was lying down.

'I'll start with your scalp stimulation,' she said. 'We'll do that first and then you can really relax. The back, neck and shoulders massage complements the regrowth treatment. Some hair loss and thinning is associated with stress.'

'So, you do all the treatments, do you?' he asked.

'The more complex and highly-skilled ones, Mr Sumal,' said Diana. Honestly, she thought, what had he been hoping for? It was perfectly clear from the front of house, website and treatments menu what sort of place Marine Heaven was.

'OK. And you can call me Raj,' he said. If I wanted to, thought Diana. It took everything she had to be polite to some clients. 'Nice and cool in here.' She had the silent fan going, but the treatment room benefitted from being at the back of the building and sheltered from any direct sunlight. Doing the massages was hot work, though, especially when it was twenty-seven degrees outside. Impossible not to feel irritable.

'I'm going to gently work this numbing cream into your scalp as the needling can be a little uncomfortable. That will be followed by the regrowth oil applied with an Indian head massage technique, then I'll be using the dermaroller. If you want me to stop at any time, just say. When hair thins, it isn't that it just falls out and doesn't regrow – the problem is that the pores, where each hair follicle comes from, close up. They become too tight. With this specially developed oil and the work of the dermaroller, we can encourage the pores to open wider, and with regular treatments, stay open so that the hair grows back thicker and stronger.'

'Sounds good,' he said.

'This preparation is gentle but highly effective. It has four key ingredients.' She paused and squinted at the label to check she was going to talk him through the right ones. 'The activating ingredient is amla oil, which stimulates the blood circulation, so your head will feel slightly warm, but not unpleasantly. It also contains organic green coffee bean tincture, cold-pressed. Caffeine's a stimulant, of course, not just as a drink, but for encouraging hair regrowth. Then brahmi oil, used in India for centuries to toughen and strengthen hair follicles. Just the name tells you it's a very fine ingredient used by the finest people.' She paused again, wondering if that sounded like an endorsement of the caste system, but he had his eyes closed already and didn't react. He probably wasn't listening. He was wearing the metal bracelet of Sikhs around his chunky wrist. She was stressing the ingredients as the stuff was expensive and she didn't want him to think it was just any old lavender oil. Upselling began the moment a customer walked through the door. 'Another key ingredient is onion oil...'

'Onion oil? I'm going to stink of onions?' he said, opening his eyes and sitting up.

'Not at all,' she said. 'The pleasant perfumes of the other oils combine to denature the onion scent compounds, but not their properties.' She'd always been good at adlibbing. 'Here—' she put a dab on a cottonwool ball and wafted it near his nose. She didn't mention his already somewhat oniony breath. She should have put on a face mask as though that were still SOP.

'OK, that's not too bad,' he said, lying back. She put the cotton wool ball down and gently placed her fingertips on one of his shoulders. It was amazing how you could control people like this – the slightest touch and they would move in the way you intended – sit up, lie down, move their head to one side or another – she enjoyed how biddable, how malleable, people were.

'Close your eyes, please. I'm going to place a muslin cloth over your face so that none of the oil goes in your eyes.' He obeyed and she sprayed a fog of it into his hair and got to work, pressing and kneading in all the right places. He relaxed and she thought he might fall asleep – clients often did.

'OK,' she said, after a while, 'Now the dermarolling isn't as nice, but think of it as stimulating. The roller is covered by titanium alloy micro-needles, completely sterile, each one less than half a millimetre wide. They activate collagen production and hair regrowth by puncturing the skin in many places and allowing the oils to penetrate to the follicles. It may feel rather odd – you'll feel it more than with the patch test – but that shows it's working.'

He winced slightly as the roller first made contact – what a wimp. He said nothing and she pressed on, working methodically across his scalp, longitudinally and then laterally.

'I can see where your hairline would have been. I'll work down to that.' Where he now had no hair, the pinpricks of the roller showed more. It left some minor bleeding in its wake. 'There,' she said, surveying her work, 'all done. Now you must keep your head covered in the sun for the next forty-eight hours. I saw you had a baseball cap. That will be fine. Now you can really relax into the massage. Loosen your watch so the blood and lymph can flow around your body, and you'll really feel the benefit.' She put the roller aside on her trolley for later sterilisation and washed her hands. 'Have you got to get back to work? It's nice to take the rest of the day off after a massage.'

'I'm the owner of Flakies, the ice cream place, and a property developer, a landlord.'

'Oh, that's interesting,' Diana said automatically. 'Holiday lets?'

'Moving in that direction. Got a portfolio in Reading and a few places here.'

'That's nice. Keep you busy, does it?'

'You can say. Endless problems, maintenance, chasing up the late rents.'

'That must be stressful,' said Diana, making her voice as honeyed as possible.

'Yeah, my son helps me out with the Reading ones, and I go up when I have to. I'll be driving up tomorrow, probably.'

'And you have some nice places here too?' she asked. So many places were becoming holiday lets. She supposed he'd be a part of that, but she kept her voice neutral and sympathetic.

'Locals are more trouble than it's worth,' he said. 'Student lets in Reading are much easier. I've got some places above shops along the high street here. Nothing but trouble.'

'Really?' asked Diana. Clients always went on about their perceived problems. She was getting to work, smoothing his shoulder blades, working around his spine, getting deep into the trapezius on each side.

'Months late at my place above McColl's...' That was her assistant, Kayleigh's place, Diana realised. And just a few days ago Kayleigh had been crying in the kitchen about her complete shit of a landlord who'd been pressuring her, wanting sex for rent arrears. She'd offered an advance on her wages, but that hadn't been necessary after Kayleigh's nan had bailed her out and then taken her off on holiday.

'Ow,' said Raj, and Diana realised she was being too firm. She reduced the pressure. She decided not to say anything – Kayleigh might not want her to – but if this man was going to continue the treatments, she'd ensure that Kayleigh was never around. She eyed her dermaroller and wished she'd pressed harder with that. What a total shit this man must be. He might own Flakies, but she couldn't imagine him actually working there. It wasn't her sort of place – all that dairy and sugar – but she knew it was busy in the season. And with rental properties, he must be loaded. She was too hot. It was as though the heatwave was inside her.

Raj Sumal was pleased that nobody knew where he was. He'd read about the treatment online, then nipped in for the patch test and to book his first treatment. He wasn't going to let anyone know he was bothered about the hair loss. And the massage could just be added to the long list of things that Sukhi didn't know about. The woman's strong fingers were doing wonders; she was probably better than a young girl would've been. The oil she was using was like one of their ice cream syrups – vanilla with orange, and something flowery that he didn't know the name of.

'Your shoulders are still a bit tense,' the woman said, pressing harder, using her knuckles. 'There.' Raj felt the knots dissolve. There was some sort of watery music playing with the sound of gentle waves breaking on a stony beach. There were gulls too, then he realised that those were just the ones outside. Lying on his front with his face poking through the hole in the couch made him feel like someone in history waiting to get their head chopped off.

The woman had finished working on his shoulders and neck now, and was rubbing his back in long smooth sweeps, over his shoulder blades and down his spine. God, she was good at this. It was lucky he was lying on his front – but she'd be used to that natural reaction from any male.

'How about a happy ending?' he asked. He kept his eyes tight shut, picturing her hands slick with the oil and ready for him. The woman said nothing for a moment, just carried on working on his back. Ever since he'd watched *The Sopranos* Raj had known, for sure, that having a belly wasn't a turn-off for women. This woman must be feeling it too. *And* he didn't wear those old-man white vests like Tony Soprano.

'A happy ending?' she said, very slowly and softly. God, she was almost purring. She worked her way back up to his shoulders and neck again. 'There we are now,' she said. 'You just lie there for a few minutes. Take your time. And I'll see you out the front when you're ready.' She stepped away from the couch.

'No happy ending?'

'That isn't on our list of treatments.'

'Aw, go on,' he groaned. 'It's my wife, she doesn't understand me. She's not like you, so good with your hands.'

Diana knew his wife by sight, and she *had* noticed her hands when she and Arthur had bought ices through the window – well, he'd had two scoops of chocolate in a chocolate cone, she'd had a single scoop of lemon sorbet which she'd later regretted. His wife's hands had looked chapped and wintery, even though it had been summer. Later, when they'd been walking home, she'd glanced in again and seen his wife mopping the floor whilst this guy sat out the front and shouted into his phone. Diana glanced at his clothes – clearly nicely ironed.

'Your wife doesn't understand you?' she said.

'She has no idea…' He raised his head, turned, and winked at her. Diana imagined a school rounders bat in her right hand, the weight of it, swinging it at his fat head.

'Clearly not,' said Diana. He turned onto his back, letting the towel slip to the floor. His hideous *member* was erect, bobbing at her through the opening of his boxer shorts.

'Your shoulders do still look a bit stiff,' said Diana. She placed her strong fingers on his shoulders again and began to massage. He relaxed back into the table. The vile thing was even bigger now.

'I do have rules for how we do this,' said Diana. 'Just lie back and relax.' She took two stretchy white headbands (the ones for customers having facials) from the drawer beside her. She slipped one around each of his wrists, twisted them, then looped them around the rails of the couch. 'Just to keep you out of any mischief,' she said, smiling. She took two more and did the same to his ankles. 'Now for a nice, fresh towel,' she said. She tore off a large piece of the clingfilm she used for moisturising wraps, spread it across a clean towel, then pressed that hard onto his face. He struggled, of course, but the headbands held firm. It only took a few minutes.

When he had stopped moving and she was sure he wasn't bluffing, she lifted the towel and put it so that she didn't have to look at his lower half. The clingfilm was damp with his slobber. She screwed it up and put it in the bin and washed her hands. She stood and regarded him for a while. He definitely wasn't breathing which was lucky – he might leave a one-star review on Google or TripAdvisor. It seemed sensible to leave the headbands so that he was still tethered to the couch. In films, the villain was never dead the first time. She didn't want him to rise up and attack her.

'I'll just leave you here to relax for a few minutes,' she said, the words she used for every client. 'You can get dressed and come on through whenever you're ready.'

She left the music playing, as always, dimmed the lights even more, and went into the front of the shop. Fortunately, there were no more clients booked that day. It was past 5pm already. She turned the sign to 'closed' and drew the blinds. She considered making herself a cup of coffee, but she never drank coffee after 2pm and didn't want to risk a sleepless night. It would have to be fennel tea. She sat behind the desk and sipped it and thought about what to do.

Perhaps she should rip her overall and say that he had attacked her and that it had been self-defence, but that might not stand up to scrutiny. Or she could say that he had had a heart attack during treatment – but there would be a post-mortem. He might well have had a heart attack too, but they'd probably be able to tell he'd suffocated. Even if she could pass it off as accidental suffocation, that would be terrible publicity.

No, it would be best to just get rid of him as quickly as possible. She put out all the lights and went into the little kitchen at the back. It had no windows. Nobody would know she was there. She hoped the boiling weather would stop rigor mortis from setting in and make him easier to move. She had no idea how long rigor mortis took to arrive, and she wasn't stupid enough to google anything like that. Instead she sat and made fantasy lists on cultbeauty.com and read on the kindle app on her phone. She was halfway through a Patricia Highsmith. She ate an apple and some sourdough crackers which were all she had in the kitchen. Eventually she made herself a mat of clean towels (the fluffiest cotton ones) and lay down for a bit. It was so annoying that she couldn't use the treatment couch herself. She would have to wait until everything, all the pubs and restaurants, had closed.

When she woke it was almost 2am. She went back into the treatment room. He hadn't moved. He was definitely dead. She hoped that he wouldn't have some sort of bowel evacuation before she could get rid of him – the cost of replacing the towels would be horrendous, apart from anything else. She had blue and white striped ones with a border of shells – really distinctive so that clients couldn't put them in their bags and then claim they were their own. The company did free monogramming, so she'd had "Marine Heaven Health and Beauty" embroidered on them. Unfortunately, when she'd mistakenly ordered some microfibre rather than cotton ones, she hadn't been able to return them. She wouldn't make that mistake again.

Now, she put on some disposable gloves, even though she knew her DNA might be all over him from the massage. She dressed him in his clothes – all of them. His jacket was heavy with car keys and his wallet, and she put his phone in there too. Oh God, his phone. That would track him. She wondered about smashing it and trying to destroy its innards, but it would already have pinned his location as here anyway. The salon was small compared to other businesses nearby. The betting shop at the top of the lane and the other places on the high street were much bigger. Fingers crossed the location wouldn't be that accurate. Probably best just to get him out of here. If she managed to tip him into the sea, perhaps that would destroy it – but all the data – who knew? And his car? Where had he parked? The salon had no dedicated parking space for clients, just one for her in the yard with the bins. Was there CCTV on Ottersea's backstreets and lanes? She had no idea. She would take him out through the back to where her own car was parked and hope. It was lucky she'd brought the car that day – she only did if she had plans or shopping that necessitated it after work.

She kicked each of the four levers that released the wheels on the couch and unlocked the back door. The moon was close to full making it quite bright. There were no lights in the yard and the lines of coloured bulbs that were strung across the nearby streets were switched off. There might still be people about – teenagers sitting around on the beach smoking and drinking and desperate parents out pushing buggies that contained children who wouldn't sleep. She considered ringing Arthur to help, but he was such a ninny and not to be trusted.

She unlocked the car and opened one of the rear passenger doors as far as it would go. This seemed better than putting him in the boot – it was less like being someone about to dispose of a body. One of Arthur's huge navy blue Oceanworld hoodies was on the backseat. She put it on as a disguise. She spread some binbags, a couple of salon couch covers, then some of the blue and white microfibre towels across the seat to try to prevent any DNA or anything to do with him remaining in her car. Then she pushed the treatment couch as close to the back door as it would go and managed to drag him into the car. She had to go around the other side to heave him in. It was lucky that he wasn't bigger. He was only about five foot five – a good few inches shorter than her.

She locked the car and went back into the salon to check around and leave everything ready for the next day. It must be because they were male that most killers got caught. They just didn't know how to tidy up properly.

Soon she was driving out of the yard. Tipping him off the harbour wall would have been easiest; she could have backed the car right up to the edge, but he would likely just bob about there and be found quickly, plus there might be fishermen and CCTV. She drove out of town towards the cliffs. She kept below the speed limit, trying to drive in as normal a way as possible, careful but casual, thinking "act natural, act natural". She met a few cars and taxis on the way. A motorbike overtook her. She resisted the urge to speed up to show the guy what her car could do. Soon she reached the Red Cliffs Nature Reserve. It seemed best to park in as normal a way as possible in case anybody else arrived, although if they were on a similar mission they could, presumably, just nod and both go about their business. Perhaps this happened all the time. She spread a couch cover on the ground and pulled him out of the car onto it. She got a big towel and kind of tucked it around him – she didn't want him leaving hairs or whatever for a sniffer dog to find. She spread another couch cover over the top of him and put another smaller towel on top of the whole lot to try to keep it all together.

The quickest way to the cliff edge was along the path through the woods. Dragging him was unbelievably hard. She had to keep stopping to catch her breath. She was so hot she gave up wearing the hood; there was nobody about anyway. An owl hooted at her and nocturnal things rustled on either side of the path, but there were no other people. The moon was so bright that she could see perfectly well. Eventually she made it through the wood and out onto the cliff tops. There was a fence near the edge. She crawled under it – there was a good few feet between it and the actual drop, but the grass was rough and tufty and the ground uneven. It would be all too easy to go over herself. She managed to drag him under the fence. She could see that the tide wasn't in – he might not even hit the water.

She started rolling him towards the edge – then he was gone. The smallest towel went with him. Bugger. She hadn't intended that, but at least she hadn't lost either of the couch covers – she didn't have that many spare. There was no sound other than the waves breaking below and the wind in the grass around her. She commando-crawled right to the edge herself and peered over. Bits of cliff stuck out; there might be a shelf that he'd landed on lower down, one that she couldn't see. He would lie there until somebody spotted him. She pictured him surrounded by pink stars of thrift, and the nests of irritable gulls. Or perhaps he had fallen all the way. She would just have to hope. She gathered the covers and towels, slithered back under the fence, hurried back to the car, and drove home.

The house was in darkness. It was almost 3am. She tiptoed

upstairs, though Arthur was such a big kid – dozy even when he was awake – he would probably sleep through anything. She brushed her hair, cleansed and toned. The sound of the waves was still there in her head. She applied moisturiser with the all-important upward-sweeping motion over her neck and cheeks and got into bed. She hoped the sea had taken him and that he would never, ever be found.

When Diana woke, she wondered if she had imagined the whole thing, but she had left her clothes (including Arthur's hoodie) on the floor – something she would never normally do – and they were dirty, particularly the knees of her trousers, which also had grass stains. She hadn't had those on her clothes for decades. Marine Heaven opened at ten. She shoved the clothes in the washing machine with a load of bedding. The shoes she'd been wearing were filthy from the nature reserve. It would be easiest just to throw them away. The couch covers and towels from the night before were there on the back seat of the car on top of the bin bags. She should have hidden them in the boot. They were filthy too. She shoved them into an old Bag for Life with the shoes so that she could carry them into the salon in as nonchalant a way as possible and deal with them later. It was annoying that she'd have to hoover the interior of the car as well, and on another boiling day.

When she arrived at Marine Heaven, she realised how utterly exhausted she was. She put the coffee machine on. With caffeine, all shall be well, and all shall be well, and all manner of things shall be well. Time to give the treatment room a quick once-over.

She put a new cover on the couch and put out clean towels. She thought she could smell the ghost of his sweat. Ha! It would be almost funny if he haunted her. What a dull and predictable ghost he would be. She was generous with the fig room spray, just in case anyone else could smell it. She fetched the soft broom from the cupboard to give the whole place a quick sweep – normally Kayleigh would be doing that, but she'd let her have two weeks off to go away with her granny.

The broom found it. His so-called smart watch. She remembered he'd kept it on but loosened it for the massage, so it must have dropped off when she'd wheeled him out. It was clearly still functioning, even without its owner. She put on some gloves to pick it up. Did these things need charging to keep functioning or just have a battery like regular watches? She had no idea. What an utterly ridiculous and self-indulgent gadget it was. She had to get rid of it. Now, if they found his body without it, that would be significant, possibly even helpful if they thought he'd been robbed. She did it up so that it was neater, wrapped it in a muslin cloth and put it in her pocket. She checked the diary – she had a good forty minutes before the first client arrived.

Diana walked briskly down to the seafront and along the promenade – *no running, act natural.* When the promenade met the harbour she slowed down, as though she was just out for a nice morning stroll. The tide was in, which was good. There were lots of people about – walkers and runners and people with dogs and to do with boats. She followed the harbour wall until she was above where the water was always deep. She checked that nobody was nearby, took the watch out of her pocket, and ever so casually leant over the wall as though she was looking at some fish below. It sank. Time to get back to the salon. She bought some oat milk and some cows' milk in the little Waitrose. Hardly any of her clients took cows' milk now but she had to have it for the occasional one who did. She was back with time to spare, pleased that buying milk had given her a mission – an everyday reason in case she had been caught on CCTV. She put on a Chopin nocturne, and it was as though none of it had happened.

Eight Arms, Three Hearts

Lottie heard the puffins long before she saw them. The Oceanworld Centre was at the end of the promenade, but you could see its aviary netting from anywhere along the seafront. That must be for the rescues, she thought, picturing herself nursing a young gull back to health and freedom. She had been there many times when she'd been little and visiting Aunt Cass, but not for a few years. Then she had probably been too excited about the under-the-sea parts to look at any birds. There had been seahorses and a glass tank of jellyfish, illuminated and sparkling, so beautiful that she'd asked her parents if it was real.

She arrived at the Oceanworld Centre at 8am as instructed. It didn't open until 10, so she hoped she'd be able to meet the creatures before the public were admitted. She knocked on the huge glass doors, but there was no sign of life – human or marine – inside. She could see the reception counter and turnstiles and lots of jolly images of sea creatures along with a thing for kids to poke their heads through so that they could have their photos taken with the body of a shark or octopus. Nobody came. She walked around the side to see if there was a staff entrance. There was. She rang the bell and waited.

The door was opened by a woman dressed in shorts and a pale blue T-shirt with the centre's logo. Her thick grey hair was in a ponytail. The pockets of her green cargo shorts bulged with Useful Things. Lottie read her name badge: Helen, Centre Manager – the woman she'd been emailing with.

'You must be Charlotte,' the woman said, extending a slightly damp hand. Lottie wondered which tank it had just been in.

'Hi – it's Lottie. Thank you. I'm really excited to be starting.'

'I'm Helen. And you're with us for the whole summer?'

'Yes, please,' said Lottie.

'Well, come through and I'll get Arthur to show you round. He's probably with Jane – he usually is.'

Helen was a fast walker. They turned a corner and there was a large tank on a platform with a label: *Common Octopus (Octopus Vulgaris). This is Jane our common octopus. The common octopus is found around the world. The waters off the south coast of the UK are their northernmost habitat. The common octopus is extremely intelligent...*

'Here's Jane,' said Helen. 'And Arthur.' The person who was Arthur turned his head slightly and smiled. He was tall with curly golden-brown hair, the colour of oarweed. He had both arms in the tank and, as Lottie drew closer, she saw that the octopus had two of her arms entwined with his, and that his were tanned and freckly, as though they had been fashioned from shingle. The Oceanworld T-shirt he was wearing was turquoise and faded – he must have been here a long time. The octopus flushed from pale rose to dark sand at her approach. Lottie stood still, not wanting to startle her, knowing that the octopus would be aware of her presence already even though she couldn't yet feel or taste her.

'Arthur, this is Lottie, our new intern. Lottie, you'll be shadowing Arthur today, though we may need you in the puffin in the afternoon.'

'Oh, I'd love that,' said Lottie, impressed that she would be feeding puffins straight away – she'd expected sweeping, hosing down, and photocopying at first. 'I've always wanted to work with puffins.'

'No,' said Helen. 'In the puffin *suit*. Out the front, greeting visitors and giving out leaflets to passers-by.'

'And getting punched in the fat furry belly by five-year olds,' added Arthur.

'Ah, OK,' said Lottie smiling.

'It's an important role,' said Helen, 'you'll be the first member of staff visitors meet. And there's a strong correlation between having someone in the suit out-front and sales of fluffies in the gift shop.'

'Cool,' said Lottie.

Arthur gently untangled his arms from Jane's and shut the hatch in the lid of the tank. There were big clips at the side. He snapped them shut and put two bricks on top of it.

'She could escape from anything,' he said.

Lottie went closer. Jane did a slow dance and kept watching them.

'How old is she?'

'About eighteen months. We've had her for over a year, so she's quite old for an octopus. She's really friendly if she likes you,' he said.

'She hates me,' said Helen. 'I don't know why.'

'Probably your smell,' said Arthur. 'She doesn't like smokers.'

'I'm a vaper,' said Helen, laughing. 'Well, most of the time.'

'She can tell everything,' said Arthur.

'Nine brains, three hearts, blue blood,' said Lottie. He smiled back at her approvingly, and Lottie noticed the sea-green of his eyes.

'Though the brains in each arm seem mostly concerned with movement,' he said.

'I know, but it's hard to imagine what being an octopus is like – how different their modes of thought must be – which parts are conscious – the colour changing, for instance, I'd love to know more about that.' Arthur nodded.

'It makes our just one brain seem a bit pathetic,' he said.

Lottie and Arthur stood and watched Jane for a while. Jane watched them and then with a swoosh, folded herself up like an umbrella and shot across the tank to her den – a construction of faux rocks. She changed colour and texture again, almost instantly matching the weird shades of sandy mustard and green that the fibreglass rocks had been painted. Then with one arm she picked up a large clam shell and positioned it on her head like a hat.

'She often does that when we're getting ready to open,' said Arthur. 'Some staff wear blue baseball caps, but they're optional.'

'I'm glad they're optional,' said Lottie, 'I'm not really a baseball-cap person.' Arthur said nothing, as he was still watching Jane.

'I don't think she is either,' said Arthur. 'I think she's mocking us for wearing them. And she hasn't even seen the puffin suit. Anyway, better get on.' Lottie looked around for Helen and realised that she had gone without her noticing.

'I'll show you round,' said Arthur. 'We'll go back to the entrance.' He led the way.

'OK, so they come in here, obviously,' he said, resting a hand on one of the little metal gates that swung open to admit visitors, 'and the first thing they see is the moon jellyfish.' The Oceanworld piped music came on – a watery soundtrack designed to make people calmer and less likely to shout, tap on the tanks, or complain on the way out.

'It's so beautiful,' said Lottie, stopping to watch the jellyfish dancing in a circle in their huge glass orb. They were illuminated by lights that cycled through pink-red-purple-blue-green-yellow-white-pink, as though the dancers were wearing magical dresses. 'It's like they've discovered the secret of perpetual motion. I hope they don't realise they're trapped in a tank and aren't in the infinite ocean.'

'They were born here,' said Arthur, 'so at least they don't know what they're missing. The tank can't have any corners, or they'd just get stuck.'

'Hope seeing this makes people stop hating them,' said Lottie. 'Maybe jellyfish will be the next craze, you know, like meercats, sloths, llamas.' Arthur looked perplexed.

'And unicorns,' she added, 'you know – on T-shirts, in ads, everywhere. But not having a face would be a negative for marketing purposes.' She read the label: *Aurelia aurita*. Could there be a more beautiful name? If she had a daughter, she could call her Aurelia, though she'd have to keep the inspiration a secret.

'They live longer than they would in the wild,' said Arthur. 'A year rather than six months, so that's a plus, assuming they aren't bored. Anyway, then most people just follow the arrows. Some of our regulars have a favourite creature and they'll go straight there, but usually it's Rainforest Zone first. The areas aren't in any kind of order. People think the piranhas will be exciting if they haven't seen them before.'

'They don't look that fierce in the tank, do they?' said Lottie. She stood for a moment and watched them.

'People always ask why they don't eat each other, but they're just like regular fish, going around in schools. Regular fish with impressive teeth.'

'Then you come back out of here and into Tropical Lagoon, people will often stay a long time in here – lots to see and they like all the colours – you get lots of people who have tropical fish at home, and often they'll ask you questions. If you don't know an answer, you can radio me. Everyone has a radio.' Lottie hoped they wouldn't be confusing to operate. 'School parties always want to see the rainbow fish, because of the book. And people like the clown fish, of course.'

'What's your favourite?' asked Lottie.

'I do like the Tanganyikan cichlids – the blue and orange seems a bit crazy. And the flowerhorn cichlids cos people are rude about their bulbous heads. I'll show you everything properly as we do the different jobs, feeding regimes, cleaning, the checks and all.' He must be a nice guy to like the flowerhorns, thought Lottie. Nobody would like them best.

They followed the arrows to an outside area – Rock Pool Zone.

'So, this is cool. People get to see local stuff and they

can touch some things. There's always a member of staff or two here supervising. We've got starfish, anemones, different crabs, various seaweeds, different shellfish. But watch out for the water – it's on a timer so every four minutes it flows out over those rocks and people's feet get soaked.' He introduced her to some of the other staff who were there already, checking on the creatures.

'Then it's through this tunnel…' They went back inside and underground to a blue and green world. Lemon sharks and smaller fish and turtles swam above and around them. 'Feeding the turtles is one of the best jobs – they have vegetables – tons of them. They like iceberg lettuces. See that one with the funny shaped shell? Her name's Humpy. She was probably hit by a jet ski, but she's doing really well here.'

'She should have another name,' said Lottie, 'if her shell wasn't always that shape. Humpy wouldn't be her real name, if she had one.'

'Ha ha, true,' said Arthur. 'I didn't think of that.' He smiled at her then glanced at his watch. 'Better get on. So, then it's back through here – Reef Zone – corals and so on, and Jane, of course.' There were healthy corals in tanks with fish as well as a depressing display showing what happened if they got bleached or damaged by sun cream. Jane came over to the wall of her tank as Arthur approached.

'I think she really likes you,' said Lottie.

'It's mutual.' He stopped for a moment and gazed at Jane. 'Then outside again, and we have the rescue seals and the otters.'

'So cool,' said Lottie. Here visitors could see the animals swimming from above ground and go back below to watch them through subterranean glass walls.

'And last of all, the puffins. We've got permanent bird flu precautions – you have to walk across this disinfectant mat.' The whole outdoor area had a netting roof attached to the boundary walls of the centre. It had been designed like a mini Snowdon Aviary, with interesting angles and planes.

'Does anyone ever try and climb on it?' asked Lottie. 'It looks tempting.'

'We sometimes get trouble with teenagers, you know, who hang out on the beach at night. But they have to be quite intrepid – the wall's really high on the other side. It's all alarmed at night. If anyone tried that, an alarm would go off and it goes straight to the police, and Helen gets called, or me if they can't get hold of her.'

'I promise not to try,' said Lottie. He looked at her and smiled again.

The Light is Brighter

A new creature was there. This one had eyes the colour of the dark weeds she remembers, the weeds where she hid when they found her and took her. But this creature just gazed, making no sound next to her own creature, the one who brings everything.

She still remembers the creatures who caught her. They scooped her up and put her in a cave with no light, a cave where she could barely move and couldn't see, could only taste the dark walls and the water which was barely enough. The cave moved and she swished and bumped inside it. The night was longer than any other night.

Then she was here. A wall disappeared and there was a light again. Creatures' arms reached in, felt her, gave her food. She tried to get out. The cave closed again. Darkness again. The cave was moved. It opened. She crept out. The light was bright and blue. The water hardly moved. There were no fish, none of her own kind, no weeds to hide in. The water became impenetrable whichever way she went. Her element deceived. Eyes and mouths of the creatures loomed before her, beyond the hardness. Arms appeared, tossed her food. There was a new cave. She went inside.

Parking Tickets and Guano

'We're back!' Kiran called up the stairs. She had collected Nindy from Brownies, leaving their mum to finish clearing up and getting ready for the next day at Flakies. Now Kiran told Nindy to go and watch TV or something.

'Mum, where's Dad?' Kiran watched as her mother loaded more tubs of cookie dough (a huge seller) into the biggest freezer.

'In Reading.'

'Are you sure?'

'Of course I'm sure. He went to Reading on, um, a few days ago.'

'But the car's by the beach. It's covered in seagull poo. We saw it just now. Why didn't he take the car?'

'Of course he took the car. He always takes the car. How could he go to Reading if he didn't take the car?'

'But he didn't take the car. We just saw it. He's got loads of parking tickets.'

'No, he's in Reading.'

'Did he ring you?'

'You know he doesn't ring me much when he goes away.'

'You should ring him.'

'You know he doesn't like me to bother him.'

'I just WhatsApped him. He hasn't been on WhatsApp for days. Didn't you notice?'

'I didn't look. I thought he was in Reading – you know what he's like.'

'Mum, I think something has happened. I messaged Bal. He hasn't seen him, He thought he was here.' Sukhi Sumal began dismantling the big mixer ready for washing. Kiran went over to help and started wiping down the surfaces ready for the next day. 'I think he might have gone, Mum, disappeared. Or something bad has happened.'

'You know what he's like, Kiran. Probably in Premier Inn if your brother's busy.'

'Then why didn't he take the car?'

'It must be somebody else's car.'

'Mum, it's our car, come and see.' Sukhi pulled a face. There was no stopping Kiran when she got an idea in her head.

'I have to finish up here.'

'I'll help you.'

Kiran finished the surfaces and mopped the floor. She and her mother were proud of their five-star hygiene rating – not everywhere in Ottersea could boast that. They knew that ignominy and ruin awaited any business that slipped. The local paper loved a story about rats in a restaurant, particularly one run by perceived immigrants.

Kiran had already locked up downstairs after the part-time staff finished. Flakies closed at 6pm. Kiran had been to Oxford where one of her schoolfriends had gone to university. There were ice cream parlours there that stayed open until midnight, but the atmosphere in the streets was different. She had loved going into somebody else's ice cream parlour and being the one to sit down at a table whilst someone brought her pancakes with blueberries and ice cream. She couldn't help but notice that the tables and floor there were sticky, though, and the place only had three stars.

Kiran found her father's spare car keys and they set off along the seafront, leaving Nindy at home, mesmerised by the TV. The tide was out. There were a few late swimmers, but most people had headed home now or back to their hotels.

The usual people were out with their dogs. Kiran looked at the ground as they walked, not wanting to see ahead to her dad's abandoned car. As she walked she noticed, yet again, how so many old people, particularly the women, wore sandals that were too small for them. They looked about to scrape their dangly toes along the pavement. Perhaps, she thought, feet kept growing as you got old, the way that old people's ears and noses seemed to. Maybe these old people couldn't accept that they now needed bigger shoes. She'd read that people's hair and nails kept growing after they died. The idea made her feel sick. What had happened to her dad? Maybe he would have been back and moved the car. Perhaps she had imagined the whole thing. She looked up. There were lots of parking spaces along the promenade now, so they could see the car from quite a way off.

'See, Mum?' said Kiran when they got close. There were six days' worth of parking tickets and bird mess.

'Where can he be?' Sukhi said, gripping her daughter's arm. They peered into the car and then opened one of the rear doors. His bag was there, hidden on the floor in the back. It contained his laptop and a folder of stuff about the lettings, but not much else.

'This looks bad, Mum,' said Kiran. 'Why would he just abandon the car?'

'He said was he was going out, and when he didn't come back, I thought he must have gone to Reading,' said Sukhi. 'Maybe the car was playing up and he decided to take the train.'

'Without his bag? I think we should tell the police. Say he's a missing person or whatever,' said Kiran.

'Should we bother the police? He wouldn't want us to go to the police.'

'Let's take the car home,' said Kiran.

'You drive,' said Sukhi. They picked off the parking tickets.

'He'll be really cross about these,' said Sukhi. 'Did Nindy see this?'

'She couldn't not, but I just said he must have forgotten

it. She was too busy telling me about her First Aid badge to realise how weird this is.'

The interior of the car smelled hot and slightly of her father and the Boss aftershave he always wore. The engine started first time, but it took a while to get the windscreen clear of guano. Kiran backed slowly out of the space. She had passed her test a few years ago but didn't have her own car, just drove the van that she and her mum used for Flakies stuff.

'Maybe he'll be back when we get home,' said Sukhi.

'Maybe.'

But he wasn't.

'Let's check around,' said Kiran. 'Maybe he left a message that we didn't notice.' But she knew he wouldn't have. Her dad didn't leave messages for them. He just told them what to do and they did it straight away. Now Nindy realised something was wrong, she began to cry, and Kiran could see that her mother was on the point of tears too. 'I'll see what you're meant to do,' she said and googled "missing person". Her mother and sister sat on the sofa. Nindy put her head in her mother's lap and Sukhi stroked her hair.

'Don't worry,' she said. 'It will be OK. He just forgot about the car. He'll be back.' But Nindy kept crying.

Kiran dialled 101. It was answered after many rings.

'Um,' she said, 'my dad has gone missing.'

'Before we start,' said the operator, 'I need to take some details.' The woman sounded kind. She had a northern accent. Kiran guessed something like Newcastle, somewhere far away. She gave the woman her phone number and the address.

'Can I ask how old you are?' the woman said.

'I'm 22,' said Kiran.

'OK,' said the woman. 'We need to check to see if a child has been left alone.'

'My mum's here, and my little sister, but they're really upset.'

'That's fine,' said the woman.

No, it's not, Kiran wanted to say. It's not fine.

'Who would you like to report missing?' the woman asked, as though Kiran might have a choice of people.

'It's my dad. His name's Raj Sumal.'

'Can you spell that for me?'

'It's just like it sounds,' said Kiran, but she spelled it out.

'And how old is your dad?'

'Um…' she turned to her mother. 'How old is Dad?'

'He's forty-six,' said Sukhi.

'He's forty-six,' said Kiran. She answered the woman's other questions – height, build, hair, eye and skin colour.

'Do you know what he was wearing when he went missing?' Kiran pulled a face and turned to her mother.

'What was he wearing, Mum?'

'I think just what he always wears, trousers and a polo shirt, a black one, I think,' said Sukhi. That was all her father ever wore. Did it have a logo? Probably Ralph Lauren – he liked that. And his shoes? Kiran went out into the hall. Her father's smart shoes and least favourite trainers were still there.

'Trainers,' she said. 'White Nike.' Her father bought himself expensive trainers; her mother just wore cheap generic ones. She told the woman on the phone about the abandoned car, the parking tickets, that they thought he had gone to Reading, but now they didn't know. The woman gave her a list of things to do: ring the Premier Inn where he stayed to see if he was there, ring the tenants to see if he had visited them, ring any friends and family who he might be staying with, ring the hospitals near Ottersea and in Reading.

'It's probably a misunderstanding,' the woman said. 'Most people just come back by themselves.'

'I hope he's most people,' said Kiran.

Toast With a Lot of Butter

Arthur was on locking-up duty and Lottie was helping. She was a few days into her internship now and loving every minute. She and Arthur went around the centre together. If somebody needed feeding, he let her do it. Jane shot over to greet them when they approached her tank. They gave her some clams for the night. It seemed a bit strange as clams were an exhibit in their own right elsewhere. They watched as Jane examined them and moved bits that she fancied towards her hidden beak.

They left the building together and set off along the promenade. Before they got to Aunt Cass's café, Arthur slowed.

'I go up here.' He nodded across the green area (you could barely call it a park) to a row of Regency houses in Edinburgh rock colours.

'Wow!' said Lottie, 'You live in one of them?'

'Yeah, it was my parents',' said Arthur, 'but they died when I was a teenager. My sister – she's a bit older than me – we just stayed.'

'Oh. I'm sorry,' said Lottie, 'I mean about your parents.'

He nodded but didn't say anything else.

'Um, well,' said Lottie, 'See you tomorrow, I—'

'Arthur!' came a woman's harsh voice. Lottie turned to see a tall and extremely neat-looking woman coming up the road behind them. She had a posh carrier bag with the unmistakeable shape of a shoebox inside it.

'My sister,' said Arthur.

'Arthur, why are you standing about getting even more freckles?' asked the woman. 'You could ask your friend inside.'

'Er,' said Lottie.

'Hello,' said the woman. 'Diana Parks.' She extended a hand with beautifully manicured orange nails.

'I'm Lottie,' said Lottie. 'I'm working at Oceanworld too.' They shook hands, though Lottie saw the woman look askance at her hands with their short nails. They probably smelled of fish tanks as well.

'Well, bring her inside,' said the woman. 'Come on.' Lottie looked at Arthur. He smiled somewhat sheepishly. They obediently followed Arthur's sister across the green and up the steps of a house that was painted a pale yellow. Up close you could see that the exterior was a bit crumbly – the whole terrace was.

A heavy wooden door with a dolphin knocker opened onto a large hall. The house was clearly inhabited by two very different people. A pair of Arthur's old trainers and some faded blue cotton deck shoes were on one shelf of a shoe rack. On the one above were multiple pairs of expensive-looking shoes and boots for every occasion. Many had heels. There was an Edwardian hat stand with a mirror, its aged silvery glass giving a kind reflection. On it were a blue and white Staffordshire bowl into which Diana dropped her keys, and a jug of fierce-looking sea holly. Lottie guessed it was a No Shoes house as far as Diana was concerned and took off her Vans. Diana put on a pair of red silk Chinese slippers.

'Shoes, Arthur. Then you can make the tea,' said Diana. 'I'll be down when I've had my shower.' Lottie watched her disappear up the wide staircase. She wondered if she should offer to leave as Arthur hadn't actually invited her in, but doing so would acknowledge that his sister bossed him about, even though she clearly did.

'Um, the kitchen's this way,' he said. Lottie followed him

down a hall decorated with watercolour seascapes and views of the town. She stopped to look at one.

'My mum did those,' said Arthur.

'They're lovely,' said Lottie.

'My favourites are her ones of birds,' said Arthur. 'I've got lots of those in my room.' He blushed slightly, perhaps, thought Lottie, because he had mentioned his bedroom and she might think that he wanted to lure her up there. He clearly didn't.

They went down a few steps to the kitchen. It had a huge old stoneware sink and a big pine table. There were more of his mother's paintings on the wall – this time of fruit and vegetables with butterflies.

'My mum loved painting cabbages, said they were more interesting than roses. That one's called *Musing Among The Vegetables*,' he said, indicating a study of savoy cabbages growing in a garden. The title was there in pale green in the bottom right corner.

'Mrs Dalloway,' said Lottie.

'Huh?'

'It's from *Mrs Dalloway*, Virginia Woolf, you know. Someone says Clarissa Dalloway is "musing among the vegetables" when she is a girl, daydreaming, looking at things in the garden.'

'Oh,' said Arthur. 'I never knew that.'

'My mum's an English teacher,' said Lottie. 'I couldn't decide whether to do English or oceanography. I chose musing among the fishes.'

'Me too, I guess,' said Arthur, 'though I never really wanted to do anything else.' Lottie looked up into his sea-green eyes and smiled. 'What would you like?' he asked, going slightly red. 'I make really good hot chocolate, but I guess it's too hot for that. Diana has every weird tea going, and we have normal tea as well.'

'Just regular tea, no milk,' said Lottie who thought that Diana might be cross if Arthur used up one of her special tea bags, she had seemed so fierce. He opened a cupboard and Lottie saw that two whole shelves were dedicated to herbal teas in pretty boxes. They looked to be in alphabetical order from African Solstice to Yarrow. There was a gap about halfway along the second shelf.

'What's missing?' Lottie asked.

'Um, rosehip. She can't get the organic one she likes at the moment. They have it on Amazon but it's about twenty quid a box there.'

He made them tea in huge Cornishware mugs and Diana's gunpowder in a bone china pot for one.

'I never understood why it was called "bone china",' said Lottie. 'I just couldn't believe anyone would do something as disgusting as make china with bones in it.'

'So many things like that,' said Arthur. 'Whalebone corsets, glue and violin strings made of gut.' Lottie made a being sick face. 'But would you like some toast? I'm pretty good at making toast.'

'Toast would be great,' said Lottie.

He took a big white loaf out of a pine breadbin with a slatted, arched lid that folded into itself. There were two other loaves inside – one of dark German bread and a small expensive-looking sourdough. It didn't seem to occur to Arthur to offer those – they must be Diana's. He cut thick slices that would challenge any toaster and put them under the grill. Lottie suspected that the breadbin had outlived his parents. She remembered lots of people having ones like that when she was little.

'Jam? Marmite? Peanut butter?' He was very generous with the butter, which was in a chipped Cornishware dish, a bit too generous.

'Just plain,' said Lottie. 'It looks so lovely. But I can do mine.' She spread the butter more thinly on her own slices. As he ate his, he added more butter when he got to the crusts and edges.

Diana appeared in a dark green silk gown with a pattern of storks and irises.

'Arthur! Must you *really* have so much butter?'

'Wanna bit?' He offered her his plate with the remaining slice. Diana shuddered.

'No, thank you. And I hope you washed your hands.' She sat down at the table opposite Lottie, who tried to hide her fingernails whilst still eating her toast.

'Honestly, Lottie, he comes home stinking of the aquarium and then eats these huge wodges of toast and butter *every day*, but it looks like you're the same.' She poured her tea. 'Your hands look rather dry, Lottie. I suppose you've been cleaning out the starfish or something? I could give you a mani-pedi if you like. It's 10% off for new customers.' Diana was, Lottie thought, someone who said new people's names a lot to establish dominion over them.

'Make your own dinner tonight, Arthur,' said Diana, 'I've got WI.'

'Oh, my aunt goes to that,' said Lottie. 'I expect you know her, Cass Green.'

'We're both on the committee. Everybody in Ottersea knows everybody else,' said Diana. 'You do look like her, though so much darker.' Lottie sipped her tea and wondered whether being a beautician made Diana think it was acceptable to comment on people's skin tones. 'Have you moved here permanently?'

'I'm just interning at Oceanworld, but I've been here loads, all the time when I was a kid.'

'You don't look much more than a kid now,' said Diana.

'I'm twenty-one,' said Lottie, and then immediately regretted it – retorting made her sound like a child. Wearing one of the centre's T-shirts and having her hair in a plait wasn't the most sophisticated look. Or the navy-blue shorts.

'Well,' said Diana, 'it's nice to meet you. Enjoy your summer, though nothing ever happens here.'

On the way back to Cass's, Lottie sat for a while on the

seawall across from The Blue Lobster restaurant. The tables outside it were full and the air was thick with the braying of rich locals and holidaymakers. The smell of mussels in garlic wafted across to her. She wondered if the mussels on the rocks nearby could smell it too and knew what it signified. She shifted along the wall to a quieter place and watched the birds checking the beach for whatever the day and the tide had left behind. When she got back to Teapot Paradise, Cass was about to leave. Her best friend Caroline Todd (whom Lottie had known her whole life) was there too. They both had crochet bags with large things in-progress inside.

'Want to come and do crochet and make bath bombs with us?' asked Cass.

'Go on,' said Caroline, 'a fun evening with your aunty and her best friends?'

'Um, thanks, but I fancy a night in. And I don't know how to crochet.' The blankets, or whatever they had in their bags, looked beautiful – many squares in greens and blues were already sewn together and they had clearly been sharing wool as they had some sparkly, ethereal greens and mauves in common. 'What are you making?'

'It's a WI project,' said Cass, 'but we can't tell anyone.'

'No,' said Caroline, getting up and giving Lottie a hug. 'And if we told you, we'd have to kill you.'

Blue Lobster, Bath Bomb

Inside The Blue Lobster, the owner, Jeremy Todd (husband of Caroline) was holding court at a table of early diners. The sleeves of his signature blue linen shirt were rolled up to reveal huge, tanned forearms. He assumed people would see the similarity between himself and Rick Stein. He had more hair left than his idol – a thick pelt of grey curls – but as yet just the one restaurant and no book deals or TV shows. Still, there was time. When he stood up you saw that his shirt was half hanging out of his chinos. His impressive belly was almost too much for the ensemble, or any ensemble. 'Never trust a skinny chef,' he always joked. He made his way back across the restaurant, pausing to check on his guests and rest a hefty paw on any bare female shoulder he could find. In the kitchen his sons (who'd been working for him for the last few years) were busy dismembering, steaming, roasting, searing, and occasionally wiping and sweeping. His boys had been in training since they were toddlers and he'd taken them crabbing off the harbour wall. Now they could pretty much run the place, but he remained in charge of the menus and decisions of importance, such as hiring the prettiest waitresses. The most recent recruits, Danuta and Catina, were dodging him between them, while collecting covers and constructing puddings for the earlier diners.

Jeremy whacked Catina's rear as she tried to circumnavigate

him. She'd got used to this and had decided that no response was the best response. She rolled her eyes at Danuta.

'That prick,' Danuta hissed. The evening stretched ahead. She longed for a cigarette, but things were just too busy.

'I didn't know that people's necks could sweat until I worked here,' Catina whispered.

'Only *his* neck,' said Danuta. 'God, he's like an elephant seal. Those ones on documentaries that crush penguins when they roll over.' Catina sniggered, but the sting of Jeremy's flipper remained.

'It's better when Caroline's in.'

When a much younger Jeremy and Caroline had opened The Blue Lobster, Caroline had been there every night, seating the diners, running the bar, totting up the bills, ensuring that everybody left happy. She didn't come in nearly as often now. She had grown to hate the way that when she got home she still moved in a cloud of fish smells. Whichever shampoo, conditioner and shower gel she used, she couldn't get rid of that smell, and Jeremy never took as long as he should in the shower, especially now that he could barely turn round in it.

The hot tub had been a twenty-fifth anniversary present to themselves. The whole family would sometimes soak there after the restaurant closed, steaming and gazing up at the stars with Caroline hoping that the scented oils she added would be enough to cover the worst of the day's odours.

At the Ottersea WI, Caroline, Cass and their friends sat around tables mixing bicarbonate of soda with citric acid. The member running the session had printed out copies of a recipe for them all to use:

Bath Bombs

200g bicarbonate of soda

100g citric acid

50g cornflour

50g Epsom salt (optional)

4 tbsp of your favourite oil (e.g. sunflower, coconut or olive)

½ tsp essential oil, such as orange, lavender or chamomile

a few drops of liquid food colouring

orange peel, lavender or rose petals, to decorate (optional)

biodegradable glitter or sparkles (also optional)

cupcake cases for presentation

'Really,' said Caroline, laughing, 'it's like pre-school, us all sitting here, mixing up glitter and cornflour and all these bits.'

'What flavour are you going to do?' asked Cass, who was sitting next to her. 'I think I'll do vanilla, I always smell of cakes anyway…'

'Lavender,' said Caroline. 'Anything sleep-inducing. But I think I'll skip the glitter – might not be so good for the hot tub.'

'Trouble sleeping still?'

'It's not me – it's Jeremy. Ugh, it's like sleeping with a cartoon character – the snoring, the burping in his sleep – sometimes he chuckles – God knows what he's laughing about – and then he's gulping and gurgling – gastro reflux – disgusting.'

'That must be painful.'

Caroline put an extra slug of lavender oil into her mixture, and then another one. She took a fistful of lavender and camomile flowers from the shared bowls in the middle.

'I think I'll have extra of these. He eats so late at night – and then downs an extra bottle of wine in the tub. There are sudden periods of quiet – I worry he's died – sleep apnoea – so I poke him awake – splutter, splutter – and then he's snoring again, while I lie there waiting for him to stop breathing again.'

'Separate bedrooms?'

'Tempting. Of course, he won't go to the doctor. But he's got a blood pressure check again next week. Chronically sky high.' The mixture was supposedly ready now. Caroline put her nose into the bowl and inhaled deeply. 'I could drift off right here.' She looked at the brown glass bottle of lavender oil. 'Sod it,' she said, and tipped the rest of it in.

The women had brought different things to act as moulds. Caroline used some of her own Lakeland silicone egg poachers. The finished bath bombs looked quite professional, though the Todds' poached eggs would taste of lavender for evermore.

When Caroline got home, Jeremy and the boys were still at the restaurant. Bliss! Soon the hot tub was bubbling. Caroline loved the smell of the warm, wet pine boards that surrounded it and comprised its walls. She took two bath bombs and put one on the little table within reach of the tub and cast the other onto the waters. The night air filled with lavender and chamomile. She hoped it wouldn't attract more than the usual number of mosquitos, perhaps it might even repel them. She should make a citronella one. Toby, her giant labradoodle, came to join her on the decking.

'So sorry, my darling,' she said. She would have loved to let Toby into the tub but the chemicals might be bad for his skin. She would rather share the tub with Toby than Jeremy. She sighed as she let her shoulders sink below the scented waters. Could anyone get closer to heaven than this? She lay back and gazed up at the stars, watching, as what must have been the international space station passed across the skies. Could the crew see her down here in Devon? She raised a hand from the water, feeling like The Lady of the Lake and waved, just in case they could. Oh, why hadn't she married an astronaut or someone in the armed forces – the absolute heaven when they were away for months at a time.

The night-scented stock and evening primrose fragrance from the garden combined with the lavender and chamomile. She lay back and closed her eyes. She might have fallen asleep if Toby hadn't been there, resting his head on the rim of the tub, and butting his head against hers every so often.

Just after midnight, a cloud of fishy garlic smells announced the return of Jeremy and the boys. Toby trotted off to greet them and then returned to rest his head beside hers again. She heard the clink of lager cans being opened and the boys retreating to the den for a game of whatever it was they played before they went to bed. Jeremy plonked a bottle of wine and a tumbler on the table by the remaining bath bomb and climbed in beside her.

'You might have showered first,' she said without opening her eyes. 'Good evening?'

'Excellent.' She opened her eyes and leant over to peck him dutifully on the cheek. He responded by giving her thigh a squeeze under the water then slid his hand up and under her bikini bottom. She pictured fish scales from under his nails floating out into the water, returning to their element. Perhaps if she and Jeremy stayed there long enough they'd be coated in them and turn into merpeople. What would the boys do? Club them to death so they could serve them up at The Blue Lobster or carry them down to the sea and release them into the waves? Maybe she'd be able to persuade them to do that to Jeremy and she could just live in the hot tub forever. She hoped they wouldn't switch off the heating, and that they'd bring her something to eat and drink every so often.

'Fuck,' said Jeremy, interrupting her speculation, 'forgot the corkscrew.'

'I'll get it. I'm practically cooked anyway.'

'Agh, don't go to bed, I haven't seen you all day.' She said nothing but climbed out and slid her wet feet into her pink EVA Birkenstocks. Toby followed her, ever faithful. She gave him a few treats then put the corkscrew on a tray along with a bowl of salted macadamias that would be Jeremy's next request. She still wondered how Jeremy could eat in the hot tub; that would make her feel sick, what with the churning water, even more so today with the heady mix of bath bomb and his fishy odours.

'Coming back in?' he asked. She opened the wine and poured him a glass and then put everything (nuts, wine, corkscrew, glass, bath bomb) together on the little table within his reach. He drained his glass and topped it up himself.

'Sorry love, it's so late.' He just grunted and but took a handful of the macadamias, dripping bubbles from his huge hand into the bowl.

Caroline went upstairs. She expected Toby to follow, but he stayed with Jeremy, resting his head on the rim of the tub, hoping for his own snack. She glanced out of the open window as she closed the bedroom curtains. The hot tub was right below, illuminated like a stage set. Jeremy was topping his glass up again. She watched as he reached for more nuts but found the bowl empty already. His hand found the bath bomb. He picked it up – took a bite – it was in a cupcake case after all – yelled 'What the fuck?' He must have bitten it. She snickered. The night air filled with more lavender. He must have dropped it in the water. Caroline hoped that Toby would come and keep her company, but he was still down there with Jeremy, who really didn't deserve his attentions.

Caroline watched as Toby lay his head on the rim of the tub, next to her husband's. Jeremy didn't seem to stir. He had probably fallen asleep already. If he'd been awake, he would have shoved Toby away or at least muttered something about "effiing dog breath". She really ought to go down there and wake him up rather than letting him cook. Toby got down. Oh good, she thought, maybe he'll come up here instead.

'Toby,' she called out of the window, 'Come on, Toby Todd, good boy.'

Toby looked up at her, then back at the tub. He put his head and paws up on the rim and butted his huge woolly head against Jeremy's. That would wake him, surely. But it didn't. She watched as Jeremy seemed to slide beneath the bubbling waters. She stood there for a while then closed the curtains and got into bed. She switched off the lamp. After a few minutes the familiar weight of her beloved was there beside her. They slept undisturbed.

The next morning found Caroline sitting on the sofa, a balled-up tissue in her hand. Tom had gone down to The Blue Lobster to put a notice on the door and ring the evening's customers to cancel. Ed was there beside her, one arm around her shoulders. There was a uniformed policeman in the armchair that had been Jeremy's and a policewoman sitting in the chair that was really Toby's. Caroline had given her statement.

'So,' the policeman said, 'I'll just read this back to you and then you can sign it.' Caroline nodded.

'"I was in the hot tub when my husband returned from work. I exited said hot tub and fetched him some wine and a dish of peanuts. I then proceeded to go to bed. When I awoke in the morning my husband had not come to bed. I went downstairs and found that he was not in any of the rooms. I proceeded to go outside where I discovered my husband deceased in the hot tub."'

'Yes,' sniffed Caroline, 'that is all true, but it isn't how I said it. And they were macadamias.'

'Which part is, er, incorrect?'

'I didn't say it like that.'

'Mum, that doesn't matter,' Ed said softly.

'I wonder if you should mention Toby,' said Caroline, and then instantly regretted it. What if it emerged that Toby had nudged Jeremy under and the police took him away to be put down? 'I just mean that Toby came upstairs with me. He's a very good dog. He always tries to keep everyone safe.'

'Mum, they don't need to hear about Toby, this is just about Dad,' said Ed.

'You want me to add something?' asked the policeman.

'Just say that Toby came upstairs with me.' The policeman looked down at his pad and added a few words.

'So, Mrs Todd, I'm now going to read your statement again and if you are happy, you can now sign:

'"I was in the hot tub when my husband returned from work. I exited said hot tub and entered the kitchen. I took my husband some wine and a dish of nuts. The dog and me then proceeded to go to bed. When I awoke in the morning my husband had not come to bed. I went downstairs and found that he was not in any of the rooms. I proceeded to go outside where I discovered my husband deceased in the hot tub."'

Caroline began to cry properly.

'I'm very sorry, Mrs Todd, I know this is distressing for you.'

Caroline nodded and sniffed.

'The dog and I,' she said.

'Just sign it, Mum,' said Ed.

She did.

She heard Tom open and then shut the front door in a way that was uncharacteristically gentle. Toby came bounding in and leapt into her lap.

'A dog always knows,' said the policewoman.

'Knows what?' asked Caroline, looking wildly about, but she quickly buried her face in Toby's fur.

'When its owner is upset,' said the policewoman.

'Yes, of course,' said Caroline, 'upset.'

'I'll take your sons' statements now,' said the policeman.

They didn't have much to add. They had gone to bed, fallen asleep, and then been woken by their mother's screams. The three of them had pulled Jeremy out of the hot tub and tried to give him mouth to mouth and get his heart started. They had kept trying until the ambulance got there, but it had been clear that he was dead and that he wasn't coming back.

Postmortem Bingo

The knife was poised, but nobody would be making bouillabaisse. A post-mortem was necessary. Jeremy Todd's death at fifty-eight had been unexpected. The coroner would try to ensure that it wasn't unexplained.

The pathologist had eaten at the Todds' restaurant on several occasions, most recently he'd had stargazy pie, the time before, lobster. Jeremy Todd, bon viveur and restaurateur, was now on the slab and became "the subject".

The subject's blood alcohol level was well over the legal limit. No point now in anyone checking whether he'd driven himself home or not. But it meant that he could easily have passed out and slipped under the water.

The contents of the subject's stomach spoke of a taster menu at The Blue Lobster and a good portion of macadamia nuts. There was nothing to suggest an allergic reaction. The chyme the stomach gave up looked like the contents of a dolphin or shark's stomach on an animal autopsy show, or like the scene in *Jaws* when they cut open the wrong shark and find things like a traffic cone. Amongst the pulverised crab and samphire, the strings of lobster flesh, and the lashings of some creamy sauce, were many chunks of some things like eels. The pathologist held one of the eelish chunks up to the light. The circumference looked too small for an eel. So elvers, perhaps, baby eels. And then he realised – it could be his dream come true. Finally, finally, he could record: *Cause of Death: A Surfeit of Lampreys*. That had been mentioned in one of the first lectures at university and now he'd be the first of his course chums to cross it off their post-mortem bingo card. He paused what he was doing to send them a jubilant WhatsApp message: Surfeit of lampreys ✓

Postmortem Bingo Card

Stepped on End of Garden Rake	Disembowelled by Cassowary, Emu or Ostrich	Running With Scissors	From Laughing	Eagle Drops Tortoise on Head à la Aeschylus
Shark Attack	Squashed by Steamroller	Historical Re-enactment Too Realistic	Stuck Kitchen Implement in Toaster	Stuck in Chimney Whilst Attempting Burglary
Lightning Strike During Imprudent Golfing	Mistook Flower Bulbs for Onions	On Stage in *The Scottish Play*	Falling Coconut	Ignored Quicksand Warnings
Slipped on Banana or Kiwi Fruit Peel	Fighting Over a Bargain	Niagara Falls Stunt Proves Impossible	Stampede of Wild Animals	Warning Sign Needed A Warning Sign
Adjusting own TV Aerial or Satellite Dish	Hoist with Own Petard	Hit by a Hearse	Malfunctioning of Own Rocket-Powered Invention	A Surfeit of Lampreys

A Body

Jim Paddon's phone woke him just after six o'clock.

'We've got a body on the beach, Sarge.'

He was down there in less than ten minutes, but a squad car and a couple of uniforms had beaten him to it. An ambulance was waiting, the paramedics standing about too. Jim hoped they hadn't disturbed anything. The area was taped off – thank you, uniforms.

Jim put on white overalls, gloves and overshoes. They always carried Vicks VapoRub – a quick smear below the nostrils blocked out the worst smells. The body was a bit below the hightide line, face down in a rock pool, not a pretty sight. Jim blinked away the thought of his little nephew Ed peering fascinated into this same pool, just last weekend when he'd come to stay. The deceased's shoes and socks were gone but the guy was still wearing trousers and a short-sleeved shirt.

'Any ID?' Jim asked the copper who was standing guard.

'We haven't touched anything yet.'

'Good, good. Who found him?'

'A jogger – that guy over there.' Jim glanced back up the beach. A man in lime Lycra was sitting on the seawall talking on his phone. Gulls were crying overhead, desperate to partake of the unusual bounty. Carrion crows strutted nearby, determined to live up to their name.

Jim looked at the deceased's feet and ankles. The skin was swollen and wrinkled from immersion. Some parts of the flesh looked nibbled by sea creatures. The parts that must have been above the water line were sunburnt. The hands were in a similar state, and with abrasions where they must have dragged on the bottom or struck rocks. It could be hard to tell, Jim knew, which injuries might have occurred before a body was in the water. He couldn't see the poor guy's face, just the back of his head. He had thinning black hair, all mussed up and full of sand, strands of seaweed and other stuff. He thought of the horrors on wildlife documentaries – seabirds' nests laced with plastic, autopsies of turtles and albatrosses who'd died from eating carrier bags and fishing tackle. He wondered what this postmortem would throw up.

The team came crunching down the beach in their white suits. The body was photographed in situ. Jim watched as it was loaded onto a stretcher. The guy looked Asian or Middle Eastern. Could this be some refugee washed up, some poor bastard who'd been trying to cross the channel and had ended up all the way down here in Devon? Possible but unlikely. The currents, he supposed, would be more likely to take a body east. But he mustn't assume anything or rule anything out. Maybe it was a cliff-jumper. They got a few of those. The clothes – what you could tell anyway – didn't look like a fisherman's or some yachtie's – more like the clothes of some regular urban type.

Jim walked down the beach to where gentle waves were breaking. The sun was already hot on his dark grey hair. He had no idea why "I Walk The Line" was playing in his head. There was still a way to go for the tide to be at its lowest. Jim scanned the sand as he went; it was possible that something else would have been washed up, though he wondered about the likelihood of things belonging to the deceased staying close to him in the sea. There were wave experts, he knew, people who would be able to track things, but then if the body had been in the water a long time – and it hadn't looked fresh – things that floated could end up miles apart.

Baseball Caps

Flakies had a notice on the door saying: "Sorry Closed Due To Family Emergency". The internal blinds were down. They were black, so gave an appearance of mourning blinds, but with the Flakies logo in pink superimposed. Raj Sumal had clearly put lots of money into this place. Could there be some Ottersea Ice Cream War happening, Jim wondered, like the legendary one in Glasgow in the 80s? Could that have been going on unnoticed? Or perhaps it had only just started. They'd have to check similar cafés, though Flakies was the only actual ice cream parlour. Other places were just kiosks or sold ice creams through the window. He could start by asking the Sumals, if any of them were up to it. He knocked on the Flakies door and waited. And waited. Mrs Sumal and her elder daughter had been to ID the body and Jim's team had taken the car to check for blood and fingerprints. Now the real investigation began. Jim had been round already with DC Grace Brown, who was very good.

After a while the elder Sumal daughter appeared. She was wearing a plain black T-shirt that was huge on her bony frame and faded black leggings which made her skinny legs look like Bassett's liquorice sticks.

'Kiran,' he said. 'How are you doing?' He didn't expect much of a reply and didn't get anything except a tiny shrug.

'Could I come in for a bit? There are a few things I'd like to ask you or your mum that could help with the investigation.' She nodded almost imperceptibly and opened the door wider.

'Do you wanna come upstairs or sit in the café?' she asked.

'Upstairs, please.' There might be things to see in the flat. *Start with the family.* 'How's your mum doing and everyone else?'

'OK. She wanted to open the café, but I said we shouldn't. I don't feel like smiling and asking if people want sprinkles. Mum thinks we should open up as soon as we can. Dad would never let us miss a day in summer.'

She led Jim through a 'staff only' door in the café and then up two flights of stairs. It was strange that the Sumals owned lots of houses and yet still chose to live above the shop. It was the way to get rich, he supposed, spend nothing on your own family – just keep investing and accumulating.

Sukhi Sumal was sitting on a brown leather sofa in the immaculate front room. Jim had a quick scan around for things he might have missed before. It was all very plain and neat, though plain and neat told a story too. There were no pictures other than family photos. The largest of these was a canvas over the fireplace showing a much younger Mr and Mrs Sumal with their son and two daughters. It was a studio job, obviously, and had an artificial sheen and a background of a faux bookcase. Jim imagined the Sumals in happier times, opting for the "extra glossy" finish. Mr Sumal and the son were wearing white shirts and dark blue ties, Mrs Sumal and the girls, salwar kameez; Mrs Sumal in turquoise with lots of gold jewellery, and the girls were pretty in pink with lots of bangles. The next largest picture, another photo canvas, was of an elderly Sikh couple, he assumed a set of the grandparents. The man was wearing a turban. Raj Sumal had been wearing a kara when he was found. Jim remembered a case where some of a man's bruises had come from being punched by a guy with his kara over his knuckles – a traditional use for them.

'Hello, Mrs Sumal,' Jim said. 'I appreciate you seeing me.' She didn't reply, just nodded.

'Do you want a coffee or anything?' Kiran asked. She was clearly the one holding everything together. The little girl came in, still in her pyjamas, and cuddled up next to her mum.

'I'm fine, thanks,' said Jim. He'd only ask for one if he wanted an excuse to stay longer.

'You can sit down,' said Kiran. He chose a chair that looked like the worst one, not wanting to sit in her father's place. There was a big leather armchair with an extendable footrest in pole position for the TV; that must have been her dad's.

'I came to let you know, there were no traces of blood in the car. No prints other than family ones. You can have it back.'

'That's good,' said Kiran, looking down at her fingers. They had all had theirs taken so they could be excluded.

'And, Mrs Sumal, I wanted to know if you had remembered anything more about what your husband was doing before he disappeared,' said Jim. She shook her head.

'Everything was as usual,' she said quietly.

'Anything at all?' She shook her head again. 'We are going through CCTV for the days when he was missing. Do you think he'd have been wearing a jacket? That could have got lost with his phone in it too.'

'He had a Timberland bomber jacket – he wore that a lot. It's gone,' said Kiran.

'Right, that's helpful,' said Jim, writing it down. 'Do you have any pictures of him in it?'

'I don't think so,' said Kiran. 'It was just plain.' She picked up her phone and started searching. 'There – it was that one.' She showed Jim an image of the jacket on a shop website. 'He only got it a few months ago.'

'That's helpful,' said Jim again, noting the name of the

jacket and the price. He turned to Mrs Sumal again, wanting to get her talking.

'Mrs Sumal, did your husband wear a hat, or sometimes a turban?' he asked, glancing up at the grandparents picture again.

'Often a baseball cap,' she said.

'Do you know which one he was wearing when he went missing?'

'I'll have a look,' said Kiran, getting up quickly. 'Wanna help, Nindy?'

'Dad doesn't like us touching his things,' said the little girl.

'Clothes are OK,' said Kiran, 'Come on, we can help the police. Do you want some tea, Mum?' Mrs Sumal nodded. 'Sure you don't want one?' she asked Jim.

'Thanks, I will. Black coffee, please. No sugar.' He smiled at her. Poor girl.

'Can you think of anyone who might have wanted to hurt your husband, Mrs Sumal?' Jim asked, after the daughters had left the room.

'Not really.'

'Did he mention anything about any other ice cream sellers or café owners?'

'No.'

'How about any of your tenants?' She shook her head.

'He didn't talk to me much about that. He and Bal, my son, do all that.'

'Where's your son at the moment?'

'He's sleeping,' she said.

'No, I'm not, Mum.' A dishevelled man in his twenties with several days' heavy stubble came into the room. He kissed his mother on the forehead then turned to Jim, extending a hand.

'Bal Sumal.'

'I'm very sorry for your loss,' said Jim. 'I'm DI Jim Paddon, the senior investigating officer on your father's case. My colleague, DC Grace Brown, will be working closely with me.'

'Yeah,' said Bal. 'Kiran said about her.'

Bal sat down on the sofa next to his mother and put an arm around her shoulders. Jim saw the son give his mother a little squeeze of reassurance. He was wearing a black Flakies T-shirt – a staff uniform one. He must have left the moment he had heard about his dad and not packed much. Or perhaps he wanted to give that impression – the dutiful son. Everyone was a suspect until eliminated – even this Mrs Sumal here in her cardigan – a bobbly grey acrylic one, too warm for most people in this heat – a cardigan that didn't look like the typical attire of a killer.

'Is Kiran making you some tea, Mum?' Bal asked. She nodded.

'So, where were you when your dad went missing?' asked Jim, pen poised.

'We don't really know when that was, do we?' he said, narrowing his eyes. 'I mean Kiran spotted his car and there were the parking tickets, when was that, Mum? You called me when you found the car, right?'

'Yes, Bal. We thought he was with you.'

'And had he been with you?' asked Jim.

'Not that week,' said Bal, taking out his phone and scrolling through something. Jim stood up, ostensibly to straighten his trousers, and saw that it was WhatsApp messages. 'He'd been up the week before, he doesn't come every week, just as and when.'

'My son manages a lot of the business now,' said Mrs Sumal.

'The business – all parts of it?' asked Jim.

'The properties,' said Bal. 'Student lets, mostly. Kiran, Mum and Dad do stuff down here.'

'Student lets?' asked Jim. Every student hated their landlord, but they didn't usually kill them.

'They're easier. You aren't going to have trouble with sitting tenants and benefits and all that shit. We're in

Reading, near where Dad grew up, but we've got a couple of lets here too.'

'And did your dad have direct contact with the tenants?'

'Yeah, sometimes, me or him. The students aren't too bad – it's their parents who get arsey. But then we send them a pic of how their precious kid left the place and they soon shut up about getting the deposit back.'

'And could you give me a list of your properties?' asked Jim.

'Sure. I can email you one. Do you think it might be one of the tenants?'

'We have an open mind at the moment. All possibilities being investigated. Can you tell me if anyone was behind on their rent? Had a grudge? Was being evicted?'

'Sure,' said Bal. 'Like I said – the students are pretty easy – we have all their parents as guarantors – it's hard for them to get behind. It's our Ottersea flats that cause more trouble, know what I mean? Dad looked after those. We might go Airbnb. One girl was behind, but Dad sorted her out.'

'Sorted her out?' Jim raised his eyebrows slightly.

'Sorted it out, I mean. I can check the books if you like.'

'That would be very helpful. And the Ottersea addresses, so we can call in on those tenants, soon as you can.'

Kiran came back in with mugs of tea and a cup of black coffee for Jim on a Flakies tray.

'I'm just gonna get Dad's hats,' she said and left the room again. She was back very soon with a nest of hats in her arms. She put them on the armchair that must have been his and sat down on its arm, just as she must have done when her dad was there. There were black and grey beanies and about eight baseball caps: a blue Reading FC one, a dark green one that also looked new, and the rest were black.

'He never wore this,' said Kiran, picking up the Reading one. 'I got it for him for Christmas, but I guess he didn't like it.' She used it to wipe away a tear then chucked it on the floor. Kiran handled the other hats more carefully, picking up each one, examining it, and then stacking them inside each other. 'There's two black NYC ones here. I'm pretty sure he had three, so it would be one of those.' She hid her face in one for a moment. And don't it make your brown eyes blue, thought Jim.

'And would the one he was wearing have been the same as those?' asked Jim.

'Yeah, pretty much,' she said. 'Dad nearly always wore a hat. He didn't want to people to know he was going bald.'

'Can I take a picture of one of those?' said Jim.

'Sure.'

'And take the hat down to the station?'

'Um, OK.'

'It will be returned to you. And it'll help us when we're looking for him on the CCTV and in any public appeals,' he said, though it was a pretty generic hat. 'Have any of you got a photo of him wearing it?'

'We can have a look,' said Bal, reaching for his phone.

'I'll get mine,' said Kiran, disappearing again.

'How about you, Mrs Sumal?'

'Mum's got an old people phone,' said Nindy, 'but she can get a new one now.'

'Why's that?' Jim asked.

'Shut up, Nindy,' said Bal. Mrs Sumal side-eyed her son. Jim sipped his coffee. Nobody spoke for a while.

'Did Mr Sumal seem angry or worried about anything or anyone? Any unusual phone calls or visitors?' Jim asked.

'I don't think so,' said Mrs Sumal.

'We haven't found his phone yet,' said Jim. He flicked back through his notes. 'You said he had an iPhone?'

'We rang it and rang it,' said Mrs Sumal, 'but nothing.'

'Are any of you connected on the find my iPhone thing?'

They weren't.

'He used a laptop?'

'Yes,' said Bal.

'Are you happy for me to take that?' Jim asked. He could take it even if they weren't.

'I don't know what you will find on it,' said Mrs Sumal. 'My husband wasn't involved in anything bad.' As far as you know, thought Jim. He saw Bal swallow. He probably had a much better idea of what his father had been like outside the home. 'All he did on it was work and play patience.' Yeah, thought Jim, a handy patience app.

'Could I take it now? There may be important information as to whether somebody did this to him.'

'I suppose,' she said. 'If it will make things quicker. We haven't been able to have his funeral...'

'And could you tell me his passwords?' Jim asked. Forensics had a black box that could unlock devices, but this would speed things up. Bal half laughed.

'He just used "FlakieKing123!" for everything, capital F, capital K and an exclamation mark.'

'What about his Fitbit?' Bal asked, turning back to Jim. 'Have you found that?'

'A Fitbit? No. What sort was it?' Jim asked.

'Just looked like a watch. Square, designer, ruched black leather strap,' said Bal. So, he had a Fitbit and an iPhone, thought Jim, whilst his wife had nothing but an old Motorola. He glanced at her wrists. She had an old gold bracelet watch, probably nothing special, probably had been a relative's or a present to her a long time ago. It was quite old-ladyish. But Sumal had a Fitbit. Why hadn't he thought of that before?

'Did he wear it all the time?'

'Yeah,' said Bal. 'He never took it off.'

'That's useful to know,' said Jim. 'Do you know what model it was?'

'I dunno,' said Bal.

'I think the box is still in the everything drawer,' said Kiran. She got up and left the room again.

'She means in the kitchen,' said Bal. Kiran soon returned with a box with a receipt folded inside.

'Excellent,' said Jim, examining it. 'Receipt and serial number. And this is definitely from his one?'

'Yeah,' said Bal, 'I got mine in Reading. Mum and the girls don't have them.'

'Good. And did he just have one email address, as far as you know?' Jim asked.

'Yeah,' said Bal, and he reeled off a Gmail one. 'Plus the "Sumal So Good Lettings" one and Flakies ones, but all the Flakies stuff is on the shop computer. Kiran did most of that with him.'

'There's not much there,' said Kiran. 'It's just for ordering and kids' parties and stuff. I do all that, and most of the accounts. Dad was hardly on there.'

'OK,' said Jim. 'We'll need to have a look at that too.'

'Um – OK,' said Kiran slowly. He could see that she was holding back a groan. A sudden death was so annoying for those left behind – whether it was suicide, murder, or even a natural one. 'Can I have it back soon, though? It's got everything on it.'

'And when can we have Dad back?' Bal asked. 'In our tradition, funerals are almost straight away.'

'As soon as possible,' said Jim. 'I know it's very hard. I know you want to make plans with family and friends.'

'Lots of plans,' said Mrs Sumal quietly. 'So many plans.'

'We do understand,' said Jim. Mrs Sumal smiled slightly and said something too quiet for him to hear, perhaps some words of a prayer, but Nindy, who still had her head on her mum's shoulder sat bolt upright.

'Really, Mum? We can get a dog?' Mrs Sumal looked down, embarrassed.

'I've always wanted a dog, just a small one, but Raj said no, no dogs. Now we can get a dog.' Interesting, thought Jim, getting up. Mrs Sumal couldn't be that grief-stricken if she was already seeing the benefits.

On the way back down to the ice cream parlour, they passed the room where Bal must have been sleeping. There was an unmade single bed, a rowing machine, loads of weights, and an exercise bike that looked to be in use; at least it wasn't currently being used as a clothes horse.

The café looked pretty sad with its blinds down and no customers. He let Kiran back up the computer onto an external hard drive before he took it out to his car. There was a lot to get through now. And plenty to think about. He glanced back up before he got into the car. Mrs Sumal was looking out of the window, but she darted back when their eyes met.

Condolences

'This is really sad,' sad Aunt Cass, pushing the *Ottersea Times* towards Lottie. It wasn't that Cass actually liked the *Ottersea Times*, but she bought it along with *The i* (chosen for price) so that she had something to put in the newspaper rack for customers. Lottie read:

"Police Identify Beach Body". Lottie's first thoughts were of dreadful articles about beach-ready bodies, but no, it seemed that a body washed up on the beach belonged to a Mr Sumal, local landlord and owner of the popular ice cream parlour, Flakies. She read on.

'Oh,' said Lottie when she had finished, 'I was in there the other day. I didn't see him – just two girls – one about my age. I guess, the daughters "left behind". God, how awful. I wonder what happened.'

'Quite a few people do jump off the cliffs,' said Cass. 'Maybe he had debts or was depressed. I didn't know him, but his wife is lovely, and the girls. There's a son too—'

'Yeah, it says.'

'I think the son lives near London,' said Cass.

'Maybe he was murdered,' said Lottie. 'A business rival or something…'

'Hardly likely around here,' said Cass.

'I guess not,' said Lottie. 'But you never know.' She

thought of the friendly girl in the café and her little sister. 'Shall we go round, with flowers and a card or something?'

'Yes. I was thinking that. It's desperately sad.'

Cass cut some pale pink roses from her garden. She stripped the leaves and thorns off, tied them with twine and wrapped them in tissue paper. She put some lemon and blueberry muffins in a box to take too.

'I wonder if people will leave flowers on the beach or cliffs or anything, you know, like when there's been a crash,' said Lottie as they set off. 'It's nicer to give them to the family, though.'

'I guess no one knows what happened yet, I mean suicide or accident. But either way, it's awful,' said Cass.

Lottie had half-expected a shrine to be growing outside Flakies with tealights in jars and bunches of flowers, but there was nothing apart from a sign on the door: "Closed Due To Family Emergency" below which someone had added "REOPENING SOON" in a different coloured pen. Cass rang the bell and they waited. And waited.

The older girl answered the door and peered at them.

'Hello. I'm Cass, from Teapot Paradise, we just wanted to say how sorry we were to hear about your father.'

'Thanks,' said the girl.

'These are for you and your mum,' said Cass, holding out the roses.

'And these,' said Lottie, holding out the white cardboard box of muffins.

The girl gave a half-smile.

'Thanks. Do you want to come in or anything?' she asked. Cass hesitated.

'Um, no, but please tell your mum that I'm thinking of her, and if there's—'

'Thanks,' said the girl, before Cass could utter the cliched "anything I can do".

'I mean it,' said Cass. 'I know cafés, or I could help with your little sister, anything…'

'Me too,' said Lottie, who was aware that she hadn't said anything yet and was just standing there like a giant muffin. 'I'm Lottie,' by the way.

The girl peered at her.

'I remember,' she said. 'Mint choc chip.' And she almost half smiled.

'She's like the woman in *Chocolat*,' said Lottie as they walked home. 'I mean knowing what flavour people will have, what their favourite is.'

'They could do with a bit of magic,' said Cass.

'But not Johnny Depp showing up,' said Lottie. 'That would be the last thing they needed.'

Cause of Death: Unknown

Jim was in the incident room when the Sumal postmortem report arrived. There was no one obvious cause of death. Jim sighed, read it through again, and forwarded it to Grace, who was sitting opposite.

Raj Sumal had suffered multiple broken bones, including his collarbone, an arm, a fractured skull and some vertebrae in his neck. There was seawater and associated fragments of debris in his lungs, but it couldn't be determined whether this had entered before or after death or if he'd died from drowning. God, thought Jim, looking at the list of what had been found. Even drowning victims were ingesting plastic now. It was also possible that Mr Sumal had died from injuries falling from a height into the sea. Jim phoned the pathologist to see if there was more to glean.

'So, "a fall from a height into the sea". How high?'

'The fractures are consistent with quite a long drop, perhaps off the cliffs. The injuries – the fractured skull, collar bone and so on would be consistent with falling sideways or tumbling. Somebody jumping is more likely to go feet first, you know, to step off. I would say that your fellow hit stuff on the way down.'

'So likely not a jumper,' said Jim, nodding.

'Likely not. It's hard to be certain and the deterioration of the skin in the water makes bruising hard to quantify. Fish nibble at dangling limbs – the fingers first, and so on. Then they and gulls go for any orifice they can – the ways into the body, obviously. Then you get sunburn on exposed skin – you've seen that before – anything above the water level. He has recent abrasions and a pinprick rash visible on the bald part of his head. I haven't seen one exactly like that before, but it's likely a combination of sun, saltwater, jellyfish, or some other creature. Curious.'

'And the stuff in his lungs?'

'Depressing, isn't it? Your standard David Attenborough stuff. Some fragments of seaweed and plastic and a few synthetic threads. But we can't tell, when someone's been in the water a while, around two weeks in this case, when exactly that stuff got in.'

'Thanks,' said Jim. 'And your two weeks is consistent with when he was last seen and when he was found. Looks like he was dead before he was even reported missing. The assiduous traffic wardens have helped us out here – guy had racked up a load of tickets. Thanks.'

'No problem, Jim.'

Jim hung up and sighed again. He called the team together to share what he'd learnt.

'So, we have the pathologist's report – various broken bones and neck, which could have been the cause of death, or happened on the way into the sea if that was from height, water and stuff in the lungs, but we can't tell if that was before or after death. So, nothing certain. He had multiple small marks on his head – probably from a sea creature – the pathologist hadn't seen exactly these ones before. We've seen the other injuries, grazing and so on, where body parts have dragged along the bottom, but not these exact marks on the head. But Mr Sumal was found in a rock pool so that probably explains that.'

'You seen those dead whales in documentaries, Sarge? My kids love that stuff. The whale sinks to the bottom and gets eaten by all these sea worms, as well as sharks and all,' said DC Andy Barns.

'Yeah, could be something like that,' said Jim. 'I'm going to see if someone at the Oceanworld Centre can cast any light, but it's probably insignificant. I'll need to put out feelers.' He imagined himself extending octopus arms, or perhaps he was more like a lobster extending its antennae. Did lobsters have two sets of them? Yes, he'd seen that when he was visiting Jane. Something was clicking. He realised it was Grace, clicking her pen. He blinked. 'Um, yes, OK, everyone. I think that's it for now.' Everyone but Grace shuffled back to their desks.

'Wanna go for a walk, Grace?' Jim asked.

'Murderers tend not to be that imaginative,' Jim said, as he and Grace walked out to where his car was parked. 'They tend not to go far to dump a body – panic perhaps – they just want to get rid of it. People are so parochial.'

'Parochial?'

'They keep things local. Let's take a walk along the cliffs. Anything has likely been blown away or walked over, but worth a look.'

There were several other cars parked at the Red Cliffs Nature Reserve. They followed the path that led straight out onto the headland.

'There's the path through the woods,' said Jim. 'But if it was dark – and you wouldn't want to dump a body or push someone off in broad daylight – I think you'd probably come this way.'

'They could drive beyond the car park and leave their lights on,' said Grace, 'but they probably wouldn't want to do that. Just torches, or a phone torch is most likely. Wonder what the moon was doing two to three weeks ago?' They stopped walking and she pulled out her phone to check the calendar. 'So what dates have we got, Sarge?'

'Reported missing on July 9th. Washed up on July 18th. First parking ticket on July 4th.'

'So, full moon on July 13th,' said Grace. 'You'd have a decent amount of light up here when he was missing, and it all reflecting off the sea.' Jim nodded.

'Not too much trouble seeing what you were doing.'

The grass on the cliff top was flattened by the wind and studded here and there with purple orchids. They walked in a straight line to the wire fence with its warning signs. They stopped there and peered out to sea, then they turned and looked back towards the car park.

'The grass looks undisturbed, no tyre marks up towards the edge,' said Grace, 'but anything might have been obliterated since then. Popular up here.' Jim squatted down, just to check. The grass did look more worn in an unofficial path toward the fence, but why wouldn't it? People would probably go that way first when they arrived. He got up and looked out to sea.

'Anyone would have to duck under this, pull a body after them, or persuade them to go over the fence if they wanted to push them off,' Grace said.

'Would they do it at the first point they came to? Probably,' said Jim. 'You wouldn't want to drag a body further than you had to.' He squatted down again and looked at the wire.

'Could be fibres,' said Grace. 'Or the wire could get bent.' But it didn't look bent and there was nothing visible on it.

'You wouldn't have to be that slim to get under this without touching it,' said Jim. He saw Grace glance at his belly. He took off his jacket, flattened himself onto the grass and slithered under the wire.

'Careful, Sarge.' He felt her hands clamp around his ankles. He peered over the edge. The drop wasn't quite straight down, the cliff face was crumbly in places, some of the sandstone looked freshly exposed. In other places plants grew, gorse and smaller things that he didn't know the names of, and something with pink flowers holding the rocks together. There were lumps sticking out – something or someone dropped off it might hit them on the way down. Further along the cliffs there was a piece of blue and white striped cloth caught on a gorse bush, though it was likely unrelated, a cloth blown away from a picnic or something. They didn't even know if the deceased had been shoved off here – it was just somewhere to start.

'There's something caught in the bushes,' he said once he was back next to Grace. 'We'll have to ask the coastguard if they can get it for us. It's further along and about twenty feet down, caught on a bush. Likely nothing.'

They walked along the cliff for a little bit. There were a couple of birdwatchers sitting in folding green nylon chairs, looking out to sea with binoculars.

'Seen anything interesting or odd up here lately?' Jim asked.

'European shags, razorbills, storm petrels' said the male of the pair, lowering his bins.

His companion glanced at him, as if for permission, before saying, 'There was a basking shark yesterday.'

Jim surmised from the matching RSPB fleeces, chairs and binoculars and the shared rucksack that they were a couple. The woman had a sweet round face and long grey hair tied back in a ponytail that looked very much like the tail of a pony. Her face was brown from outdoor activities. She was wearing flat, girlish shoes with straps and a Velcro fastening.

'Interesting,' said Jim. He looked out to sea, hoping to spot one himself. There was the usual motley crew of yachts and passing boats. 'Do you come up here every day?'

'Only at peak times of year,' said the man. 'We're from the Ottersea Wildlife Society. We've a rota for counting in the arrivals and departures, the migrants.' Jim pictured an airport arrivals hall with twitchers holding up signs with different bird names.

'Thanks,' said Jim. 'I'm DI Jim Paddon and this is my colleague DC Grace Brown.' He took out a couple of his cards and gave them one each.

'We're investigating a possible crime up here. Have

you seen anything unusual, suspicious, any unusual cars or activity? People who don't look like the usual walkers…'

The woman looked towards the man. Definitely married, thought Jim, and seeming to ask for permission to speak. Her arms were covered by the sleeves of a fleece despite the hot weather. He wondered if these were hiding bruises.

'No, nobody unusual,' said the man.

'I don't think so,' said the woman.

'Would you have a copy of your rota, or a list of members who might have seen something up here?' Grace asked.

'Um,' said the woman.

'Wouldn't that contravene data protection laws?' said the man.

'Only if we were to hold personal information about individuals on the computer without their permission, which we wouldn't in this case,' said Grace.

'A serious crime may have been committed,' said Jim, thinking, "what a wanker". 'We are looking for potential witnesses or anybody who might have seen something unusual.'

'I am the Treasurer of Ottersea Wildlife Society. I think I can make an executive decision to show you our rota.'

'Graham, dear, they could just go and look at it pinned up in the church hall if they wanted to,' said his wife. He grunted something and gave a little kick sideways towards her shoes.

'Don't keep the officers waiting, Katie,' he said, and she started to rummage in their rucksack. First to come out was a yellow cotton bag embroidered with daisies. She put this on the ground and Jim saw that it contained some sort of knitting. There was a stainless-steel thermos flask, two copper water bottles and an elderly Tupperware box containing sandwiches, another one containing flapjacks, a smaller one with two hardboiled eggs, and finally, a brown paper bag of apples.

'I told you not to put the apples at the bottom after last time,' said the man.

'Sorry, they must have slipped down.'

'I don't want to be eating my way around bruises again.'

'Sorry.' She pulled out a much-mended plastic pocket, the sort punched with holes so that it could go in a ring-binder and tentatively offered it to Grace, who was standing closer to her.

'So, you have people up here most days? Mind if we take a photo of this?'

'Go ahead.'

'Much appreciated,' said Jim.

'Would you like a flapjack?' said the woman, offering them the plastic box. Jim saw a look of displeasure cross the husband's face. Was he anti-law enforcement, or just worried about missing out on part of his lunch? The sticky slabs were studded with green chips of pumpkin seed and looked unpleasantly wholesome.

'Not while I'm on duty,' said Jim, though Grace took one. Jim looked back down at the list. 'So, you are Graham and Katie Grayling?' he asked. 'Would you be able to give us a contact number, in case we want to talk to any of your members?'

'Sure,' said the man and he rattled off a local phone number which Jim wrote down, Grace being too busy with her flapjack.

'There must be an age divide where if you ask for someone's number, they'll give you their landline rather than their mobile,' said Jim as they walked back to his car. 'Let's get back to the station and see how the uniforms are getting on.'

They stopped at a coffee shop. Jim bought not just his Americano and Grace's latte, but a few extras for the officers who would be doing the long, tedious, but so essential work of trawling through the CCTV.

In the incident room a couple of uniforms down from Exeter were going through CCTV of the streets around where Raj Sumal's car had been found. There was a huge, bald, plate-faced one called Gavin Poltree and a shorter, equally bald and equally plate-faced one called Will Potterton. Jim knew them both slightly.

'Coffee, guys,' he said. They paused the footage on their screens before turning.

'Cheers, Boss.'

'Thanks, Sarge.'

It was going to be a long process. There were cameras on the promenade – they already had the footage from those – and they would be collecting whatever they could from local shops and businesses. They could put out a call for dash cam footage too once they knew which days and times were of most interest. They'd been in touch with the traffic wardens who were pretty assiduous in Ottersea, but the tickets might not have told the whole story. Raj Sumal might have got lucky (before being so catastrophically unlucky) and either missed getting tickets or had returned to his car and thrown some away before leaving again. Plus, someone might have moved his car.

'Anything yet?' Jim asked.

'It's tough, Sarge,' said the PC Poltree. 'There's crowds, all these people with their kids and dogs, almost all wearing hats that block their faces, as well as other people's. Bloody heatwave.'

'And loads of them are walking along with umbrellas against the sun or kids on their shoulders – and then the bloody kids have hats,' added PC Potterton.

'And what about the car park – the little one down the alleyway?'

'We're waiting on that, Sarge.' Jim saw Potterton's eyes dart towards the clock and then to a box of Krispy Kreme doughnuts that someone must have got at a garage on the way down.

'If you're going to eat doughnuts at work,' said Jim, 'at least buy them from a local baker.'

Poltree and Potterton wouldn't have looked quite so sheepish if they'd seen what hung above Jim's parents' mantlepiece: a photo canvas of The Tumble Weeds, Jim's parents' Country covers band mid-set. There they stood, his mum holding the microphone, dressed mostly in white – white Stetson, white cowboy boots, a white denim flouncy skirt that finished above her knees, and a white waistcoat with rhinestone trimming. The only splashes of colour were the red checks of her gingham blouse, her flaming locks of auburn hair and her eyes of emerald green. His dad had a matching white rhinestone-studded waistcoat, but wore blue jeans with his cowboy boots. His floppy wing of black hair (hair that Jim had inherited) was mostly hidden by his white Stetson. His dad played the guitar. Behind them, Jim's uncle (also called Jim) was on drums and Uncle Steve, who wasn't an actual uncle, was on keyboards. Jim and his sister were there too. Loretta had a mini version of her mother's outfit whilst Jim wore a miniature cowboy outfit complete with sheriff's badge. Jim and Loretta were sitting on the front edge of the stage. Jim wouldn't have known which particular summer fete or half-hearted festival the picture had been taken at – almost every weekend of his childhood summers had involved his parents playing somewhere – but his mum had told him that this was at someone's wedding near East Coker. His sister had enjoyed getting up on the stage, shaking a tambourine and singing along, but Jim preferred to sit somewhere inconspicuous and eat whatever was on offer – fairy cakes, lollies, popcorn, little clear plastic bowls of strawberries with squirts of artificial cream – and to practice drawing his cap gun from the brown plastic holster that had come with the outfit: Stick 'em up! Hit the dirt! The events often went on late into the evening and Loretta and Jim would end up drowsing on the scratchy tartan travel rug that went with them to every gig. Jim would lie and look up at the stars, alone on some wild prairie, one hand on his sheriff's badge, the other on his gun, ready for anything until he fell asleep. His parents now lived in assisted-living accommodation in Surrey where they'd moved from their native Devon to be closer to Loretta and her family. Jim's mother was doing everything she could to slow his father's slide into dementia; weekly line dancing club and the constant playing of songs whose words Jim's father would, fingers crossed, never forget, seemed to be helping, at least for now.

Jim made sure now that none of his colleagues knew he'd been a miniature sheriff with a Country and Western band. What was harder to hide was the soundtrack of his childhood still playing non-stop in his head. Sometimes he couldn't stop himself from whistling or humming the odd chorus or lyrics from leaking into his speech.

'Ottermouth, oh Ottermouth…' he belted out to the tune of "Galveston" as he drove back from a late shift, or he might growl along to "Highway Patrolman", or become the "Wichita Lineman", not just because of the soundtrack to his childhood, but because, a few years ago now, his girlfriend Eva had picked a fine time to leave him.

When Your Dad is a Bit of an Arsehole and Then He Dies

Lottie spotted the girl from Flakies sitting on a bench on the promenade as she walked home from work.

'Hi,' she said. 'How are you doing? Sorry, stupid question.'

'That's OK. You're nice to ask.'

'It must be really tough,' said Lottie.

'Yeah,' said the girl. 'It is.'

'How's your mum?'

'It's like she's asleep, just really shocked. Some of my aunties have come to stay. I kind of wish they'd all just go away. Mum and I usually manage everything by ourselves, I mean Flakies and everything.'

'I can imagine,' said Lottie.

'And we still have no idea what happened.'

'Do you wanna get a coffee?'

'Not really – cafés, you know.'

'I know, my aunt's Teapot Paradise, it can be pretty crazy.'

'Just being here is nice,' said the girl. 'I'm Kiran, by the way.'

'Lottie,' said Lottie.

'It's like he just disappeared,' said Kiran. 'I mean, they found him and all, but we just don't know why, or what he was doing. He didn't believe in mental illness or anything.'

'That doesn't mean...' said Lottie. 'Sorry. I didn't mean to imply – as if I'd know anything.'

'No, you're OK. But he seemed fine. And Bal hasn't found anything, I mean with the rentals, and I know all the Flakies stuff. Maybe he just slipped, or fell, or there was a freak wave.'

'That can happen, freak waves,' said Lottie. 'A ship can go by or a boat, sometimes not even seen from the shore.'

'Maybe he just had a heart attack and he got swept out. I think that's the best we can hope for. That's what I've been telling my mum. I don't know if she believes me – or anything that's happening at the moment – she's just drifting about. Not saying much.'

'I'm really sorry,' said Lottie. Kiran rubbed away some tears.

'Stop saying nice things to me or I'll really cry,' she said.

'Maybe you should.'

'I've probably cried enough.'

'I doubt it,' said Lottie, putting an arm around Kiran's shoulder, which felt bony and angular through her black T-shirt.

There seemed to be dads everywhere – dads pushing kids along in buggies or on those little trikes with sticks for the parent to hold, dads carrying beach stuff, sunburnt dads in terrible shorts with fat bellies, grandfathers queuing up at the kiosk for cups of tea and ice creams, dads in ill-considered Lycra cycling past; it wasn't fair.

'Actually, my dad was a bit of a dick,' said Kiran. 'He always did what he wanted, but was pretty controlling of my mum. He didn't like her working where people could see her, so she was upstairs in the freezer room a lot of the time. Now it's like someone opened her cage door, but it hasn't occurred to her that she can go out. He was away quite a lot with the properties, so we didn't notice when he was gone for a few days until I saw the car all covered in tickets. We thought he was in Reading with Bal, that's where most of the properties are.'

'Mm,' said Lottie, 'It must be so hard. My dad died when I was twelve, so I can imagine a bit. He had a heart attack – just suddenly died – even though he wasn't that old. It turned out he'd had a heart condition that we didn't even know about. One minute he was fine and the next, gone.'

'I'm sorry,' said Kiran and she put *her* arm around Lottie's shoulders. They sat there for a while, just watching the waves breaking on the shore. 'It's worse for my little sister, really, to have something this bad happen when you're so young. It was her and me who spotted his car all abandoned. I tried to act like it was nothing too weird, but since then with the police coming round – she's not been shielded from it all.'

'It's probably better that she isn't. I wanted to know everything when my dad died.'

'And she was really daddy's little girl – I don't think she had much idea that he wasn't actually the perfect dad, that he was a bit of an arsehole.'

'There's no such thing as the perfect dad, or the perfect anyone,' said Lottie.

'There is when you are nine. I'm a bit worried what the police might uncover, to be honest. We don't really know what he got up to when he wasn't here.'

'That must be awful.'

'They've got access to lots of his stuff, so any contacts, anything online, they'll find that out. And I don't want Mum to know if it's anything awful.'

Maybe there was a secret family, thought Lottie, or a mistress or mistresses, or maybe he was involved with drugs and Flakies was just a front, but surely Kiran would have realised that. She hoped it wouldn't be anything too awful; bad enough losing your dad without then discovering he was a *total* shit and having it all made public.

Plastic Carrier Bag

Katie Grayling was always sorry if Ottersea Shanty Crew practices and Ottersea WI meetings fell on the same evening. Tonight there was a Shanty Crew practice at the same time as the unofficial meeting of the WI for them to work on the crochet and knitting project. The benefit of Graham being gone in the evening was lost if she was out too. The Shanty Crew would practise in a backroom at The Ship and stay for many pints afterwards. She would often hurry home after WI meetings so that she had some precious time alone in the house before Graham got back. On rare occasions when the Shanty Crew finished first and none of them were staying in the pub, Graham might come and lurk outside the WI meeting. She'd see his shadowy figure sitting on the wall waiting for her. If one of her close friends spotted him too, they'd give her a sympathetic look or her arm a little squeeze. They all knew what Graham Grayling was like – a sneaky bully who pretended to be nice. Distant acquaintances thought he was a lovely man and that they were a lovely couple, so well suited.

They had met at university in York in the 70s. Nineteen-year-old Katie had known that a grayling was a butterfly – one that was a master of camouflage and mostly brown with washed-out orange markings. There had been long afternoons in the students' union coffee bar and trips on coaches to London for protests. Graham was the founder of a new university society – Men Against Patriarchy – and he arranged the meetings (which were never that well attended) to coincide with meetings of the Women's Campaign Group; how considerate that had seemed. He had lurked for her outside the meeting room to ensure that she got back to her room safely. What a beautiful boy he had been, with his golden curls and big green jumpers – he could have been an elf from the Flower Fairies books she'd loved so much. Time had turned him from elf to goblin. His curls were now grey and he had an expansive beard like the one that the ungrateful dwarf in *Snow White and Rose Red* gets stuck in a tree. He sometimes stole her embroidery scissors to trim it. She would find them on the side of the sink with bristles adhering to the blades. The Graylings' bathroom was testament to their green credentials. No aerosols were allowed and they had been early adopters of shampoo bars. They grew their own loofahs to use for scrubbing themselves and their saucepans.

Graham had been somewhat depressed lately; Katie had been as supportive and sympathetic as possible. The source of this depression was that he sent weekly videos of himself talking about some aspect of their garden or allotment to *Gardeners' World,* but they had yet to feature any of them. Every Friday he would watch, waiting for the moment when one of his planet-saving hacks would be featured, only to be disappointed. Katie had been in love with Monty Don for many years. She had once thought that having curly hair guaranteed niceness; Graham had proved that wasn't the case, just as Dr Harold Shipman had proved that being mild-mannered and bearded didn't mean you were a trustworthy fellow.

The WI get-together had finished first and Katie had scurried home. She decided to do her crochet sitting up in bed. She could pretend she was asleep if Graham came upstairs feeling amorous, as he often did after a night with the Shanty Crew. She made her cup of camomile tea and took that and her crochet bag upstairs. As well as the WI project, she wanted to start work on a pink and white elephant for a niece's baby. She had some new bamboo and cotton yarn from Maddy Knits. Here it was in her crochet bag, but damn, she had forgotten to hide the plastic bag Maddy had put it in. Katie's life was measured out in cotton tote bags, but on this occasion, she had forgotten to take one with her.

The elephant involved a complicated pattern consisting of many rosettes that would combine to make a delightfully textured toy. She got started with the trunk but found she was more tired than she'd realised. She decided she would just close her eyes for a minute.

'And what the hell is this?' Katie awoke to Graham standing over her, brandishing the carrier bag. He was breathing fire, or at least real ale fumes. 'Did you buy this? How could you have let this into the house?' He flapped it in her face and then crumpled it, making as much noise as possible.

'Graham, I'm sorry,' she said, knowing meekness was the best policy for de-escalation. 'It was a mistake, we'll do something good with it, I promise…' She nearly said, 'treasure your plastic' but stopped herself in time – quoting Monty Don would only make things worse.

'We do not have plastic bags in this house! You want to kill turtles, do you?' He slammed his fist onto the pillow beside her.

'Of course not, Graham. I'm sorry.' He harrumphed and stomped off to the bathroom where he made more loud noises.

Katie definitely didn't want to kill turtles, though she did hate documentaries about them. Seeing them lay their eggs in the sand was so disgusting – something that she had never confided in Graham – and the footage of the babies being captured and eaten as they tried to traverse the perilous few yards between their nest and the waves – it was too heartbreaking. Graham would watch any documentary, the gorier the better.

'It's the circle of life,' he'd say if he caught her looking away or thought she was being sentimental. 'Nature seems wasteful, but one creature's loss is another's bounty.'

Now he was back and standing over her.

'I'm sorry, Gray, let's just go to sleep,' she said, knowing that falling back to sleep would be impossible for her.

'I am not sleeping with this monstrosity, this pollution near the marital bed!' He did his best to hurl the carrier bag out of the room. The gesture was pretty ineffectual and it landed just outside the bedroom door. 'I want that out of the house first thing tomorrow. You brought it in. You deal with it.'

Katie kept her eyes lowered but nodded rigorously. She put her crochet away, hoping that the bad vibes wouldn't pollute the present for the baby. She would wash it in the most pure and gentle of eco-liquids before giving it to her.

Graham collapsed on the bed beside her and was soon snoring like, well, she didn't know what. A giant weasel? A walrus? She drank her camomile tea and lay there for a while. They lived close to the Oceanworld Centre, so they could often hear the cries of the birds kept there. She could hear the waves breaking too and every so often, the laughter and cries of young people who'd be drinking and smoking on the beach, lucky things.

There was no way she was going to get back to sleep. She got up and went to the bathroom. The carrier bag was still where Graham had thrown it, an obvious slipping hazard.

A rebellious thought swam through her mind like a tiny silver fish: let him pick it up himself. She went back to bed and eventually drifted off.

At 2am Graham woke, the first effects of the shanties and real ale having worn off. He was thirsty and needed to pee. He stumbled out of bed and would have made it to the bathroom if he hadn't stepped on that carrier bag. He slid, unstoppable on the natural fibre carpet, tried to grab the banister but fell headfirst down the stairs.

Katie, in her dream, heard a cry. She was outside the Oceanworld Centre. The captive birds were rising up against the netting of the aviary and screaming to get out. The puffins were making their eerie sound. In her dream the puffins had forgotten how to fly.

'Go on, puffins,' she told them, 'fly free!' She had her embroidery scissors in her hand. They sparkled and glinted in the sunshine, as though they were new and Graham had never sullied them with his bristles. She cut the netting. The puffins remembered they could fly and rose up with the other birds through the hole she had made and out into the greater blue.

When Katie awoke the next morning having slept far better than usual, Graham wasn't in bed, which was odd. She always got up first and brought him a cup of tea. But wherever he was, he hadn't thought to bring her one.

There were no sounds coming from downstairs. She got up and put on her slippers and her dressing gown.

He was lying by the front door. Oh dear, she thought. She spotted the carrier bag halfway down the stairs. She stopped to pick it up and fold it neatly into her pocket so that he wouldn't see it and be annoyed again. But when she reached him, he was already cold.

'Oh, Graham,' she said. She knelt beside him and stroked the curls that she had once loved so much. He didn't look very dignified in his pyjamas. The plastic bag rustled in her pocket. 'You were right,' she said, starting to cry. 'Killers. Hazards to wildlife.' She dialled 999 and asked for an ambulance although it was clearly too late. Whilst she waited for it to arrive, she fetched a throw that she'd crocheted herself and put it over him. She wondered if she'd be arrested. They might think that she'd planned the whole thing.

They said that the ambulance would be there as soon

as possible. She sat on the bottom step and waited. Then it occurred to her that she was still in her nightie. She hid the carrier bag in the kitchen bin under some other non-recyclable rubbish. She hurried back past Graham and upstairs where she had a wash and brushed her teeth and put some clean clothes on. She took her long grey hair out of its night-time plait, brushed it, and put it up in a bun. Would this make her look more guilty? *Me thinks the lady hath bothered to brush her hair.* Then, with a devil-may-care attitude, she picked up her crochet bag; there was bound to be a lot of waiting about. She might as well make the most of the time that was now hers. She was just wondering about coffee when the ambulance arrived.

A few hours later, when Graham had been taken away, Katie was sitting alone on the sofa whilst Cass made yet more tea. Cass'd had several mugs already – Katie kept letting hers go cold. The phone rang.

'Is that Katie Grayling? This is DI Jim Paddon, we met on the clifftop. Do you have a moment?'

'Yes,' she said quietly. So, they were onto her already. She wondered if she should just confess now or wait to be handcuffed and led out to the waiting car with the neighbours looking on.

'I wondered if you and your husband could help us out with some contacts for the other members of your club.'

'My husband – um—'

'So, I have the list you gave me—'

'My husband died,' she said. 'He fell down the stairs in the night.'

'What?' said Jim. 'I mean, I'm so sorry to hear that.'

'Last night, he'd been out to Shanty practice and he got up in the night, well he always gets up in the night, but more after Shanty practice…'

'I'm very sorry to be bothering you at a time like this,' said Jim. 'I'm very sorry for your loss. I'll call back another time.'

Katie thought 'OK' but after a while realised that she hadn't said that aloud, or anything else.

'Are you alright, Mrs Grayling? Have you got anyone with you?'

'Yes,' she said. 'My friend Cass is here.'

'Ah, that's good,' said Jim. 'My condolences. Again, I am so sorry for your loss.' And he rang off.

Lutra Lutra

Otter feeding at 3pm always attracted a big crowd. Lottie was doing it today, delighting in the way that Star, Ollie and their cubs squeaked with joy and feasted in full view before making sure they all had clean whiskers and returned to diving, rolling and chasing each other in the water behind the glass wall of their tank. The crowd clapped when it was over before drifting on to the next exhibit, apart from a lone woman who accosted Lottie as she climbed down the little ladder from the feeding platform.

'I don't know how you can work here. It's just disgusting that you keep them in these conditions,' the woman said. She was wearing a sleeveless pink blouse and expensive-looking white linen trousers with the sort of loafers that had a shiny metal bar across the front.

'All our creatures are kept in the best possible conditions,' said Lottie. 'The Centre is really careful about that. Animal welfare comes before anything else. Their diets are carefully monitored, and they are all checked many times each day.' She put down her empty fish bucket and tried a smile before she turned and pushed the ladder to the feeding station back up and locked it. Then she went through the gate to the public area, locking that behind her too.

'Well, the environment here,' said the woman, waving a beringed hand at the otters' enclosure, 'is clearly lacking in their most basic requirements. It is really cruel to be keeping them here without any wood or trees to work with.'

'Wood or trees?'

'They have to gnaw. They should be able to build a dam. It's what they do. And their teeth. Their teeth must be really blunt and painful without any wood to work on.'

'They have plants, and water plants – look,' said Lottie. 'Otters love swimming in this eel grass, they have plenty of that.'

'Those aren't otters,' said the woman. 'Those are beavers. And beavers need wood. Who's in charge here? I want to speak to them.'

'Really, madam,' said Lottie, 'These are otters. They are definitely otters. The parents were rescued separately as cubs, and they are really happy here in their family group. They have everything they need.'

'No,' said the woman. 'These are beavers and beavers need wood.'

'They are definitely otters,' said Lottie again. 'Look—' she indicated the display. 'Eurasian Otters – Lutra lutra. Beavers are rodents and have big front teeth and broad, flat tails. They're much rounder. Otters are long – look at them swimming. They're in the weasel family. See how their tails are furry and pointed – not like a beaver's rubbery paddle. I can show you a picture of some beavers on my phone if you like…'

'You can't fob me off like that. Who's in charge here?'

Lottie hadn't had anyone complaining before. All the staff kept an eye out for any fish who had died or looked ill, for slippery floors and dropped litter, and the loos were checked every hour – they needed to be with all those people changing nappies.

'These really are otters,' said Lottie. 'They don't need wood to gnaw on, but I can call someone.' She took off her gloves and balanced them on the side of the bucket and unhooked her radio:

'Arthur to the otter display, please.'

'Beaver display,' the woman said loudly, leaning towards Lottie's radio. Lottie took a step back. A family with two little girls dressed in pink fairy dresses arrived.

'Ah, look at the baby otters,' said the mum.

'I think you'll find that these are beavers,' said the woman. The children rushed up towards the glass. The otters obliged with some squeaks and dives.

'Arthur to the otters, please, Arthur to the otters,' Lottie said again. Her radio crackled:

'On my way, Lottie.' Moments later he appeared.

'Everything OK here?'

'Everything is *not* OK,' said the woman. 'I'm horrified by the conditions you are keeping these poor animals in, and I want to make a formal complaint.' The family with the fairy daughters turned to watch. 'These animals are being kept in cruel conditions, deprived of their most basic needs. Where is their wood?'

'This lady,' said Lottie, 'thinks these are beavers and that they should have wood to gnaw on and to build dams with.'

'Beavers?' said Arthur, smiling, 'These are definitely not beavers. Look—' he pointed to the display board – "Eurasian otters."

'Don't give me that,' said the woman. 'I know a beaver when I see one.'

'Yeah, me too,' said the fairy girls' dad, sniggering.

Lottie had read the Visitor Complaints Procedure on her first day – it had been in the file they'd given her to look through, but she couldn't remember exactly what it said. Probably just to be polite and get the duty manager to talk to the person. Well, she'd done that. Now she watched as Arthur shoved the fingers of his left hand up through his curls. He tilted his head to the side slightly and spoke kindly and calmly:

'Really, Madam, these are otters, not beavers. I can assure you that they are otters. They don't need wood to chew on. We make sure that they have everything they need and do all we can to enrich their environment with the best food and constant opportunities for play, grooming, rest away from the public, and family bonding.'

'This is despicable. You should be shut down. I'll be reporting you. What's your name?' She went right up close to him and peered at his badge. 'Right, "Arthur Parks, Aquarist" – and that sounds like something made up in case people complain – I'm going to do everything I can for the welfare of these beavers. They are a protected species, you know.' Arthur backed away, but she kept moving closer and he was soon pressed up against the otters' tank.

'Madam, they really are otters and they are happy in there together.' Behind him Star, Ollie and the cubs did tumble turns. The woman narrowed her eyes and peered at them.

'They are brown. They are beavers. Beavers deprived of their basic rights. You haven't heard the last of this!' She swivelled on one loafered heel and left.

'God,' said Lottie. 'I thought she was going to start jabbing you. How did you stay so calm?'

'I've had worse,' said Arthur.

'Does this happen often, I mean, angry visitors?'

'Not really,' said Arthur, 'but my sister has a bit of a temper – I guess I'm used to it. Some people get cross if they miss feeding time or something's fully booked. Often it's things they just imagined we'd have and they say they saw it advertised on the website. One dad went crazy when we didn't have a great white – he'd promised his kid he'd see one on his birthday. We gave them a rubber shark from the gift shop, not that they deserved it – but you have to be so careful. Reputation, reviews – you know. You should see some of the things that get shared in the aquarists' Facebook group. I think we're quite lucky here – it's not the biggest aquarium – but people still try their luck. A lot of the time they lie about stuff to get their ticket price refunded or free chips in the café. Owners just have to build it into the overheads now.'

'Do you think she believed us?'

'I dunno,' said Arthur. 'Perhaps she just didn't want to admit she was wrong.'

'Perhaps she could be fobbed off with a free key ring,' said Lottie.

Safe, Safe, Safe

The one with eyes the colour of the darkest weeds where she hid is there again with the one she loves. There is no threat. This creature has a steady pulse – safe, safe, safe – just like the one she loves – slow, slow, slow.

She remembers when he was first there, his skin tasting already of the water and of salt, the kind arms not flinching or retreating. Safe, safe, safe. His one heart beating. And each time he came, he brought her things, but never the open sea.

Cheatin' Heart

Jim bought black coffee through the window at Flakies from a hapless-looking youth then sat at one of the pavement tables to drink it. Kiran Sumal came out with antibacterial spray and a cloth. She had dark circles under her eyes and her hands looked raw – she must spend a lot of time cleaning. Jim had clocked Flakies' five-star hygiene rating which was doubtless down to her and her mum – he couldn't imagine Raj Sumal had spent much time mopping and wiping. Kiran glanced his way. He knew what she was thinking before she said it out loud:

'Shouldn't you be busy solving crimes?'

There wasn't an answer to that. He should be. But this was a part of it – the watching, the thinking. And it was actually his day off, not that he always took them.

'How's your mum doing? And you and your sister?'

She pulled a face. 'Mum wants to keep going with Flakies. I know she's thinking Dad would be cross if we didn't stay open.'

'Was he easily angered?'

'Not really, not that much.'

'Have you thought of anything else that might help us?'

'No.'

'You can talk to me, you know. Here, or in private somewhere. I just want to find out what happened.'

'Me too.'

'Was everything alright with your mum and dad?'

He saw something flicker across her face and she bit her lip.

'Yeah, well, nothing had changed.'

'They got on well?'

'Mostly. It's his car being left I don't understand. He'd never just abandon it.'

So, Jim thought, Sumal wouldn't leave his car, but might he leave his family? Maybe there had been a girlfriend somewhere, someone whose own partner had found out. Jim looked beyond Kiran for a moment, across the promenade and out to sea. Two paddleboarders were moving slowly across the bay. A lone canoeist overtook them. Jim remained fascinated by that canoeist case – the guy who'd staged his own drowning, hid in the attic, let his own kids think that he'd died, and then ran away to Costa Rica. What kind of person let his own sons think he was dead while he was hiding in the attic? Perhaps the Sumals had been cooking up something like that, but then he'd drowned anyway. The car was pretty convincing if that had been part of it. This daughter didn't seem to be in on anything; the wife though, seemed strangely unmoved. Was she in shock? Glad he was dead? Had she been involved?

'We're doing everything we can to find out what happened,' said Jim.

'What do you think happened?'

'I couldn't say yet,' said Jim. 'We'll keep you informed. Grace will be by again soon and you can call her or me anytime.' Kiran sighed. 'I'll always pick up,' said Jim. 'Even on a day off like today.' He drained his coffee.

Jim felt Kiran's sad eyes on his back as he walked away. He decided to try to get some extra uniforms to speed up looking through the CCTV, but that was always a struggle. Perhaps Sumal had been meeting someone and had got into *their* car – they had to check for that too. Jim continued along the seafront towards the Oceanworld Centre. He had an annual membership, something that none of his colleagues knew about.

The honking of the puffins grew louder as he approached. The place was a bit like a young offenders' institution; he didn't like to think of the creatures' lack of freedom, but he kept coming back, drawn to the soothing blue light in the subterranean exhibitions. Subterranean homesick blues, he thought, each time he visited. He knew not to come until the hour before closing time. By then the families with noisy children and the objectionable people who tapped on the glass (despite the admonitions on every tank) had always left to get their fish and chips. He pulled his annual pass from his wallet and nodded to the girl on the admission desk – a new one, he noted, pretty with curly dark hair and tawny eyes, early twenties, he guessed, about the age of Kiran Sumal. Her name was Lottie, her badge told him, and she was here to help.

He said a quick hello to leafy seadragons. Most people lingered longest in the glass tunnel where sharks and turtles cruised over their heads, but he walked on through. He passed the illuminated column of jellyfish and bubbles and had his usual thought that it was like a lava lamp. He was headed for his favourite place: the bench in front of the tank where Jane the octopus resided. There at last, he leant back against the faux cave wall. The prickles of its strange surface, some sort of extra spiky textured paint, pressed into his back, but he didn't mind. It felt like the stings of tiny jellyfish. It might leave tiny pink dots on his back under his shirt. But how would he know? He only looked in the mirror to shave, almost never in a long one, and wouldn't ever crane his neck to get a rear view. And he had nobody to tell him.

Apart from wanting to visit Jane, Jim wanted to talk to Arthur about the marks on Sumal's scalp. Arthur knew that he was a copper. They often exchanged a few words about Jane. Jim liked Arthur and admired how calm he seemed – it must be from spending his time in this blue world – the world outside could do with more guys like Arthur.

Jane had been hiding in her cave, exhausted or bored by the visitors, but she came out to see him, as she always did, jetting towards the front of the tank. She extended a tentacle to the glass and held it there. He gently put his own hand on the tank, mirroring her gesture, and they stood there, suckers and fingertips divided only by the glass.

'Hello, Jane,' he said, voice low. He knew that she heard as she extended another arm to be met with his other hand. They stayed there for a few minutes, then Jane broke the gaze and shot away to the other side of the tank. She picked up one of her collection of clam shells and walked across the shingly floor of her tank back to him. She held up the shell to him and he smiled and nodded.

'That's a beauty, Jane.'

She amused herself and him by passing it from arm to arm like a juggler in training.

'You're the best, Jane,' he said, and she changed colour from the brownish green she'd been when he arrived to a paler sandy colour. He knew that paler colours could denote pleasure. And then she was off, jetting back across the tank to another corner where most of her toys were. Jim had never seen any of the staff actually *in* her tank – they just opened a panel of the lid to interact with her – so he surmised that she must have been the one to put them into what looked like an art installation.

There was a series of jars with screw-on lids lying on their sides in a line – big-small-big- small-big-small. Each of these contained pebbles and shells. Behind these were a coil of jute rope (not the plastic kind), a lobster pot into which Jane had put a collection of clam shells after she'd eaten the inhabitants, a huge steel saucepan (the kind people had for making jam) that was big enough for her to sit inside in a horrible parody of the fate that befell so many of her kind, a mirror designed for a toddler that had a frame like a daisy, a cricket ball (somewhat battered), and the bleached-white jaws of a small shark. Other toys floated – a tennis ball, a football, a ring frisbee, and some plastic stacking cups in primary colours. He had noticed that the toys changed – Arthur must be trying to keep her entertained. Jane got into the saucepan and then reached out to pick up a hard plastic toy shark which must have come from the gift shop. She morphed and disappeared below the rim of the pot.

Jim was in no hurry to leave, but he glanced at his watch – 4.45pm. He had a little while yet before the centre closed. When he looked back up he saw a blurry reflection of himself in the glass of Jane's tank – he had been looking beyond that before. Tank Jim looked how he felt – dishevelled and tired and not that different from the first time he'd been in here, over seven years ago, although then his hair had been more black than grey and he'd also looked shocked.

It had been an accidental visit. He'd knocked off work and had been walking along the seafront to clear his head before heading home. Eva, with whom he'd then been living for three years, had said she'd be working late. She was in charge of publicity and marketing at Ottersea Arts Centre, so she often worked evenings, and what with his hours, some weeks they barely met. It had been summer half-term and the promenade and beach were packed with families. He'd stopped to watch slightly enviously as a dad and three kids played with a frisbee in the shallows. He and Eva had talked about kids, but she said she wasn't ready yet. After a while he'd turned away. He would walk past the arts centre on the way home. He thought of calling in, but he didn't want to get stuck in some dank private view where the only drinks available were warm white wine or stomach-cramp-inducing orange juice from a paper cup. There were people up on the roof garden where they had a café and held events. He glanced up, hoping to see Eva. And there she was. She was leaning on the rail around the edge, and as he watched, a man came up behind her, not just any man, but the centre director, a tall, skinny guy called Jago who wore velvet jackets in winter and white linen ones in summer. It was a white linen jacket night. He handed Eva a paper cup that would be half-full of the awful white wine and kissed her on the forehead. And she had smiled up at him, taken a sip of the drink, and then kissed him, quickly, on the lips. Those kisses were worse, he'd thought afterwards, than if they had been big romantic ones. They looked like kisses of familiarity, kisses between two people who were already together, an accepted couple. Jim had stood there gawping. Perhaps sensing him there, Eva had glanced in his direction, and he'd scarpered. He didn't want to go home. The first place he'd come to was the Oceanworld Centre. He'd gone straight in and bought a ticket, even though the boy on the desk said they'd be closing in half an hour. He'd stood in the glass tunnel and watched the sharks. He remembered wondering why they were allowed to be in the same tank as a couple of big turtles. Why weren't they attacking the turtles in some gruesome feeding-frenzy way? Now he knew that the aquarium's sharks were of the blacktip reef variety; they looked impressive but only ate smaller fish like mullet and groupers and never ate people. He'd carried on through the tunnel and found the bench where he was now, in front of the octopus tank. The octopus at that time had been another common one. He'd watched it eating something. It had ignored him. What he'd just witnessed between Eva and that shit Jago couldn't have been nothing. Nobody kissed someone else on the forehead unless they were already with them. And what did that make him? Cuckolded. That old word was perfect for it. Jago was somebody that they'd made jokes about, or thinking about it, he had. How long had this been going on? He was a detective who'd failed to detect something right in front of him.

Eva had got home late, later than would be normal for some private view. He'd been sitting there in the dark without the TV on. A storm had blown in, the sort of late spring one that brings down trees.

'Hello, Eva. Long day?'

'Just the usual – private view and then some of us went for supper.'

'Some of us? Who is *some of us*?'

'Jim?' He had never spoken to her like this before and he hated the way it made him sound – suspicious and bullying – but he went on.

'I was walking home along the seafront. I saw you – being kissed by Jago in his fucking linen jacket. And you kissed him back.'

'I was… it was…' She sank down in the armchair opposite, not where she normally sat on the sofa beside him. 'I'm sorry.'

'How long has it been going on?'

'A while,' she whispered.

'Jesus!'

He'd taken his car and driven to the clifftop carpark, not with thoughts of jumping, just to be buffeted by the wind and to hear the waves crashing below. He slept in the car and awoke, shivering, at 5am, and drove back home. Eva was asleep or doing a good impression of a sleeper. He showered, shaved, changed his clothes and went into the station early. When he got home that evening, she was gone. A few months later, Eva and Jago were married, and a year after that they had a baby. It wasn't that she hadn't wanted to get married and have a baby, she just hadn't, in the words from one of her favourite movies, wanted to do that with him.

Now, standing there with the watery music playing, Jim decided that Jane wasn't going to emerge from her saucepan. He went over to the glass to say goodbye. He gently leant his forehead against the cool glass, hoping that she might emerge again.

'See you soon, Jane,' he said, but only in his head. He expected she had powers of telepathy along with all her other complex and remarkable senses.

He heard soft footsteps coming through the glass tunnel behind him and then a gentle young voice:

'We'll be closing in a few minutes, sir.' He turned. It was the pretty new girl from the reception desk.

'Thanks.'

'Have you spotted her?' she asked.

'She's in that big saucepan.'

'Yes, she loves that,' said the girl. She came and stood beside him. 'A bit tactless, isn't it, giving her a saucepan? But luckily, she doesn't know.'

'As far as we know,' said Jim. He had watched a documentary where desperate squid fought to save their fellows from a fishing boat, some giving their lives. They obviously knew a terrible fate awaited any that were hauled aboard that ship of doom, though no survivors could have returned to tell the tale.

'We're just about to check things for the night, see that the top of the tank's secure,' said the girl. She disappeared behind a 'staff only' door and then reappeared on a platform behind the tank from where she checked the temperature of the water. 'They are escape artists. I read a book where an aquarium octopus escaped from her tank at night but because the floor was still wet from being cleaned, she died from the bleach and stuff.'

'Nasty.'

'Horrible.'

'I haven't seen you before,' said Jim. She looked at him from across the top of the tank and smiled.

'I'm here for the summer, doing an internship.' Arthur came through the same 'staff only' door and stood beside her. He and Jim nodded to each other.

'If you've got a minute, Arthur,' said Jim, 'there's something I'd like to ask you about.'

'That sounds serious,' said Arthur. He checked the lid of the tank too and then joined Jim in front of it. 'Lottie, could you go on to the hospital tanks?'

'I'm working on a case,' said Jim, when she'd disappeared and Arthur had come round to join him. 'Body on the beach. What I'm looking for is an expert opinion. If it goes to court, we'll be looking for an expert witness, but just informally, could you give me a steer?'

'Sure,' said Arthur.

'So, the guy's head was in a rock pool. You're going to get lots of scratches and so on – a possible fall or otherwise from the cliffs and a spell in the water. But where this guy is balding, he's got these red dots and little scratches. The pathologist hadn't seen anything exactly like this before. What do you think?'

'Hmm,' said Arthur. 'How big?'

'Mostly like pin pricks, but with redness around them.'

'There's lots that could do that. Look at this,' said Arthur, showing Jim his forearm. 'These little dots – scars from jellyfish stings – got those in the sea, not at work.' He stepped closer to the illuminated tank so that Jim could better see them. 'You can get stung just from loose tentacles in the water. Or if it's in a rock pool – it could be sea anemones. Or maybe a starfish. Did you see what was living in there?'

'Didn't think to look closely at the time, but there's pictures of the body in situ.'

'How long ago was it?'

'Just a few weeks.'

'If there were sea anemones then, they'll probably still be there now. You can get jellyfish stings at any time of year. The blooms aren't at their peak yet, but they're always about.'

'Thanks,' said Jim. 'So, do you think these dots sound unusual?'

'No,' said Arthur. 'Nothing unusual.'

Jim headed home to his empty house and empty fridge. He wondered what his sister Loretta and her family were doing, then realised that they'd gone on holiday. He should have picked up something to eat on the way home. He wondered what Grace was doing. She'd probably be cooking something proper. She often brought in boxes of leftovers to heat up for lunch – Caribbean food that smelled delicious. He dialled the Chinese takeaway and waited for his usual to arrive.

9am Briefing (No Doughnuts)

Jim sat on the desk at the front of the room waiting for the stragglers.

'OK,' he said, as the last person sat down. 'So here's where we are with the Sumal case. The coroner says it's suspicious – but could be suicide. Nothing obvious to trigger that at the moment, so we keep looking at everything and everyone. We need to rule everything out. We're nowhere near having a prime suspect. Still lots of loose threads. Our guys in Reading haven't come up with anything. Sumal hadn't been there for a few weeks, and it seems like his son does most of the face-to-face with their lettings, so any grudge might presumably be against him.

'The son, Bal, his alibi checks out and there's no clear motive – no apparent tension there. Got on well. We've got him and his car on CCTV in Reading pretty much constantly for the week before his dad was last seen alive. Bal Sumal wasn't in Ottersea for two weeks before his dad went missing, then not until after the body was found. Seems like an OK guy – been very open with passing the tech on. The finances all look healthy. We haven't found any debts apart from buy-to-let mortgages, and they're creaming it on those. Definitely doesn't seem like financial troubles pushed him over the edge or debts made him a target.

'Mr Sumal was last seen in the bookies at 4.17pm, but

he wasn't, from what we know so far, a big gambler. No financial problems.'

'What about life insurance, Sarge?' someone asked.

'He was well covered. His wife and the kids will be well looked after.'

'Could that be a motive?'

'It could. He was the one who took it all out. She's the beneficiary, then going to the kids equally. The policy is a few years old, so she was biding her time, if it was her.'

'What's your impression of Sukhi Sumal, Grace?'

'She's very reserved, but when she does say anything, it's something random – like suddenly saying she wants to get a dog.'

'Maybe she's just worried about security?' said DC Andy Barns. 'I mean, if your husband has potentially been murdered and you've got two daughters at home…'

'No, she wants a spaniel or a bichon frise – hardly a guard dog. Sounded like she just always wanted a dog, and now he's gone, she can get one. Maybe he was allergic or something, or he just didn't like them. They seem to have lived different, separate sort of lives. You look at his stuff – it's all designer and brands – he had the latest iPhone and she has some old Motorola and wears acrylic cardigans. Why's that? It seems like she was kept behind the scenes at Flakies, always stuck upstairs in the freezer room. Her life is her kids. No social life. No social media. And she said she likes going for walks by herself.'

'We need to go further down this avenue,' said Jim. 'Public appeal and see how they all react. Maybe he was a bully, coercive control and she finally cracked. We need to think about the oldest daughter too, Kiran, though it seems pretty unlikely. What are your thoughts there, Grace?'

'Seems she's the one holding it all together. Very capable. Obviously close to her mum and the rest of them, less so to her dad. Doesn't have a motive unless he was abusing any of them, and I haven't got that vibe about her and the little one.'

'What about the other staff at their ice cream place?' asked Jim.

'They seem to do almost all of it themselves. They get various sixth formers or whatever each year. Kiran and her mum work really hard,' said Grace.

'OK,' said Jim. 'Grace, can you talk to the family about doing an appeal, and we'll get as much publicity for that as we can. Let's put them under the spotlight, specially the mum.'

Impromptu Cuticle Work

It wasn't that Diana was feeling guilty – he'd had it coming – but she did want to see Mrs Sumal properly for herself. She locked up Marine Heaven and went into Waitrose where she stood for a while looking at the flowers. She wanted to get something nice, but it couldn't be *too* nice or they might wonder why. She settled on two bunches of lisianthus, one purple and one white. With their green foliage and the Waitrose wrapping they had a nice suffragette look which seemed appropriate. She needed a few things herself so she picked those up too – some miso paste, a bag of rocket leaves (even though she was officially against bagged salad), some English strawberries and a punnet of organic blueberries. She had thought of getting some chocolates for the Sumal children (she knew there were some) but presumed it would be coals to Newcastle as they ran an ice cream parlour. Plus, she didn't want to encourage bad habits, even if they were in mourning.

It was just before 5pm when she arrived at Flakies; things seemed to be calming down for the day. There were families sitting over disgusting concoctions of whipped cream, ice cream, bananas, glace cherries and chocolate. A group of teenagers sat in a booth at the back drinking coke, and an old couple who should have known better were tucking into plates of waffles. Diana wondered if there was a choice of syrup; maple syrup being preferable to golden as it had a lower GI index. She had read an article about its cancer-preventing properties (though that might just be because Canadians were a healthy bunch). It was even supposed to prevent periodontitis, which seemed counterintuitive. Or perhaps Flakies offered some sort of stevia option, not that she would ever opt for anything to do with waffles or syrup.

She joined the queue. There was a pretty young woman in her twenties behind it, presumably a Sumal daughter. The girl had good hair and skin, but dark circles under her eyes that needed attention. There were only a few people ahead in the queue, but they took forever deciding what they wanted. Perhaps, Diana wanted to say, if people were only allowed *one* scoop of ice cream, they wouldn't take such an age. At last it was her turn.

'What can I get you?' the girl asked.

'Actually,' said Diana, 'I wondered if I could give these to your mother. I heard about your sad loss and wanted to give her my condolences. I'm chair of the Ottersea WI.' She held up the flowers.

'Thanks,' said the girl. 'She's actually there at the back, or I can give them to her.' Diana looked to the back of the café where in the last booth a smallish Asian woman was sitting with a little girl – a younger version of the one behind the counter.

'Can I buy her a cup of tea, or whatever she'd like, and something for you and your sister?'

'Um, OK,' said the girl. 'And what about you?' Diana glanced up at the huge menu on the wall. There was no fennel tea.

'Just a black tea for me.'

'Cheers,' said the girl. 'I'll do a small smoothie for Nindy and a cup of tea for Mum. I'm OK.'

'That's good,' said Diana. 'It must have been a great shock.'

'I meant I don't want a drink or anything,' said the girl. She turned away and started loading pre-cut mango and banana into a blender. Diana shuffled along to where the till was and waited to pay a spotty teenage boy. The girl soon had a tray ready with two big white mugs of tea, one with milk, and a tall glass of smoothie with a bamboo stirrer and a stripy paper straw that looked too thin for the liquid. Diana paid and put a pound coin in the pink plastic bowl for tips.

'I'll carry the tray over for you,' said the girl. She turned to the waiting queue: 'Be right back.'

Diana followed her to the table.

'Mum, this lady's come with some flowers from the WI and she got you this tea and the smoothie for Nindy.'

'Very kind,' said Mrs Sumal. 'Everyone is being very kind.'

'The least I can do,' said Diana. 'Can I join you for a moment?' Mrs Sumal gave a tiny nod.

'Thanks,' said the child called Nindy.

'You can bring the tray back, Ninds,' said the big girl going straight back to her station.

'My Kiran is such a good girl,' said Mrs Sumal. 'She and Bal and Nindy are all being so good.'

'I'm so sorry for your loss,' said Diana. 'It must have been a terrible shock.' Mrs Sumal just nodded. 'I'm the chair of the WI, the Women's Institute. I brought you these.' She put the flowers down on the table.

'Very nice,' said Mrs Sumal. She looked at them but didn't pick them up.

'Do you want me to cut them up and put them in the Orangina bottles?' asked Nindy.

'They're for your mum, for all of you, not the café,' said Diana. 'But of course put them in the café if you prefer.'

'What's WI?' asked Nindy.

'Women's Institute. It's a club for ladies. We do lots of nice things, your mum could come if she wanted to.'

'What, like trips?' asked Nindy.

'Sometimes. We meet every month. It's something different each time. Here, I brought you a leaflet.' She took one out of her bag. Mrs Sumal didn't take it, so Diana but it down on the table. 'You'd be very welcome.' Nindy picked it up. It was made from a sheet of A4 card, folded triptych-style.

'Making bath bombs – can kids go?'

'I'm afraid not,' said Diana. 'It's usually just for ladies. And I'm afraid we've already had the bath bombs evening.'

'Aw, not fair.'

Diana picked up her mug and took a sip of her tea. Mrs Sumal did the same. Nindy began to drink her smoothie. The straw was soon soggy and unusable, so she gulped it instead.

'Your older daughter could come with you, if she's over eighteen,' said Diana. 'Our deputy-chair, Cass from Teapot Paradise has a niece staying and she might come. We welcome young women.'

'Will Bal look after me, then?' asked Nindy.

'He could,' said Mrs Sumal. That didn't sound like an agreement to come, thought Diana, but at least she had offered. She would ask Cass to drop round too – people always warmed to Cass. She was good at this sort of thing, and she wouldn't wonder why Diana was suggesting it – being neighbourly and offering condolences would seem natural to her. Though knowing Cass, she'd have been already. Mrs Sumal's hands and fingers around her mug looked sore and dry. Her nails were in a terrible state with ragged cuticles.

'I'm a beautician,' said Diana. 'I'd be very happy to give you a complimentary manicure. I can do a mini-mani for, um, Nindy too.'

'What's a mini-mani?' asked Nindy.

'To make your hands and nails smarter,' said Diana. 'I use lovely, scented cream for your hands to make them soft and smooth, give you a hand massage, and then strengthen, shape and polish your nails.'

'Free?' asked Nindy.

'As a treat for you and your mum,' said Diana. 'It's important to look after yourself when sad things happen.'

'Mum's hands are always cold from the freezer room,' said Nindy.

'Nindy, ssshh,' said Mrs Sumal.

'Cold and wind are the enemies of hands,' said Diana.

'It isn't windy in there, but it is really cold,' said Nindy.

'I also do a hot wax treatment,' said Diana, 'that's lovely. The hands are gently coated with naturally organic paraffin and beeswax and then placed in specially heated gloves.'

'I once got some candle wax on my arm,' said Nindy. 'It hurt.'

'Oh, this doesn't hurt,' said Diana. 'I'm very careful not to hurt my clients. Anyway, I think I have one of my own leaflets in my bag.' Diana always had one of her leaflets in her bag, they were there in an envelope under her cosmetics pouch. Taking one out now, she realised it was an old one that still listed dermaroller hair loss treatment and other "Treatments for Gentlemen". Well, if people behaved like gentlemen, their treatments would go as planned. She looked up at the now fatherless little girl and smiled rather wildly. She pushed the leaflet across the table to Mrs Sumal.

'Thank you,' said Mrs Sumal, 'you're very kind.'

'Not at all,' said Diana.

'What's in your flowery bag?' asked Nindy, reaching for the make-up bag that Diana had put down on the table too.

'Things I always carry with me,' said Diana. 'Lipstick, mascara, powder, essential creams, cuticle trimmer, nail files, that kind of thing.'

'So, you could do me and my mum a hand thing right now?'

'A massage and manicure,' said Diana. 'I don't have everything with me, but I can do a taster.'

'Me first!'

'Nindy,' said Mrs Sumal, 'I'm sure the lady's very busy.'

'This cream smells of roses,' said Diana. 'Here, would you like a smell?' She squirted a tiny bit of the cream out so that it stayed on the end of the tube.

'Mmm,' said Nindy. 'Can I try some?'

'It's up to your mum,' said Diana.

'Mum?' asked Nindy. Mrs Sumal blinked. 'Mum, can I try it?'

'Perhaps I should go,' Diana said.

'Mum?'

'I don't mind,' said Mrs Sumal. Nindy took a huge squirt of the cream.

'Attar of roses is very precious,' said Diana, eyeing it. 'It takes two hundred and fifty pounds of rose petals to make a single ounce.'

'What's an ounce?' asked Nindy.

'A big spoonful,' said Diana. 'Now you rub it in. Your hands will be lovely and soft. And the scent of roses is healing and uplifting.'

'I think I've got too much,' said Nindy. 'My hands are all shiny.'

'Rub it gently into your mum's hands, if she doesn't mind,' said Diana. She sat and watched as the little girl did that. The mother and daughter's hands slipped around each other like the pair of otters she'd once seen at Arthur's sealife place. Mrs Sumal began to smile.

'It does feel much better,' she said. 'My hands were dry.'

'Please,' said Diana, 'Keep it. And this one's for your nails.' She drew another, slightly smaller tube out of the bag. 'You rub it into your nails and cuticles a couple of times a week. It's very strengthening.'

'Strengthening,' said Mrs Sumal. 'That's good.'

'What's cuticles?' asked Nindy. 'Sounds rude.'

'I thought that when I was your age,' said Diana. 'Cuticles are the parts at the bottom of each nail, the places where the nails start to emerge. They can get very ragged, sore, and unsightly if they aren't looked after properly. So, you rub the cream in and gently push them back, like this.'

'Can you do it for me and Mum?' asked Nindy.

'I never touch people without their permission,' said Diana.

'Mum, can this lady do our nails?'

'I'd be delighted,' said Diana. 'It's the least I can do. I don't have everything with me, just the basics that I always carry, but if you're happy with that…'

'It would be very nice,' said Mrs Sumal.

Diana looked at Mrs Sumal's nails. They were cut rather short and had traces of some pale pink polish – not a colour Diana would have recommended for her – something more coral would have suited her skin tone better.

'I'll just do a quick file, buff and hand massage,' said Diana. 'But do come into the salon if you'd like the full treatment.' She took a few napkins from the plastic holder and spread them out on the table. 'There, that will make it a bit more hygienic and easier to clean up. And no one will see us, here at the back.'

'We get everything in here,' said Mrs Sumal. 'People brush their hair and do their make-up when they've had their ice creams. When they're on holiday, they think it doesn't matter how they behave. Kiran had to stop a customer from changing a baby's nappy on a table last week.'

'Ugh,' said Diana. 'Well, this isn't quite as bad. And it is *your* café.'

'I suppose it is now,' said Mrs Sumal, 'mine and Bal and Kiran and Nindy's. It seemed like my husband's before, everything did, though Kiran has been doing so much since she left school.'

'So, Kiran's looking after things, is she?'

'Yes, she's a very good girl.'

'And you have a son too?'

'Yes, Bal, he works very hard on the lettings, he was already working with his dad. He knows what to do. They both do.'

'So, they both know what to do for the businesses, that's good. I know things must be very hard,' said Diana, 'but it's great that you have such capable children.' She started by getting rid of the remnants of polish with remover wipes from the little round tub she always carried with her and then filed and buffed Mrs Sumal's nails and cut off the worst of the frayed cuticles. If only she'd had her remover with her, she'd have been able to do it thoroughly.

'And does Bal live nearby too?' she asked. Hopefully he wasn't a complete shit like his dad.

'He lives in Reading where most of the properties are.'

'Oh, he lives in Reading, that's nice.'

'But he visits a lot.'

'He visits a lot, that's good.'

Using the rose cream, she massaged Mrs Sumal's hands, gently loosening each joint. She felt Mrs Sumal's hands relax and warm in her own. It was nice to work on a client that really needed it and was so appreciative; so many of her regulars just took it all for granted.

When she was younger, Diana had wondered how it was that grown-ups could talk to each other about nothing with such ease, but when her father had been ill and in hospital, she'd noticed how the nurses kept conversations going with patients by just repeating things back to them. She never talked incessantly when she was doing treatments, aiming just to soothe and listen. Now, she finished the massage in silence, but there was the chatter of customers nearby, the sound of Nindy drinking her smoothie, and Motown hits playing in the background. Diana supposed that Kiran behind the counter got to control the music and must make choices based on pleasing the customers whilst choosing stuff that she could also tolerate.

'That was very nice,' said Mrs Sumal when Diana had finished. 'You're very kind to come and visit us.'

'The least I could do,' said Diana, again. 'Would you like me to do Nindy's?'

'Yes!' said Nindy.

'Go and wash your hands first, then,' said Mrs Sumal, indicating the Ladies room at the back of the café with a tiny jerk of her head.

When Nindy came back her hands were still slightly damp, but they looked clean, at least for a child's. Diana patted them dry with some more of the napkins.

'You have very pretty nails,' she said. 'They look like little shells, but they are too soft and delicate for me to file at the moment. I'll just do the massage.' Nindy smiled at the compliment.

'Say thank you, Nindy,' said Mrs Sumal.

'Thank you.'

'My pleasure.' The little girl's hands were rather dry. Diana wondered what bath and handwash products they used, probably some industrial-scale things they bought for the café.

'When I was a little girl,' said Diana, 'I used to love temporary tattoos. Do those still exist? They came in these lovely paper bags called jamboree bags that had sweets and things in.'

'We have mehndi for weddings – Mum and Kiran are really good at that.'

'I'd advise against *ever* getting a permanent tattoo,' said Diana. 'I see lots of people in my salon who either now regret them, or as they get older and the tattoo fades, it really doesn't look very nice. You should keep your lovely young skin unsullied.' Had the child's father had a tattoo? She didn't remember one. She would have remembered one. 'And people forget their original purpose was for sailors – and who wants to look like some old sailor when they've got such pretty skin as yours?'

'Why did sailors have them?'

Oops. Now she realised why the idea of tattoos had come into her mind – it was so that if sailors or their body parts were washed up after a wreck, people might be able to identify them. It seemed rather tactless to explain. She needed to change the subject.

'I don't know. I expect they got bored on long voyages,' she said. And she'd just read an article about chopped off feet in trainers being washed up somewhere in Canada. People had thought it was some foot fetishist serial killer, but it turned out that it was just that trainers were so floaty and preserved the foot inside them when everything else was eaten away.

The child's skin looked much better with some moisture in it. Hers and her mother's had been so grey and neglected before she'd begun. They were likely lacking in vitamin D too, being darker skinned and living in England. If Mrs Sumal spent her days indoors, that was pretty much a certainty.

'It's really important to look after yourselves, particularly after a tragedy. Are you taking vitamin D, for instance?'

'Vitamin D?' asked Mrs Sumal.

'It's very good,' said Diana. 'Most people don't realise that they are deficient in it. It's called the sunshine vitamin and it's just so important for bones, skin and good sleep.'

Kiran appeared at the table, ready to take the tray.

'This lady has been so kind,' Mrs Sumal told her.

'It's Diana,' said Diana. 'Please do drop into the salon if you'd like a manicure on the house, and do come along to the WI meeting – we're a very friendly lot, a group of us go swimming together too.'

'Are you the ladies who go to the pool in the rocks together?' asked Mrs Sumal.

'That's right,' said Diana. 'Do you like swimming?'

'I did. There was a lovely pool where I grew up – we would all go after school. But the pool here – I don't like that sculpture.'

'Nor do I,' said Diana. 'I just try not to look at it when I'm there. Once you're in the water, it's easy enough to avoid looking up at it. Do join us one day. I'll drop a new salon leaflet through the door – this one has smoothie on.' That was a good excuse to put it back in her bag and ensure they didn't read about the hair loss treatment she used to offer.

Puffin Suit

Another day. Lottie stood on the promenade zipped into the puffin suit which smelled of sweat and general fishiness. She hoped that the smell was just internal to the costume and that the people she was accosting with "Kids Go Free" leaflets wouldn't think that it was her, not that anyone would recognise her unless they came up really close and peered under the beak to where the eyeholes were. There were also holes for her hands on the undersides of the wings to give her just enough manoeuvrability to give out the leaflets. You were meant to wear giant orange furry feet too, but she had sneaked out wearing just her green strappy sandals in the hope that a bit of ventilation at the bottom would prevent her from dying of heat exhaustion. Small dogs with small-dog complexes barked at her and the occasional sensitive child burst into tears, but she was impressed by how obedient people were; most of them automatically took a leaflet when it was thrust towards them.

In the distance she saw Kiran, the girl from Flakies, walking towards her and "The Girl from Ipanema" began to play in her head. It made a change from the medley of sea-related songs that had been stuck in her head since her first day at the Centre: "Beyond The Sea", "Octopus's Garden", "My Bonnie Lies Over The Ocean" (which they'd sung as a round at primary school), "Orinoco Flow" and "Sailing".

Kiran really was tall and tan and young and lovely, although the way she walked was not with a samba. She was wearing a big black T-shirt with the Flakies logo in pink across it, black leggings and trainers, an outfit that Lottie suspected was her year-round uniform. As she approached, Lottie smiled, but then realised that Kiran wouldn't be able to tell it was her in the puffin outfit. But she was wrong. Kiran came straight up to her.

'Alright, Lottie.'

'How did you know it was me?'

'The sandals. I noticed them before – they're really nice. You must be boiling in there.' Lottie flapped her wings.

'It's horrendous and it stinks of other people's sweat.'

'How long have you got to do it? Can you take a break?'

'A quick one.'

'Come on then,' said Kiran.

Lottie waddled and Kiran walked over to the nearest bench overlooking the sea. Once they were sitting down, Lottie undid the Velcro down the front of the suit. She kept the head part on as the beak made a convenient sunshade, as though she was wearing a huge baseball cap pushed back on her head.

'Wait here,' said Kiran. She went to the kiosk by the entrance to the pier and came back with a bottle of water for Lottie. She had her own one already and took it out of her bag.

'I shouldn't be seen drinking out of a plastic bottle,' said Lottie, 'but thanks. I was about to expire.'

'Hide it in your flipper,' said Kiran.

Lottie laughed. 'My wing. I'm meant to be a puffin but loads of people think I'm a penguin.'

'Penguin – puffin – what's the difference?'

Lottie could have explained but decided not to. 'The puffins here are the only ones I've ever seen,' she said. 'Every holiday my parents took me on, we'd go on a boat trip to try to see dolphins or puffins or whatever, but somehow we never did. We even went to a place called Puffin Island, and the moment the boat set out, the guide said that there wouldn't be any puffins as the breeding season had finished. Puffin Island – No Puffins.'

'We never really went on holidays,' said Kiran. 'If you live at the seaside and the holidays are your busiest time, you aren't going away to some other beach.'

'I guess not,' said Lottie. 'How are you all doing?'

'It's just really weird. Weird and sad. Sometimes, just for a minute when I'm busy, I forget, and then I remember again, and I can't believe it. We still haven't been allowed to have his funeral. Mum's downstairs more now, so that's good. And people are being nice. People we don't know have been bringing cakes and lasagnes and things. This lady from the WI came in yesterday and she sat with Mum for ages. I looked round and she was only giving Mum a manicure. She has a posh little beauty salon – the sort of place that Mum would never go to in a million years.'

'What did she look like?' asked Lottie.

'Skinny. Tall. Dark hair. Sort of super neat.'

'I think that was probably Arthur's sister. Arthur works at the centre. She's older than him – really bossy. It was probably her.'

'Well, she offered us free manicures.'

'You should go.'

'And she was saying Mum should go to the WI.'

'My aunt's in that. It's just women doing nice things together. A gang of them go swimming all the time and they do crafts and stuff.'

'Mum might feel like the odd one out.'

'I'll go if you go,' said Lottie. 'Then she wouldn't be the odd one out.'

'I knew you were desi,' said Kiran, 'Or mixed anyway. And part penguin.'

'Puffin,' said Lottie.

'Whatever. But yeah, that would be nice. Or something else.' Kiran took out her phone and Lottie put her number into it.

Planticide

Diana took her second cup of green tea with lemon into the front room to enjoy a few moments of tranquillity by the bay window before she had to leave for work. She was proud of the front garden – it was just as good now as in her parents' day. They would have been pleased to see how well the yellow tree peony was doing. She kept the lavender bushes that bordered the short path to the front door neatly trimmed, never allowing the woodiness to take over or cutting too deeply into the old growth which could kill them. The one time she'd asked Arthur to tidy them up she'd had to replace one – and he was meant to be good with living things. The view beyond the front garden should have been across the little park and to the sea, but there was a great stupid palm blocking it. Why on earth, she thought for the thousandth time, did people here think it was a good idea to grow these beastly things, *just because you could*? The Ottersea palms had been planted twenty years ago as part of a promenade regeneration project to great fanfare in the local press. She'd seen them covered in snow and their fronds tossed by each year's named storms, but they refused to die. She'd watched Monty Don cover his in sacking each year to preserve it as they could be killed by frost. Nobody bothered to protect them in Ottersea, where any snow or ice soon melted. They hadn't grown tall, just fat, and now looked like giant bloated pine cones that should have perished with the dinosaurs. She hated the one blocking her sightline down to the sea. Perhaps, she thought, she could take a travel mug of ice cubes each day on the way to work and tip them into its scaly heart. That might do the trick. She downed the last of her green tea, wincing though the bitterness was familiar, and went into the kitchen. She had prepared a box of salad the night before – spinach with walnuts and cherry tomatoes, topped with some nasty vegan grated cheese that she'd wanted to try but had discovered to be vile. She wasn't going to waste the money, although now that she'd read an article about the dangers of coconut oil, she should probably just put it in the bin. She filled her William Morris travel mug with ice cubes. It had been a present from Arthur. He should have realised that she despised William Morris and that they only had William Morris curtains from their parents' time because the windows were so big that changing them would have cost a fortune.

There was a convenient bench in front of the offending palm. Nobody would want to sit there with its spiky fronds tapping them on the shoulders. When no one was looking, she casually leant back and poured the ice cubes between some of the wooden scales of the trunk.

'Take that, you hideous interloper!' she hissed. 'You don't belong here.' She smiled as she walked away.

Fibreglass Cow

The uniforms said they had gone through the CCTV, including the recordings from the Freddy's Racing. Now they were eating doughnuts, as per.

'So, what have we got?' Jim asked.

'Here he is going up to the bookies,' said Gavin Poltree. And there was Raj Sumal, seen first from the front, looking slightly shifty, pulling his baseball cap down, and then heading into Freddy's Racing.

'He looks a bit worried,' said Jim. 'Wife probably didn't know he gambled, or how much.' And everybody always looked a bit strange on CCTV – either insubstantial, or shifty, or as though they were already a ghost.

'Seemed his wife didn't know much about what he got up to,' said Grace.

'What about inside?' asked Jim.

'Here,' said Will Potterton. The recording on his screen had been stopped, he rewound it a little. And there was Raj Sumal, sitting on one of the stools looking up at the screens. But he wasn't there long. Potterton speeded up the footage. Raj Sumal left. The street CCTV had him again, but only briefly. He headed down one of Ottersea's twisty-turny sideroads – a shortcut down to the seafront called Cobble Lane.

'No CCTV there,' said Gavin Poltree. 'And we can't find

him on the promenade. He disappears. Or we just can't spot him in the crowd. It's busy. We keep going over it.'

'Go through *everything*,' said Jim. 'Traffic cameras, shops' CCTV. I'll put out a request for tourists' pictures – he must have been caught somewhere, maybe in the background of a pic on someone's phone. Dash cams, maybe doorbells. Come on, Grace, let's get back out there.'

They started at the bookies and Kenny Roger's "The Gambler" began playing in Jim's head. Jim and Grace knew the manager, Steve, who was a dead spit of Walter White. He was used to their inquiries and called them out himself to the odd fight or if a drunk and lairy punter decided to bed down in the shop loo and wouldn't shift.

Now there were only a few punters in the shop. Jim figured that the rise of online gambling must have taken its toll. Steve was behind the counter with his deputy, Jackie, who had worked there for a thousand years. There should be rules, Jim thought, so that people over a certain age didn't have to wear crappy work uniforms. It seemed demeaning that a woman of Jackie's age had to wear a polycotton polo shirt with the company logo and an "I'm Jackie, I'm here to help" badge. He'd noticed that Steve almost always wore a brown woollen cardigan or an old tweed jacket over his polo shirt, so he must feel the same, or perhaps he just found the aircon too much. Jim pulled out the pictures they'd taken from the shop's CCTV to show them.

'Yeah,' said Jackie. 'He was in quite often, maybe twice a week.'

'And what was he like? Did he spend much?'

'Not big,' said Steve. 'Ten or twenty pounds a slip. Seemed like he could afford it. Landlord, wasn't he?'

'That's right,' said Grace. 'And owned Flakies, ran it with his wife and kids.'

'I saw it on the news,' said Jackie. 'Sad. So do you think he topped himself?'

'Can't say yet,' said Jim. 'Do you think he had a problem?'

'Not really,' said Steve, 'he was pretty laid-back.'

'We've been through your tape,' said Jim. 'Cheers for that. So, we know he was in here on the last day his family saw him. Did he mention where he was going afterwards?'

'Nah,' said Jackie, 'not that I remember anyway.'

'Why would he?' said Steve.

'From the tape, we have him leaving here just after four o'clock,' said Jim. 'But nothing after that. The tape made it look as though he was by himself in the shop. Have you noticed him with anyone before?'

'No,' said Steve. Jackie shook her head. 'He was a friendly enough guy, though,' said Steve. 'Would pass the time of day with you.'

'OK. If you do remember anything, or anyone comes in asking after him, give me a call.' Jim slid two of his cards across the counter to them. And he and Grace headed back outside.

'OK,' said Jim. 'Let's follow his likely path. He must have kept going this way, down Cobble Lane, or he'd reappear on the high street cameras.'

A seagull was staring at itself in a shop window. Jim wondered briefly about a gull's sense of self but didn't bother to say anything to Grace. A few steps further and they were outside Aunty Dolly's Fudge Shop with its distinctive old fibreglass Jersey cow, which was more the size of a large goat. People were compelled to pat it as they went by so that the paint on its back was worn away. Jim noticed Grace start to reach out as they approached, but then snap her hand back: no patting fibreglass cows whilst on duty. It was a short lane and Jim and Grace couldn't imagine that Raj Sumal would've been interested in any of the shops: Aunty Dolly's Fudge, The Olive Grove (a Christian bookshop), Crazy Daisy (a hippy clothes shop), a beauty parlour, and a shop selling frumpy shoes for retirees. They knew Raj Sumal bought himself expensive trainers – he was hardly likely to shop there.

They worked their way down the lane, starting with Aunty Dolly's, which had no need for CCTV as the fudge was all kept in glass counters. Customers were served by local teenagers who tried to neutralise the uniform mob caps by using huge amounts of mascara and eyeliner. The owner, daughter of the original Dolly, said that the only crime they had was people helping themselves to too many of the free samples.

'Shall we even bother with this one?' Grace asked. 'I mean he was a Sikh.'

'No stone…' said Jim, wearily. But after a quick chat with the shop owner, a woman with extremely long mousey hair held back by a white linen headband that looked like a misplaced dog collar, he had to admit that Raj Sumal having been in there was pretty unlikely. It was a similar story at the sensible shoes shop, and neither of those places had CCTV.

The owner of Crazy Daisy (a piratical seventy-something in a stripy T-shirt and black cargo shorts) said he knew Raj Sumal by sight, but couldn't recall him ever coming in; most of his customers were holidaymakers and teenagers. He had CCTV as shoplifting was a problem and was happy to give it to them but didn't think it would be any use. Annoyingly, his cameras were all trained on the interior.

As Jim pushed open the door of Marine Heaven Health and Beauty he knew Grace would be thinking 'Really, Boss?' and he was inclined to agree. Inside, a highly-groomed woman of about forty was sitting behind the counter, seemingly engrossed in a magazine.

'Hello. I'm DI Jim Paddon and this is DC Grace Brown,' said Jim. 'We're investigating the disappearance of a local man whose body was found on the beach last week. Can we have a chat?' The woman gave them a tight-lipped smile. 'Are you the owner? Can I take your name?'

'Yes, I'm Diana Parks, the owner. I'm rather busy, though, and I've got a client due soon. It's just me here on Wednesday mornings. Would you like a glass of water? This heat's never-ending.' She indicated the glass flagon on counter. There were slices of lime floating in it and a tray with glasses beside it. Jim could have murdered a coffee. And he had always been a bit suspicious of lime. And grapefruit, which always smelt a bit sweaty. Grace helped herself. Jim saw the woman's eyes flick to Grace's hands.

'And do try the lotion,' she said, gesturing towards an expensive-looking bottle of something on the counter. Grace made a tiny movement towards it but then, Jim was pleased to see, stopped herself. This could, of course, be a crime scene.

'Not while we're on duty,' said Jim, drawing out the pictures they had of Raj Sumal. 'This is the person whose movements we are trying to trace,' he said. The woman peered at the picture.

'He *certainly* wasn't a client,' she said and gave a little laugh.

'No, well. We think he walked down this street on the day he disappeared. Do you have CCTV or a video doorbell?'

'I'm afraid not,' she said, with the same brittle laugh. 'Just a "No Cash Kept On The Premises Overnight" sign. Almost everyone uses cards nowadays anyway.'

Behind them, the salon door opened with a tinkle of little brass bells and shells. Jim turned, expecting to see some lady coming in for a manicure or whatever, but it was a delivery guy with a large Dell box.

'Diana Parks?' the guy said.

'Yes,' she said, 'I've been waiting for this.'

He put the box down on the counter – it took up nearly all the space and shoved the bottle of lotion and a rack of leaflets precariously close to the edge. The woman tsked, but then said:

'Would you mind awfully carrying it through to the back for me? Just through here.' She glided out from behind the counter and opened a door to her left. Jim took a step forward, just to see. It was only a small kitchen. There was a table with some magazines and paperwork, a sink, fridge and microwave. Plus floor to ceiling cube storage holding folded blue and white stripy towels and the tools of her trade – lotions and potions and the like. It all looked very clean and organised. The woman signed the delivery guy's handheld with her finger. After he'd left she sanitised her hands. This Diana Parks was clearly running a tight ship.

'Is there anything else I can help you with?' she asked.

'Did you notice Mr Sumal walking by on July 4th, or any kind of altercation in the street? Did you notice anyone going by who looked distressed, confused or the worse for wear?'

'Hmm, no. I certainly don't remember anything. Most days are pretty much the same here,' she said. 'I have my regulars and often holidaymakers come in to get their nails done or to have a little treat. Almost always ladies. You'd be amazed at how much better a nice mani-pedi can make you feel,' she said, looking rather pointedly at Grace.

'Here's my card,' said Jim.

'Thank you.' She glanced at it and put it down out of sight.

Grace took one of the leaflets, folded it in half and put it in her jacket pocket. The brass bells tinkled again.

'Ah, my next lady.'

'Hello, Diana, sorry I'm a bit early.' The client sank down into one of the cane chairs in by the window.

'Lucinda, lovely to see you. I won't be a minute.' Diana Parks held the door open for Jim and Grace. 'Good luck with your search.' The bells tinkled behind them.

'God,' said Jim, when they were a few steps down the road. 'People go to those places to relax?' He rubbed at his nose. 'Just the smells would drive me crazy.'

'I guess scented candles aren't your thing.' That was the last of the shops. There was a little alleyway off to the right that led to a small short-stay car park, though people didn't use the cut-through much as it was full of bins.

'He could have gone down there,' said Grace.

'Hmm' said Jim. 'Probably no CCTV in the alleyway, but we can get it from the car park at the other end.'

'I don't think many people use that cut-through,' said Grace. 'It's pretty gross, with all the rubbish.'

'No stone,' said Jim.

'And no binbag either,' said Grace. They continued on to the seafront.

'Might as well get back to the station and get the uniforms onto it,' said Jim. He was longing for a cup of tea. His head was pounding from the salon and now rubbish smells and the sun's glare. If only it would rain. It must be the heat, he thought, making people careless; three middle-aged men in a small town having stupid deaths within a few weeks of each other was unusual, but probably, if you looked at it over a longer period, there would be nothing remarkable.

'Terribly sad business,' Diana told her client. 'They're looking for any sightings of that poor man who was washed up last week.'

'He owned Flakies, didn't he?'

'Did he?' asked Diana. 'I haven't really been following it. Anyway, your usual? You're here to forget about anything unpleasant. Come on through.' The woman looked down at her nails and smiled. 'I've got some new shades here,' said Diana.

A Blockage

Only occasionally did a visitor ask where the Oceanworld's water came from. Most people, if they wondered at all, probably thought it was like a swimming pool, circulating and filtered and cleaned but not changed very often. It came from the sea. Beneath the centre floor and under the promenade was a network of pipes that brought water in, filtered it many times and then supplied it at the correct temperature for each exhibit. Unwanted creatures were kept at bay while the centre's inhabitants were not flushed away. The inlet pipe was some way out to sea and covered by a grille that stopped most big things from getting into the system, but occasionally, perhaps pushed by a strong current, things did make it through and Mike, the chief maintenance guy, had to clean them from the series of filters in the centre itself. Condoms were the worst; they managed to sneak through along with wet wipes – the sorts of things that laid the foundations of fatbergs elsewhere. On one wall in the Our Seashore section they kept a display of rubbish that staff had picked up on the beach – fishing gear, crabbing lines, plastic bottles, lost spades, spent "disposable" vapes and barbeques, Crocs and flip-flops, polystyrene cups and trays from take-aways; all the usual suspects. They didn't pin up condoms or laughing gas canisters or sanitary towels, though they were often found too. If Mike picked up anything interesting or unusual from the inlet filters, he would give it to Helen, the centre manager: 'Something else for your rogues' gallery.' The used water was pumped away and out to sea. There weren't any grilles on the outlet pipe as it was assumed that creatures wouldn't get through the filters inside their tanks, but if one did, it would be carried straight out to the ocean.

The system was showing that the inflow was sub-optimal. Mike went to investigate, expecting wet wipes, bane of his life. Instead, he found a blue and white striped hand towel. He fished it out. It was tar-embellished with bits of gravel on it, otherwise it would have just floated. It felt like the towel his wife used for her hair; it had the same knobbly texture that grabbed at your skin. There must be some damage for that to make it through the first grille – he'd have to get it checked. He gave the towel a rinse and chucked away the wipes and bits of unidentifiable gunk that had been with it and took it to Helen's office.

'Nice one, Mike. Definitely one for the display. Why can't people just use cotton towels or bamboo nowadays? Who had to go and invent towels that won't ever biodegrade?'

'And clog the bloody filters,' said Mike.

'I'll put it up with all this tar and stuff still on it – the grosser the better.'

Back at the station, Jim ordered the CCTV from the car park at the end of the alleyway and set the uniforms to go through it when it arrived.

'We're looking for Sumal coming out of the alleyway and any vehicles that belong to him or known associates in the car park. It's the period from when he went missing to when he was found. Particularly July 4th, the day we have him at the bookies.' He gave them a list of people to look out for: Sumal himself, his wife, his three children (the youngest being an unlikely suspect, but still), the family's car and van, the Sumal tenants, and all the usual Ottersea lowlife suspects.

He made another cup of coffee and one for Grace and stared at the glass screen. It was the sort that they always had in movies now. You could write on it with drywipe pens and stick stuff on it, and in movies or TV shows, that led to the breakthrough.

'Correlation doesn't mean causation,' he said aloud.

'Pity, that,' said Grace.

He had never quite seen the point of these glass screens – from behind all you saw was mirror-writing and the backs of Post-it notes and other bits of paper. But looked a bit smarter and more hi-tech than the old whiteboards, and he supposed that was good for morale. The idea was that once you'd drawn the web of connections, the spider at the heart or lurking on the edge of it all would be revealed. The Sumal web was still pretty undeveloped, and no likely spiders had appeared. So perhaps they should be looking for the *unlikely* spiders. Maybe it was Bal, the son, or Mrs Sumal, or one of the daughters. If it was one of the girls, the others would be protecting her. Maybe Sumal had been a child-abuser. The whole family had seemed in shock, but perhaps that was something else at work. Mrs S had hardly said a word. Maybe her husband was abusive and had been about to start on one of the girls. Maybe she'd pushed him down the stairs or off a cliff. Maybe, maybe, maybe. They should have heard from the digital forensics guys by now. That was where most people's secrets lay. When they got that, they'd have some new directions to go in.

Jim powered up his laptop and opened his emails. The digital forensics *were* in. He went through the info and called a briefing.

'We still haven't got his phone,' he began. 'That's still missing, but it last pinged outside Ottersea at 2.19am on July 5th.' He wrote this on the glass screen – 'That's early in the morning on the day after the family last saw him. The family gave us his laptop, so we have lots of messages, but not a complete browsing history of what he did on his phone. We don't know all the apps he had on that. There were no threats or surprises in his emails or WhatsApp – he'd used that on his laptop for calls, so we've got at least some of his messages. His Fitbit is still missing.'

'What was he into? What came up on his laptop?' asked Grace.

'Wasn't into kids. Just all the usual stuff, nothing particularly nasty.'

'What about other women?' Grace asked. 'Or men?'

'Nothing from the laptop, emails or messages. Just a real bugger that we don't have his phone.'

It was all pretty tedious. So much of policing now came down to trawling through people's messages and checking CCTV. It wasn't what Jim had imagined when he'd signed up, though that was back in the early 90s when most people weren't even online. Things had started to change when Blackberry came in, though Ottersea hadn't been a town of early adopters. The mobile signal had been dreadful for years, what with the cliffs around the bay.

After a while of staring at Sumal's browsing history, Jim'd had enough. He walked along the seafront, back to the end of Cobble Lane. He sat on the wall, but facing away from the sea. It seemed that nobody used the cut-through to the car park – it must be too off-puttingly narrow and smelly with all the bins. A local might use it though, he supposed. Someone in a hurry.

The air was full of the sounds of summer, just as it ought to be. People were walking by with buggies or holding the hands of older children, or returning from work or the shops, others were gliding by on mobility scooters – the many ages of man. He wondered if he would make it to the mobility-scooter stage – he kind of hoped not – particularly if he was still on his own. He closed his eyes against the sun and the mobility-scooter people changed to turtles, or maybe basking sharks. He opened his eyes and swivelled round to face the sea. There were inflatable unicorns and swans everywhere. People stood, post-swim, like monks in their towelling robes. He was tempted to go down and join them. He hardly ever went in the sea. He imagined taking off his shoes and rolling up his trousers and going for a paddle, but didn't.

Toddlers in brightly coloured rash suits were playing by the water's edge. He watched as a little girl filled and emptied her pink bucket again and again in a cascade of diamonds. A little boy a bit like his nephew, Ed, was digging a huge hole. When he'd last seen him, Ed had, at eight, discovered The Beatles and had spent the whole weekend telling Jim about them and singing their songs. 'I look at all the lovely people,' Ed had sung in his sweet high voice. Jim wasn't going to be the one to tell him that all the people were lonely. Ah, all the lovely people. A family of many generations had set up camp just to the side of the steps down to the beach, clearly not bothered that they were in the busiest part. They had chairs and a yellow and orange windbreak and multiple cool boxes and stripy towels. They were soon joined by another member of the family with a tower of pizza boxes.

'Bloody hell! How many did you get, Connor?'

'They were doing twofer so I got us two each.'

The smell of pizza, mostly, he detected, with pepperoni, drifted towards him as the family tucked in. They were like a party of urban foxes, he thought, adapted to a new environment and making the most of it. Jim had caught the end of a wildlife show the night before. Urban foxes were evolving shorter snouts and getting smaller brains. That seemed about right. These urban foxes enjoying their pizzas were glossy and well-fed and definitely not suffering from mange. He wondered if they bothered to hide their bushy tails when they went swimming.

He loved to see these normal, not dead people, the grandparents, some fit with lithe, tanned bodies and legs that defied their ages, others exposing big, doughy arms and thighs, all in their holiday garb. He found it cheering that these people had shopped for and packed these clothes – the Hawaiian shirts, the strappy dresses that exposed sunburnt shoulders, the Panamas and bucket hats, as well as lots of baseball caps. He liked seeing women in floppy straw hats that gave them a 70s look. His mum had had one like that. He remembered the way it cast delicate shadows on her face, a bit like the patterns they'd made at school, crayoning over paper doilies, how hard it had been not to rip the paper and spoil the pattern. He had been good at drawing, mostly at copying things. He was careful and accurate, though his pictures had always looked a bit static. His little sister's had always been so much better, her people looked as though they were strolling across the page, his were more like photofit sketches: *Have you seen this man?* Loretta was an art teacher now, not the Great Artist she had hoped to be, though she had her own website, selling prints of her acrylics of gardens, flowers and cats. He wished he could see the world the way that she did, but he knew too much, had seen too much. Knew that the guy in the humorous T-shirt over there might be smashing his wife's face in later that night. Some things couldn't be unseen. If Jim couldn't hang out with his Loretta and her husband and Ed, there was only one person he wanted to talk to.

The Oceanworld Centre was close to closing when he arrived, but the woman on the desk nodded him through. He walked past the smaller tanks and the column of swirling jellyfish, with "Islands in the Stream" playing in his head. He went straight to Jane's tank.

She was in her den behind a new construction of clam shells that she'd built since his last visit. She had impressive building skills – they were carefully arranged so that even with the swirling water from the oxygen pump, the wall of them stayed firm. She had placed them all concave side down – such skill and planning. He could do with some officers as diligent. He went up to the glass and whispered, 'Hello, Jane. I've missed you.'

Figurines, Desktops, Breadmakers

'I really couldn't smash up a china dog,' said Katie.

'Me neither,' said Caroline, 'definitely not a dog. Not even a pitbull.'

'When I had my last blood test,' said Cass, 'I had almost no testosterone. I wonder if that means I won't have any rage.'

'Rage isn't a male preserve,' said Diana. 'I think that's rather the point of this.'

They were waiting at reception in Exeter Rage Room. The walls were lined with shelves of things that people could choose to destroy – fat desktop computers, grubby looking laptops, TVs, breadmakers, vast quantities of crockery and ornaments that were now considered ugly.

'A few years ago, there would have been those hideous German lava vases from the 60s and 70s, but people like those again,' said Caroline.

A door opened and a party of university students came out laughing, though some had tears on their cheeks. They were followed by the woman who'd come into Teapot Heaven. She was wearing, Cass noted, the same sunflower-patterned dungarees.

'Thanks for coming! Don't forget to review us online!' The woman turned to the waiting friends. 'Welcome to Exeter Rage, if you'd like to come this way.' She led them into another room where there were more shelves of doomed items and they were given forms to fill in, disclaimers to sign, and overalls and safety googles to wear. There was no choice of weapon, only scaffolding poles. They were going to be able to watch each other's smashing sessions on a big screen.

'I don't know what Graham would think,' said Katie.

'Oh, it says they recycle everything they can,' said Caroline. 'And what they can't was just going to landfill anyway. Maybe we can go in together.'

'I'm sorry,' said the owner, 'it has to be one person at a time.'

'People might run amok with the scaffolding poles,' said Diana.

'Exactly. Or hit each other accidentally. Now who's up first?' They all looked at each other.

'I will,' said Caroline, standing up in her head girl-ish way and adjusting her ponytail in its pristine velvet scrunchie. 'I think I'd like china, as long as it's ugly.' She chose a box of hefty beige crockery patterned with darker brown ears of corn. Once inside the smashing room, she turned to the webcam and waved to her friends, knowing they'd be waving back and cheering her on.

She raised the pole.

SMASH!

BLOODY
JEREMY
DYING!

CRASH!
LEAVING ME ALONE WITH A BLOODY FISH RESTAURANT!
BLOODY JEREMY LECHING AFTER EVERY FEMALE ON EARTH!
THWACK!
MAKING ME NOT BOTHER TO HEAVE HIM OUT!
SMASH!
LOOK WHAT YOU MADE ME DO!

THWACK!

BLOODY STUPID WOMAN LETTING HER BLOODY STUPID HUSBAND DIE!

CRACK!

BLOODY RESTAURANT! BLOODY DINERS EATING ALL THE BLOODY FISH!

BLOODY COMMERCIAL FISHING -- DROWNING DOLPHINS -- BLOODY PLASTIC FISHING STUFF--

SMASH!

BLOODY VEGANS
SHOWING US
WE'RE WRONG!

KAPOW!

BLOODY GLOBAL WARMING!
BLOODY DYING OCEANS!
BLOODY WORLD! BLOODY
HUMANS! BLOODY MEN KILLING
EVERYTHING! BLOODY PUTIN!
BLOODY WESTERN CIVILISATION!
BLOODY WARS! BLOODY
TALIBAN! BLOODY MEN!

Out of breath, she looked down. She was surrounded by shards and fragments. There was still more to go.

She could enjoy this more. She threw a side plate into the air and smashed it, tennis-style.

NOT BAD,
CAROLINE!
YOU'VE STILL
GOT IT!

KAPOW!
KAZAM!
CRASH!

She bowed to the webcam and laughed.

Up next, Cass vs a breadmaker and more beige china. She smiled and waved at her friends through the webcam, then felt rather silly. What good would smashing anything do? Shouldn't they be building and fixing things, soothing and healing? Then she thought of the news the night before, the children abducted from Ukraine. Landmines. The mothers whose sons would not come home. The bombs falling on schools and apartment blocks and playgrounds. She raised her scaffolding pole:

PUTIN!

ARMS MANUFACTURERS!

SMASH!

BLOODY ENDLESS WARS!

BASH!

BLOODY DISASTER CAPITALISTS!
THWACK!
BLOODY GOVERNMENT!
BLOODY HOSTILE ENVIRONMENT! BLOODY WAY TO TREAT REFUGEES!
JOHNSON! PRITI PATEL! REES-MOGG!
BLOODY BREXIT!

BASTARD
POLICE
MURDERER!

She paused, hot and sweaty.

BLOODY MENOPAUSE!
BLOODY MIDDLE-AGE!
BLOODY HOT FLUSHES!
BLOODY *LIFE!*

BASH!
BASH!
BASH!

She wiped her forehead on with the back of her hand. She was done. She surveyed the damage and hoped the fragments of china could be used as crocks in the bottom of plant pots, but really, that pottery was so hideous, it was better to take it out of circulation before someone decided it was nice again. She sank down onto the bench by the wall, took off her goggles, and gave the webcam a big wave. Then, just like Caroline, she helped the sunflower dungarees woman to sweep up.

'You were brilliant!' cried Katie when Cass came out. 'A virago, a vengeful angel! I really don't know if I can do it, though.'

'Go, on,' said Diana. 'Go next – it'll be good for you.'

'Stages of grief,' said Caroline. 'It did feel therapeutic.'

Katie's head was so small that she had to wear the kid-sized safety goggles.

'I'm so glad I'm here with you all,' said Katie. She didn't need to add "and not Graham". He would have gone berserk, either with the smashing or about the way something might be disposed of. There were so many things she could have said to him, so many things over the years, but smiling and nodding and biting her lip or digging her fingernails into the palms of her hands had been the safest option. Now she was alone in a room with a scaffolding pole, a flatscreen TV, and a huge box of chipped vases. She put the pole on the floor and took the vases out of the box one by one. It was true, they really weren't worth salvaging, not even with that lovely Japanese method of mending things with gold. One of the vases had a scene of foxhunting – well, that could go. She raised the pole

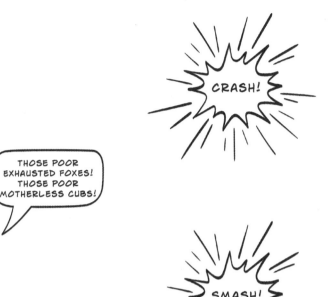

Even if foxes weren't always very nice people, they couldn't help it. Graham had gloried in reading Roald Dahl books to the boys. The cruelty—

The screen smashed.

NO MORE QUESTION TIME!

SMASH!

NO MORE GRAHAM SHOUTING AT THE TV!

WHACK!

NO MORE GRAHAM EXPLAINING EVERYTHING!

SMASH!

MORE
VASES!

CRASH!

NO MORE STEELY
FINGERS GRIPPING
HER ARMS!

NO MORE
ENDLESS
PLACATING!

SHE COULD WATCH
BAKE OFF AND *SEWING
BEE!* NO MORE
INTERRUPTIONS!

When the vases were all smithereens and the TV was a mess of broken glass and plastic, she stopped, out of breath, and put the pole down, took off the goggles, waved at her friends.

It wasn't a rage room – it was a joy room. Her friends hugged her. She couldn't stop smiling.

'I don't mind if you all need to get back,' said Diana, glancing down at her nails, which today were a particularly subtle pink.

'Don't be silly – you have to have a go,' said Cass.

'I'm really very calm inside, spin class is all I need, spin and swimming.' But she was already standing up, ready to don the goggles. The pole felt familiar in her hand, though she hadn't handled a scaffolding pole before. A car would have been nice to smash, or a whole house. She had to look casual, to act nonchalant. She had chosen a lamp and a box of plates and china oddments. The woman had said she should fill the box. She'd hoped for a gluggle jug – God she hated those hideous fish – or a plastic Barbie house, but there hadn't been any of those – probably all listed on Etsy for a fortune now.

There were some simpering figurines in the box, already chipped. She laid them down the workbench and smashed them, one by one. It was hard to be as poised and precise as she wanted to be, but she did her best. She waved to the webcam. The lamp had a yellow plastic shade—

The base was white china crackle glaze – she'd give it crackle glaze –

A hideous cheap gold planter, probably from a Christmas bulb kit – still mud-stained – God, why did these things even exist? God, she hated amaryllis. And bulbs – poking their stupid, phallic green shoots out of the ground.

Again—

A plate.

Another—

A ceramic swan.
Why did his stupid, fucking, hideous body have to wash up?
Teapot – no lid

THWACK!

BASTARD -- A HAPPY ENDING! SHE'D GIVEN HIM ONE--

CRASH!

MORE PLATES! MORE CUPS! CHEAP GLASS VASE! MAUVE VASE -- SHE HATED MAUVE--

SMASH!

HASSLING KAYLEIGH!

CRASH!

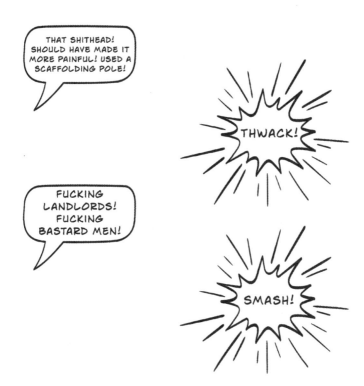

The box was empty – she wished she'd brought in more. She was out of breath.

She removed her goggles, wiped her forehead on her sleeve – God – what had come over her – she would never normally do that – would discreetly use a cleaning wipe. She smiled and waved to the others but waited until her breathing had returned to normal before she went to join them.

'Diana, you were magnificent!' said Caroline. 'You could do that for a living.'

'Thanks.' They were all hugging. Normally she hated to be hugged, but it felt good.

'Maybe I need a career change,' she said, laughing.

'I do feel a bit guilty about all the destruction,' said Katie, 'though it was fun.'

'Don't be silly,' said Diana. 'Feeling guilty is a waste of time. You should never feel guilty and never apologise. *Je ne regrette rien.*'

'Exactly,' said Caroline.

Exeter was heaving with shoppers and tourists. Everywhere was packed so they bought cups of iced coffee from a posh little van and went to sit in the cathedral close.

'I can't remember the last time I drank coffee in the afternoon,' said Katie. 'Graham was so against any caffeine after two o'clock. Now I suppose it doesn't matter if I break our routines.'

'We have to find our own routines now,' said Caroline, putting her arm around Katie's shoulders. 'You have to learn how to please yourself. Smash your old routines with a scaffolding pole. Or keep them of course, if they help.'

'It's all so strange,' said Katie. 'I never would have been able to do this, the smashing, if Graham was still here. He would have had some detailed plan for the day that he would say I'd forgotten about.' Cass gently took her hand. 'I'm too hot with the long hair, even when it's up. I only kept it long as he protested so much at any mention of a change.'

'It's very pretty,' said Caroline. 'I'm always seeing things on Instagram about silver sisters.'

'A bob would frame your face very well,' said Diana.

'I might just do that,' said Katie. They all smiled at her.

'We should definitely book for the whole group,' said Cass. 'And it's nice to support a business run by two women. I wonder if any other WIs have been – we might be the first. It does seem like quite a young-people thing, you know, like escape rooms.'

'We're the pioneers,' said Caroline. 'The ground-breaking, cutting-edge WI. We should be more radical in what we do.'

'The knitting project might cause quite a stir,' said Katie.

'I guess we could get more involved in some of the national campaigns.'

'Or do local things,' said Diana. 'Look for who the local bullies are and take them out, I mean campaign against them. The polluters, the bad landlords.' She rattled the ice cubes in her paper coffee cup. 'I mean, who knows how corrupt and evil some of the local politicians and police are. Judging by the news...'

'Oh, let's not talk about the news,' said Cass. 'It's all too appalling. That beautiful, young woman – a primary school teacher. Imagine having to explain that to your child, to her class. Now I'm talking about the news. Sorry.'

'If only it was like *Minority Report*,' said Caroline. 'Planning on raping someone – you're dead. Thinking about invading another country? Vaporised.' They all nodded.

'I think it's going to take more than guerrilla crochet projects to change things,' said Katie.

Katie was right, Diana thought, as she lay in the bath when she got home. It was going to take more than guerrilla crochet projects. Well, at least she'd done her bit with Raj Sumal. But the world was full of bullies. At least Katie and Caroline were free of their pigs of husbands now. Cass had been unencumbered for ages since she'd been traded in for a younger model – and she seemed the happiest of them all. What if the WI took out the whole Shanty Crew, one by one, or in some carefully orchestrated event. She lifted one elegant leg out of the Neal's Yard geranium-scented bubbles to admire her beautiful teal toenails.

Three Hearts

Lottie and Arthur were cleaning the exterior glass of Jane's tank. Jane had watched them for a while, but now was busy rearranging her clamshell wall.

'Did you know that octopuses have a sense of left and right?' Arthur asked.

'Really?'

'Yeah, with some species, the males squirt the sperm into the funnel that the females use to breathe, but with others, they hand it over, like a present, and the female will always use her right arm to take it. We don't know why yet.'

'Maybe it's just polite, like shaking hands – you just do it with your right,' said Lottie.

'There was a thing with Scouts – you were meant to shake hands with your left hand, kind of weird,' said Arthur.

'Secret handshake? Kind of Masonic?'

'I dunno,' said Arthur. 'There's so much we don't know about them, octopuses, not Scouts. And we aren't going to find it all out by looking at them in captivity. I'd really like to spend time with them in the wild.'

'And why do you think she walks across the sand at the bottom of her tank like that when swimming looks easier?' Lottie asked.

'Strangely, swimming takes more energy. You wouldn't think that, but it does. When she's swimming the heart that pumps blood to her organs stops beating so that's going to tire her out.'

'Mmm,' said Lottie, 'three hearts.'

They stood watching Jane rearranging the shells in her construction.

'Do you think it's a wall to hide behind, part of her den?' Lottie asked.

'I guess,' said Arthur. 'But I think she's also doing it for fun, like playing with Lego. We can't know without asking her.'

'She does seem to enjoy just rearranging them,' said Lottie. 'Look at the way she examines them and seems to weigh them and then rearranges them. I think she's making aesthetic judgements. She's an artist,' said Lottie. 'And I guess she does have time on her hands, her suckers. An intelligent creature has to fill it somehow. Nine brains and all those neurones. Like constant hyperaesthesia. But I guess they're used to it.'

Arthur turned to her and smiled. 'And three hearts, I wonder if she's aware of that. If she thinks about them, is aware of them. Are other creatures aware of their heartbeats? You'd think they would be, I mean, if they are running, or galloping, or swimming really fast and get out of breath, they must be aware of panting and the pounding in their chests, or in her case, her gill hearts.' He was aware of his own heart, beating a little faster than usual. He wondered what Lottie would do if he reached out and took her hand.

'God, it's hotter than usual today, even in here,' said Lottie. She took a step sideways away from him and began fanning herself with one of the centre leaflets.

Arthur said nothing. They stood watching Jane rearranging her wall until she seemed satisfied with it and disappeared into her den.

'Talking of hearts, I met this girl,' said Lottie. 'Kiran. Her dad was the man whose body was found on the beach.' Arthur pulled a face of sympathy.

'I was at school with her. Comes in with her little sister sometimes. She always seemed nice. I didn't know her that well – she was friends with all the popular kids – she was one of them. Half of everyone who was at school has moved away now.'

'That's sad,' said Lottie.

'Jobs, you know.'

'But you came back.'

'I didn't mean to, but then when I finished my MSc and the job was here, and Diana was ill... she looked after me after our parents died, and then Jane arrived, so I just sort of stayed.'

'Is she OK now?'

'She's fine. She had this mystery illness – it was really worrying – but then it turned out she was allergic to some obscure ingredient in one of the potions she uses. It had grape pips in, and just a whiff of it. They were the pips of some very particular type of grape. She isn't even allergic to grapes. You wouldn't believe some of the stuff she buys and uses on her clients, but maybe you would, you are a girl.'

'Yes,' said Lottie, 'but not a very beauty parlour one.'

'Diana did a degree in nursing then said she was sick of seeing ill people. I think she must like doing weird treatments on people. Some of my first memories are of her friends coming round and doing beauty things to each other, making disgusting stuff out of yoghurt and instant coffee and bananas to put on their faces, washing their hair with eggs. I never know what might be food and what might something else in the fridge. Anyway, we'd better do the other tanks.'

On the way home, Lottie went into K's Market, a sort of cheap everything shop that sold beach toys, begonias, and hideous things for pets. She skirted a display of water pistols and headed for the plastic flowers at the back, where, as she'd guessed, they had net bags of glass pebbles for people to put in vases. They were only £1 a bag. She chose six, two aquamarine, two dark green, one amber and one pink.

Would those be colours that an octopus liked? Would Jane see colours the same way as a human? She had a view of tropical fish tanks across the room, so would be familiar with lots of bright colours, plus, Lottie supposed, she must see the bright clothes of visitors. She walked back to Teapot Paradise with the glass pebbles clinking in her bag. Could an octopus learn to read and write? It seemed likely that one could learn to recognise images, but letters? Probably too abstract. What if she made flash cards of different treats and toys to see if Jane could indicate which she'd prefer? If Jane could learn to write or communicate with humans, what would she say? *Stop those cruel idiots banging on the glass? Are there no other creatures like me? Let me go back to the sea?*

Lottie helped Cass with the wiping and sweeping and putting the remaining cakes away.

'Fancy a swim?' Cass said. 'Sea pool?'

Sea Pool

When they arrived at the sea pool, most of the day's families had already, thankfully, gone. A line of deluxe flip-flops, Crocs and sandals were grouped together in the shadow of *The Wild Swimmers* statue and indicated that Cass's fellow WI committee members had arrived before them. The shoes of the other committee members were easily identifiable:

- Turquoise Birkenstocks (Size 6): Caroline Todd, recently widowed owner of The Blue Lobster.
- Rainbow fabric sandals with soles made from recycled tyres (Size 3) bought at a festival some years ago: Katie Grayling, retired teacher, also recently widowed.
- Black leather Fitflop clogs (Size 7): Diana Parks, owner of Marine Heaven Health and Beauty.

Cass waved hello and slipped off her yellow linen dress. She had her black one-piece on underneath. She put her own cyclamen crocs, this year's pair – so useful and comfy for Teapot Paradise – with the gang of shoes. Lottie took off her own green sandals and the stripy T-shirt dress that was her after-work garment of choice. It was a faded Seasalt one that Aunt Cass had given her, saying that it was too short on her.

The water, after a day in the sun, was several degrees warmer than the sea itself, even though it was washed over and replaced (at least in part) with every high tide. Lottie decided not to think about the hundreds of children who'd have been peeing in it all day. The salinity level, she knew from her many days studying rock pools, would be much higher by now than in the sea. She lowered herself in and swam to the far side where she could look out over the sea. She could measure the salinity and then perhaps she and Arthur could bring Jane for a trip. But would that be a kindness – to give her a look at the world she was missing out on? And there was not much, as far as Lottie could see, living in the pool – not much for Jane to find to eat and few places for her to explore or hide. She'd seen videos of octopuses walking across beaches. If Jane knew that the wider sea was there, she would be able to clamber out of the pool, down across the rocks and away. She was pretty sure that Jane would be able to catch her own food – she showed lots of initiative with what was given to her in her tank. And she had been taken from the sea when she was very small. She'd probably have some memories of the world she had lost and her instincts would return, given the chance. Lottie held onto the edge of the pool and gazed out to sea, gently kicking her legs for a bit of exercise, aware that she was in the company of women who observed a no-splashing etiquette. She turned and saw that Cass and her friends were swimming companionable lengths, all doing a non-splashy breaststroke, apart from Diana, Arthur's sister, who was doing a strange kind of backstroke that involved energetic breaststroke legs. She looked like a powerful frog on her back, though Lottie thought she had the best swimming costume of them all – it was a 50s-ish number, black with white polka dots. Diana must feel a bit caught between the generations, Lottie supposed, she was younger than the other WI lot, and yet becoming responsible for Arthur when their parents died must have made her feel almost as old as them. Perhaps once you started to feel like that, there was no going back. But Arthur was a grown-up now, even if Diana didn't believe it. If I were him, thought Lottie, I'd move away. She could picture Arthur and his sister getting old together – that would be sad. Old and unmarried, Arthur in ancient T-shirts and hoodies from the centre, winning an award for the longest serving member of staff, although he'd never be older than their oldest giant clam. If he spent his whole working life there, he would witness the lives of many octopuses, and that was another sad thought. An octopus's lifespan was so short for something so intelligent. Perhaps all that sensing and feeling and having so many beating hearts meant that life was exhausting and completed quickly. How sad that they hadn't evolved to have more than one experience of mating and having (in the female's case) babies. The male was quite likely to mate and then get eaten by the female. Diana would probably do that, if she ever did find a mate.

Lottie started to swim lengths, falling in beside Cass and her friends, imagining herself as a sea otter, swishing though the kelp forests, but after a while she was too lazy and turned to float on her back and gaze up at the sky. Gulls were circling overhead. In the distance she could hear the mournful sounds of the puffins back at the Centre. She tried not to think of them stuck beneath their aviary netting, watching the birds who were free to come and go. Cass swam over to join her.

'Heaven, isn't it?' she said.

'Uh huh,' said Lottie. 'Though I try not to look at the hideous sculpture. It's best to just look at the sky or out to sea.'

'Even the artist's mum doesn't like it,' said Cass. 'I don't think anyone does, apart from the artist.'

'Maybe even he doesn't,' said Lottie, 'and that's why he got it dumped down here.'

'He said it was inspired by the people of Ottersea. That's why we hate it so much. Give us some dignity! There was quite a campaign when it was installed,' said Cass. 'We haven't given up.'

Two policemen walked past, both carrying things from Subway. Diana stopped her vigorous frog-leg stroke and began to swim more sedately.

Important Instructions

At home after her swim, Diana took a shower then got dry and dressed in her usual speedy way. She adhered to strict rules, ensuring that she was dressed with her hair extremely neat before anything could happen to her. She had done this since the sad day when she'd found her mother collapsed after her bath. To be found like that, not decent, your hair in a damp mess that would dry to something worse, your toenails needing painting – it was to be avoided at all costs. She had brushed her mother's hair and put some clothes on her before the ambulance got there, even though it was already too late. She still regretted not putting socks on her mother's poor dead feet. They had looked so sad and vulnerable poking out from underneath the blanket as she was wheeled away. Diana ensured that no scruffy underwear or clothes ever resided in her wardrobe in case she died and people discovered that she'd been capable of socks with holes in or multipack knickers that had seen better days. Now that she should probably worry about a sudden banging on the door, cries of 'Police! Open up!' and being marched off to the cells, her precautions were even more important.

In the drawer of the kitchen table was the file she had made for Arthur many years ago when she'd first gone away for a weekend, leaving him alone in the house. She had kept it updated with information on the house insurance along with the card of the plumber they used for emergencies. Although she now did everything online, she had printed out details of the gas, electricity, water and council tax accounts. Did Arthur remember that this file was there? He was so dozy. She would have to remind him about it. She made herself a cup of fennel tea then sat down with her laptop to write a page of extra instructions for the file:

In the Event of My Sudden Death or Incapacitation, Arthur, please ensure that you follow these procedures:

1. *Ensure that I am properly dressed.*
2. *Please brush my hair as best you can. Do this whilst waiting for any ambulance to arrive. Do not allow me to be taken away with bare feet. House shoes are acceptable. (By house shoes, I mean my pink cashmere slippers or my red silk ones, depending on the season.)*
3. *Ensure that the ready-packed washbag on my dressing table is brought to me wherever I am.*
4. *Ensure that all clients with appointments booked are contacted and asked to postpone as necessary if my current assistant cannot carry out the appointments. If I am incapacitated for some time, the business should be mothballed. Please email all clients to say that I will reopen as soon as possible.*
5. *Ensure that most plants are watered weekly. The ZZ plants in the bathroom and spider plants can go far longer. It is better to underwater than overwater.*

Diana knew she had form when it came to violent outbursts. At preschool when a hateful little boy called Toby Hickly had planted a slobbery kiss on her face she had whacked him around the head with a tambourine. The metal discs had left him with a set of neat slashes (really not *that* deep) across his stupid freckly cheek. She was still outraged that *she* was the one who'd got into trouble. She hoped that now the incident would be seen differently. Her mother had been asked to stay for a chat at the end of the session. Diana remembered sitting on one of the little chairs next to her mother – the adults had to sit on those chairs too – whilst the preschool lady (who until then Diana had liked) said that she (Diana) had to learn to control her temper and use her words to express her anger.

'He put his wet mouth on my face,' Diana had said, using her words to express her anger.

'He did it because he likes you,' the woman said, and her treacherous mother had nodded. 'Though he might not like you anymore.'

'Good,' Diana said, folding her arms. 'He smells of eggs. I don't want him to like me.'

There had been other incidents at school – her school milk, horribly warm after being left by the radiator had been shoved away in horror. She hadn't meant it to go all over Kimberley Finch's stupid painting, but she also hadn't minded that it had. Kimberley Finch cheated in spelling tests. She'd written "separate" and "accomodation" on the inside of her pencil case. Diana hadn't told her that it had two "m"s, or told *of* her – it seemed better to keep the information in case it was useful in the future. And Kimberley Finch was stupid anyway, not just at spelling, but at everything. She stuck her tongue out a bit when she was drawing the slow, laborious flowers with stupid smiley faces that she always did in art. Everyone knew that flowers didn't have smiley faces, and nor did the sun. The milk had made the colours of her picture run and look much better, but that hadn't stopped Miss Lucas from making Diana wipe it all up with paper towels. Diana still remembered the way that the scratchy green paper of the towels had disintegrated in the milk, not drying it, just smearing it over a wider area.

There had been another incident – a lucky escape really – at secondary school. Boys and girls usually did PE and Games separately, but if the weather was truly awful, they might join together in the gym. It was one of those days.

Diana remembered that she'd had chilblains; she could feel them, itchy and painful and being made worse by having to wear plimsolls with their thin cold soles. Perhaps a lot of crimes were committed by people exasperated and distraught from painful foot conditions – somebody should study that. Having been a chilblain sufferer meant that now she didn't mind doing foot treatments for people. Plus, her clients were usually people whose toes were in tip-top condition. Marine Heaven didn't attract the sort of people who had fungal nail conditions. Anyway, that day at school they'd been playing indoor rounders and the team she was in was batting. When it was her turn to face the pitcher, she'd bent down to pick up the bat and Derek Collett, who was behind her in the line, had slapped her on the bum. She'd yelled and turned, bat in hand, and swung at him. Luckily for him (and, she guessed, for herself) she'd got him on the upper arm, not the head, or, as Miss Bussey had said, she might have killed him.

'He whacked me on the bum!' she'd protested. But Miss Bussey said that was irrelevant. You didn't use PE equipment as an offensive weapon. And she'd been sent to sit in the changing rooms whilst Derek Collett just carried on playing. It was the final lesson of the day. There was no way she was going to sit about in that stinking prison surrounded by people's muddy shoes. She walked out of school and went home. Her mum, who was a primary school teacher, wasn't yet back from work. Diana had found the chilblain tablets which came in a tiny bottle with a snowman on and made her heart race. Then she'd run a really hot bath with Satsuma Body Shop bubbles and lain there soaking and fuming. The hot water on her toes was bliss, though she knew she would pay for it in the long run. Derek Collett had attacked her. Why was she the one in trouble for defending herself?

In books the young Diana liked, the heroine often had a hot temper that she had to learn to control. A hot temper was an acceptable character flaw, unlike being mean, sneaky or two-faced. Anne of Green Gables had smashed her slate down on

Gilbert Blythe's head; he had deserved it. And witness Darrell Rivers in *Malory Towers*, who was always shaking people or shoving them into the swimming pool. There was nothing wrong with a bit of righteous indignation. Perhaps Darrell Rivers had grown up to smother sexual predators, although rolling their bodies off the cliffs at night might be seen as sneaky. Diana still regretted losing the towel that had gone off the cliff with him. The salon operated on tight overheads and she couldn't afford to lose stock like that; plus there was a chance that it might be washed up, though she'd say that clients sometimes stole them, particularly people on holiday, which they did. It would be circumstantial.

She printed out the list of instructions and put it in the file which she left out on the table. She would remind Arthur about it over supper.

The Flat Above McColl's

'We'll go through the tenants next,' said Jim. 'We'll start with any that have been in arrears. We've got the details from the son. The Devon ones are most likely, but who knows? We'll see what the Reading crew come up with.'

He began to look through the spreadsheet Bal had given him – addresses, names of tenants with their phone numbers, rent payments – it was all laid out for them. There were only a few in Ottersea – most of the empire was in Reading. It seemed likely that a tenant with a grudge or who'd struck out in anger would have done it in their home town. One of the Reading ones *might* have travelled to Ottersea, but would someone in rent arrears do that? Unlikely.

'Let's start with this one, they had arrears for a few months,' he said. 'Kayleigh Evans and Jake Miller. We'll go round now – they'll likely be home from work.'

The flat was above a McColl's at the wrong end of the high street. "Our Town" by Iris Dement played in Jim's head. They knocked at the flat door and waited. "There's A Guy Works Down The Chip Shop" took over. Eventually a woman, early twenties, answered the door. She looked worried when he and Grace said who they were.

'Are you Kayleigh Evans?' asked Jim.

'No, I'm her friend.'

'Is Kayleigh in? We need to talk to her. She's not in trouble – we're just hoping she can help us with something.'

'Um, no, she's not back from work yet.'

'Will she be back soon? Can, we come in and wait?'

'Can you just give me a couple of minutes?'

'Sure,' said Jim. She shut the door. Through the glass they could see her slight shadowy figure running up the stairs. They exchanged glances and then looked up to see that the flat's windows were being opened wide. She returned a few minutes later and led them up some narrow stairs. The carpet, a nasty shade of brown, was stringy and faded. Some hasty tidying had occurred. A scented candle was starting to give off a headache-inducing aroma of something fruity, peach, perhaps, and something like biscuits. Neither the candle nor the breeze from the open windows covered the smell of marijuana.

'We're also hoping to speak to a Jake Miller who lives here.'

'Is he who you want?' the woman asked, brightening at this idea. 'What's he done?'

'Nothing that we're aware of,' said Jim, 'but we'd like to ask them both some questions.'

'He moved out, a few months ago,' said the woman. 'He and Kayleigh split up.'

'Right,' said Jim. 'Would you mind telling us your name?'

'Georgia,' said the woman, 'Georgia Shaw.'

'Thank you,' said Jim and he and Grace smiled in what they hoped was their most reassuring way.

'Georgia, you aren't in any trouble. Could you tell us where Jake's moved to?'

'Plymouth or somewhere, I dunno exactly. Kayleigh does – she forwards stuff to him sometimes, but God know why she bothers – he was a real shit to her.'

'Really?' said Grace. 'How do you mean?' Jim took a step back, sensing that Grace would be better at drawing things out, woman to woman.

'Cheated on her. So, what's he done?' This Georgia looked only too happy to drop him in it if she could.

'Do you live here now?'

'Um, yeah, why?'

'It's about your landlord, Mr Sumal.'

'He was a real shit too,' said Georgia.

'Really? Why do you say that?' asked Grace. Georgia paused, clearly wondering how much to say.

'Oh, you know, landlords…'

'You know he was found dead?'

'Yeah. I know you're not meant to say bad stuff about dead people.'

'In what way was he a real shit?'

'I don't know if Kayleigh would want me to say…'

'It might be helpful, we're trying to work out where he was in the days and hours before he died. Anything you can remember about him might be useful – we're trying to get as complete picture of him as possible.'

She bit her lip.

'I didn't know him before I moved in, though. I haven't even met him – I just did all the rent stuff through Kayleigh.'

They heard the front door opening below them and then footsteps on the stairs.

'Kayleigh!' Georgia called out, 'Some police are here!' The footsteps stopped. Then after a moment, they started again, but slower. In came a young woman of the type Grace had once described as a "perky brunette". Her shiny brown hair was up in a high ponytail. Her face was polished clean. She was wearing a white overall with a mandarin collar over some black leggings. She had on a pair of chunky pink flipflops with huge yellow plastic flowers on the straps. Her toenails were painted alternately cyclamen pink and sunflower yellow. Were those her work shoes? Jim glanced down at his own sturdy DM shoes and Grace's plain black slip-on trainers.

Kayleigh glanced around the room. He saw her eyes rest briefly on a small enamel box next to a spider plant, presumably where they kept their stash, and the two women exchanged glances. He considered saying: 'Look, we're not interested in that.'

'Hello, Kayleigh,' he said. 'I'm DI Jim Paddon. and this is DC Grace Brown. We're looking into the disappearance and death of Raj Sumal, your landlord.'

'I saw about that,' said Kayleigh. She sat down, rather heavily, on the sofa. 'Found on the beach, wasn't he?'

'That's right,' said Jim. 'We're talking to all his tenants, all his contacts. When did you last see Mr Sumal?'

'Um, a few weeks ago? Before Georgia moved in and saved me.' She smiled at her friend.

'Saved you?' said Jim.

'He was really hassling me for the rent. My ex, Jake, moved out and I was stuck. It turned out Jake hadn't paid the last two months – I'd been giving him my share but then I found out he'd put it to a deposit for another place with someone else. Then Georgia moved in, and my gran helped me, and we managed to catch up.'

'How do you mean, hassling you?'

'He came round a few times. I don't really want to say.'

'You might be able to help us,' said Jim. 'Do you mind if we sit down?' He and Grace were still standing and he knew that being so tall, he must be towering over Kayleigh and Georgia. He'd noticed how young people often didn't realise that if the visitor was old school, they would stand until offered a chair.

'Course,' said Georgia. As well as the sofa where the two young women were sitting, there was an old Ikea chair with a bentwood frame and what had once been a cream-coloured fabric seat and a wooden kitchen chair. Jim took that.

'In what way was he hassling you?'

'For the rent,' said Kayleigh. 'He rang me up. I didn't even know we hadn't paid. Then he came round one morning.' She looked down at her knees. 'He said he'd let me off, if I, you know, would have sex with him. He said I had a choice – I could do that or be evicted. I didn't know what to do. My mum's got a new boyfriend and I didn't want to move in with them.'

'And what happened?' said Grace, gently.

'He was here, and I was feeling really pressured, and luckily my phone rang, and I could see it was my nan, and I picked it up, I said I had to in case something was wrong. I acted like she was an old lady who might have had a fall. She's not like that really. She does Pilates and everything. And he was just standing there, too close to me when I was on the phone to her, and I burst into tears. He left without saying anything. Later that afternoon he texted me and said he'd be round again soon, but he didn't say when.'

'That must have been awful,' said Grace. Kayleigh nodded.

'And who did you tell?' Grace asked.

'Hardly anyone – I mean it was really embarrassing about the rent and Jake and everything first of all, without that.'

'Hardly anyone?' Grace asked.

'Well, my nan. And then Georgia – and it was really lucky she could move in.'

'And can you remember anything else? What did you do after he'd been round?'

'I just went to work, my boss is really arsey if I'm late.'

'Where do you work?' Grace asked. 'Did Mr Sumal know where you worked?'

'I don't think so. I work at Marine Heaven. I was an apprentice and then Diana, that's my boss, kept me on. It's minimum wage and not many hours, but sometimes there's tips. But I never could have paid all the rent we owed or afford this place on my own. I did Hairdressing and Beauty at college, but I like Beauty better, it's more interesting.'

'Marine Heaven?' asked Jim, jotting it down. 'And where's that?'

'Down Cobble Lane. Actually, I did tell my boss a bit. I don't normally tell her much stuff, but he texted again in the afternoon and I was upset. She was nice about it, said I could have an advance.'

'And what happened next?' asked Jim.

'Well, I went round my nan's for dinner that day, and Georgia came round too.'

'My mum and dad live next-door to Kayleigh's nan,' said Georgia.

'And my nan was really kind. She wanted to go round to his ice cream place and have it out with him, but of course I didn't want her to – it would have been so embarrassing, and I was officially behind with the rent, even though I hadn't known about Jake not paying and all that. Anyway, my nan said she'd give me the money to catch up, she was a health visitor and she's got a really good pension. She's always going on holidays with her friends. She just took me to Turkey too. So, she sent me the money the same day and then I could tell him to fuck right off. Sorry.'

'And did you see him again?'

'No. I was going to give my notice and move out, cos he was such a creep, but then Georgia said could she move in, and we decided to stay for a bit anyway, though we've both applied for jobs in Exeter, so if we get those, we're gonna move anyway.'

'And have you had any other contact with Mr Sumal or his family since then?'

'I had to change the direct debit – but I did all that online and with Bal, his son, he's OK – he was in the year above us at school.'

'And Kiran Sumal was the year below us – that just made it extra gross,' said Georgia. 'God, he was really old, well, maybe not old enough to die, but old as in old and disgusting.' Jim couldn't help but smile at this. 'Sorry, no offence.'

'What about Jake?' Grace asked. 'Did you tell him about what had happened?'

'Um, no,' said Kayleigh. 'And he's a real coward, I mean, he couldn't even tell me he was breaking up with me. Even though half of the late rent was his. Plus, it's all sorted now.'

'You did really well, hun,' said Georgia, putting her arm around her friend's shoulders.

But had she done anything else? Jim wondered. Her story seemed plausible. Would she tell them about Sumal's sex-for-rent coercion if she had killed him? She would likely just keep quiet. It seemed to have come to nothing when her grandmother had bailed her out. It *seemed* like it had stopped there. But if he had been pushing this girl for sex, he had probably done it to others in her situation. Jim had read an article about it – the practice was rife.

'So, where were you on July 4th?' Jim asked.

'I know that,' said Kayleigh. 'I was in Turkey with my nan. Her friend had Covid so I went at the last minute instead.' She stretched out her right arm to inspect her tan.

'And how long were you there?' asked Jim.

'Uh, ten days. I can show you the stuff on my phone. By the way, I didn't kill him.' She started flicking through photos on her phone and then got up to show them to him.

'That's me and Nan on the balcony when we'd just got there, and that's our first dinner – it was all inclusive – and that's by the pool – you can see the dates.'

'Can you send me a copy of the booking and flights so we can eliminate you from our enquiries?'

'OK. My nan did it all through On the Beach. I'll have to get her to do it.'

'Here's the email address. If she could do it today, that would be very helpful.' He gave her one of his cards and Grace gave one of hers.

'Course,' said Kayleigh. 'I don't wanna be arrested for that creep.'

'Well, thanks,' said Jim, getting up. 'You've been really helpful. If you remember anything else, please let us know.'

'Good luck with the job applications,' said Grace. 'I'm really glad your nan could help you with the rent too. That must have been a horrible thing to go through. I'm glad it worked out OK for you.'

'Thanks,' said Kayleigh. 'Now I just feel sorry for his family. Bal Sumal's OK, but I still wanna move.' Jim and Grace saw themselves out.

'Interesting insight into Sumal,' said Grace, as they drove away. 'If someone does that to *one* of their tenants, you can guess...' Jim nodded grimly.

Later that evening, he got an email from Kayleigh's grandmother. They had both clearly been out of the country when Sumal had disappeared and for a good week afterwards, so even if they *had* wanted to kill him, they were likely in the clear.

Where the Water Ends

A change in light and shadow. A shape she knows looms where her element ends. She extends a tentacle, pours herself out of her cave and dances across the distance until she can press one arm along the place where the water becomes solid.

He does the same with one of his own thick appendages, extends his stumpy suckers and through the wall they meet – pleasure – she shivers and pales as she relaxes. He is dull and limited, can only turn a little darker. He can open his mouth and show his teeth in a curve like a fishbone. She has seen him make drops of water by his eyes, but he cannot change the way she can. He is slow – remains on the base of his own place – sometimes he is there but more often he is not.

If she could go beyond where the water ends she would zoom up towards the brightness. She remembers the big blue above. She remembers the time before.

'Hello, Jane,' Jim whispered. 'I'm a bit stuck on this one. No leads. Haven't got anything much yet. The guy is there in the betting shop, then a couple of weeks later he's dead, washed up on the beach. Looks like he came down the cliff – but jumped or pushed? No idea. You know what it's like – when you're dead, you're a dead pecker-head.

Tempting just to say suicide and be done with it. But no note, no obvious troubles. We like a mystery, though, eh?'

The bell rang. He saw Jane darken. She clearly didn't like it. They should have thought of that. Sea creatures hated alien noise – whale songs were drowned out by offshore drilling and the booms of the super tankers – everyone bloody knew this now.

A recorded voice came over the tannoy:

'Ladies and gentlemen, boys and girls, the centre will be closing in ten minutes. Please make your way to the gift shop and exit through there. The gift shop remains open for twenty minutes after other areas have closed. Thank you for visiting.'

'Bye, Jane, see you soon. Wish I could take you with me.' She whooshed to the side of the tank nearest the exit, as if she wanted to accompany him as far as she could. Poor bugger, he thought, trapped in here. And he wondered yet again whether she would survive if she escaped or if somebody smuggled her out. *Local Copper in Octopus Theft Shame*. Worth the risk? He thought she'd have a pretty good chance. Nobody knew how smart they really were. He'd read that some octopuses carried Portuguese man o' war tentacles to use as weapons. Any creature that could do that…

Jim wished he could avoid exiting through the gift shop, but there was no other way out. He walked through the next room – they were more like caves really – 'Our Local Seashores'. There was a logjam of buggies at the exit turnstiles into the shop. Jim waited beside a display of garbage that had been found on Ottersea Beach. It was all the usual plastic crap – people should know better. He knew this would be an edited version – there would be needles and nitrous oxide canisters and condoms and stuff that they wouldn't want on the wall in a tourist attraction. Something blue and white caught his eye, a piece of cloth, some sort of towel. They'd given it a label: "Microfibre is an artificial fabric and contains plastics. It takes longer to break down than natural fibres and when ingested will harm sea creatures. Clothes made from artificial fibres like polyester are a major source of pollution in our seas. Try to choose clothes and furnishings made from plant fibres like cotton, linen, and bamboo instead." Those blue and white stripes looked familiar, but then practically everything in Ottersea was blue and white striped. Then he remembered – it was exactly like the thing he'd seen when he peered over the cliff edge. He'd asked the coastguard to try and retrieve it. Had it been done yet? Nobody had reported back on it. He returned to the station to find out. Thanks, Jane, he thought, again.

Back at the station, he checked for messages from the coastguard – there was one he'd missed in his emails. They had gone to the cliffs to look for anything that might have been tipped off and got caught on the way down, the cloth he had mentioned and anything else, but there hadn't been anything.

Well, thought Jim, perhaps the thing had ended up in that display at Oceanworld, but there was no way of knowing, or if it had any relevance. Nevertheless, he called the Oceanworld Centre and left a message on their machine, saying that someone would be round first thing to collect the cloth, and could they please ensure that nobody touched it before then.

Helter-Skelter

Lunchtime. Arthur and Lottie's breaks coincided so they went to sit outside together. A pair of black swans, perhaps visitors from Dawlish just along the coast, were floating on the sea in front of them.

'It's so clever of swans to go on the sea as well as freshwater,' said Lottie. 'They seem to be feeding – I wonder what on. Perhaps they're on their honeymoon at the seaside.'

'That mating for life business is true,' said Arthur. 'But probably more feeding and looking for territory than an actual honeymoon.' He opened the bamboo box that he brought his lunch in and groaned. 'Diana made my lunch – I should have said no – it's vegan cheese and spinach. Ugh. I knew she had an ulterior motive in making it. She bought these vegan cheese slices and they're so disgusting she wants to use them up on me. I had a fight to stop her making my school packed lunch – it was a running joke – *What's Arthur Got In His Lunch Today?* It would be quinoa salad before that had even been invented, or giant couscous with mung beans and raw garlic and then she had a craze on pickled everything. Everyone else was just buying chips or a baguette. I ended up making my lunch for the next day the moment I got in from school just to stop her.'

'Have some of mine,' said Lottie, 'if you aren't allergic to nuts.' She passed her box to Arthur and he took one of the cashew butter and lettuce sandwiches on the sourdough used in Teapot Paradise. 'Not too mad for you?'

'No,' said Arthur, eying another one, 'pretty good. Let me buy you some chips, though.'

'That's OK. I've got more stuff here – my aunt gave me some fruit cake too.'

As they walked back to the Centre, it seemed that everyone who wasn't a tourist said hi to Arthur or waved. As they passed the helter-skelter, a middle-aged man in a khaki T-shirt and long shorts yelled, 'Good on yer, Arthur!' Arthur raised a hand in a friendly but resigned wave. 'You stick with him, love. He's a keeper!' the guy called to Lottie.

Lottie didn't know what to do, so she just waved back. Was Arthur "a keeper"? He wasn't hers in any way, let alone to keep. Arthur was blushing. Her sunglasses were big enough to cover most of her face and her own reddening cheeks.

'Who's that?' she asked, mostly for something to say.

'That's Malcolm, owns the helter-skelter and those rides. He's like that to everyone.' Oh, thought Lottie, so I'm to think it doesn't mean anything. Arthur nodded towards some kiddie rides – some hot air balloons that went round without actually going up and down and a little merry-go-round train called "Florida Adventure" in the form of an alligator. 'My first job was with him.'

'What did you have to do?'

'Stand at the top and check that kids sat on their mats and tell them to stay sitting down and keep their arms in.'

'Did you get bored?'

'Not really. Only when it was busy. When it wasn't I could just look out to sea. I saw quite a few basking sharks, and the dolphins whenever they went by.'

'It must have been nice at the end of the day when you got to come down the slide.'

'You didn't. You have to put up a board and stuff in case drunks get onto it at night. You do that and then you have to come down the stairs. Then you lock up at the bottom. It's all made of metal so it was like being in charge of a giant Dalek.'

'A pink and yellow stripy Dalek. Did people ever get stuck?'

'All the time – great big parents and grandparents taking their kids down. Malcolm would warn them at the bottom, and they'd say, "OK, I'll just go up the stairs and help them onto the mat," but then they'd change their mind on the way up.'

'Too fat for a helter-skelter – embarrassing,' said Lottie.

'You could tell people to go sideways, but if they had a kid on their lap, that wasn't going to help. They'd have to try to shuffle back. It was pretty bad. And Malcolm wouldn't want to call the fire brigade or he'd be in the local paper for the wrong reason and he might get shut down.'

A loud cawing made them turn and look back. A carrion crow was now sitting on top of the helter-skelter.

'But the corvids love it,' said Arthur. 'I mean the helter-skelter – not people being stuck – there's nearly always one sitting on top of it like that.'

'I bet they love people getting stuck. I bet they caw-laugh. Crows must have a sense of humour.'

'Maybe,' said Arthur. 'You see it with quite a few creatures – Jane squirting people, cetaceans, parrots, monkeys and apes. Animals play. Perhaps they like watching people go down it – like a marble run.' They stopped to watch the crows and gulls on the beach.

'I think they're also learning from the gulls,' said Lottie, 'following them, watching them.'

'The helter-skelter is definitely their eyrie, their castle. Someone has to go down slowly each morning to clean off any mess – you can stop yourself sliding if you wear trainers – it's not really that slippery – that's why people are given the mats. One crow always hung out at the top with me. I would sneak it little bits of food, but I had keep it secret from the gulls – you don't want to get divebombed. I've always wanted a crowfriend, not a pet, but a friend.'

'Me too,' said Lottie.

'The helter-skelter was loads better than doing the gator ride – that's really noisy. And I hated that it was alligators.'

'Don't you like alligators?'

'They're OK. But why tell kids it's a "Florida Adventure" when we've got so many brilliant animals here? It should be a seal adventure, or an otter adventure with an otter train to ride in. I guess the designers might not think otters are exciting enough. We've killed all our big predators.'

'I know,' said Lottie. 'It's so sad – but there's hope with rewilding – one day the wolves and lynx will return.'

'I wish everyone was like you,' said Arthur. Lottie blushed again. 'I mean, optimistic,' he added, thinking he had said too much. But she smiled. Now, he told himself, just put your arm around her or something. But they were almost back at the centre and Helen was coming towards them, vaping. Lottie waved and Helen waved back. The moment was gone.

Morning Dredging

Kiran had woken at 6.39am with tears on her cheeks. She hadn't known that you could cry when you were asleep. She put on her black leggings, a hoodie and her trainers and went downstairs to the café. It smelled unpleasantly of floor cleaner, but apart from the smell, everything was ready for the day, for the hundreds of ice creams she would serve with sauces and sprinkles and flakes.

She unlocked the door and went outside, then turned to lock it again, putting the keys in her kangaroo pocket. She went to sit on a bench and look at the sea.

The Ottersea morning people were already doing their stuff. The dog-walking beach area was busy. A woman with two French bulldogs went past. Those dogs shouldn't be allowed, thought Kiran, they couldn't even breathe, and they had stupid mean faces. She should help her mum find a dog though, she'd always wanted one. It would make things better. But not one of those over-bred dogs. A friendly mongrel would be nice. Her dad, if he had allowed a dog, would have wanted something impressive and fierce. Friendly and cuddly would be better. She had no idea where you started with buying a dog. Perhaps there were lots of unwanted lockdown dogs online. They would let Nindy choose its name. A dog would be so good for Nindy.

The dredger was at work as usual, clearing the path into

the harbour. She'd once thought it belonged to some lazy fishermen who couldn't be bothered to go out to sea. Further out, the last of the furloughed cruise ships was still moored, sending its plume of pollution into the blue sky where it hung in a stream that reached for miles. There had been five of them during lockdown and a container ship.

During the first lockdown, Kiran had hoped that people would change, that there would be no more crime and everyone would be nicer to each other. She remembered going outside with Nindy and her mum to clap and bang metal ice cream scoops on stainless steel bowls every Thursday. Nindy did a picture of a rainbow and they put it up in the Flakies window. Their dad approved and when the sunshine faded the felt pen colours, he asked Nindy to do another one. When Nindy's school was closed and Kiran was in charge of helping her with the online lessons, they'd made rainbows with Hama beads and hung them like bunting on a string.

Middle-aged people in fitness stuff ran by, loads of them terrible runners. She had forgotten what running felt like. Perhaps she should go running everyday like them. At school she had been on the athletics team from her very first term and the PE teachers were always on at her to try out for other things. She ran for the school because then there would be a minibus, but when it came to other events, her mum was always working and looking after Nindy and her dad was often away, so going would have been too tricky. Plus she was expected to work at Flakies at the weekend, and that got worse when Bal left home. He'd been really good at football, but it hadn't been the same for him. He just did what he wanted and made sure it happened, getting lifts with mates' parents when he needed to. Kiran hadn't known the other girls on the athletics team that well – they were mostly posh girls who lived in the big houses up on the hill that overlooked the town.

Sometimes she hated humans. They made such a mess of everything. The bins just along from her bench were overflowing with the debris of the day before. The crew would be here to empty them soon, but in a few hours there would be more people stuffing them with more rubbish until they were overflowing again. At least with Flakies, she thought, people ate the containers, the cones, or if they had tubs, they were given waxed paper ones which would decompose eventually, well, more or less.

The bin guys arrived. Anticipating the heat, they were wearing just hi-vis vests over their bare chests. Surely it would be cooler to wear something cotton rather than have that stiff plasticky stuff next to your skin?

'All right, love?'

She smiled and nodded, hoping that the tears from earlier had dried. She walked further along and sat down again. That woman, Diana Parks, who'd been round with flowers and her leaflets and hand massage stuff, was sitting on a bench with a Waitrose Bag for Life beside her as well as a blue leather crossbody one. Kiran put up her hood. The last thing she wanted was another Nice Chat with that weirdo. Diana Parks took a posh-looking travel mug out of the Waitrose bag. She swished it around – typical of that woman to take her own coffee to work rather than supporting a local place – but instead of drinking it, she looked around and then tipped the contents right into the palm tree behind her. Whatever it was caught the light – was she hiding crystals? No, ice of course. Definitely a weirdo. She tipped the last drips out of her mug and put it back into the bag. Then she took out a face mask and some disposable gloves and put them on. She got out what looked like a bottle of kitchen cleaner. Was she going to clean the palm tree? A pair of runners were approaching. She put the bottle back in the plastic bag until they had passed. As soon as they had, she took it out again, stood and turned and then sprayed loads of the stuff right into the heart of the palm tree. Kiran huffed, then realised it was the first time anything had made her almost-laugh for days, but it wasn't really a laugh, more like the half-bark of some stupid asthmatic dog.

'Kiran! I was so worried! I thought you'd gone too!'

Her mum was in front of her, wearing her coat over her nightie. She would never have gone out like that before.

Kiran stood. 'Don't worry, Mum, I'm not going anywhere. I wanted some fresh air before the day started. I was just coming back in. I'll make you some tea.' She put her arm around her mother's shoulders and they walked home together, back along the seafront.

An hour later, Arthur stood looking at the staff rota whiteboard. He saw that he and Lottie had a day off in common. He often came in on his day off, just to see Jane and be there if he was needed, but perhaps not this time.

'Day off tomorrow, Lottie?' he asked as they cleaned out the puffins. It was like looking after chickens, Helen said, but you had to be careful not to step on them. He and Lottie were leaving the burrows – some of the puffins had eggs – and just getting the worst of the mess out with brooms.

'Yeah,' said Lottie. 'I ought to offer to help my aunt in the café. Puffins make the weirdest noise, don't they? Like creaky doors or old men groaning. Maybe we've got it all wrong about them being these jolly birds – sea parrots, clowns of the sea – and they're all chronically depressed. Perhaps somewhere there are happy puffins who make a completely different noise, but nobody ever hears it because they hate people and if anyone comes near, they make their call of despair.'

'What about hidden recording devices, wildlife cams?' said Arthur, laughing.

'No,' said Lottie. 'They're smart as well as miserable. They know when someone's spying on them. And they're depressed about the decline in sand eel populations. You know, I hate those spy-cam documentaries. I'm doing an animal ethics module next year.'

'Plenty to think about here,' said Arthur, looking up at the netting that kept the birds captive.

'Some of it seems OK, I mean the rescue creatures, the ones that couldn't survive back in the wild, we're assuming they're happier to be alive here than left to die…' She looked up and realised that a small crowd had gathered to watch them doing the cleaning; people often seemed more interested in watching the workers than the animals. Ethics would have to wait. She got on with the sweeping.

'Miss,' a little girl with a pink velour unicorn headband called. 'Can I stroke one of the puffins?'

'Sorry,' said Lottie. 'They can be a bit pecky and they're quite shy if they don't know you.' Plus, the bird flu exclusion rules had only just been called off, and there was strictly no admittance for the public to any of the bird enclosures. The staff were wading through disinfectant every time they entered or left an exhibit. Bird flu, thought Lottie, yet another way we've messed up the world.

'Can you get one for a pet?'

'They wouldn't make very good pets,' said Lottie. 'They need lots of space and special food.' She went over to the edge of the enclosure so she could chat properly to the little girl. 'Have you got any pets already?'

'A dog called Luna. She's a cockapoo.'

'Ah,' said Lottie, 'I'm afraid that means that you couldn't have a puffin anyway. Dogs and puffins don't get on. Or puffins and cats or rats or mink. Puffins don't want to be chased and they don't want anything that might go down their burrows and steal their eggs.'

'What about a rabbit?' asked the little girl.

'A rabbit might be OK, *if* you were able to have a pet puffin. I don't think a rabbit would bother them.'

'And they could share a burrow?'

'Well, perhaps,' said Lottie, 'but I think they'd get in each other's way.'

Arthur watched impressed. Lottie was a natural. He loved the way she could just chat about anything. Chatting had never been his strong point. He realised he was staring. She had her hair in two plaits today and from behind she didn't look much older than the little unicorn girl. Lottie's hair was brown, but since she'd arrived it had gained extra colours – reds and chestnuts and golds, he guessed from all the sunshine. He was surprised Diana had been friendly to her and made Lottie come in for tea. They were polar opposites. You would never catch Diana mucking out some puffins or choosing to chat to a little girl with a unicorn headband. Diana loathed unicorns.

'Are you going to come and see us feeding the otters?' Lottie asked. 'We'll be doing that in about half an hour.' The little girl turned to her parents.

'Can we?'

'Course we can. Come on, Derry.'

Derry, thought Lottie. She hadn't heard that one before. She turned to start sweeping again.

In a few more minutes they were done. They let themselves out of the puffins, locked the gate and checked it, went through the disinfectant footbath and off to get the fish for the otters.

'So,' Arthur said, as they weighed out the fish, 'we've got the same day off tomorrow. I wondered if you'd like to do something. My friend does cruises around the bay, we could see if he's got any spaces. I help him sometimes, with the cruises, not fishing, he does a bit of that too.'

'Sure,' said Lottie.

And just like that, she had said yes.

Foraging for Food and Fun

Diana was relieved that the foraging walk was heading away from the part of the beach where Sumal had been found. Although she had no regrets, she didn't particularly want to go there either. There were rock pools at both ends, but he'd been found in the ones near the harbour wall. Today they were going to the wild end.

'God, did you see the news last night?' said Cass, as they set out across the beach. 'I just wish that we could have some acknowledgement in the press that almost all the problems in the world are caused by men, by male aggression and testosterone.'

'I couldn't agree more,' said Diana. 'We should have an international committee of WI members – delegates from each country running things. Men cause all the problems.'

'Not *all* males,' said Caroline, as she bent to let her beloved Toby off the lead. 'Women do bad things too.' Katie, who was walking beside her, nodded.

'I know,' Cass said, loftily waving a hand as if to indicate the whole world. 'Not all men.'

Katie stopped for a moment and stared down at her feet on the sand.

'Have you spotted something?' asked Cass.

'No. Not really,' said Katie, 'but it's true. Women do terrible things too, just not as many or as often.' Caroline linked her arm through Katie's – the WI's two most recent widows, united in their grief.

They were being led by an artist and forager who had an Insta account with three hundred thousand followers and a book deal. Diana saw that Cass had brought along Lottie, the pretty niece who was working with Arthur; she was up ahead, chatting to the foraging woman. Lottie could be just what Arthur needed – she seemed so lively – useful if he had to cope without her. This outing would have been just Arthur's sort of thing too. It was also a litter-pick and each woman carried two bags, one for edibles and one for rubbish. So far, they had lots of rubbish but nothing to eat. Well, the other women did. Diana didn't like touching other people's garbage. She had a pair of disposable gloves in her bag as she knew that she'd have to give the appearance of joining in.

'One egomaniac, psycho male can cause all this suffering, to say nothing of the young men *who are nice* being forced to fight,' Cass said. 'All the problems of the past and present, all around the world – it's all the same cause. War. Domestic violence. Trafficking. Really, I despair.' She stopped for a moment and stared out to sea. 'Lottie says it's in animal societies too. But, God, I'm so sick of it all. Of male musk ox banging their stupid heads together, of the rutting season, of black grouse lekking, of male tigers killing a rival's cubs. But humans are the worst – by far the worst.' They had reached the more interesting part of the beach now where there was shingle, plants, wildness and rock pools. 'All I want to do, all most women want to do, is live in peace and dream and grow potatoes. That's what Tove Jannson said, though it was through Moominpappa.'

'Plenty of existential dread in Moomin Land,' said Caroline. She'd had all the books and tried reading them to her boys, but they had never got into them. 'But you're right, of course. It's like with cars, planes, the fishing industry. It's staring us in the face that these are terrible things, but nobody wants to say it.' She picked up a hideous hank of blue nylon rope. 'Some massive percentage of ocean plastic is from fishing. I shouldn't be running a fish restaurant. Even our vegetarian alternative – battered halloumi – comes with a side of airmiles. We've been carrying on – it's what the boys want – they seem to be almost enjoying not having their father in charge, and they're perfectly capable. But I'm starting to think I want out. I haven't told them yet.'

'Don't move away!' cried Cass. 'I'd miss you so much!'

'I don't think I could – I mean the boys are still at home – the house, the restaurant, all of you. Everything I love is here,' she said, looking at Toby who was down by the water, chasing birds. 'Toby wouldn't want to move either – all his friends are here.' Another piece of nylon rope, this time orange, was a few yards down towards the sea. She went to pick it up. 'See – horrendous. But at least it's washed up, not inside some dolphin's stomach.'

'That's just what Arthur would say. I told him he should come,' said Diana. 'I didn't think any of you would mind – it's not as though it's a normal meeting.'

'He's such a sweet boy,' said Cass. Diana noted with pleasure that Cass looked at Lottie when she said this. Lottie and the guest speaker had walked up beyond the high tide line. 'Oh, I think she's going to start. There's lots of samphire and sea peas and so on up there. I expect she'll tell us about those.' It was hard for the committee to find speakers with any knowledge that they didn't already have.

'Well, hello ladies!' said Sarah, aka @foragingqueen. 'So, this is a really good place to start as we have shingle and pebbles. We can go down to those rock pools and then if you like, into the woods up there,' she said, indicating the Red Cliffs Nature Reserve up on the cliffs. Diana hoped they would stick to the beach.

'So here at Ottersea, you mostly have sand. You can sometimes find nice things to eat in sand – wild leeks can be very good. And dewberries, and in times past, people would be catching rabbits in sand dunes, but none of you look like the sort to skin and gut rabbits.'

'You'd be surprised,' muttered Diana.

'Also, most sand dunes are protected now, so I can't encourage anyone to go picking things there.'

Plus, we don't actually have any sand dunes here, thought Diana. Oh, why had she come? She had been trying to act naturally since what she'd come to think of as The Disposal, and that meant going to WI meetings, but this was one that normally she might have skipped, even though she was the chair. This foraging woman was rather beautiful, she had to admit, even if she was wearing rather cliched clothes – faded purple linen dungarees over a stripy T-shirt. Her hair was a gorgeous honey colour and done in a messy French plait. Her skin had lots of sun damage though, far too many freckles. Diana wondered if she should have a quiet word and offer her a consultation. Judging by the state of her nails, she'd never had a manicure in her life.

'So, can anybody spot anything we might find useful around here?' A taxi home would be good, thought Diana, but they were a long way from any roads. 'How about this?' The woman bent and picked a few stalks of what they all knew was samphire but were too polite to say.

'Well, this is samphire, and you'll find it on many menus in top restaurants. It tastes like asparagus and it grows freely, so you needn't worry about taking a little just for yourself. And that's the rule – never take it all – only take a little – if there are three flowers, only take one.'

'If there are only three, I don't think you should take any,' said Diana, this time audibly.

'Well, no, not if it's something rare. I would never suggest anyone pick anything endangered. Now let's see what else we can find.' Most of the women bent to take a few stalks of samphire. Diana wondered if there was a sewage outlet nearby.

'How do you know if things are full of pollutants?' she asked. 'I only eat organic.'

'Good question. As locals, I'm sure you'll know, and the

Surfers Against Sewage website is very good – they have a map and track what the water companies are doing.'

'I've never met a surfer I'd trust,' Diana said, quieter this time.

'Well, I'm a surfer, and so are my boys,' said Caroline. Of course Caroline, with her long blonde hair, was a surfer. And she probably wore the same size wetsuit as when she was a teenager.

'Oh, I didn't mean you. Just surfers generally – Newquay types with their dude mentality. I know your boys are lovely, and it must be so tough with what you've all been going through. They were just marvellous at Jeremy's funeral, that speech they made together…'

'Thanks, Diana,' said Caroline, but she moved right to the front of the group as though she didn't want to miss what would be said next.

'Now, what about this?' asked @foragingqueen.

Caroline put her hand up. 'Sea kale,' she said.

'That's right. Sea kale. Has anyone tried it?' They used it at The Blue Lobster; like samphire it was a menu fixture. Nobody said anything. 'Well, it too can be delicious. It's a brassica and you can eat all parts of it. I'm not going to take any of this as there are just a couple of small plants here, but you can grow it in your garden and treat it like savoy cabbage. The flowers have a gorgeous honey scent. The Victorians loved it, and it became very depleted in the wild. It's good with eggs. Or in Chinese or Thai recipes. Like with cabbage or spring greens, you won't want to eat the really tough stems. For a sea vegetable, it doesn't have a very salty taste, so that's good too.

'But what I should have said, before we even started, is that of course you have to be careful. There are some things that might look tasty, but can be deadly. Come over here.' She led them off the beach to where a little stream ran down towards the sea. 'Look at these – they look good, don't they? – but don't even touch them. They're sea parsnips and must be completely avoided. They're also known as water hemlock or water dropwort – clue's in the name – you would drop dead, maybe not immediately, but pretty soon. And dogs might be tempted by them – they're deadly to dogs too. They often grow by streams near the shore, like here.' The women crowded closer to look. 'It was in the papers earlier this year when lots washed up on a beach in Cumbria. But don't get any ideas about bumping off your partners, ha ha. The leaves smell like parsley and the roots, which are even more deadly, look and smell like parsnips, or like mooli, if you know what that is.'

'Of course, we all bloody know what mooli are,' muttered Diana, who had come to the front to see the poisonous plants.

'And does anyone know what this is?' asked the woman, moving away from the sea parsnips and back onto the beach.

'Sea radish?' asked Lottie when everyone had gathered round again.

'Yes, that's right – sea radish. There's lots of it so we can take a bit. Look out for these clouds of flowers – so pretty. Up close the flowers are very simple – just four petals in a cross shape – it's in the Cruciferae family, same as lots of garden plants like aubretia and wallflowers. It's really useful if you happen to be shipwrecked as you can eat the leaves, the stalks and the seedpods, but they're only nice when they are young. It grows all year round, which is useful if you're looking for something in the colder months.'

'Let's go and take a look in some of the rock pools,' said @foragingqueen. 'We'll keep an eye on the tide, that's another one of the rules. Always take your phone, and always let someone know where you're going.'

Honestly, thought Diana, they weren't children. She went with the group down the beach towards the rocks, but then found a nice dry one to sit on where she hoped it would look as though she was listening intently. She was all for seaweed, and many of the preparations she used at the salon and for herself contained it, she just didn't really want to have to gather it herself. The foraging expert continued:

'This is dulse and it's one of the most useful seaweeds for just eating as a straightforward vegetable. Lots of people think it tastes a bit like bacon, so it's used as vegan bacon. You can eat it raw, or lightly fry it – anything really. I always wash it in sea water before I take it home – I don't want to take any little creatures with me – you never know what might be in a rock pool.'

Yes, thought Diana. People really don't know what might be in these rock pools, what with all the tourists, and the water companies discharging sewage, and all the dogs capering about. There had been even more badly behaved dogs since Covid. But she did know what else you might find: a body that had been in the sea for a couple of weeks.

The wind and sand were stinging her eyes. To her absolute horror, she realised that she was almost crying. She dug her fingernails hard into her palms to stop herself and then found her sunglasses and a tissue in her bag.

'Are you OK, Diana?' Cass sank down on the sand next to her 'Don't you fancy seaweed for supper?'

'I try not to eat after six o'clock.'

'Goodness, that must be hard.'

'It's just a routine. Easy once you're in it. The system needs to rest.'

'She was saying that dulse in omelette is very good. It seems that eggs and seaweed go together, like eggs and spinach. It's used in lots of ice creams too, apparently. Oh, Lottie said that you went round to the Sumals – that was kind of you – and gave the mother and the little girl hand massages. Lottie's made friends with Kiran, the elder daughter. We went round too, but didn't go in. So appalling for them.'

'Yes, appalling.'

'Lottie said Mrs Sumal thought it was really kind, and that you talked about swimming. Kiran's going to persuade her to join us. I don't know how the family are coping. I hope he had life insurance and it pays out, I mean, if it's ruled suicide – would it pay out for that, or is that just something in books and films?'

'I don't know. I've never really thought about it. When my parents died, it was medical – no question. Perhaps he had some terrible diagnosis and couldn't face it. Or debts or was a gambler. I don't suppose we'll ever know.'

'These things always come out in the end,' said Cass. 'I just hope it won't make things even worse for the family. An accident is the best anyone can hope for now.'

'An accident. Must have been.'

'I'm sure the police will get to the bottom of it. They always do eventually.'

'I doubt it,' said Diana. 'They all seem to be corrupt or complete clowns.'

'Maybe,' said Cass. 'I suppose we can hope. Oh look, Lottie's going for a paddle, perhaps we all should.'

'Good idea,' said Diana. She slipped off her shoes and left them neatly on the rock with her bag and she and Cass walked down to where the waves were breaking.

'I wonder if she's going to talk about foraging oysters,' said Cass. 'I hope it doesn't seem rude that we're not joining in. But you did look a bit down, sitting there by yourself.'

'Cass, you're always so kind, but I'm fine. It's just been a long day with lots of demanding clients – holidaymakers – they're the worst. They always think things should be *so* much cheaper here than in London, which they are, but then they want new customer discounts and all sorts of extras and think I don't know what I'm doing.' This was a lie, but, Diana observed to herself, she ought to brush up her lying skills, just in case. Cass took her arm in a companionable way as they reached the water.

'I expect we look like The Walrus and The Carpenter,' said Cass.

'What?'

'Oysters, you know. I'd be The Walrus, of course.' And she went on:

'"A loaf of bread," the Walrus said,
"Is what we chiefly need:

Pepper and vinegar besides
Are very good indeed —
Now if you're ready, Oysters dear,
We can begin to feed.""

'Cass, I know you're a baker, but you should know I hardly eat bread. Not even with oysters. Apart from sourdough, and then only occasionally.' This too was a lie. Sometimes when Arthur was out she would make herself a marmite sandwich with the white sliced Hovis that he bought, a sandwich just like her mother had made her. She would eat it slowly, discarding the crusts and hiding them in the bin so that Arthur wouldn't know she had erred.

In twos and threes the rest of the WI took off their shoes and came to join them until they all stood there, chatting and laughing as the sun began to go down and sent a path of pink gold towards them across the water. Beside her, Cass was telling Caroline that the sea was wet, the sands were dry, and that there wasn't a cloud in the sky or any birds, even though there were lots of birds around. And now they were even holding hands like schoolgirls. Perhaps I should get out of here, thought Diana, sell the business, sell the house, make sure it doesn't look suspicious, but *just go*. If only she didn't have Arthur to think of. If she left him to his own devices he would probably turn into one of those awful men who wore cargo shorts all year round.

Boat Trip

Day off. Arthur came down the stairs whistling. His sister was already up and eating her weird breakfast of avocado and eggs without toast.

'Honestly, Arthur,' she said. 'Do you have to wear those awful cargo shorts? Look at the pockets – they're bulging and rattling with *stuff* – and they really need a wash.'

'These are my favourite shorts,' he said. 'Anyway, day off and I'm going out with Joe on one of his tours.'

'Well, wouldn't you want something a little warmer then?'

'It's boiling. They're fine, sis.'

'Why don't you see if that nice new girl from your centre would like to go?'

'There's a thought,' said Arthur, and he couldn't help smiling. He put some bread in the toaster – it had to be on the highest setting – all they had was her favoured sourdough. Surprisingly, she didn't say anything even though she was watching him take the last two slices. Instead:

'I've been thinking. Maybe we should sell the house and move. We don't need to stay here. There isn't really anything to tie us here.'

'Nothing to tie us here? I can't leave! What about Jane?'

'I knew you liked her, but you've only just met her.'

'Not Lottie, if that's who you mean, and she's just a friend. Jane.'

'But who's Jane?'

'Jane the Octopus. The creature I've been looking after for over a year. I can't leave Jane! And why would we sell the house? The house is fine.' He watched as she put the last piece of avocado in her mouth and chewed it in her neat way. She had this thing about chewing everything (even things that other people barely chewed) about a million times. She would never speak until every fragment was swallowed. Even if she had to yell "fire!" she would probably do her hundred chews first. She aligned her knife and fork in the centre of her plate and took a sip of her coffee. Anyone else would be chasing the last fragments of scrambled egg around their plate, but Diana never did that. She had never given up telling him off for doing that at the end of meals. She thought it made people look either greedy or poor or, she said, both. His counter argument about wasting food was dismissed with a wave of a hand and the flash of whatever colour her nails were that day.

'We might not want to stay here forever. *I* might not want to stay here forever. We don't have to stay in this house together just because we were both born here and we own it.'

'What? Why suddenly say this now? I thought your bookings had picked up again!'

'I just think we should consider it. Perhaps it's time for a change. Or we could rent the house out. Airbnb – whatever. See the world. Go to South America or somewhere. Just think about it.' She got up and scraped and rinsed her plate before putting it in the dishwasher and leaving to get ready for work.

His toast popped but he was too stunned to react. What was Diana thinking? It was insane. His phone dinged. Lottie.

"Leaving in fifteen. See you soon x" And the smiley cat emoji she always used to sign off. He figured the x was just punctuation. Joe said that he should go on Tinder and other apps. He was the only person, Joe said, who wasn't, but he wouldn't have known where to start. How could you message someone that you didn't even know?

Lottie had a longer walk than him. He buttered his toast

and put marmalade on it, but it tasted like dust and slime. He tipped it all into the bin.

Lottie was waiting for him on the harbour wall. She was wearing a pair of dungarees with an impressive number of pockets and a T-shirt. He'd only ever seen her in the work clothes before. He hoped she wouldn't have the same scathing thoughts about his shorts as Diana. But then Lottie always seemed too busy noticing the *actual* world to look at what other people were wearing. Now she wasn't watching out for him, she was sitting on the wall and looking down at the water in the harbour.

'Hey, Lottie,' he said as he approached. He didn't want her to think he was sneaking up on her like a stalker or startle her so she fell in. She turned and smiled and waved hello.

'Lots of fish down there,' she said. They sat and watched them together for a few minutes. There were other people milling about too, probably also there for the boat trip; a family with two children in yellow sunhats which would probably blow away, a middle-aged couple, an elderly one, and a young couple who looked as though they'd just had an argument. The man was staring at the Otter Cruises leaflet whilst the woman stood looking at her phone.

'Here comes Joe,' said Arthur. A boat with banks of seats came chugging into the harbour laden with the people from the early morning trip. Joe was at the front, doing the talky bit whilst his dad (who'd taken over Otter Cruises from *his* dad) was steering. Joe and his dad were RNLI volunteers too. Arthur had been at Joe's many times after school when the alarm had sounded and Joe's dad had to drop everything and go running down the street to the station. Now Joe did the same. They were pretty much local heroes. Perhaps he shouldn't have brought Lottie to meet him.

They watched as Joe and his dad tied up the boat, helped the people off it, and then made the checks ready for the next excursion. Then Joe came up the steps to meet his new lot of trippers. He went round with his battered clipboard, ticking everyone's names off. He came to Arthur and Lottie last.

'Arthur, my main man!' He grinned and whacked Arthur on the back. 'And you must be Lottie. Good to meet you.' Lottie jumped down from the wall and picked up her bag.

'Thanks for the spaces.' She smiled, clearly not realising that Arthur had booked and paid for them like anyone else.

The elderly couple were first down the steps to the boat. Everyone else went slowly behind, making sure they didn't get too close and make the old people feel as though they were being too slow. Arthur wondered if the old people realised. Presumably they would have done the same when they were young. Had they now forgotten? One of the yellow sunhat kids had to be held back.

'Can we go at the front, Mum?' Everybody else held back so that they could. Arthur smiled at how human beings could be so kind and considerate to each other.

'If you could go on one boat in the world, which would it be?' Lottie asked him as they were putting on their lifejackets.

'SS David Attenborough,' Arthur said without missing a beat. 'And I'd get to control Boaty McBoatface.'

'Me too,' said Lottie. 'Ever since *Thunderbirds*, I've wanted to be in charge of something like that. "We'll need Pod 4, Gordon." But this is pretty cool.' They stopped talking to listen to Joe's dad make the safety announcement while Joe cast off. Soon they were out of the calm waters of the harbour and bumping over the waves.

'So,' Joe said, standing up in the bow, 'I know lots of you will have seen the photos on our website and social media. Please share your pics and remember to tag us. You're probably hoping to spot some dolphins. We often see dolphins, harbour porpoises, the occasional basking shark, and if we're extremely lucky, a minke or even a humpback whale. I can close to guarantee seals. We'll be taking you to some of the quieter coves where they like to hang out. You might be hoping for otters. This is Ottersea, right? I don't think we'll see any of those. Any otters around here live upstream in the rivers. And we'll also be looking out for birds, peregrines who nest on the cliffs, guillemots, shags...' Arthur had heard this spiel countless times – he and Joe used to go out with Joe's dad all the time. The wording hadn't changed. He wanted Lottie to have a good time, but he hoped she wouldn't be too impressed by Joe. 'If you think you spot something – and I can see lots of you have your binoculars ready – give me a wave or a shout. And we'll go as close as we're allowed and take a look at it. We'll also go see the cruise ship that's been moored out here for the last two years. We'll go right up close and you can give the poor old crew onboard a wave. They have to flush every loo and run every tap every day to stop Legionnaire's disease. We have about a seventy-five per cent chance of seeing some dolphins – I know they're most people's favourites – for every four trips, we see them on about three. We've seen sunfish too in the last few hot summers. That's not something my dad ever expected, did you Dad? And we've got some extra experts on board today – my best mate, Arthur and his friend Lottie from the Oceanworld Centre. So, if I don't know what something is, you can guarantee they will.' Everyone turned to look at Arthur and Lottie who were sitting at the back. Arthur smiled; Lottie waved.

'I thought you looked familiar,' said the middle-aged man of the couple who were sitting in front of them. 'We were there the other day. Saw you feeding the otters. Very nice.'

They chugged on out to sea. Joe pointed out the different types of rock and the cove that had been used by smugglers, then dancing towards them came the dolphins.

'There, Arthur!' cried Lottie, pointing, and then, to his complete joy – she squeezed his hand. The trip delivered everything Arthur had hoped – not just the dolphins, but seals hauled out on the rocks, peregrines perching on the cliffs and kestrels hovering above them, and more shags and guillemots than you could shake a stick at.

'Would you, um…' said Arthur, as they climbed back up the slope from the jetty.

'Like to get some coffee?' Lottie asked, 'We could go to Flakies – I want to see how Kiran's doing. It must be so awful for her.'

'Sure,' said Arthur.

They walked back along the promenade. Bal was behind the counter at Flakies along with Nindy and a couple of local teenagers.

'Is Kiran around?'

'She's upstairs. With my mum.'

'OK,' said Lottie. 'Maybe I'll message her. I'm Lottie, by the way.'

'OK,' he said. He gave them their coffees and turned to the next customers who looked as though they were going to ask for complicated orders of waffles and smoothies and pancakes.

Arthur and Lottie went to sit outside.

'So, were you at school with Joe?'

'Yeah, known him for ever. Lots of people move away, but he'll stay. He does the tours, plus he and his dad have lobster pots. They used to do more fishing, but they just do those now, and Joe does deliveries from the fish market, stuff like that.'

'Do you ever go out with him to get the pots?'

'I have done, but not anymore.'

'I know it's people's livelihoods, and everything, but…' said Lottie. She didn't know how much she should say – criticising small-scale fishermen might be a bit out of order in Ottersea, and Joe was clearly Arthur's mate.

'Say what you like,' said Arthur. 'There's people now who go and buy live lobsters from the fish markets and restaurants – you know when they have them in tanks – just to put them back.'

'It just seems so, well self-indulgent, when a lobster can

live to be – um – really old. And a person comes along and just has them for lunch. Something that may have been living in the sea for decades and may have decades of life to go.'

'The oldest recorded lobster was seventy-something,' said Arthur. 'Some people think lobsters are—'

'—immortal?' said Lottie. 'But they aren't. They just don't age the way we do.' A couple in almost matching blue and white checked shirts and beige bucket hats were approaching. They hadn't grown to resemble their dogs – two black labs – but they had grown to resemble each other, unless they always had. Lottie stopped talking. The couple were followed by a man on a mobility scooter. He had a Davy Crockett tail on an old aerial attached to it. He was really motoring and parped his horn. The checked shirt couple and their dogs got out of the way just in time.

'I guess the Davy Crockett thing is a vestigial tail of his Mod days,' said Lottie. Arthur smiled. They drank their coffee and gazed out to sea.

'Yeah, lobsters just get bigger,' said Arthur after a while. 'Imagine if we did that – just taller and taller until we died. It must be exhausting, shedding your shell again and again.'

'I wonder if people would be even more impressed by height, if that's what humans did,' Lottie said, 'or if they'd still fetishize youth and thinness. I guess if people didn't get wrinkly and doddery as they got older…'

'My sister would be out of business,' said Arthur.

'I'm sure there would still be things people wanted done,' said Lottie. 'Height enhancement treatments, manicures or whatever.'

'Probably just a matter of time before people start making face cream out of lobsters,' said Arthur, staring sadly into his coffee.

Lottie was going to tell him that she'd seen face cream made from snail slime on Amazon and how that was a thing, and that fish scales were often used in lipstick for their iridescent properties, but he looked so sad, she decided not to.

A man wearing a tan anorak, despite the heat, and an elderly border terrier were now limping along the promenade towards them, followed by an old lady with a shopping trolley that she'd decorated with plastic flowers. As she passed, they saw that it also had a sticker that said: "My Other Car's A Porsche".

Lottie kept quiet until they'd passed.

'Maybe the lobsters start displaying old lobster behaviour though, you know like wearing anoraks in summer and wanting the heating on all year round, buying those half-cans of baked beans...'

'I did go out with Joe and his dad, you know, to collect the pots, but I stopped after I started volunteering at the Centre. It was just too weird – feeding some creatures and hauling other ones to their deaths. And they don't go to get the pots every day, so you can have things in there eating each other – it's not great.'

'I guess it's just part of life, and death, around here, though.'

'I guess,' said Arthur. 'This morning my sister suddenly said she wanted to sell the house and move. Just out of the blue.'

'Really? What do you think? Do you want to move?'

'I haven't thought about it much since Jane arrived. I didn't mean to come back and just stay here. I used to want to do a PhD or go and work on an interesting project somewhere – not just with animals in captivity. You know, do something good.'

'That's what I want to do after my degree,' said Lottie. 'But I don't know what or where. Maybe you should think about it.'

'I couldn't leave Jane, though.'

Beyond Ice Cubes

After a week of daily ice cubes, the palm looked no different. If anything, it appeared healthier. She supposed that as they hadn't had rain in weeks it must be enjoying the chilled water. It looked as though it could withstand a nuclear blast, but then, thought Diana, its ancestors probably had when the comet struck and the dinosaurs were wiped out. Now it was sprouting a nasty protuberance, some sort of hideous flower. So, no more Mr Nice Guy. She would have to get tough if she wanted it out of her view. At the supermarket on her way home there was nothing that looked powerful enough. She took a detour to the old-fashioned hardware store. Here an ancient man in a brown overall sold the sorts of things that had been banned many moons ago, chemicals that would give Arthur conniptions if he knew about them. She eased past the glue traps for rodents, the dog chews made of pigs' ears, and the boxes of dusty millet for pet birds until she found the garden-destruction section. Here were slug pellets and things in plastic bottles for killing every species of flora and fauna. She eschewed the ready-to-spray bottles of weedkiller – dilutable would be better, that way she could make it extra strong. She spotted something that claimed to kill tree stumps and picked up a bottle of that too.

'We can sell this again, thanks to Brexit,' the old guy told her.

'One of the many benefits of it,' said Diana, smiling.

Sarcasm would be lost on the old fool. Much of his stock had been here since at least Mrs Thatcher's time. There was a faded portrait of the queen behind the counter along with a promotional calendar from a power tools company and banks of shelves with little pull-out drawers containing washers and batteries and radiator keys and other things that nobody could ever possibly want.

'You want to be careful with that stuff, though,' the man went on.

'Yes, I know,' said Diana. 'I am always extremely careful.' He put the bottles into the sort of skinny plastic bag that most places in Ottersea had stopped giving out years ago. She paid with cash. Best not to leave a digital trail.

That night, once Arthur was asleep, she put on dark trousers and shoes and one of his dark blue Oceanworld Centre hoodies. She took the sharpest knife from the kitchen and hacked into the palm. It was easy enough to see what she was doing with the light from the moon on the sea and the strings of coloured bulbs. Once she had a big enough cavity, she painted on lashings of tree-stump killer. Then she climbed onto the planter wall and poured the glyphosate weedkiller all over the palm, hissing 'Die, you ugly brute!' She poured the rest of the tree-stump killer over it for good measure, then with Arthur's hood still in place, she climbed back down and walked briskly home. She put the bottles in a bin bag and straight out into the wheelie bin so Arthur wouldn't see them. She had always wondered why more criminals didn't just put things into their bins – as long as nobody searched their rubbish before it was collected, the weapons or whatever would surely be lost forever. And why did robbers in movies always run away? If they just walked briskly nobody would know they were fleeing the scene of a crime. The trouble with so many criminals was that they were stupendously dumb.

She washed her hands and went to hang Arthur's hoodie back up on the peg, then with a pang of conscience she decided she should just put it straight in the washing machine.

The weedkiller was, after all, lethal to fish and pondlife. He had loads of hoodies, identical but for their varying degrees of fadedness, and would never notice which ones were available. She was so tired by now that she couldn't be bothered to put the kitchen light back on. It was only when she tossed it into the machine and it caught the light that was still on in the hall that she saw that the script on the back (that she'd thought was just in a contrasting green) was actually in fluorescent lettering and might incriminate the wearer if they were caught on CCTV from behind. But anybody who knew her would know that she wouldn't be seen dead in one of Arthur's hoodies.

After a few days, when not much seemed to be happening, Diana started half-filling the travel cup she'd used for the ice cubes with weedkiller each morning and chucking it at the palm on her way to work. She was very subtle about it. Nobody would notice what she was doing.

Chapped Lips

The room they were waiting in at the police station in Exeter
had nasty yellow strip lighting and no windows. The main
room they'd be broadcasting from was just as bad – they really
couldn't have given Jim a more depressing venue for the press
conference. Mrs Sumal, Bal and Kiran clearly hadn't twigged
that it was intended to expose the grieving relatives to stress
and see their reactions, as much as appeal for information.
Jim was pleased they hadn't brought the little Sumal girl.
He was waiting with the rest of the family and Grace in a
side room. They could hear people in the main room, and it
sounded like a good turnout of local TV and press; hopefully
it would be picked up nationally, or at least in Reading. He
wondered if that might throw something more up – nobody
liked a landlord.

Bal, the son, had clearly dressed up and was wearing a new
white shirt (you could still see the creases from the packet),
smart black trousers (probably ones he wore to weddings)
and shiny shoes. He was clean-shaven and his hair looked
recently cut. He clearly hadn't felt too distraught to make
time for a trip to the barber. Jim had the impression that his
dad had cared a lot about that stuff too. The pictures he'd
seen of him showed him in expensive clothes – much more
expensive than the things his wife wore. She was wearing a
white salwar kameez with a white cardigan over the top, even

though it was going to be hot again, and her hair was covered by a white cotton scarf – mourning clothes. She was carrying a battered maroon handbag. The fake leather was peeling in places, exposing the black fabric base. Kiran was wearing her Flakies get-up – black leggings and a Flakies T-shirt and trainers with her hair hanging down her back in one long plait. She had no make-up on, but just before they were about to go in, she found a lipstick and some mascara in her bag.

'Here, Mum,' she said, 'you want to look your best.' Mrs Sumal sat back in her chair and Kiran applied a little of both which such tenderness that Jim had to look away.

'You're taking such good care of your mum,' said Grace, and Kiran gave her a half-smile.

'Put some on too, Kiran,' said Bal. Kiran sighed and put on a bit of mascara.

'Lips are too chapped for anything,' she said.

Grace took a tube of Blistex out of her purse. 'Here,' she said, 'a squirt of that will help.' Kiran rubbed some in. It smelled strongly medicated even across the room where Jim was sitting. 'It really works,' said Grace. 'Keep it.'

'Thanks.'

'I'll see if we can start,' said Jim. He put his head around the door into the main meeting room. 'Good turnout,' he said. 'Looks like we have two TV crews and a few press and photographers.' He didn't add that he knew the local press loved these events because it made a difference from their standard fare of potholes and kids being sent home from school for having the wrong uniform.

The cameras were running when they stepped out of the room and as soon as they sat down, the flashes started. He sat one end of the table; next to him was Bal, and then Mrs Sumal, Kiran, and Grace at the end. The Sumals held hands under the table in a way that seemed spontaneous and natural. If one of them was the killer, Jim thought, the others either didn't know or were helping to cover it up. Mrs Sumal started dabbing at her eyes with a tissue, even before Jim had started to speak.

'Thanks for coming everybody,' said Jim. 'I'm DI Jim Paddon, the senior investigating officer on the case. With me here are DC Grace Brown and three of the Sumal family, Mrs Sukhi Sumal and two of her children, Bal and Kiran.'

Behind him were display boards with blown-up pictures of Mr Sumal, his car, its number plate, his NYC baseball cap (though God knows, that was pretty generic), the type of Fitbit they thought he'd been wearing and his model of iPhone.

'This started off as a missing person case, but very sadly, Mr Sumal's body was washed up on the beach – some of you covered that,' Jim said, thinking "no pun intended", and nodding at the reporter and photographer from the local paper. 'What we are trying to do now is establish the circumstances of Mr Sumal's death.' He turned to the Sumals. Mrs Sumal's hands were now in her lap, and he saw her digging the nails of one hand into the back of the other's fist. Her son had his arm proprietorially around her, with his hand gripping her shoulder. It looked as though he was trying to hold her still. Was he trying to keep her quiet, or just calm? Kiran, with her head slightly bowed, was staring determinedly at the edge of the table in front of her, clearly not wanting to make eye contact with any of the press. But why would she? The whole situation, whatever had gone on, was horrific and must be beyond surreal, a nightmare.

'Mr Sumal was last seen by his wife and daughters on the morning of July 4th. They thought he was travelling to Reading where he had business interests, but it seems he didn't leave Ottersea that day. When his car was found on the promenade a few days later they were unable to contact him and reported him missing. Sadly, his body was found on the beach here at Ottersea on July 18th. He had been in the water for some time but had broken bones and injuries consistent with a fall from a great height, and considering the circumstances and location, quite probably from the cliffs.

'We would be really grateful for the public's help in tracing Mr Sumal's movements in the last days of his life, particularly from when he was last seen on CCTV on the afternoon of July 4th until his body was found on July18th. Any information at all will be much appreciated. We ask people to come forward even if they think what they can tell is too trivial to be useful – it could just be the missing piece of the puzzle we need.

'When Mr Sumal went missing, he was wearing black chinos, a black Ralph Lauren polo shirt, and a black NYC baseball cap like the one you can see on the boards. We are particularly keen to trace his iPhone 11 and Fitbit, both of which are still missing. Robbery is a possible motive, so it's essential that we trace these items. We ask any member of the public who is offered a second-hand iPhone 11 or Fitbit to please get in touch with us. Officers have been going door-to-door in Ottersea and Reading. We ask the people of Ottersea to please check any dashcam or doorbell footage they have for images of Mr Sumal, particularly on 4th July, the last day his family saw him and the day that his car was abandoned on the seafront.' A few press hands went up, but Jim hadn't finished. He went on:

'Were you in the high street branch of Freddy's Racing that day? We know Mr Sumal visited it. Did you see him park his car, or walking along the seafront, or on the cliffs? We'll be grateful for maximum publicity for the case so that this grieving family can know what happened to a much-loved husband and father.'

Jim turned back to the family. Mrs Sumal was staring straight ahead, her son's hand still clasping her shoulder in that restraining way. Both Bal and Kiran were now looking towards their mother, though she seemed oblivious to this. Kiran looked as though she was willing her mother to do or to not do something. Collapse in tears? Confess all? He didn't know. Maybe Bal had done it – he was the most likely after all – and she was covering up for him. Though he had been in Reading at the time of the disappearance and his alibi stood up. They hadn't traced Mr Sumal to Reading – but who knew – maybe this appeal would throw up something new. Perhaps he had got a lift with someone.

'Now I'm going to hand over to Mr Sumal's son, Bal, who is going to say a few words on behalf of the family.'

Jim watched as Bal stood up and took a sheet of folded A4 out of his pocket. The moment he took his hand off his mother's shoulder, she began to sway gently backwards and forwards. Kiran turned to her and put her arm around her mother's shoulders in just the way her brother had. This seemed to still Mrs Sumal; she became calm and stared straight ahead again. The two of them were clearly ensuring she held it all together. Or kept it all in. Bal began to read:

'Er, thank you very much for coming and for helping us find out what happened to my dad. Dad was a good husband and father, and we are all missing him, especially my mum and my little sister.' (So, not you and Kiran so much, thought Jim). 'We were an ordinary family and we never thought something like this could happen to us. My mum and dad moved to Devon when I was a kid and they built up Flakies together. My dad taught me everything I know about the property business. Lots of people here and in Reading knew him, so if anyone knows what happened, please come forward cos we just want to know the truth and find closure.'

Jim was always amazed by the way people were so quick to say that they wanted to "find or achieve closure" – the person they had lost was barely cold! There was no real moving on from loss and grief. They were like politicians: "Let's all just draw a line and move on". And maybe it was "Let's just draw a line and move on so that nobody finds out what we did". Or maybe he was just parroting the clichés and saying whatever he thought he was meant to because he had no other words.

Kiran now had tears on her cheeks, but Mrs Sumal, nothing, despite the previous eye-dabbing. Maybe that had been a reaction to the mascara. She just stared down at her lap. They would have the TV footage to work with, and colleagues in another side room were taping things and observing in case that didn't come good. Bal sat back down. He folded up his speech again and put it back in his pocket. Jim was impressed that it had been on a piece of paper – many people would have just read from their phones. A printed-out speech showed more planning.

'Very good, Bal, well done,' whispered Mrs Sumal, and Jim saw her give a little smile. It was the most animated she'd been all morning.

'We can take a couple of questions,' said Jim. Some hands went up again and there was a bit of general shuffling.

'Max Smith, *West Country News*. Do you think Mr Sumal's death is connected to his business empire?'

'It's not exactly an empire,' Bal said before Jim could reply.

'We're keeping an open mind. There may be nothing suspicious. This could also be an accident or Mr Sumal may have taken his own life. That's why we need the public's help,' said Jim.

'Follow-up question. Could this be a racist attack?'

'We don't know. We're keeping an open mind. The Sumals have lived in Ottersea for over twenty years and were a part of the community. If anyone has any information about anyone with a possible motive, we urge them to come forward. The number's there,' he said, gesturing to the display board behind him.

'Lily Salmon, *Look South-West*. Could this be ice cream rivalries, something that's led to killings in other parts of the UK?'

'Again, we're keeping an open mind,' said Jim.

'Tell them everyone loves Flakies,' Mrs Sumal whispered to her son. He stood up.

'Like the detective said, we don't know. But Flakies has been here a long time. We're on good terms with all the other local businesses. We never had any racism in the business either.'

'And everyone loves ice cream' said Mrs Sumal, louder this time. 'The business is for my children now and we don't want it to have this bad publicity.' Jim and Grace exchanged the quickest of glances at this odd response. Jim saw Kiran bite her lip and press the flat of her hand on her mother's knee beneath the table, as if to say "shut up". Another hand went up.

'Harry Dean, *Ottersea Echo*. Have you found a murder weapon?'

'We don't yet know if this is murder, but no weapon has been found,' said Jim.

'Are you looking for one?'

'There are some unusual factors in this case, so we have to keep an open mind.'

'What kind of unusual factors?'

'We don't know for certain if Mr Sumal was still alive when he entered the water. His manner of death is, as of yet, unconfirmed. We are investigating a number of possibilities.' This caused a bit of chatter, but there didn't seem to be any more questions. 'Thank you all for coming,' said Jim. 'As you know, we really value the media's help in appealing for information. We ask everybody to please come forward if they know or noticed anything, however insignificant it might seem. Please also keep a look out for Mr Sumal's iPhone and Fitbit and check your doorbell or dashcam footage. Thank you.'

'What do you think, Skip?' asked Grace, once the Sumals had left with Bal driving them back in his car.

'The son and daughter were understandably protective of their mother. But she seems a bit odd. How about you?'

'She doesn't seem exactly heartbroken, but maybe he wasn't that nice – maybe she's relieved he's gone. Or maybe she had something to do with it. They went for a walk and she shoved him off the cliffs.'

'Think that's likely, Grace?' asked Jim. "Ode to Billy Joe" began playing in his head.

'Maybe he was a bully – coercive control. She doesn't seem to have much of a life outside home. Maybe he told her something or she found out what he got up to.'

'Hmm,' said Jim.

'We shouldn't discount her. That interjection about the kids and the ice cream was odd – as though she didn't really care he was gone. No tears the first time we saw her either.'

'Just in shock?' Jim suggested. 'Lots of them don't cry until the funeral.'

'I know, Sarge, but we shouldn't rule her out because she doesn't look the type. And do you remember, when someone asked what she was going to do now, she said she was going to get a dog?'

'Yeah, that was odd. I guess she could have meant for protection, but they haven't seemed that worried about someone coming after him or them.'

'Little Nindy said something about a cockapoo – you don't get those for protection.'

When Jim got back to his desk, the forensics from the washed-up towel were waiting for him. There was nothing, at least nothing of Raj Sumal. He hadn't expected much, after all, it had been in the sea, perhaps for a long time, and then caught up in the Oceanworld filters. It was just some bit of meaningless cloth.

Pimm's and Sympathy

After Graham Grayling's funeral, when Katie's sons would have left her all alone again, Cass invited herself round.

'Oh, do come,' said Katie. 'We can get on with the project too. Shall we invite some more?'

'I don't want to put you to any trouble,' said Cass, 'that wasn't the plan.'

'It's no trouble. Nice to have some company.'

'Well, I'll ask Caroline,' said Cass, thinking, same boat. And then she saw Diana in Boots, and mentioned it, and now Diana was coming as well. The four of them often met as the committee, so it made sense.

Now here they were in Katie's front room, all with their knitting or crochet, apart from Diana who hadn't thought to bring hers – she wasn't much of a knitter even though she was all for the project. She had brought a bottle of Pimm's and all the makings, and they were on the second jug. The doors to the garden were open in the hope of a breeze blowing through – it was still sweltering, not really knitting weather, but they needed to get the project finished for August Bank Holiday.

'We could make Pimm's ice lollies for the bank holiday,' said Cass. 'I wonder if that would work?'

'Mmm, with strawberries in,' said Caroline. 'Though strawberries are so horrible frozen, but all the other things.

What about raspberries – so much better frozen, though strawberries are traditional.'

'We'd have to be careful that children didn't buy them,' said Katie. 'Awful if the WI were accused of getting children drunk or poisoning anyone.'

'Ha,' said Diana. 'It's a good idea, though. It would be nice to have something new on the stall.'

'We took over three hundred pounds last year,' said Katie. The town's bank holiday fete, held on the green in front of Diana's house, was always a money-spinner for local groups – the last hurrah of the summer holidays. 'If it's this hot, the cakes won't go as well as usual.'

'It is going to be so strange,' said Katie. 'No Graham and no Jeremy in the Shanty Crew.'

'We'll stick together,' said Caroline. 'But you don't have to go, of course. We can stay in if you like.'

'I don't deserve nice friends like you!' cried Katie, putting down her crochet and starting to cry. Cass was already sitting next to her and put an arm around her. Caroline knelt on the floor in front of her and took her hands.

'I'll get you a tissue,' said Diana, only moving to reach into her bag.

'Don't deserve nice friends? Katie, that's ridiculous. Nobody could be more lovely than you!' said Cass. 'You have no idea how much people love you.'

'No, no,' said Katie, 'they wouldn't if they knew what I was like.'

'You silly thing,' said Caroline 'you're exhausted after everything.' Katie shook her head from side to side, as though she could get rid of a thought. Diana got up from her armchair and gave Katie a tissue, even though there was a box on the coffee table with a blue cotton cover to which Katie had appliqued daisies. Katie dabbed at her eyes and Diana sat back down.

'I have to tell someone, or I'll burst,' said Katie. 'If you feel you have to tell the police, I understand.'

'Katie, you can tell us anything,' said Cass.

'It was all to do with my crochet,' said Katie. 'It was all my fault.' Cass and Caroline exchanged glances. 'The night Graham died,' said Katie, looking over to his empty chair. 'It was Shanty Crew. I'd gone to bed early with my crochet. I had new yarn – lovely bamboo and cotton to make an elephant. I'd bought it that day, but I'd forgotten to take my own bag – I told you it was all my fault. Maddy put it in a plastic bag for me. It was all so stupid of me. Graham was so firm about plastic bags – I should have hidden it and then secretly taken it to the Scope shop. But I fell asleep, and he came up to bed and spotted it. I told you it was my fault.'

'None of this is anything bad,' said Cass.

'There's worse, much worse. He was so angry. He threw it out of the bedroom, but you can't really throw a carrier bag. It was barely out of the bedroom door – just on the landing. He said I had to pick it up. But I didn't. It wasn't that I forgot – I decided not to. Then later, in the night, he got up – he always does... did, more if he's been to the pub. And he slipped on it. That's why he fell down the stairs.' She started to cry again.

'Oh, Katie, you couldn't have known he would. It was just an accident!' cried Cass.

'And I think I heard it happen in the night, but I just turned over and went back to sleep! And I slept so well without him there in the bed. I even had a lovely dream about puffins. Then when I woke up – there he was at the bottom of the stairs – and it was too late – and there was the bag. He must have slipped on it.'

'But all of this was an accident,' said Cass. 'You couldn't have known any of that might happen.'

'But I should have known. We've always thought about tripping hazards. Graham used to do a monthly health and safety walk through the house, checking for anything dangerous. It was on the calendar. And he was expecting me to pick it up.'

Cass pursed her lips, not wanting to speak ill of the dead, though there was plenty they could all say about Graham.

'It was an accident,' said Caroline, 'just an accident.'

Katie shook her head. 'When the ambulance came, they didn't suspect me – nobody did. They just thought he had fallen down the stairs.'

'He *did* just fall down the stairs,' said Diana, with Cass and Caroline nodding. 'It wasn't as though you pushed him, though nobody would have bl...' she thought better of finishing the sentence.

'I keep expecting him to come back and tell me off,' said Katie.

'That isn't going to happen,' said Diana. Katie drained her glass. Diana poured her another and topped up everyone else's.

'I hid the bag before the ambulance arrived and I haven't told anyone – not the boys, not anyone.'

'You don't have to – there's nothing to tell. He fell down the stairs. That's all,' said Cass. 'Let's go outside and look at the stars. It always helps.'

It was still ridiculously warm outside. Katie's night-scented stocks were in full bloom and her evening primroses were luminescent.

'Graham would say something about light pollution,' said Katie as they reclined their wooden garden chairs to better look up at the sky.

'You mustn't feel guilty,' whispered Diana. 'Apart from there being no point, he was the one who threw it near the top of the stairs. Why should you have been the one to pick it up?'

'It was just an accident,' Cass added. 'And you don't know that he slipped on it – maybe he just fell anyway.'

'No,' said Katie, in a tiny voice. 'It was on the stairs – it was obvious what had happened.'

'Well, he'd clearly been drinking,' said Diana. Cass gave her a look, though Diana either didn't see or ignored it. 'These things happen all the time. More Pimm's, anybody?' She topped up everyone's glasses again.

'I don't know,' said Katie. 'I could have stopped it happening.'

Caroline reached over and took her hand then she

glanced around. There was no light or noise coming from the neighbouring gardens.

'You aren't the only one,' she whispered. 'I didn't tell anyone what happened when Jeremy died – and it's worse.' They all turned to look at her. She took another sip of her drink. 'You mustn't tell anyone.' They all nodded. 'It was the night of the bath bombs, remember? I did lavender, but I put in so much – they were really strong. I had one in the tub – it was just me and Toby, well, Toby's not allowed in it, but he was keeping me company. Jeremy and the boys were still at the restaurant. When they got back, Jeremy got in, stinking of fish, as usual. I got out and went to bed, but Toby stayed down with him. He had some wine – Jeremy not Toby – he always did after work. He wanted me to stay with him, but really, I didn't fancy it. I went upstairs. As I closed the curtains, I saw him take a bite of a bath bomb—'

'A bite? Was he poisoned? Oh, Caroline, how awful!' said Cass.

'Oh, no,' said Caroline, 'not that.'

'Oh, thank goodness,' said Katie. 'How awful if the WI had poisoned someone!'

'I did laugh, though. I was watching – he must have thought it was a cake – the muffin cases we used – it was quite funny. He just chucked it in the tub, though. So much lavender oil. He lay back and must have been drifting off – and then Toby nudged him – you mustn't tell – he might be put down – and I saw Jeremy slide under the water. This is so much worse than you, Katie. And I did nothing. I got into bed and just waited for Toby to come and sleep at my feet.'

'You let the dog on your bed?' asked Diana.

'He's a very clean dog. Labradoodles don't shed. But I should have gone back down. I should have pulled him out. He was drowning and I just got into bed and went to sleep.'

'Oh, Caroline!' said Cass. 'I'm sure you weren't to know.'

'Perhaps you thought he was just ducking under for a minute,' said Katie.

'I don't know what I was thinking, but I should have gone back down.'

'What about your boys?' asked Diana. 'They could have fished him out.'

'They were in the den gaming. They didn't know. It was my fault. But I didn't tell anyone. I'd be in jail, and worse, what would happen to Toby? You mustn't tell.'

'Of course not,' they all said.

'It was very unlike Toby. I just can't get over that. Dogs are meant to protect their people.'

'Maybe he was trying to,' said Cass.

'Yes, he's usually such a good dog,' added Katie.

'Maybe he was trying to protect you, not Jeremy,' said Diana.

'Diana!' cried Cass, forgetting to whisper.

'No,' said Caroline. 'I wondered about that – maybe we were secretly in league. Maybe he thought I'd be happier.'

'Oh, Caroline,' said Cass, reaching across the gap between their chairs to stroke her friend's arm. 'I know things weren't always great.' She had seen Jeremy in action at The Blue Lobster.

'At least I have my boys,' said Caroline, 'but if they ever knew…'

'Well, they must never know,' said Diana. 'Nobody is suspicious.'

'I suppose,' said Caroline. 'I'm glad I told you all, I had to tell someone.'

'Me too,' said Katie.

'We're the WI,' said Diana. 'Middle-aged women. We're invisible.'

'You're not middle-aged, Diana,' said Cass.

'Well, no,' said Diana. 'But it's true. We could do anything, and nobody would notice. We should make the most of it. More Pimm's, anybody?'

Wildlife

It was the Ottersea Wildlife Society's monthly meeting. Arthur had missed the last one because he'd had a late staff meeting at the Centre. When he arrived, he went straight to talk to Katie Grayling, who had an empty chair beside her, though he remained standing. He'd emailed her his condolences when there'd been a message from the society's chair about Graham's sudden and unexpected death, but not seen her since it happened.

'Hello, Katie, how are you doing? I was really sorry to hear about Graham.'

'Thank you, Arthur. It was such a shock. Just a terrible accident. One little slip.'

'I'm sorry I couldn't come to the funeral – my boss was on leave and I couldn't get the time off. You must be missing him so much.' She looked down at her hands and nodded and then reached for her knitting bag. She took out a ball of creamy coloured wool with speckles of pale green and orange that made it reminiscent of Sandwich Spread and buried her nose in it. When she looked up at him again, she had a half-smile.

'The boys have been brilliant, but of course they are devastated.'

'They must be,' said Arthur. 'Losing their dad.'

'I know you know all about that, and you were much younger,' said Katie, patting the chair beside her. Arthur was reluctant to sit in what was so clearly Graham's empty chair – it seemed a bit disrespectful, even though it was just one of the old stacking chairs, but he had no choice but to sit down. He did move the chair to the side and back a bit so that it didn't look so much as though he was in Graham's place. The other members were arriving too and Arthur was relieved when Peter, the Chair, sat down on the other side of Katie and put an arm around her shoulder.

'Thanks everyone for coming,' said Peter. 'You will all have heard the news of the very sad passing of our treasurer and long-term member, friend, and Katie's husband, Graham Grayling. Graham has been a stalwart of OtterseaWildlife Society since the 1980s. He will live on through his meticulous recordings of the birds and animals of our little patch. I know we all offer our condolences to Katie and the whole family. Before we start, let's have a minute's silence to remember Graham in our own ways.' He removed his arm from Katie's shoulder – she looked relieved – and everyone bowed their heads.

Arthur closed his eyes and thought about what an efficient treasurer Graham had been and how nobody had ever been allowed to fall behind with their membership fees. Graham had always been ready with the financial statement at meetings and been guaranteed to have some Other Business (even though Treasurer's Report was a fixture on the agenda) and how he'd offered his opinion on every other item. Meetings would now be significantly shorter.

When Arthur opened his eyes, he saw that Katie had, within that minute, silently taken the rest of her knitting out of her bag and was quietly unravelling whatever it was she had been making. He remembered seeing in films how one person would hold up their hands for the other person to wind the wool on, but she seemed to be doing very well quietly wrapping it back on its ball instead. He wouldn't have wanted to offer that anyway – too intimate. The unwound wool had a nice zig-zagginess to it, like that sort of linguine, but thinner. He wondered if she had been making a jumper for Graham and was now going to use the wool for something else. Graham would have approved – he had hated waste of any kind; perhaps that was why Katie was smiling.

Arthur remembered Graham really losing it at Katie when she had put some used paper plates in a black binbag someone was passing round at the society's annual picnic. He'd said that they should be composted even if they were too soiled (his word) to be recycled. Katie had just put her head down and apologised and then Graham had stalked off whilst everyone else finished clearing up. Arthur had been a new member then, only seventeen and the youngest there by a good few decades. Now he hoped that if something like that happened, he would have the guts to say something, but he hated any kind of conflict and feared that he would duck out of doing anything, the way he always did when Diana was on at him.

They got through the agenda faster than usual without Graham's interjections, constant corrections, and points of order. Everybody's favourite part came at the end: This Month's Notable Sightings when they shared news of what they'd spotted. Lots of them shared pictures on the society's Facebook page, but some of the older members didn't have the internet so the agenda item stayed. Mavis said she thought she'd seen a hoopoe in her neighbour's garden, but as it was after her cataract operation, it might just have been something yellow on their washing line. Last to share their sightings was Katie. She and Graham had always been in charge of maintaining the society's trail cams at the Red Cliffs Nature Reserve.

'I'm sorry,' she said. 'Since Graham died, I'm afraid I don't know how to get those little card thingies out of the trail cams. Sorry. I should have worked out how to do it, but somehow, I just haven't had time.'

'Of course you haven't had time,' said Peter.

'I can do it,' said Arthur. 'You could show me where

they are, and I can either do it or show you how – whichever you prefer.'

'Thanks, Arthur. If you have time,' said Katie.

'Course I do,' said Arthur.

'I'll minute your offer, thanks, Arthur,' said the secretary. Then for the first time in many years, there was no other business.

Trail Cams

A few days later, Arthur borrowed Diana's car to pick Katie up. She took a couple of minutes to answer the door and when she did, she was holding one of her walking boots; the other one was on, but still unlaced. Katie looked a bit different. He realised he'd never seen her arms before – she'd always worn long sleeves.

'I'm sorry, Arthur,' she said. 'I seem to take forever to get ready now without Graham rattling the car keys at me.' She smiled and sat down on the bottom stair to finish putting her boots on. Arthur stood on the doorstep, determined not to look in the slightest bit impatient. He had the car keys in his hand and put them, as silently as possible, into his cargo shorts pocket.

'Absolutely no hurry,' he said. There was a little wooden table with the telephone on in her hall. On top of it was a photo of her and Graham on their wedding day. Beside it was a small vase containing a couple of flowers seemingly made from black binbags and pipe cleaners. The front garden was full of real flowers – lavender, pinks, sea holly, buddleia, hollyhocks and foxgloves, so these homemade artificial ones seemed an odd choice, but then, Arthur mused, Graham had been such a committed reuser and recycler.

'There!' said Katie. 'Ready at last. Thank you for being so patient.'

'I wasn't,' said Arthur. 'I mean it was only a minute.' She had a little rucksack ready packed and swung it up onto her shoulder.

'Just the essentials,' she said. 'Binoculars, coffee, biscuits.'

'Cool,' said Arthur. 'Thanks. I've got my laptop so I can download the images from the SD cards and we can put them straight back in while we're there.'

'That's the bit I wasn't sure about,' said Katie.

'I'll show you how – it's easy,' said Arthur.

'Easy for a clever young person,' said Katie.

'I don't mind doing this with you every time,' said Arthur. 'It's no bother. And it's always exciting to see what's been caught. We might get a surprise.'

'That's what I always thought – maybe we'd get the Beast of Bodmin on holiday, but Graham said that was silly.'

'You never know,' said Arthur. 'But everything caught on the camera is important.'

The drive up to the nature reserve on the cliffs only took about ten minutes, but as it was a steep climb on a hot day, walking would have taken much longer.

'So, how many trail cams have you got?' said Arthur after he'd parked.

'There's only two,' said Katie. 'They belong to the society, really, not me and Graham, though Graham has always looked after them. There's one near the little path and one in the woods. We usually get some nice shots of badgers – one's by the sett. But you know that, of course, from the meetings. They do sometimes get shots of people, but the badgers use the path too, so it's worth it.'

They used the main car park and set off through the woods. It was the middle of the day and the birds were silent, though Arthur and Katie could hear gulls in the distance and soon the hush, hush of the sea.

'I don't expect we'll see any badgers,' said Arthur.

'No, but it's always nice to know they're there, leading their secret lives,' said Katie. 'It's weeks since Graham and

I did this. I hope the cameras are OK, not that it's rained for ages. I suppose the batteries will be completely dead. Should I have brought some more? I don't know what kind they use.'

'They're probably fine – they have a battery life of months if they're just taking photos. They're all excellent nowadays, designed for use in jungles and on mountains. What Ottersea throws at them won't be as bad as Borneo or the Himalayas.'

'Oh, that's good. I was probably silly to worry. Graham always spent ages looking at the *Which?* website and reading reviews of things. He loved leaving reviews too, even for things that *I* bought.'

Arthur could imagine this: *My wife bought these shoes in the sale and she's generally pleased though the laces are, in my opinion, somewhat longer than ideal meaning she keeps me waiting while she puts them on.*

'Sounds like Graham,' he said. He wondered if Graham's life had flashed before him as he fell down the stairs. Had he thought about all the time he'd taken posting online reviews and thought, "A life well spent"? Graham would probably be writing TripAdvisor reviews of heaven now: *The weather is generally cloudy. The ambient music can be annoying and there isn't much to do. Three stars.*

Arthur and Katie went to the badger sett camera first, following a little trail off the path through the woods. The camera was on a tree opposite one of the sett entrances. The sett looked well used and Arthur picked up a tuft of brindled fur and put it in his shirt pocket. There were some fallen trees used for scratching and claw sharpening; one was worn almost smooth in places.

'That's one of the places they like to play,' said Katie. 'We've had some great pictures of the cubs from there.' They stood and looked at the used bedding – dried bracken, leaves and long grasses – and the sandy, freshly-dug earth around the entrance. Katie sat down on a tree stump whilst Arthur showed her how to get the SD card out of the camera.

'What I'll do,' he said, 'is get both SD cards and then we can sit down on a bench somewhere and I'll show you how to upload the images onto a laptop and then we can put the cards back. OK?' Katie smiled and nodded.

The other camera was further along the main path to the clifftop and was fixed higher up.

'Ah, this is the stump one,' said Arthur, noticing how it was pointed at a place where some birds clearly dismembered their prey.

'Yes, this was Graham's favourite. He loved seeing what they got up to. Definitely worthy of *Springwatch*.' There were feathers in many colours and tufts of what looked like rabbit fur on the ground.

'Yeah,' said Arthur, smiling, 'you must get some pretty gory scenes up here – it's quite a spot.'

'We've seen goshawks here a few times – the ghosts of the woods.' Arthur gave an impressed whistle.

They removed the SD card and followed the path out onto the clifftop where they had both been so many times with other Wildlife Society members, counting the notable arrivals and departures. They sat on one of the benches and Arthur got his laptop out.

'I don't know which card is which,' he said, taking them both out of his pocket. 'Though that doesn't matter – we'll know when I get the images. So, your laptop will have a little thing at the side like this and you just put the card in, this way up, like this, and then push the little tray back in. Then the computer will tell you what to do.'

'OK,' said Katie. 'I didn't know about that little tray. I'd have had no idea where to put it. I had a camera ages ago with one of those cards, but I just used to give it to the lady in Boots to sort out.'

'It's the same principle,' said Arthur. 'And we could print off some pictures if we wanted – let's see what we've got.'

'I didn't know you could do this outdoors. Graham always used to do it in his study and then come back with the little cards another day. Have you got the internet up here?'

'No,' said Arthur, smiling again. 'But that doesn't matter. I could make a hotspot from my phone, but I don't need to.' Katie looked slightly baffled. 'I can email you the best pictures later and upload them anywhere you want me to.'

'Thank you,' said Katie. 'Coffee?'

'Please. So, the laptop knows the SD card is in there – and I'm just going to keep clicking "yes" then we can look at the pictures. Here we go – oh, it's the badgers one.' The pictures had uploaded – there were tons of them. He rested the laptop on the grass and Katie handed him an enamel mug of coffee.

'It's already got oat milk in – I hope that's OK.'

'Course it is,' said Arthur. His sister cycled through different plant milk choices almost by the week. He never minded which one they had and was happy to just buy whichever one she was currently dictating.

'Biscuit?' said Katie, offering him a packet of Choco Leibniz.

'Cheers,' said Arthur.

'Graham always insisted on homemade flapjacks and cookies and so on. It's actually quite nice to just buy a packet of what I fancy. I even forgot to look out for palm oil until I got home, but it turned out they're OK on the Ethical List website Graham always checked.'

'And they're really nice,' said Arthur. 'Diana is pretty anti-biscuit, but I can have them at work. Not posh ones like this though.'

'I don't know what I'd have done if they did have palm oil in. Graham would have said to take them back to the shop, but I might have put them in the food bank box instead. But then is it better to give away biscuits with palm oil in than eat them yourself? The orangutans aren't going to be helped by you giving them away – the damage of buying them is already done…'

'Um,' said Arthur, his mouth too full to reply properly. Then, 'Does a good deed mitigate a bad one – interesting question.'

'Have another,' said Katie. 'They're getting quite melty so we may as well eat as many as we like.' Arthur ate another two, then wiped his hands on his shorts and uploaded the pictures from the other card. An elderly couple with two small dogs walked past them and said good morning. Katie gazed after them wistfully.

'It's so nice of you to come up here with me. I've got lots to get used to. I've been thinking of getting a bench for Graham, perhaps up here. He did like it here. I don't really know how one goes about getting a bench for someone...'

'I suppose it must be quite straightforward – Ottersea's full of them.'

'Ageing population retiring to Devon, and all those people with happy childhood memories here. Yes, we're two-a-penny.'

'Well, everyone likes a bench,' said Arthur.

'And up here on the cliffs is the perfect place to remember someone,' said Katie. 'I'd have to make sure it was responsibly sourced wood or Graham wouldn't like it.'

'Oh, the photos are loaded,' said Arthur. 'Let's see what we've got.' But the sun was now so bright, they couldn't see them properly.

'It does feel a bit silly to be sitting here looking at a computer screen,' said Katie, 'when we can just look at the sky and the sea and all this *life*.'

'I'll have a look at home and send you all the good ones,' said Arthur, shutting his laptop. They sat there for a while, watching the gulls and listening to the waves breaking below.

'It really is the perfect place,' said Katie. 'I think I'll put his bench up here. I'll talk to the boys about it. How could you not be at peace up here?'

Arthur smiled and patted her arm. They tipped their enamel mugs upside down to drain the last drips of coffee from them and then retraced their steps to the car, stopping to replace the SD cards in the camera traps on the way.

'Hope we caught something good,' said Arthur as the second one clicked into place.

That evening, Arthur had nothing much to do. Diana was out at yet another knitting event, even though she didn't like knitting. He sat on the sofa with his laptop and, because Diana was out, put his feet up on the coffee table, nudging aside a pile of magazines. He had become almost blind to the ridiculous sentence fragments on their covers but every so often, one even more stupid than the common herd would make him blink or snort in disbelief: *Say No to Water*; *Achieving Glass Skin*; *The Inside Scoop on Lactic Acid.* Diana took great pains to read them neatly and never in the bath so that when she took them into the salon, they looked as fresh as possible.

Arthur put on the TV and found a documentary about the Indian Ocean. It had already started, but he didn't mind. Some turtles had just arrived at an underwater beauty salon where some fish were cleaning their shells. They had travelled miles for this – nautical miles, he supposed – he wondered if they had a way of calculating distances themselves, a way of telling themselves how far something was. And if they did, would eels and salmon and everything else do the same? If they did, it was all the more impressive that they embarked on such long journeys, rather than just thinking, 'Sod it. I'll just stay here to lay my eggs rather than swim thousands of miles to get back to some random bit of river.'

He had the photos from the camera traps to go through. He wanted to send them to Katie without her asking him, although she probably wouldn't, she'd clearly put up with lots from Graham. He hoped the WI ladies would be being especially nice to her tonight.

There were some excellent pictures of the badgers – a large family group with several boars and sows (he would never think sows an appropriate name; badgers deserved their own gender nominatives) and three cubs. The badgers looked pleasingly healthy and well fed and he could see how the cubs were growing across the captured images. It had been a few months since Graham had downloaded the last lot. A fox sniffed around the outside of the sett on many occasions, and later on in the series, some cubs came with it. The badgers were clearly sett-proud, bringing out the old bedding and then arriving with new stuff.

The SD card from the camera that pointed at the plucking post had shots of sparrowhawks and goshawks coming in with an impressive variety of birds. It was particularly bad luck for the sand martins, Arthur thought. Imagine flying back all that way only to get nabbed by a hawk. Lots of other creatures came sniffing around the stump at night. The camera was by the path, so it picked up lots of walkers and their dogs too. Someone bearded sat on the stump (they wouldn't if they knew what it was used for, thought Arthur) to take off a Croc and tip a stone out of it. Really, these people would make a good enough wildlife show. Somebody clsc sat on the stump for a while only to drop a cigarette butt on the ground. The camera only picked up movement, so each thing was just a freeze-frame. He was pleased it wasn't videos. Taking pictures of people without their knowledge seemed a bit unethical. Arthur sat clicking "delete" for each of the ones with humans in. Graham would have kept the one with the smoker to raise the matter under Any Other Business. Arthur remembered when two guys had dragged an old mattress, and then some cushions and finally an old sofa past the camera to dump them in the woods. Graham had got on to the council straight away, but they hadn't been able to identify the perpetrators just from their trainers and tracksuits and they'd had their hoods up so their faces hadn't been caught.

But the next human was caught walking backwards, dragging something covered in striped cloth. He knew that bowed head. He knew those shoes. But it couldn't be Diana, surely? What would she be doing dragging something through the woods in the middle of the night? He stared at the screen. It definitely looked like her, but she would never wear a big dark hoodie like that. He could see some of the writing on the hoodie's back and a slice of her face. It *was* Diana and she was wearing one of his Oceanworld hoodies and dragging something that looked like an Egyptian mummy. He looked at the date and time: July 5th and 2.27am. What was she doing? It looked as though she was dragging a body, but that was absurd. In the next shot she was gone – there was a fox sniffing the ground where the mummy had been. And then the next shot, taken twenty-three minutes later, was of her mid-stride going in the other direction. She was cradling a bundle of what now looked like sheets scrunched up in a huge ball. He stared at the picture. You couldn't tell for *sure* it was Diana, but it really looked like her.

He went back and looked at the first picture again. It oscillated between Diana and Not Diana. But what was this person dragging? It looked like a body wrapped up, but how could that be possible – Diana dragging a body through the Red Cliffs Nature Reserve? The more he looked from one picture of the figure to the other and back again, the more it seemed like her. But it couldn't possibly be a body. It must be that she was fly-tipping something from her salon. That was the only explanation.

He could use *Finding Bigfoot* methods. He and his student housemates had loved that show. The programme's team would go wherever the possible bigfoot had been sighted and recreate grainy photos by sending Bobo, the giant of them, to stand where the possible creature had been so they could gauge its height. It always turned out to have been taller than Bobo and at least eight foot. You could use the bird of prey's post in the picture for scale and the bushes behind this possible Diana and try to work out the size of what she was dragging. It was clearly something or someone about as long as she was tall. He minimized the picture and went to make a cup of tea. He would just have to ask her about it.

Arthur stood in the kitchen staring out of the window while the kettle boiled. The whole thing was ridiculous. There must be some sort of innocent explanation for it, even one that involved Diana fly-tipping stuff from her salon into the woods.

He made his tea, adding the last of Diana's organic barista-style oat milk then worrying that she would be annoyed.

If it was Diana with a body, he thought, still standing and looking out into the gathering darkness, would he be compelled to testify against her? Perhaps there was some rule for siblings like the one for married people. He could google that. Or he could just pretend that he had never seen it. Delete it and forget all about it. That might make him an accessory to the crime (whether it was fly-tipping or body-dumping) and it might mean that he was aiding and abetting an offender, or whatever. He went back to the laptop and carried on from the walking back with the bundle image, clicking through the pictures, making swift decisions about what to save and what to delete. Once he had just the best ones left from both SD cards (if you ignored the strange ones), he put them in a folder to send to Katie. It was 10.15 and Diana would be home soon. He didn't feel like talking to her now. He took his laptop and went up to bed. Not long afterwards he heard Diana come in and start clattering around in the kitchen, making her chamomile tea and whatever elaborate and disgusting thing she had planned for her lunch the next day. It was stupid. Of course, Diana couldn't have been hiding a body in the woods. He opened his laptop again. The photos were there in his downloads as well as in the file he'd saved them to back on the clifftop. He looked at them again. It was ridiculous, but he couldn't understand it at all.

The next morning, he took his laptop to work. He was on an early shift, checking all the creatures, fishing out any casualties, all the normal stuff. Perhaps if he looked at the pictures again, he would see that it wasn't Diana or be able to understand what she had been doing if it was in fact her. He was soon busy with the routine of the day. Helen had called in sick so he was in charge. A paddletail snapper had a nasty-looking growth in its mouth so he had to call the vet and then stay late to help; it was impossible to know how bad it was without a biopsy.

'Try not to worry,' the vet said. 'Sometimes things look sinister, but they really aren't.'

'Hope so,' said Arthur.

Lottie helped him with the checking and locking up routines.

'Do you feel like going for a drink tonight?' she asked. 'We could get supper too, just somewhere cheap. But no worries if you're busy.'

'Yes. Great,' said Arthur. 'We could go straight from work if you like.' Then he might be able to avoid Diana entirely for another evening.

'God, no,' said Lottie. 'These clothes smell of puffin lunch.' She pulled up the neck of her T-shirt and sniffed it. 'Euugh.'

'Um, OK. How about quarter to seven?' That seemed like the shortest amount of time Lottie might need to shower and change.

'Cool. Meet you by the harbour?'

He hurried home, the rucksack with the laptop feeling heavier than normal on his shoulders. He didn't go into the kitchen as he usually would but went straight upstairs for a shower. Diana had always managed to weasel things out of him when he was still at school; she was better than his mum had ever been at that. He knew the whole thing was stupid and that he should just ask her about it, but now he was meeting Lottie, he had a good excuse not to. He showered and threw his clothes into the washing basket. He supposed that he must always smell of the puffins' lunch but had just got used to it. He took the rucksack with the laptop in when he went out again. Diana used to snoop through his stuff when he was a teenager (not that he ever had anything contraband) so she still might. She always said she was looking for school letters that he'd forgotten to give her and or wanted to sign his homework diary. He had probably been the only kid whose homework diary had been checked and signed every day.

Arthur arrived early to meet Lottie. He sat at the place where the beach and the harbour met, thinking that it would be nice to go for a walk along the curve of the wall with her and look at the boats. He watched the last of the day's families packing up their stuff while the gulls and crows checked for picnic leftovers. There was a broken blue plastic spade in front of him on the sand. He jumped down with his rucksack and retrieved the spade before it could be carried out to sea. There were cigarette butts too. It looked as though people had been emptying car ashtrays everywhere. He spotted a McDonald's bag by the seawall – that would do for the fag butts. He dumped his rucksack and spent the time he had gathering as many of them as he could see. He'd read an article about gulls becoming addicted to nicotine from eating them. There seemed no end to the horrors humans were inflicting. The spade was the sort of plastic that could rarely be recycled so, with a heavy heart, he put it in a bin back on the promenade with his sack of cigarette ends. His hands were going to stink of something as bad as a bucket of fish. Luckily there was a tap for people to wash the sand off their feet. The water splashed on his legs and shoes. Now he looked like a sad wino who'd pissed on himself. He looked up and Lottie was walking towards him in a blue dress. He hadn't seen her in a dress before. It was the blue of a Lake Kutubu rainbowfish. She had strappy flat green sandals on that looked as though they were made from plaited seagrass. He realised that she might have asked him on a date.

Lottie saw Arthur long before he spotted her. He was putting what looked like a McDonalds' bag and something that was blue in a bin. She saw him sniff his hands and then go and run them under the feet-washing tap. Would he still want to get something to eat? She hoped so, she was starving. He looked up and spotted her and she waved then had to do that embarrassing walking-towards-a-person-from-some-distance thing.

'Hey, Arthur.'

He smiled. 'Hi. I'm sorry my trousers are all wet – I had to wash my hands.'

'Have you eaten already?'

'Not yet. Where would you like to go?'

'Oh, cool. I'm hungry, but I can wait a bit if you want to.'

'Shall we just walk along the harbour wall? What do you feel like eating?'

'Oh anything. That Pizza Shack always has good smells. It would be nice to eat outside.'

They walked along the harbour wall for a bit. Arthur didn't seem inclined to speak.

'When Tennyson went to Lyme Regis,' said Lottie after a while, 'he said something like "don't show me some boring historical thing, just show me the exact spot where Louisa Musgrove fell from The Cobb".'

'Oh,' said Arthur. Then, 'I'm sorry, who was Louisa Musgrove?'

'In *Persuasion*,' said Lottie. 'My mum told me that. She's an Austen fanatic. We went to Lyme Regis last summer and she gave me *Persuasion* to read.'

'Oh no!' cried Arthur. 'I left my rucksack on the sand!' He looked back east along the beach. 'Sorry – I have to go back.' And he was off. He wasn't the fastest runner, but then who could run fast after a surreptitious McDonalds? Lottie sat on a bench and watched him. He didn't slow down once. The tide was coming in – the waves were licking almost all the way up to the seawall. When he got to the end of the harbour wall, he jumped down onto the sand – that jump would have hurt her ankles. There was only a tiny strip of sand left. She saw him pick up something black and then he had to half-walk-half-paddle to the steps back up to the promenade. When he was there, he gave her a big-armed wave. She stood and waved back. The rucksack must have got a bit wet – she could see him taking something out of it and wiping it with his T-shirt. Then he gave the rucksack a good shake and put it over one shoulder. He carried the other thing under one arm and started walking back towards her. Even from this distance he looked sweet and klutzy.

When he finally made it back to the bench, she saw that his trainers and the bottom of his shorts were soaked and that the thing he'd been trying to dry was his laptop.

'Oh no,' she said. 'I hope it's alright.'

'The bag was wet, but the inside was just damp. I dunno if I should switch it on, or if that might short it.'

'Yeah, it might,' said Lottie. 'Sit down, I'll google it.' He opened the laptop and sat with it upside down in a balanced V on his legs.

'Yeah,' said Lottie. 'It says to wipe it dry, keep it upside down, take out any USB things – but you haven't got any in, have you? And take out the battery.'

'Thanks,' said Arthur. 'Can you hold it for a minute? Sorry about this.' He balanced it on Lottie's legs and she put a steadying hand on top of it while he took out his Swiss Army knife for the Phillips screwdriver.

'It looks pretty dry,' said Arthur. 'It was really dumb of me. I went down on the beach cos there was a plastic spade and then loads of cigarette butts – you know how birds can get—'

'Addicted,' said Lottie.

'And I forgot and left it there.'

'Well at least it didn't get washed out to sea,' said Lottie. 'It could have ended up in the beach rubbish display. Embarrassing to have something of yours in there.' He grimaced.

'It was stupid of me to bring it tonight, anyway. God. Really dumb.'

'Why did you?'

'It's well, that's kind of ridiculous too.' She raised her eyebrows at him, but he just looked away out to sea and then down at the laptop.

'It's nothing – probably nothing. Let's forget about it. Let's go. Pizza Shack?'

'OK.' She smiled, but it was odd. Arthur had always seemed really straightforward and sensible before. She hadn't ever seen him look rattled, even when they were doing something really tricky, like when a sea dragon had got its tail stuck in a filter and he'd had to delicately ease it out. But now she thought about it, the time when his sister made her come in for tea when she'd only just met him, then he'd looked kind of sheepish.

They walked along the promenade to Pizza Shack and managed to get a table outside and as far as possible away from the families with fractious or noisy children.

'I've really had it with kids by the time we close each day,' Lottie whispered as they sat down.

'Yeah, me too,' said Arthur.

Lottie spent a long time deciding which extra toppings to have, finally settling on grilled aubergine, black olives and extra tomatoes.

'Just a margarita,' said Arthur when the boy, who looked about twelve, came to take their order and that made Lottie wonder if he'd think she was greedy or fussy, or maybe he was bored of her and just wanted the evening to be over. He wasn't saying much – just giving his laptop worried looks.

'It will probably be OK,' she said. 'You could put it in lots of rice when you get home.'

'Yes,' said Arthur. 'Sorry. It's got photos on it, but it doesn't matter.'

'Aren't they on your phone?'

'Not these ones. I was helping Katie, this lady in the Wildlife Society. Her husband died suddenly and I went and got the photos out of the trail cams for her. He'd always done it.'

'So many people die suddenly around here. Kiran's dad,

plus Jeremy who ran the fish restaurant – did you see that? He was married to my aunt's best friend. He drowned in his own hot tub. And then the husband of another one of her friends fell down the stairs and died.'

'That would be Graham Grayling' said Arthur. 'Katie's husband.'

'Cass said it's seeming like a bit of a plague, or at least a trend. Middle-aged husbands in Ottersea having strange accidents. And their wives are in the WI, but not Mrs Sumal. Maybe they have some sort of *Neighbours on a Train* thing going on.'

'What? No – it must just be coincidence. I mean statistically, if you looked across a wider sample, the numbers are probably not significant – there's just a cluster. Well, probably.'

'Yes,' said Lottie, as their pizzas arrived. 'I was only joking.'

When Arthur got home the laptop seemed pretty dry, but he didn't want to take any risks. He considered putting it open and upside down on some rice, or filling the battery compartment with rice, but that seemed unlikely to do much. One of his university flatmates had hoarded those hateful little silica gel packets in his desk drawer for times like this. But Arthur hated those – they might get dropped outdoors and eaten by a hedgehog. He always put them in the bin straight away. Instead, he left his laptop in the airing cupboard overnight.

Cass was downstairs at Teapot Paradise when Lottie got back, prepping things for the next day.

'Hi honey, nice evening? You're back earlier than I expected.'

'It was OK. We went to Pizza Shack.'

'Only OK?'

'Yeah, wish I hadn't asked him out now,' Lottie said,

looking down at her dress. 'Maybe he only likes girls when they smell of mackerel.'

'You look gorgeous.'

'Thanks. He was just really distracted. Hardly talked. He'd brought his laptop for some reason – I mean who brings their laptop when they go out to dinner? But then he left the bag on the beach when he was waiting for me and the tide was coming in. He went running back – that bit was quite funny – and the bag had got wet, and he spent most of the time fretting – putting it upside down and just looking at it.'

'Well, I don't suppose they pay him much at the Oceanworld Centre – those jobs are always done for love.'

'He definitely prefers octopuses and turtles to people.'

'Well, fair enough, if it's people in general, but not if he prefers sea creatures to *you*.'

'Hmm,' said Lottie.

'Arthur has always been such a sweet boy.' Cass turned to take a chocolate cake out of the oven. 'Maybe he's got something else going on. He seemed keen on you before.'

'Well, his possibly broken laptop was more interesting than me tonight.'

'Fancy an ice cream or a cookie or something?'

'Maybe a gin and tonic.'

'I'll join you.'

They sat in Cass's little garden, which smelled of evening primroses. Cass had left the back door open and wafts of the baking smells drifted out to join them along with the evening smells of Ottersea – chips, cannabis, the sea air and something a bit drainy.

'This is better than any dumb aquarist,' said Lottie. She reclined her chair to gaze up at the sky. 'Maybe we'll see some of the Perseids.'

'Close your eyes, there are suns beneath your lids,' said Cass, quoting Louis MacNeice.

'He probably doesn't know who Louis MacNeice even is,' said Lottie. 'He didn't know who Louisa Musgrove was.'

'Well probably not many males of his age have read *Persuasion*,' said Cass. 'Plenty more fish in the sea, even if there aren't plenty more nice-looking guys in the Oceanworld Centre. A holiday romance would have been nice, though. Wouldn't it?'

Lottie just smiled and shrugged and asked, 'How was your evening?

'Oh, fun,' said Cass. 'It was unofficial WI here – just the crafters. We're doing a guerrilla knitting project.'

'Cool,' said Lottie. 'I hope it's something big.'

'It is,' said Cass. 'Very big.'

The next day was Lottie's day off, so she helped Cass in the café and tried not to think about Arthur. Back at Oceanworld the following day, he greeted her all crinkly-eyed in the staff room:

'I think Jane missed you when you weren't here. It was as though she was looking about for you when I fed her. Helen came by and she gave her a squirt and then shot away, like she was running away laughing. But I think it was also cos she was hoping for you to come.'

'Oh, that's so nice,' said Lottie. 'So, what's on today?'

'Er, you're down for the puffin suit this afternoon.'

'The intern's lot,' said Lottie. 'And it's going to be boiling again.'

'Sorry,' said Arthur.

'You're not the one who did the rota,'

'And I'm sorry about the other night,' said Arthur. 'I know I was distracted.'

'How's the laptop?'

'I haven't put it on yet. It's still in the airing cupboard. Thought I'd try after work – it's probably as dry as it's going to get.'

'Good luck.'

'Thanks, um, I wondered if you might like to go out again...'

'I'm quite busy with my aunt for the next few days. I said I'd help her with some stuff,' said Lottie, though it wasn't true.

Mystery Promenade Plant Deaths

OTTERSEA ECHO

Council bosses are mystified by the state of a promenade planter. Local resident, Crystal Curtain contacted the council when she saw how the plants behind her mum's memorial bench were suffering.

'It's awful,' said Crystal Curtain (37). 'The planters are usually kept really nice and all the others are lovely, but everything is dying in the one behind my mum's bench. The big palm tree looks really ill and all the flowers around it have died. I go there every week and often do a bit of weeding and I've put some of my own seeds in there. I want it to look really nice for my mum. My dad's had a stroke. We take him down there in his wheelchair but now I don't want to. It's depressing. It looks like someone just sprayed weedkiller all over it.'

A spokesperson for the council said 'We

are sorry to hear about the state of the planter and for any upset or inconvenience this has caused. Our gardeners take real pride in the seafront displays and will be looking into this straight away. Ottersea's parks and planting are the pride of the town and give great pleasure to residents and visitors. We will be checking CCTV to see if there has been deliberate criminal damage and the plants will be replaced as soon as possible.'

'Look at this, Dave,' Crystal Curtain said. She WhatsApped the article to her husband rather than walk across the room to show him. She was on the sofa with the dog and her feet up, just back from work, whilst Dave was in the recliner with his feet up too.

He read it and smiled.

'Well done, love. You're famous.'

'I don't care about that,' said Crystal. 'I just want the planter sorted. And if the palm tree's dead they should take it out.'

Not Some Weird Fish

Arthur put the battery back into the laptop. He held his breath and then switched it on. Everything seemed normal. As he waited for it to be ready, he thought about how ridiculous he had been – as if there would be someone, let alone Diana, dragging a body past the trail cam in the reserve. He must have imagined the whole thing. He knew that when he looked at the pictures again (if he even bothered to look) it would be:

    a. Not Diana and / or

    b. Someone doing something with a reasonable explanation
       of sorts such as dumping garden waste.

If only he hadn't wasted the evening with Lottie, particularly when she was the one who had asked *him* out. What a dolt he was. And now she'd given him the brush off. She must have thought he was a real plonker, fussing about his laptop and having nothing to say. Maybe he could explain how he'd had this crazy idea that his sister had been dumping a body and they'd laugh about how ridiculous he had been.

He faffed about for a while reading what people had spotted in the last few days on gobirding.co.uk.

He ordered himself some new underwear for the first time in ages, knowing even as he clicked "buy now" that this was displacement activity. Then he opened the file with the photos and started to click through.

There was the figure. In the days that had elapsed it

hadn't transformed to look less like Diana and the bundle to look less like a body wrapped in striped cloth. He enlarged the section with the hair and slice of face as much as he could. It just made it look even more like Diana; the same with the image of the person returning. When he enlarged a section with the bundle, he realised that it looked like towels. Diana had striped towels – loads of them at her salon. He returned the picture to its normal size and carried the laptop downstairs.

She was in the front room filing her toenails. She had the tools of her trade on the coffee table and the room smelt disgustingly of acetone. If he had done anything to his feet in that room, she would have thrown something at his head.

'Hey, sis.' She looked up and then back at her toes.

'Can I show you something?'

'If it's some weird fish, I'm not interested.'

'It's not a fish.'

'Let me finish this,' she said. He sat in the armchair, not wanting to be next to her until she was done. She had a wooden paddle thing by her side that she used for dry skin on her heels. Arthur wanted to stay clear of the human dust it generated. He wondered if criminals knew not to file their feet at the scene of a crime – they really would be spraying DNA everywhere. She carried on – she was at the painting nails stage now. He got up and walked over to the window.

'That palm looks as though it's getting smaller, shrinking a bit,' he said.

'Good,' said Diana, without looking up.

'Looks like some of the leaves are dying. Maybe it's just a seasonal thing, but the others all look OK. I wonder if they'll replace it.'

'They'd better not,' said Diana. 'There. Done.' She stretched out her legs and feet to better admire her now navy-blue nails.

'Want a cup of tea?' asked Arthur.

'Please, fennel.' She packed the many bottles and implements into her toolbox. When Arthur came back in, she was reading a magazine.

'I just want to show you something,' he said, putting the mugs down on the table.

'OK.' She didn't look up so he sat beside her on the sofa.

'I was helping Katie from the Wildlife Society with the trail cameras.'

'Katie, yes, whose husband fell down the stairs, though she's better off without him.'

'Hmm, anyway, when I downloaded them – there were these two images.' He clicked to wake up the laptop and there was the one with the fox sniffing where the dragged thing had been.

'It's a fox, Arthur.'

'Not that one. This one,' he said, clicking backwards through the reel.

There was the figure dragging the mummy. Diana gasped.

'How did you get this?'

'The Wildlife Society has trail cameras at Red Cliffs, two of them.'

'Oh my God! I didn't know.'

'So it is you?'

'Who's seen this?'

'What were you doing?'

'Arthur – this is—'

'And this one,' said Arthur, clicking past the fox and onto the one of the figure returning with the bundle of towels. 'What were you doing?'

'Nothing. I mean, who says it's me? You have to delete these.'

'What were you doing?' She tried to snatch the laptop, but he held it firmly with both hands.

'What were you dragging?' He had never seen her so pale.

'Give it to me. Let me look.'

Arthur stood up, still holding his laptop. He closed it

and clamped it to his chest with both arms. 'What were you dumping? What was it?'

'I, I, I can't tell you. You don't need to know.' She stood up too. Arthur put himself in front of the door.

'Is it a body? Did someone die in your salon? It looks like you're dragging a body.'

'Arthur, you have to delete these.'

'Tell me what you were doing.'

'Give it to me.'

'No. It's my laptop!' cried Arthur.

'Arthur, please. Just let me see them again.'

'Only if you tell me what you were doing.' He saw her eye the laptop and raise one leg to kick him. He jumped sideways and she missed.

'Only if you delete them.'

'Sit down,' said Arthur.

'You sit down.'

'You're not the boss of me,' said Arthur, like he had when he was thirteen and it was just the two of them.

'But I am your sister.'

They sat down on the sofa again.

'There,' said Arthur, showing her the pictures again but keeping a firm hold of the laptop with one hand and covering the mouse with his other. 'I thought it was you the moment I saw them.'

'Has anyone else seen them? What about Katie? Did you send them to her?'

'No,' said Arthur. 'Nobody else has seen them.'

'But are they still on your spy camera?'

'Trail cam. And no.'

'You have to delete them, please, Arthur. This could be really bad for us both. Oh, God. I'm going to be sick.' She ran from the room. Awful sounds came from the downstairs loo. After a while he heard her go upstairs and shut the bathroom door. He sat back down in the armchair and put the laptop on the coffee table. The more he looked at the pictures, the clearer it was that it was Diana, and her reaction left him in no doubt. She hadn't even tried to deny it. Perhaps, if he hadn't caught her off guard, she would have. She had to tell him what she'd done. His mind raced with possibilities. Perhaps it was a hit and run victim that she was hiding – but surely an accident would have been reported and there would be witnesses and CCTV. Maybe she was just dumping rubbish – but then why the anger and vomiting? Perhaps one of her ladies had died in the salon – but then why hadn't she just called an ambulance? Her salon was everything to her. Perhaps something had happened, and she didn't want any bad publicity. But then surely that person would have been reported missing and traced. There would be searches for any woman who went missing. There would be stuff on the news and posters up everywhere. He looked back at the first picture. Whatever she was dragging, it was as long as her.

He heard Diana coming back down the stairs. Her face looked scrubbed and she had changed her top. He picked up the laptop again, closed it and held it tight.

'Arthur,' she said, 'you have to delete those pictures.'

'Tell me who or what it was.'

'I can't,' she said. They stared at one another. 'Please, Arthur, you have to do it, for me.'

'What have you done? Just tell me. Was it a person who died in your salon? Why didn't you just call an ambulance?'

'I can't tell you.'

'Why, would you have to kill me?'

'Don't be stupid.'

'I'm not the one being stupid here. You're the one dragging something that looks like a body through the woods at night. Who was it?'

'I can't tell you.'

'Why not?'

'Like *The Sopranos*,' said Diana. 'Plausible deniability. I just want to protect you.'

'Protect me? I'm finding out that my sister's a serial killer and she wants to protect me?'

'I'm not a serial killer. But you have to trust me. Just be a good brother and delete them.'

'I can't believe we are having this conversation.'

'Nor can I,' said Diana. 'So, you just have to do what I ask you and then we'll never talk about it again.'

'Who was she? Someone must be missing her.'

'It wasn't a woman,' said Diana.

'What?'

'He was a complete shit. A landlord. He was there for a treatment and asked me for "a happy ending",' she said, almost spitting the words. 'And when Kayleigh was behind with her rent, he wanted sex instead. Well, he didn't get either.'

'God! Was it Mr Sumal? Kiran's dad?' He should have thought of that – looked for what happened around the date of the trail cam images on the local paper website.

'Nobody knows,' said Diana.

'So did Kayleigh kill him?'

'No. It wasn't Kayleigh. She doesn't know. But I'm not going to tell you anything else,' said Diana. 'And you have to promise not to tell anyone. Please, Arthur.'

'God,' said Arthur, burying his head in his hands. She crouched down beside him. She almost never said "please" to him, never asked him nicely for anything.

'Look, it's done now. Nobody knows what happened. Nobody has to know.'

'Did he hurt you? He didn't…'

'No.'

'I can't believe this – how could you kill someone and hide a body? Are you insane? If it was self-defence, you should just tell them.'

'It's too late for that now.'

'What did you do with him?'

'Tipped him over the cliff. But he washed up. Please, Arthur, delete them.'

'I don't know – it's not right. Nothing's right. He had kids.'

'Let me do it then.' She took the laptop off his knees and opened it up. He watched as she deleted both photos. 'What were they on, I mean originally?'

'An SD card, it's back in the camera, but I emptied it before I put it back. I did that before I even looked at them.'

'And they aren't anywhere else?'

'No,' said Arthur. 'They're gone now. Just empty the recycling bin, and they're gone.'

She did that.

'Thank you, Arthur. Now promise me you won't go to the police.' Arthur closed his eyes and exhaled.

'I won't go to the police.'

'Thank you. I know I can trust you. Just try to forget about all of this.' She got up and left the room.

The pictures would still be there in his downloads. She hadn't thought of that. He wished that they weren't, but they would be. He went upstairs too and emailed the file from there to himself and put the laptop in a bag under his bed.

How could he forget this? How could he rearrange everything he had ever known? His sister was a killer and he was helping her cover it up. It was like being underwater. Like being in a tank with no other creatures. There were weird sounds in his ears. He could hear his blood pumping with the rhythm of a filter, but it was more than that, his whole life, everything he knew was swishing around him.

Salt Water

Arthur went in slightly early the next morning – he had to avoid Diana. He knew he couldn't avoid her for the rest of his life, but for now it seemed the best thing to do. He took his laptop in his rucksack.

He had to walk past Flakies. It would normally have been closed at this time, but the door was open and there were lots of cars and minibuses parked outside and people milling about. They must be having Mr Sumal's funeral. Oh God, he thought, this was all Diana's fault. It seemed extra cruel that the Sumals must have had to wait weeks to get his body back, and that they would have kept picturing him lying in some giant fridge. Kiran's little sister was standing outside the café door with her big brother. Arthur put his head down and hurried on.

At work he started the morning routine of checking for fish who'd died. Being early gave him extra time for Jane so he lingered above her tank. She came straight to him and seemed to know he was upset. She gently coiled an arm around one of his and gazed up at him.

'What should I do, Jane?' he whispered. 'What should I do?' Salt water was coming out of his eyes. A tear plopped into her tank. She didn't seem to mind and instead raised another arm and seemed to stroke his other hand where it was holding the edge of the glass.

'I'm sorry, Jane,' he said. 'I didn't mean to change the salinity or make you sad.' Without extricating himself from her, he managed to wipe his damp cheeks on his shoulders. If anyone saw him, they would probably just think that Jane'd splashed him. 'My sister is a killer,' he whispered. In the octopus world that wouldn't be a problem. Maybe Jane would approve of Diana killing Mr Sumal. A male octopus was likely to get eaten if his attempts at mating weren't welcome. 'Our rules are different, Jane. We don't get to kill or eat people we don't like.'

He had hardly allowed himself to think about Kiran and her family since Diana had told him. Surely, they deserved to know the truth. But if the truth was that your dad or husband was a complete shit, was it better to find that out if he was already dead? He could tell the police, but how many more lives would that ruin? 'And she is my sister,' Arthur whispered. 'How can I do that to her?'

He felt another gentle arm on his shoulder and turned his head. Lottie.

'Arthur, what's wrong?'

'Nothing,' he said. 'Jane splashed me, that's all.'

'Really? You look like... you look really sad.' Jane slid away from them and down to the bottom of the tank. She picked up a mother-of-pearl clam shell and brought it up and gave it to Lottie.

'She really loves you,' Arthur said. He wiped his face on his sleeve.

'Thank you, Jane,' said Lottie quietly. 'She'll never love anyone as much as she loves you. Am I allowed to keep this?' she asked, looking at the shell. Jane stayed at the surface and put a tentacle back onto Arthur's hand and another onto one of Lottie's so that the three of them were in a ring.

'She gave it to you – it's yours.'

'Has something bad happened? Do you think Jane's ill?'

'Jane's fine,' said Arthur. 'I'm fine.'

'You don't look fine.'

'I am. It's nothing.' Jane's tentacles climbed further and further up their arms.

'You can talk to me,' she said.

Helen appeared on the other side of the tank.

'Hey, you two, you three. Stop the love-in and do some work!'

They gently unfurled Jane from their arms and she danced back down towards her cave.

'You seen the rota?' asked Lottie. 'I've got to help in the giftshop this morning – someone called in sick. Then meet and greet in the puffin suit this afternoon – again.'

'Ah, bad luck,' said Arthur.

'If only it would rain, or just cool down. See you at lunchtime?'

'Sure,' said Arthur. 'Thanks.'

Lottie hated the giftshop. Although the centre liked to boast of its green credentials and its conservation work, it was part of an empire of attractions and entertainment facilities across the UK, so the bottom line was getting people through the doors and selling them as much stuff as possible. Nowhere was this more evident than the giftshop. All around the centre, visitors saw signs exhorting them to use less plastic and to recycle it or dispose of it properly, but when they got to the giftshop, almost everything on sale was plastic, even things like pencil cases and mugs which had no reason to be. The notebooks they sold had thick plastic covers with holograms of different sea creatures embedded in them. There were shelves and shelves of snowstorms with different creatures in them – as if it snowed under the sea – and these were all plastic. There were racks of doorplates with kids' names on – all plastic. Even the teddies and cuddly toys were made of artificial fibres which would shed filaments of plastic whenever they were washed. She tried not to think about any of this as she worked. Then hers and Arthur's lunchbreaks were at different times, so she didn't see him then.

Puffin Lottie spent the afternoon on the promenade outside

the centre, greeting visitors and giving out leaflets with a 10% discount code. There were a few drops of rain which studded the acrylic fur of the puffin suit like diamonds, but then the sun and the heat returned. The puffin's fluffy tummy was an irresistible punch bag to the more violent toddlers; fortunately, it was also well padded.

Arthur now seemed so different from when she had first met him. Then she'd thought he was all calm seas. She had got him wrong. She'd been annoyed after their so-called night out and decided that he must be one of those awful people who think that if you're going out to dinner, the eating is the main thing. God, she hated those people. And the way he'd fussed over his laptop. She hated fusspots. But now it seemed that there really was something wrong, something serious.

Once she'd managed to offload all the leaflets, she hopped back inside; moving like a puffin was the main pleasure of wearing the outfit. There was only fifteen minutes until closing, so soon she could help with the locking-up routines, but she had a few spare minutes and could spend them watching the seals. She took off the puffin outfit in the staff room. Someone had stuck some chewing gum on its tail without her realising. Luckily, the acrylic fur was so dense that she could just snip it off without it showing. She felt blissfully cool out of the costume but couldn't help wondering if she smelt a bit after so long in the sweaty suit.

She envied the seals in their pool and stood and watched as they glided through the water. She would have loved to be able to swim with them and like them, though they definitely had fish breath. Bowie could have put seals instead of dolphins in "Heroes". She felt sorry for the seals here. They were all rescue ones and wouldn't have survived in the wild, but they had nothing to chase and no kelp forests to hide in. They had some toys, but UK law prohibited feeding live creatures to other animals, so they never got to chase their dinner. A fish that one had chased and caught must taste so much better than one lobbed to you from a bucket.

Gloria, the oldest of the seals, had only one eye. Management had decided, when she'd been brought in years ago, that she would never be able to live in the wild again. She had a big old scar across her face too – she had probably been hit by a jet ski or similar. Children asked if she'd been attacked by a shark. Lottie always replied that it was a possibility, but added that a jet ski or boat was more likely. All the seals were female. The centre had no interest in establishing a breeding colony. Male rescues went to other places.

'Do you mind that?' Lottie asked as Gloria swam by. 'Do you even know?' If Lottie were a rescue seal, she would quite happily live in an all-female colony, assuming that she couldn't go back to the sea. Wasn't that rather what Cass and her friends were doing? They hardly socialised with any men, and their husbands were all dying or had left them for younger women, but they all seemed pretty happy. She hoped the seals were happy too in their cloistered life.

She went to help with the closing procedures. Arthur was doing something complicated to one of the filters in the turtle area. She lurked around for him in the staff room, but then decided he might be trying to avoid her, so she left the centre and went to sit on the wall by the sea outside, hoping he might come and join her if he wanted. She sat, swinging her legs, and watching the families on the beach. Scores of old people in deckchairs were fast asleep and looked as though they would only wake when the tide started lapping at their feet.

'Lottie!' She turned.

'Hi, Arthur,' she said. 'You OK?'

'Um, yeah, sure. You?' She noticed he had his rucksack with him and that it now had a saltwater line around its bottom.

'Feel like getting an ice cream on the way home? We could go to Flakies,' she said.

'Flakies? Um, I can't go there.'

'Why?'

'Um, I just can't,' he said.

'We could go somewhere else then, just get one from the

Kelly's kiosk, but I hope Kiran won't see us. It wouldn't seem very friendly.'

'Um, no. But I guess she wouldn't know.'

'Has something happened with you and Kiran? I didn't realise…'

'Me and Kiran? Um, no. It's not that.'

'What is it then? I don't mean to pry, but, something seems wrong.'

'I'm fine. Really.'

'You don't seem it.'

'Um, it's just some stuff with my sister, that's all.'

'Oh. I'm sorry. I hope she's OK, not ill or anything.'

'Come on, let's go.' They walked in silence for a while.

'You can always talk to me,' said Lottie.

'Thanks,' he said gruffly. They carried on along the promenade, Lottie trying to think of things to say.

'So, how's the laptop doing?' she asked.

'Um, OK. It's fine. It dried out OK. I don't think any water really got in it. I should probably get a new one anyway, get rid of this one.'

'Mmm,' said Lottie. Laptops weren't a very interesting conversation topic.

There were only a few people in front of them at the kiosk. Lottie studied the flavour board, unable to decide between mint choc chip and fruits of the forest.

'This is on me,' said Arthur. 'I wasn't much fun the other night.' He got her ice cream (mint choc chip as usual) asking for an extra flake and a chocolate cone, but just got himself a cup of tea.

'Now I feel like a kid, you being so grown-up, just having tea,' said Lottie. They sat with their backs to one of the big planters. The palm in it looked really ill. Some of its now brown and crackling fronds were hanging down and kept tapping them on their shoulders.

'Sorry,' said Arthur. 'I just didn't feel like ice cream.'

'Things must be bad if you don't feel like ice cream,'

said Lottie. 'Oh look, there's your sister.' Diana was walking towards them. She was wearing what Lottie took to be her beautician's outfit – a white linen dress with a nurse vibe and low-heeled black shoes. Lottie waved. Diana nodded and raised one hand in greeting. She didn't look very friendly and certainly not how she had been when they'd first met and she had practically forced her to go in for tea.

'Hi Diana, how are you?' Lottie asked when Diana was close.

'Well, thank you. And you?' Diana and Arthur just nodded at each other. Lottie scanned Diana's face to see if she looked ill. She did look thin, although she'd had a lean and hungry look when they'd first met. It was hard to tell. She was pale too, although Lottie expected she'd be into high-factor SPF and would have a special one for her face.

'How brown you've grown over the summer, Lottie,' said Diana. Perhaps she could read minds. 'I suppose you're working outdoors a lot, when you aren't in those dank caves with the fish. But then you are very dark complected. It doesn't give you full sun protection, though, did you know that?'

'Of course she knows that,' Arthur snapped back. Diana ignored him.

'Well, see you soon I suppose,' Diana said to Lottie.

'Maybe,' said Lottie. 'I'm only here for a few more weeks.'

'That's a shame,' said Diana, with a tight little smile that might have been genuine or sarcastic.

'Is your sister really OK?' Lottie asked, once Diana was out of earshot.

'She's always like that, more or less,' said Arthur. 'I think she's just being extreme Diana at the moment.'

'She doesn't seem to like me much,' said Lottie.

'Oh, she doesn't like anyone,' said Arthur.

'It must be hard being a beauty therapist if you don't like people,' said Lottie. 'Hairdressers are meant to be the happiest people. Maybe that doesn't carry for what she does.'

'Always an exception, I guess,' said Arthur.

'Well, they have to do loads of disgusting treatments – waxing and so on. My friend kept getting this thing done where she had a long beeswax candle put in her ear and set alight – it was meant to help with ear infections. Then she realised that she just had to stop getting so much water in her ears when she washed her hair. It sounded quite exciting though, having your head almost on fire, but not quite.'

'Anyway…' said Arthur, and Lottie realised that he must be meaning to say goodbye.

'Oh, OK, bye then. See you tomorrow.' She got up and left before he could say anything else. She could feel his eyes on her back as she walked away but she didn't turn around and wave.

Diana was in the shower when Arthur got in. He made himself a pile of peanut butter and tomato sandwiches and two huge mugs of tea – enough so he wouldn't need anything else all evening. He started browsing Netflix on his laptop. If this was how the rest of his life was going to be lived, lurking in his bedroom eating sandwiches, he would have to move out. They could sell the house, split the proceeds, and go their separate ways. Now he understood why she'd suggested moving. Who lived with their big sister anyway? He imagined going to the police, or anonymously sending them the images. But he couldn't do that to his own sister. He blinked the thoughts away and found an episode of *Walking With Dinosaurs* (his go-to show for when he felt down) and settled on the bed to watch it.

Ding! Arthur woke. He'd somehow fallen asleep. The sandwiches were still there beside him. He was desperately thirsty. He knew this feeling – it was more than just hunger and thirst and the discombobulation of waking after a deep sleep in the day – it was how he'd felt in the weeks after his mother had died. Retreating into sleep had been how he'd got through it – that and the way that Diana had taken over and kept everything going for them. He remembered how he hadn't been able to stop sleeping – he'd come in from school and fall asleep. Diana would wake him up for tea, he'd eat it with her, do his homework whilst she sat beside him, and then start falling asleep again. He'd fallen asleep in class again and again, even in PE. The teachers, apart from the PE guys, had just let him get on with it and Joe would wake him at the end of each class. His phone dinged again. It was a message from Joe, nudging him awake again:

"Blue Anchor?"

Arthur downed his cold tea in one and messaged back a thumbs up. He ate one of the sandwiches, cleaned his teeth and headed out with the laptop in his rucksack without seeing Diana. He didn't tell Joe about Diana or the photos – just being with him and out of the house was enough for a while.

Crystal Curtain Reports a Crime

'Hello. I want to report a crime and I've got pictures of it happening.'

'OK,' said Linda, the 111 call-handler, 'is the crime happening now?'

'No, it was this morning.'

'And are you in any danger? Is anybody hurt?'

'Well. Not exactly, but it's important.'

'And can I take your name and address?'

'Yes, it's Crystal Curtain, 378 Seaside Road, Ottersea.'

'And is this the best phone number to get you on?'

'Yes.'

'And where did the incident take place?'

'It's a crime, not just an incident. On Ottersea Promenade in Ottersea, that's in Devon.'

'And can you tell me what happened?'

'Yeah, so it's been in the local paper already, someone's been vandalising one of the planters, killing the plants. It's the one behind my mum's memorial bench, and it's been really bad. The council said they'd replace the plants, but all they've done is just pull up the dead ones, but not the big palm tree that looks like it's dying too.'

'OK.'

'So, I've been sort of staking it out. My dad had a stroke

268

and he's disabled and he loved going to visit Mum's bench, but now it's just sad.'

'Mmm hmm.'

'So, I walk my dog, he's a rescue, every morning on the beach.'

Linda the call-handler was more of a cat person. She had a cushion embroidered with "Cat Hair Don't Care". Dog hair would have been another matter. She had noticed how often dog owners were compelled to tell people that their dog was a rescue, as though they'd been the ones to go into a burning building to get the pooch or had descended into an ice crevasse to fish it out.

'And what happened?'

'Well, we were just getting near the bench. My phone went off, so I stopped to have a look. It was my cousin asking if I'd have *her* dog for the day. So anyway, I stopped, and I was half-looking at my phone, when I saw this woman, smartly dressed, sitting on my mum's bench, and she really deliberately stood up and poured what was in her cup onto the palm tree – you know how they have all those scales on the trunks? She stood up, and acted like she was yawning but still holding her cup, and really deliberately poured it into the tree. And I got pictures. The first one is a bit blurry, but then I got some of her, and you can zoom right in on the face.'

'You'd like to report this as a crime?'

'Yes, with my pictures. And I'm going to send them to the council, and maybe they have CCTV of her doing it.'

'There's a strong possibility of that if it's on a busy road,' said Linda.

'So, anyway, I took pictures of this woman and then I went right up to her, but of course she denied it. So I said, "If that's nothing in your cup, let me see you have a sip of it."

'But she just said she'd already drunk it, but I saw her pour a whole cupful of whatever it was into the plant. And she had this *other* travel cup in her bag, and she took that out and showed me it was coffee. She was really rude. And she walked off, and I had to go anyway, as I always go round to do my dad's breakfast and then my sister was going to come and drop her dog off. He's a rescue.'

'Well, perhaps it was all innocent,' said Linda, 'and this woman has nothing to do with the plants dying.'

'It's definitely a crime and I've got evidence, so you ought to be sitting up and investigating.'

'We'll do our best,' said Linda. 'I can pass your information on. Do you know who this person is?'

'No. But I can send you the pictures.'

'OK,' said Linda and gave the woman the email address. 'And I'll give you an incident number.' She didn't bother to add that the likelihood of her uniformed colleagues doing anything about this possible plant killer was close to zero.

Family First

'So,' Jim said, surveying the room. 'This is where we are...' He summed up the progress, or lack of it. 'One thing that I think we need to look more at, is the PM report. So, we still don't know how the bone breakages happened and where they are in the sequence of events. These, including the neck, could have been because he was pushed or jumped – but perhaps the fractures happened before, or at least some of them.'

'Family first,' said Andy Barns. 'That's what you always say, Boss.'

'Well, the son would be the most likely – but he was nowhere near Ottersea in the two weeks before his father disappeared.'

'Contract killing? Maybe the son paid someone,' Andy suggested.

'We've got nothing there. Other ideas, anyone?'

There were none.

'Do we know how the inheritance goes?'

'Everything goes to the mother,' said Grace. 'She told me she'd nothing to worry about financially. So, if it *was* Bal, her son, he wasn't in it for the money, or at least he'd have to get to it through her.'

'Maybe it's her then. Maybe we just haven't looked closely enough at her because we think she's this polite woman who wouldn't do something like that. What do you think, Grace?' said Jim.

'Well,' said Grace, 'they don't seem to have been that close – but that isn't a reason to kill your husband, is it? We shouldn't stereotype her – just cos she seems like a traditional Asian woman, doesn't mean she's meek. I've seen her at work – she's tough, works really hard, hefting about huge tubs of ingredients, going up and downstairs with them. One of their bedrooms has weights in it. I asked whose they were, and she said everyone's. She's pretty fit. I got them to show me some family photos, and quite a few of them are of picnics on the cliffs – it's clearly a place they know.'

'You got a sense of whether she knows what her husband got up to?'

'She hasn't mentioned anything.'

'We've got the story from the tenant about the sex for rent threat. Seems unlikely that was a one-off, but all the houses in Reading are student ones where I think he'd be unlikely to do that – strengths in numbers. Plus, the son runs those. Maybe another trawl of the CCTV, not just for her, but for whatever she drives.'

'They have a van as well,' said Grace.

'OK. I hoped the uniforms had done that already. I'll check.'

Like Something in a Fairy Tale

At The Blue Lobster, Tom and Ed had begun chopping and prepping for the day. They'd found that they could manage pretty well without their dad – they liked being in charge, though they missed him like crazy, of course. Danuta and Catina certainly didn't miss the bottom slapping. The girls (as they thought of them) had just arrived when Joe came in through the back door with crates from the fish market on his sack truck.

'Good stuff for you today,' Joe said. Tom went over to see the nature morte laid out in the ice of each crate – oysters, mussels, scallops and cockles in one, lobsters with their claws bound by rubber bands in another, and two crates of fish at the bottom.

'Cheers,' he said. 'Nice stuff.' The bottom crate contained pollack.

'Look at this big bugger,' said Joe. 'Biggest one caught all year.' He put the crate onto the big steel table next to the others. Tom ran an appraising finger along the biggest fish's lateral line.

'Must be nearly a metre long,' he said. He looked at the invoice and gave an appreciative whistle, just like his dad would have. 'Just over ten kilos. Cheers, mate.' The fish's dead eye stared up at him. Joe left. Tom gave his hands a rinse and got his phone out. This fish was insta-worthy. He put it on a marble slab for the perfect shot along with some halved lemons and samphire. "Get a load of this beauty – over ten kilos and caught this morning." #beautifulfish #Devon #linecaughtpollack #TheBlueLobster

Soon his mum arrived to do front of house stuff. She'd seemed quite ambivalent about The Blue Lobster since his dad had died, talked about selling it sometimes, but with the season going well and him and Ed managing on their own, they'd just kept going. She did front of house stuff and especially liked chalking things up on the boards as she had such pretty writing and liked drawing borders of seaweed.

'Hey, Mum, look at this huge pollack. Joe said it's the biggest landed all year. It's up on insta already.'

'Yes, I saw,' said Caroline. She looked down at the fish somewhat regretfully. 'I wonder how old it would be. It's very fat, I mean for a fish.' She stepped back as Tom raised his knife ready to gut it. 'I don't want those guts on this shirt,' she said. 'It's new.'

Tom glanced at what she was wearing – a white linen shirt like 100s of others she owned, jeans and a pair of silver flipflops – the fat expensive sort that middle-aged women wore.

He sliced along the fish's belly and the guts tumbled out. There was a strangely angular lump in them. He poked it with the knife. It was curiously hard. He carried the plastic tub of guts over to the sink and sliced through the intestines either side of the lump. Something big slid out.

'Bloody hell – look at this – this pollack ate a watch!' Ed and his mum appeared beside him.

'Ugh,' said his mum, 'that stinks.'

'Hope it's some yachtie's Rolex,' said Ed. Tom hooked the watch, which was still done up, over the knife blade.

'We need to get this online,' said Ed. 'Let's get pictures of everything.' He turned the tap off. 'Before and after pics. Maybe we can reunite it with its owner.'

'People won't want to see that gore all over it,' said Caroline. 'Just get it clean. Ugh.' They ignored her and took some pictures of the watch covered in muck. Danuta and Catina came in.

'Look at this, girls,' said Tom. 'I found a watch inside a fish.' He ran it under the tap. 'Some guy must be missing this.' The strap was ruched black leather. Fragments of gunk were stuck to it.

'It's going to take some cleaning,' said Caroline.

'Oh, it's a Fitbit,' said Tom.

'Pity it's not a gold Rolex,' said Danuta.

'Or a gold ring – like in a story,' said Catina.

'Oh, yes,' said Caroline. 'But it is like something in a fairy tale – *The Fish and The Ring*.'

'Yeah, or like the Greek myth, Polycrates,' said Ed, who had Classical Civilisation A level and had been obsessed by Ancient Greece when he was a boy.

'What's that one about?' asked Catina.

'Fortunes change, but you can't escape your fate. Polycrates was a tyrant – threw away his emerald ring so he wouldn't be thought of as too lucky and successful, but it came back to him in a fish, as they do. Ended up murdered, obvs.'

'Uhhgg,' said Caroline, 'that smell.' She put her hand over her nose and mouth.

'Might be your fate to throw up, Mum,' said Ed.

'Hope that's all,' said Caroline. She backed away and went through the door to the restaurant.

'I guess it's totally dead,' said Tom, poking the Fitbit. 'But we could try charging it up.' He'd got the worst stuff off it now. The screen was completely dark. He put it down next to the fish amongst the lemons and samphire and took some more pictures. 'This is so cool. Let's give it a chance to dry out. I'll put it on the socials.'

'We should ring the local paper too,' said Ed. 'Maybe Mum'll do that. Don't chop the pollack up yet – we might need more pictures of it.'

'OK, bro,' said Tom. He put it in one of the fridges and turned his attention to some of its smaller relatives.

Local Chef's Fishy Tale

OTTERSEA ECHO

Chefs Tom and Ed Todd were surprised this morning when they cut open a giant fish to find it had swallowed a Fitbit. The locally-caught pollack weighed in at a massive 10.2 kilos and was delivered fresh this morning, but it turned out some of that weight was down to the fish's unusual diet. The brothers, who've been running The Blue Lobster since the tragic death of their father earlier this summer, are hoping to reunite the Fitbit with its owner.

'It was weird,' said Tom (26). 'Joe from the fish market brought the pollack in this morning. It looked pretty special being so big, but when I gutted it, I saw there was this strange lump which turned out to be a Fitbit. Someone must have lost it when they were swimming or sailing.'

'We googled it,' said Ed (24), 'and it turns

out they're waterproof to fifty metres, so it might still work. We're giving it a chance to dry out before we charge it up. It's like something in a myth or a fairy tale. It will be really cool if we can trace its owner. Although they might find out the pollack was fitter than them,' he joked. 'We've put it on the restaurant's social media so hopefully someone will see that or read about it thanks to you guys.'

Comments

DevonBoy66: Something fishy going on here!

BigMike: Know your plaice DevonBoy66

DevonBoy66: Good cod! They've gotta be joking

BigMike: Haddock up to here with you

OldBeachBabe: Weren't the police looking for a Fitbit from that poor bloke who was washed up? Has anyone told them? @OtterseaEcho do your job!

'Local paper on the line, Sarge,' said PC Potterton. 'Chef at The Blue Lobster found a Fitbit inside a big fish. The paper ran the story before they made the connection. Says it's completely dead, but it has a black leather strap like the one in the appeal.'

'I'll go down there myself now and take it straight up to Exeter,' said Jim.

'Maybe it's the breakthrough we need, Sarge.'

'Can but hope.'

Jim drove to Exeter listening to Springsteen's "Nebraska". God, he loved "Highway Patrolman". He arrived at HQ just after 4pm. It was a Friday. He'd rung to say he was coming to ensure that Liam, the most useful of the tech team, didn't bugger off early. Liam was at his desk, which was covered with dirty take-out cups. His bin was overflowing with packaging and bags from the local bakers.

'Been having a party?' asked Jim.

'Ha. Just Friday cake run,' said Liam. Jim took the Fitbit, now in an evidence bag, from his pocket.

'What do you think you can do with this? It's been inside a fish.'

'God,' said Liam. 'Maybe nothing – we'll see.' He took the device and turned it over. 'Looks like one of the newest ones. They only hold their data for so long – rely on being near the user's phone and sending it to the app there. What are you hoping for?'

'First of all, whose it is. We know our guy had one like this. We have the receipt and original box for it, here.' He passed Liam another bag with it in.

'Good. You can only find the serial number in the settings – it's not on the exterior of the device. If I can get it going, we'll easily see if it's his. You got his phone?'

'No. That's still lost. Maybe at sea.'

'Hoping for another fish?'

'Something like that. Been wondering if we could call in those military dolphins like the Russians have to look for it,' said Jim.

'Ha ha.'

'I know there won't be physical forensics after being eaten by a bloody great pollack. So, what might you be able to get off this?'

'When it was last used. The last days of readings if we're lucky – steps, heart rate, GPS, flights of stairs.'

'Could be extremely useful.'

'Would you know his password?'

'The family said he used the same for everything. Here, I'll write it down for you.' Liam passed him a pad of Post-it notes. And Jim wrote down the one the family had given him: *FlakieKing123!*. Liam nodded at it.

'Did he have kids, pets, in case it's not that?'

'Three kids, these are their names,' said Jim, adding them to the list. 'But I'd be surprised if he used those. Does a Fitbit show if someone was swimming?'

'Yup,' said Liam. 'You're not a Fitbit type are you, Jim?'

'Ha – no. So that could tell us if he was alive when he went into the water, if he was wearing it, and swimming in a regular kind of way.'

'Probably.'

'How long might this take?'

'Depends on its condition – we might not be able to get anything. But pretty quick if it's not damaged and we can get into it easily enough. I've never had to go to Fitbit for passwords before – that would delay things.'

'Can you start now?'

Liam sighed and glanced at his own watch which Jim saw was a so-called smart one. He clearly didn't use it for fitness. Ah well, thought Jim, the road to hell and all that.

'I'll give it a go.'

'Cheers, mate. Appreciate it. We could use a break with this one.'

Jim left and drove back listening to Gram Parsons. He sang along to "Streets of Baltimore", his favourite song. Meanwhile Liam opened the Fitbit up. There was a little dampness. He got to work drying it. It looked as though it might be OK.

Minutes of Ottersea WI Committee Meeting

17/08/2022 7.30pm at Teapot Paradise.

Present: Diana Parks (Chair), Katie Grayling (Secretary), Caroline Todd (Treasurer), Cass Green (Membership Secretary), Rachel Brown, Asha Sharma, Jenny DeSoto, Gill Baker.

Apologies: Ulli Jansen,

Matters Arising from July Meeting
1. Diana, Katie, Caroline and Cass visited the new Exeter Rage Room. A fun time had by all. Concerns about environmental impact of rage rooms discussed. Agreed we will offer to take home broken crockery for gardening or possible mosaicking. Agreed to book an autumn trip for all interested members. Katie to enquire about possible Tuesday or Wednesday evenings in October.
2. Katie has written to Sarah Shelley to thank her for the beach foraging evening walk.

Chair's Report
On behalf of us all, condolences offered to Caroline and Katie for the recent losses of their husbands. Diana reported

that she visited Mrs Sumal, who was also recently widowed, to extend the WI's sympathies. She left a leaflet and invited Mrs Sumal to join us for swimming, regular meetings or other activities.

Diana thanked the committee for coming. An August meeting only necessary to confirm Extravaganza plans.

Autumn programme close to finalised (see attached draft). Katie has written to speakers to confirm dates. Only bonsai expert yet to confirm. Ulli suggested an evening on using slow cookers, air-fryers, cooking on a budget if we have a gap.

1. Christmas Do
Agreed to usual pot-luck supper rather than restaurant. Must bear in mind cost of living concerns.

2. Treasurer's Report
See attached. Caroline reported that over the last year we have raised £723.47 for Women's Aid. Agreed to continue with collection of toiletries at each meeting as well as non-perishables for Basics Bank.

3. Ottersea Extravaganza
Katie confirmed that the stall is booked. We have two long tables. Copies of the autumn programme to be ready by then, with tbc if the bonsai expert is still elusive. All members to be emailed about cakes and produce. Caroline to organise Pimm's lollies – adults only. She will also make clear signs about alcohol content and oversee sales. Discussed having a child's alternative but decided against due to danger of confusion / alcoholic poisoning of children. Cass to coordinate scones, cream and jam. Asha and Jenny strawberries from PYO. Diana is making courgette and parsnip chutney. Rachel, green tomato and runner bean. Diana suggested mini ploughman's or cheese and biscuits so we have an alternative, and offered to bring the makings. Katie offered homemade cheese biscuits to accompany. Agreed on cheese scones (Cass to supply) with

Diana and Rachel bringing cheese and homemade chutney. We have ample catering bamboo plates, forks, bowls, etc. from last year. Cass to bring Teapot Paradise napkins.

4. AOB
There was no other business.

5. Date of Next Meeting
14/9/2022 7.30pm at Teapot Paradise.

Cuppa With a Copper

It was the third Thursday of the month and Ottersea Community Hub (the place formerly known as Ottersea Library) was busy with toddlers and their associated adults making garden wind spinners as part of Storytime. There had been a horrible accident on the M5 north of Exeter, and with so many people on leave, Grace was covering the police drop-in. It was up on the constabulary website and had been tweeted about, plus the poster behind the library desk invited people to "Have a Cuppa With a Copper and Meet Your Neighbourhood Police Officers". Grace wasn't expecting to have to do much. When she arrived she was tempted to ask if she could join in with making a wind spinner, though she really ought to catch up with online paperwork, but there were already six people waiting in the so-called comfy chairs. So much for getting through the paperwork.

The first person Grace talked to was a guy who wanted to complain about how much water he thought his neighbours were using to fill their paddling pool. As they chatted, she realised it was more that he found the neighbours' children annoyingly loud. He was, he said, hoping for a hosepipe ban.

'Well,' said Grace, pushing the box of biscuits that she'd brought with her towards him. 'How old are the children?'

'I don't know. About eight and ten. They look too big to want to play in a paddling pool. And they don't really play in it – just use it to fill up these giant water pistols they have and then run around screaming.'

'I can imagine how noisy that must be. Have you tried having a gentle word with them? This hot weather probably won't last, and then they'll stop.' The man harrumphed and put a couple of biscuits in his pocket for later. Grace wasn't sure what else to suggest.

Next was a woman who said that her neighbour had been fraudulently using a disabled parking bay outside her house, one that had been put there for her late husband. The woman said that she didn't have a car herself now, but that it was disrespectful and the principle of the thing.

Another lonely person, thought Grace. She got the council's parking website up on her laptop and saw that the street was in a residents' parking zone. Really, it was a parking enforcement problem, not a police one.

'Have you told your neighbour that it makes you sad for her to park in your late husband's space?' she asked.

'Yes,' the woman said. 'She just said something that I won't repeat and that as they have three cars, they have to.'

'I'm so sorry to hear that,' said Grace. 'Now let's report this on the council website and see if they can have a word with your neighbour.'

'My son already did that,' said the woman. 'He lives in Gloucester, but he does all the online stuff for me.'

'Well. that's good,' said Grace.

'No, it's not,' said the woman. 'They just said that as my husband's passed on, they'll be round to paint over the lines, so he won't even have a space anymore.'

'Oh,' said Grace. 'And did they say when they'll be doing this?'

'Yes,' said the woman, 'tomorrow. I just wanted to make a complaint before it's too late.'

'I understand,' said Grace, although she barely did. 'Perhaps you and your son could do something special to remember him by, a nice plaque somewhere, or sponsoring something, There are lots of nice things like that you can do in Ottersea, benches, trees. When my granny died, we sponsored one of the donkeys at Sidmouth Donkey Sanctuary for her. She loved going there.'

'Thanks love,' said the woman. She patted Grace's hand and got up to go. 'You must miss your granny, but at least you have a nice donkey to remember her by.'

'I couldn't help overhearing,' said the next woman, sitting down in the vacated seat, 'but memorial benches can lead to trouble too. I'm Crystal, Crystal Curtain.'

'DC Grace Brown,' said Grace, 'but call me Grace.'

'I've got an incident number already,' said this Crystal, pulling a notebook decorated with golden retrievers out of her bag. 'I got that from 111, but nothing seems to be happening, so I've done my own detective work.' She put her phone down on the desk too and opened the photos app. 'So, this is on the seafront – it's my mum's bench.' She showed Grace a picture of a bench with a polished brass plaque. 'And it has one of the big planters behind it. The council keep it quite nice, but I put marigolds and some of my mum's favourites like nasturtiums in there too, just to brighten it up. I take my dad, he had a stroke, there a lot – we just like to sit there and chat and think of Mum.'

'That's nice,' said Grace.

'So, I walk past it every day with my rescue dog,' said Crystal Curtain, 'and I noticed that the palm tree looked like it was dying, but none of the others were – they all looked fine. And then I saw that some of the plants at the bottom were all withered up, as if someone had been putting weedkiller on them.' She swiped through some photos. Grace made appropriate noises of concern at them. 'Then one morning, I saw this woman throw the contents of her travel cup really deliberately into the tree, and it splashed onto the dead plants. So, I asked, all polite, what she was doing, and she was really rude. It was really suspicious, and she had this whole other travel cup in her bag – I mean who takes two travel cups with them?'

'That does seem odd,' said Grace.

'So anyway, I've reported it on 111 but heard nothing. And it was in the paper, but still nothing. Then, cos I do the walk every day, I keep seeing her, nearly every morning, and she often does the same thing with one mug that she never drinks out of, just chucks the contents at the palm tree. I'm pretending not to notice, but I lurk along the prom in one of the shelters – she goes in the other direction, so she never sees me. And I've got these pictures by zooming in.' She swiped through some more pictures – they were interspersed with pictures of dogs, children, and plates of food – but they did show, sometimes blurrily, a woman on different days throwing the contents of a travel cup at a palm tree in one of the promenade planters.

'But why would anyone want to kill a palm tree and damage all the flowers, I mean on a permanent basis? They might get vandalised, but not usually like this,' said Grace.

'Well, I have the answer to that. So, I don't know her name or anything, but one morning, I decided to follow her to see where she goes. I figured she must be going to work as she does the same thing at the same time.'

'You have to be careful doing things like this. There are laws about stalking and harassment.'

'Yeah, but I checked, and if someone's in a public place, you can take photos of them, and there's no law against just walking through your own town.'

'Hmmm.'

'And this is where she works.' She swiped through some more pictures of dogs and dinners to a picture of the woman, taken from some distance, unlocking the door of a shop in one of Ottersea's lanes. The next picture was of the shopfront, only it wasn't a shop, but a beauty salon: Marine Heaven Health and Beauty.

'OK,' said Grace, wondering if this Crystal had another reason to be trailing the mystery liquid-chucker. There was often another story when people made bizarre complaints about others. Perhaps there was some family feud or the liquid-chucker had slept with this woman's partner. 'Do you have any other connections with this woman?'

'No. Only that she's been poisoning the plants behind my mum's special bench.'

'And you don't know her name?'

'Not for certain, but if you go on the website for her salon and she's the owner, then she's called Diana Parks.'

'Well,' said Grace. 'This does look like criminal damage, so we can definitely look into it.'

'At last! But I've got more. So yesterday, I happened to be walking back from town at the time she closes her place, and I happened to follow her, and she lives here...' She swiped to a photo of one of the big houses that fronted the little park on the promenade. 'I waited for her to go in – I didn't knock or accuse her or anything – not after the first time when I thought she might turn nasty. But I got this picture – and you can see the house number. And I walked past and on for a bit, and then when I went back past her house, I realised why she was doing it. The planter with my mum's bench is right in a line from her house to the sea. I bet she wants to kill it cos it's blocking her view. And there's your motive. And you've already got the method – poison!'

'Well,' said Grace, 'we don't know for sure that she had weedkiller in her cup, but we can definitely look into this. Can you send me those photos? Here's the email address. And I'll need your contact details. But don't worry, she won't know who made the initial complaint. From now on, though, please stay well away from her and the whole business.'

'I'm not staying away from my mum's bench.'

'No,' said Grace, 'of course not. But I would keep away from this woman and be careful. And I hope the council will get the plants replaced soon.'

'Well, I won't hold my breath. But I'll be getting onto the MP about this if nothing happens.'

'You can do that,' said Grace, 'but I'll look into this, and I'll let you know what we find.'

After a woman who had trouble with youths kicking a ball against her wall and two people who really did just want a cuppa with a copper and the free biscuits, Grace was done.

When she got back to the station, Jim was staring at the map of Ottersea they had on the wall with Raj Sumal's significant places marked – his home, Freddy's Racing where he was last seen, where the car was found, the flats he owned, where his body was found.

'Anything new, Sarge?'

He shook his head.

'He goes to the bookies and then just disappears. We don't see him get into any cars.'

'Maybe someone killed him in the toilet of the bookies and then took his body out some back way,' said Grace.

'He didn't go into the loo there,' said Jim. 'We've been through the CCTV from the whole day. He leaves and just disappears. I think we need to go back out and take another look around.'

'Sarge,' said Grace. 'On Cobble Lane you remember we went into that beauty place?'

'Yeah, they didn't have any CCTV or security cameras. We couldn't get anything down that lane – that's our problem.'

'I was just covering Cuppa With A Copper. This woman comes in with a complaint about this lady who she says has been putting weedkiller in one of the planters. She's really upset as her mum's bench – you know with a plaque – is by this planter and the council haven't replaced the dead flowers.'

Jim sighed and raised his eyebrows.

'Well, the woman has been staking out the bench and taking photos of the person she thinks is killing the plants. She showed me all the pictures – it does look weird. The woman keeps pouring some liquid into the palm tree, and now it's dying. So, then she followed the woman to see where she goes, and it turns out she works at that salon – Marine Heaven. Then another day, she follows her home from work, and she lives in a big house opposite the promenade with a view straight down to the sea. The woman reckons she's got it in for the palm tree.'

'So?'

'What I mean is, what kind of person pours weedkiller on municipal flowers? What kind of person would try to kill a palm tree? I think we should go back there, to the salon or round to her house. I told the woman I'd follow up with the possible plant poisoning anyway. Let's go round about that for starters and just do some general snooping.'

Jim laughed and shrugged.

'OK, Grace. We might as well. But I think we need to keep pushing with Mrs Sumal too. She's where we should be focusing our attention.'

Bells and Shells

At 10am the next day, Jim and Grace met at the bottom of Cobble Lane. Grace had dressed smarter than usual, wanting to look like someone who went to beauty salons. Instead of her usual trainers, she had on a pair of sandals. She was wearing a pair of the black trousers she lived in for work, but instead of her usual plain T-shirt, she had put on a white linen shirt and more jewellery than she usually wore. Her toenails were painted lilac.

There was a tinkling from the string of shells and Indian bells hanging on the door as she went inside. A woman came out from a side room, well, more of a girl really. She had a blonde ponytail high up on her head and skin that looked scrubbed clean. Her fingernails, which were as short as Grace's own, were painted a pretty pale green. It would be hard, Grace supposed, to give massages and that kind of thing, if you had long scratchy nails.

'Mrs Alverston?' the girl asked.

'No,' said Grace, 'I just wanted to ask about some treatments.'

'Oh, sorry,' said the girl. 'I thought you must be my ten fifteen come early.' Grace stood up and went to the counter.

'What I was wondering – it's for a present – do you do treatments for guys – it's for my brother?'

'Um, yes, of course,' said the girl.

'Is Ms Parks here?'

'Not this morning. But you can book for either her or me. I'm new, but I'm fully trained. When would you like it for? Let me just get the diary up.'

'So, what would you recommend for a guy?' asked Grace.

'What sort of thing does he like? We can do a mani-pedi for men, not polish, just polishing, unless he likes polish, of course. Then facials, Indian head massage, massages…' She picked up one of the leaflets and pointed to the bit about massages. 'Oh, I forgot it's Ladies Only for those. I must be thinking of the last place I worked.'

'Hmm. It's hard to choose,' said Grace. 'Maybe, I'll just take the list and have a think and come back later.'

'We do gift vouchers too,' said the girl. 'Anything from twenty pounds up.'

'Thanks,' said Grace. 'I think I'll come back.'

She left to the sound of bells and shells and walked back down the lane to where Jim was waiting.

'It was interesting,' she told him. 'But Diana Parks wasn't there. I got a price list. They don't do much stuff for men. There was a different woman working there – said she was new – so I don't know any more about if Raj Sumal and Diana Parks were connected.'

'OK. We'll doorstep Diana Parks about the weedkiller.'

Jim and Grace walked up the path to Diana Parks's house and knocked. A youngish man answered the door. Jim recognised him and the turquoise Oceanworld T-shirt he was wearing – Arthur, the mild-mannered octopus keeper. He had his name badge on too.

'Hello, Arthur,' said Jim. 'I'm DI Jim Paddon and this is DC Grace Brown. I know we've met at the Oceanworld Centre, haven't we?'

'Is everything OK there?' Arthur asked. 'I've got a late start.'

'Everything's fine,' said Jim and Grace nodded. 'But we

would like to talk to Diana Parks.' Arthur blanched and his hand went towards his mouth, in shock, Jim thought. 'Is she in?'

'Er, what's it about?'

'Just a local matter,' said Jim again. 'Could we come in?'

'Um, no,' said Arthur. 'I mean I'm not sure. Do you have a warrant?'

'Not at present,' said Jim, 'but most people prefer to discuss things quietly inside rather than in front of their neighbours. Can you ask your wife to come talk to us?'

'It's my sister,' said Arthur. 'She's my sister.' He stood there blocking the entrance, clearly not wanting to fetch her.

'Is that my delivery, Arthur?' came a voice from somewhere behind him.

'Er, no,' he called back, 'It's some people to see you – some police.'

There was no reply.

'Can we talk to you for a moment please, Ms Parks?' Grace called.

There was no answer, but then a door opened at the end of the passageway and a tall woman with dark hair strode towards them. She stopped just behind her brother and folded her arms.

'Hello, officers,' she said. 'Is there some sort of problem?'

'It would be easier to talk about this indoors,' said Jim. 'Could we come in?'

'Of course,' she said. Arthur stepped out of the way, though she still didn't move. 'This way please. Though I can't imagine what it's about. I hope there isn't a problem at my salon – I'm a beautician – it's my day off – my assistant should have rung me. She rings me for the slightest thing – would rather call me than look in a cupboard to find something… We do sometimes get trouble from an HMO nearby, but there hasn't been anything much lately.' She flashed them a wide smile which made the tendons in her neck stand out. Not a real smile, Jim thought, a bit desperate, but then nobody gave a real smile when the police showed up on their doorstep. 'Would you like a cup of coffee, perhaps?' She was one of those people who could talk nonstop as a diversionary tactic.

'No, but thanks,' said Grace.

'No thanks,' said Jim, 'not right now.' Depending how things went, asking for one might be a useful way of seeing more of the house or of getting the brother, who he'd always thought of as a thoroughly decent but somewhat other-worldly guy, to leave the room.

Jim glanced along the passageway. There were two doors – two reception rooms and then the kitchen where she had emerged from. It was a nice house, old fashioned, with ridiculously high ceilings. So, brother and sister lived together – unusual nowadays – in what he surmised was the home they'd inherited. Diana Parks opened the door to the front room. They all followed her in.

'Do please sit down,' she said, but he walked over to the window. The view was straight down to the sea – and there in the centre of it was the planter with a palm tree that looked sick. Many of its fronds were brown or splotched with brown.

'Nice view you've got here,' said Jim.

'Yes, isn't it?' she said. 'We're very fortunate.' People who say they are "fortunate", thought Jim, don't really think they are. It was an expression used by people who know they have more than others but think they deserve to. He turned back to face the room. Grace was now sitting on the edge of an armchair. Diana Parks was sitting on the sofa in what was clearly her spot – there were women's magazines in a wicker rack beside her. Arthur still stood by the door, looking worried, fists clenched. 'Are you sure you wouldn't like a cup of tea or a glass of something cold? Arthur can easily fetch you one.' Poor guy, living with her, thought Jim. There must be quite an age gap between them – maybe fifteen years – she must have been bossing him about for his whole life.

'No thanks, we're fine,' said Jim.

'So, what can we help you with?' she asked.

'It's just you at the moment, Ms Parks,' said Jim. He took out his tablet. 'We've some photos we'd like you to have a look at…'

'Arthur!' she cried 'You…' she stopped herself. Arthur raised his hands in a "stop" gesture and gave a tiny brisk shake of his head.

'Can you have a look at these please?' Jim held up his tablet. There was the woman who looked very like Diana Parks pouring something onto the palm tree, and again, seemingly chucking liquid from a travel cup at it.

Diana Parks exhaled loudly.

'Well, that could be anyone,' she said.

'We believe it is you. Somebody has been damaging the plants in the planter right opposite your house, the palm tree that is right in your line of view to the sea.'

'What?' said Arthur. 'God!' He went and looked at the picture. Jim swiped from one to the next and back again.

'That does look very like you, Ms Parks. What were you throwing at the tree?'

'You can't possibly say that's me,' she said. 'And whoever it was was probably just emptying the dregs of their coffee. Honestly, what a fuss about nothing.'

'What do you think, Mr Parks? Does that look like your sister?' asked Grace. Jim saw Diana Parks shoot her brother a glance.

'Um, I don't know,' said Arthur. He backed away.

'We have a likely case of criminal damage here,' said Jim.

'This is ridiculous,' she said. 'As if I would damage some municipal planting!'

'These photos were taken on August 3rd and 5th. You can see the times in the corner. Can you tell us what you were doing on those days at those times?'

'I have absolutely no idea without consulting my work diary,' she said. 'Though I can assure you, as can my brother, that I'm not the sort of person who damages plants.'

'Perhaps you would like to consult your work diary, then,'

said Jim. 'There is also another matter that we'd like to talk to you about.'

'I'm happy to help in any way I can,' she said.

'Good,' said Jim. 'Because we're also investigating an unexplained death, that of a Mr Sumal. We came into your salon, if you remember, trying to trace his last movements.'

''Scuse me,' said Arthur. 'I've got to go. Need to check something at work.' He left the room and then they heard the front door shut. Jim and Grace exchanged a glance.

'Ah, yes, the gentleman from the ice cream parlour who was washed up – so sad. And wasn't he last seen in the bookies – really very sad. But as I told you before, we don't have any kind of CCTV inside or outside and he wasn't a client. I would have remembered. I hardly treat any gentlemen.'

'Perhaps you'd like to show us your work diary, your bookings,' said Jim.

'Of course. My laptop's right here.' She indicated a shiny blue bag which was patterned with a design of peacock feathers. Jim had always been suspicious of peacock feathers – his mother had said that you should never have them in the house or on jewellery or hats as they brought bad luck. Diana Parks either didn't know that or didn't care. She took her laptop out of the bag and switched it on. It was impressively clean; the police confiscated so many devices that were filthy from people with grubby mitts. They usually examined laptops where the spaces around the keys were full of crumbs and grease. Sod the contents of the stomach at a PM – you could tell what some people had eaten for the last few years by dusting their laptops. As it came on, he saw that it still had the protective film over the screen.

'Looks nice and new,' said Jim.

'My last one was a complete dinosaur,' said Diana. 'Almost steam-powered.'

'So, when did you get this one?'

'Quite a few months ago. I think it was just after Easter.'

'And do you have all your bookings on here?'

'Yes – let me show you.' She went to the Marine Heaven website and logged in at the top then clicked on "Bookings". 'What was his name? Mr Somar, was it? I can search for that. I really don't think he was a client, though I hope you understand we operate a strict policy of client confidentiality. You can imagine that my ladies wouldn't want anyone to know their secrets, certain treatments they are having. Feminine mystique must be maintained.'

'It's Sumal,' said Grace. 'Raj Sumal. S-U-M-A-L.'

'Of course – I did see it on the local news, but one doesn't always remember that sort of thing.' She typed "Sumal" into a search bar at the top of the diary. 'No, look – nothing.'

'And do people always give you their real name?'

'Why wouldn't they? Almost everyone pays by card – so I'd see their name anyway, and we take contact details for bookings, of course.'

'Try Raj, please,' said Jim. She did. Again, there was nothing.

'It really is mostly ladies,' said Diana.

'And how far do your records go back?'

'Oh, at least five or six years. Before that I used a regular diary, a desk one, A4. I think I still have that at the salon if you'd like me to have a look.'

'Perhaps,' said Jim, not wanting her to think he was giving up. 'And what did you do with the last laptop?'

'That old thing? It didn't even seem worth giving it to one of those repurposing charities. It just went to the dump. But this Mr Somal wasn't a client. I have a very good memory for my clients and would certainly have remembered a gentleman with that name.'

'Sumal,' said Grace. 'His name was Raj Sumal.'

'Mr Sumal was a landlord too,' said Jim. 'We're looking into his business and property connections.'

'Well, landlords aren't the most popular of people,' said Diana. 'I can imagine you'll find plenty of suspects that way. But I own my little salon. There isn't a landlord. I'm sorry I can't be of more help.'

'And what about as a friend, or some other closer relationship?' asked Jim.

'Good Lord, no!' said Diana with a little laugh. 'I don't think our paths ever crossed. We certainly weren't friends or anything more. Anybody who knows me would say that was preposterous.'

'OK,' said Jim. 'But back to the plants. I have officers going through the CCTV at the moment looking for evidence of deliberate criminal damage.'

'I can help you there,' said Diana. 'I've often seen a woman digging around in the planter. She's probably the one you want.'

'Really?' said Jim. 'That's interesting.'

'Yes,' said Diana. 'That will be the person you want. She's probably been damaging the root systems or something. Why would anyone dig around in something they are paying their council tax for?'

'Some people,' said Grace, 'take special care of the planters near to where they have a memorial on a bench.'

'I expect it's somebody who is a terrible gardener,' said Diana. 'There. I think I've solved your case for you.' She stood up. 'Now if there's nothing else, I do have to go out soon – I need to get some things for a project my WI is working on. You should come along,' she said, turning to Grace. 'We'd make you very welcome. Or perhaps you'd like to do a talk for us sometime. We'd love to have you. I'll give you one of our leaflets. And if there's nothing else…'

'Not for now,' said Jim. He and Grace stood up. Diana took a cream-coloured card folded triptych-style from a side pocket of her peacock bag.

'Here,' she said. 'I'm afraid you've missed most of these. We're putting together the autumn programme now.'

Grace took the leaflet and looked at the back.

'So, you're the chairperson?'

'For my sins,' said Diana with a little laugh. 'I've always been a good organiser,' she said.

'Yes,' said Grace. 'You do seem like one. Well, thank you for your time.'

'I'm sorry I couldn't be of more help,' said Diana.

'We'll see ourselves out,' said Jim. But like most people, she followed them to the door anyway and shut it behind them.

'So, Grace, you joining the WI?' he said when they were back in the car.

'Look Sarge,' said Grace. 'Look at this committee. Chair: Diana Parks, Secretary Katie Grayling, Treasurer, Caroline Todd. Those names mean anything to you?'

'Bloody hell,' said Jim. 'Two dead husbands in one summer and a palm tree killer. Ha!'

'Maybe we should look into this more – I mean it is a bit of a coincidence.'

'The WI Killers – ha – no – we have two accidental deaths – sad accidents, that's all.'

'You don't see a pattern here, Sarge?'

'Ha. That would be funny. Ottersea WI criminal masterminds.'

'I'm just saying, Skip.'

'No, Grace. There were no suspicious circumstances there. But this, it did look like her chucking stuff at the plants, but it would be hard to make that stick. Criminal damage is hardly top priority at the moment. And if she was doing something – she'll likely stop now she knows we're on to her.'

'Another thing, though,' said Grace, 'when we went round to Marine Heaven the first time – she was unpacking a new laptop – that was soon after his body was found. Just now she said she got it around Easter. Interesting, huh? She's clearly not dumb.'

'Motive? Means?' asked Jim.

'I dunno. Maybe she waxed him to death,' said Grace.

'Bad way to go,' said Jim. 'I don't think we can quite rule out her and Raj Sumal having an affair. The way she talked

– "Good Lord" and "preposterous" – sounded like acting. Would give him a reason to go down Cobble Lane – and then maybe his wife spotted him, found out. Bumped him off.'

'The way she and Arthur reacted when I mentioned the photos was pronounced,' said Grace. 'But then if there'd been an altercation with the women with the bench... Her brother disappeared smartish.'

'Or maybe Arthur and Kiran Sumal had something going on and Arthur got into a fight with her dad,' said Jim.

'OK. What's next?' asked Grace.

'You go and talk to Kiran Sumal – see if there's any connection between the families. I'll go and see Kayleigh Evans again – maybe she can shed some light on any relationship between Diana Parks and Raj Sumal. And I'll have a chat with Arthur Parks sometime.' It would be a good excuse, if he needed one, to see Jane too.

Grace and Kiran

Grace waited until she knew Flakies would be almost closing. Kiran was there, cashing up behind the counter with Nindy, whilst one of the teenagers they employed part-time mopped the floor and another wiped the tables. They both looked slightly stoned. Grace imagined that they would all try hitting on Kiran. It was an unpleasant thought. It didn't seem much of a life for Kiran, just here with her family; but family must be what kept her here, and now with her dad gone, leaving, if she ever wanted to, would be even harder. Ottersea wasn't the easiest place to be Black or Asian – Grace knew that only too well. Wherever you went, whatever you did, you would be in the minority, always sticking out a bit.

'Turn the sign, Nindy,' Kiran said, and the little sister came out to do that, shut the double doors and put the bolts down.

'Oh, hi Mrs Policelady,' said Nindy. 'We're just closing.'

'Hello Nindy. Don't worry, I just want to talk to your big sister about something.' Kiran shut the till drawer and looked up.

'Hey Grace, what's up? Anything new?'

'Not quite, maybe, we've some new leads and wanted to ask you some things.'

'Good,' said Kiran. 'About time.'

'I know,' said Grace. 'We are doing all we can, exploring every avenue.'

'Want a coffee? Ice cream?'

'I'm fine,' said Grace. 'Have you got time now?' Kiran looked around the café and glanced at her phone for the time.

'You guys can go now,' she said to the teenagers, and they sloped off to get their stuff from the backroom. Once they reappeared, she let them out through the front door and locked it behind them. 'Nindy, you can go and watch TV if you like,' she said.

'But I want to stay with you, or you won't tell me stuff.'

'OK. And I do tell you stuff. Everything I know, you know too. We just don't know enough.' Kiran turned back to Grace.

'How about just one scoop of our cappuccino ice cream? I can tell that's what you'd choose.'

'You're right,' said Grace, smiling, 'but no thanks not until we've solved this.'

Kiran slid into a booth opposite Grace and Nindy slid in beside her. Grace didn't mind her staying – children were often the most observant witnesses and almost never told lies. They were also liable to blurt out truths. 'My mum's not here, she's just gone to the shop. Bal's back in Reading.'

'That's fine,' said Grace. 'I can ask them about this if I need to. So, we've seen some slightly odd behaviour from a couple of local people and want to know if there are any connections between them and your family.'

'Who?' said Nindy, leaning forward with huge eyes. Grace and Kiran both smiled, and Kiran put her arm around her little sister's shoulder.

'The Parks – Arthur and Diana. Do you know Arthur Parks?'

'Arthur? No way would he ever do anything. We were at school together – he's just a really sweet guy – you know Arthur, Nindy, who works at the Oceanworld Centre.'

'He gave me Occie,' said Nindy. 'That's my octopus plushie. I only had enough money for a pencil.'

'We were at the Centre and just leaving. Nindy was looking at all the plushies, but I said they were too much. He found one out the back with a tiny hole in one of the legs so it couldn't be sold. I thought he might have just made the hole – he's just a really nice guy – I can't imagine him ever doing anything bad to anyone. He was really quiet at school, never got into fights or hassled anyone.'

'Was there ever anything between you and him that your dad might have disapproved of, that could have got them into a fight?'

'God, no. He is NOT my type. And if anyone was angry with him – he'd just back away. No, I've seen him more since Dad died, but we've never been anything or even that good mates.'

Grace wondered, unprofessionally she knew, who Kiran's type might be.

'Was there anyone else,' Grace asked, 'who your dad might have got into an argument with, for any reason, that you haven't mentioned to us before?'

Kiran thought for a minute. 'No,' she said. 'But I don't know much about the lettings – Bal always did that with Dad. Haven't you talked to all of those yet and gone through the books?'

'Yes,' said Grace, 'of course. And I also wanted to ask you about Arthur's sister, Diana Parks, She's quite a bit older than him.'

'I don't think she knew my dad – why would he know her?'

'She runs a beauty salon. It's near Freddy's Racing where he was last seen. Did your dad ever mention that, it's called Marine Heaven Health and Beauty?'

'Dad *was* pretty vain,' said Kiran.

'He took the longest in the bathroom,' said Nindy, 'and always told everyone else to hurry up.'

'But he never went and got his nails done or anything like that. Nor did my mum. But Diana Parks, she did come in after he died. I thought it was a bit weird but then she said she was coming from the Women's whatsit.' Grace nodded, thinking, Ottersea WI again – the heart of Ottersea affairs. She coughed in what she hoped wasn't too obviously false a way.

'You want a drink?' asked Kiran, immediately under-standing. Grace nodded. 'Nindy, please can you get Grace some water and make it pretty – ice, straw, umbrella… and you can have whatever you like with no cooking or blending.'

As soon as Nindy was behind the counter, Grace said in a low voice, 'I know this is difficult, but do you know if your father had any affairs? I know we asked you that before and you, your mum and Bal all said no. But have you found anything that makes you think he could have been? And with Diana Parks?'

'He was away a lot,' said Kiran, slowly, 'and we don't know what he got up too. He was pretty patronising to my mum. She was always here working – he had more of a life. But I never saw anything or found anything. And Diana Parks – God – she did seem a bit of a weirdo when she came in. I dunno. You don't like to think of your parents doing stuff like that.'

'What was she like when she came in? Did she seem upset?'

'Nah. She gave Mum a leaflet and tried to persuade her to go to their meetings and swimming with them. But lots of people came in and left flowers and food.'

'In what way was she weird?'

'She stayed longer than you would expect from a stranger, longer than other people. And she gave hand massages to Mum and Nindy. And she filed and polished their nails here in the café. I was working so I didn't hear everything she said, but she offered Mum a free treatment. I just thought she was being nosy really – trying to be kind, but also nosy. Ghoulish. Some people were like that.'

'Did she ask anything about your dad?'

'I don't remember – I was still really spaced out – we all were.'

'OK. Try and remember if there was anything.' Nindy returned with a tall glass of water with ice and lemon, a red and white stripy paper straw and two paper parasols – both blue.

'You've got blue umbrellas cos you're in the police and

they have blue uniforms, but we haven't got dark blue – only turquoise – and blue is my favourite colour,' said Nindy.

'It's mine too,' said Grace. Nindy went back behind the counter and returned with a silver metal dish with three scoops of strawberry ice cream, a flake, a wafer and strawberry sauce.

'Three scoops, Ninds?' said Kiran.

'You said I could have anything I wanted.'

'That does look good,' said Grace.

'You can have some,' said Nindy. 'Or I can make you your own one.'

'That's OK,' said Grace. She waited until Nindy had taken a few spoonfuls and would be in an ice cream-induced state of relaxation before asking:

'Nindy, do you remember when a lady called Diana Parks visited after your daddy died and gave you and your mummy a manicure?' Nindy nodded and took another spoonful of ice cream. 'Do you remember anything she said about your daddy or what had happened?'

Nindy thought for a moment.

'Yes,' she said. 'She wanted Mummy to join her club and go swimming and she said that Mummy had very dry skin and she should go and have a free hand-thingy.'

'Did she say anything about your daddy?'

'Um, I don't know. But she looked like she was just acting being kind. When she rubbed our hands with cream it was nice, but a bit funny.'

'Really,' said Grace, 'that's interesting.'

'Kiran! Girls!' came a voice from out the back.

'Here, Mum!' Kiran yelled. 'Police Grace is here, Mum!' Grace wondered if she might be tipping her off – maybe Kiran knew something about her mum. But anyone would warn someone coming in that there was a copper in the house.

Mrs Sumal came in with two big reusable bags stacked with shopping.

'Hello, Grace,' she said, putting the bags down. Grace smiled and said hello.

'You sit down, Mum,' said Kiran. 'We'll get the stuff in.'

'You want a hand?' asked Grace.

'Nah, we're good. Haven't you got to go?'

'Not yet,' said Grace, wondering if Kiran wanted her out of there. Kiran fetched her mum a glass of water and then she and Nindy disappeared out back to get the shopping. 'When you've recovered, can I ask you some questions, Mrs Sumal?'

Mrs Sumal took a sip of her water and slipped off the cardigan that she was wearing, despite the heat. Her arms were impressively toned.

'Of course. Have you any news?'

'Not yet,' said Grace. 'But I want to find out if there was any connection between the Parks family and your husband. Arthur Parks and his sister Diana. Do you know them?'

'I don't think so,' said Mrs Sumal.

'Arthur was at school with Kiran. He works at the aquarium. Diana Parks is his older sister. Her beauty salon is on Cobble Lane near Freddy's Racing where your husband was last seen. Do you think he might have known her?'

'No. I don't think so. He didn't always say to me where he was going.'

'I have to ask again, Mrs Sumal, do you think your husband might have been having an affair?'

'I don't know anything since he went. I thought everything was just business. I can't say now. I don't know all the answers.'

'Do you know if he went for any treatments, like massages, or to have his nails tidied up? Lots of men do. They have their backs waxed, their eyebrows done – all sorts of things. Have you ever found any receipts for that or seen things on the bank or credit card statements?'

'Raj liked cash. He would always pay cash. Even in Covid when everyone used cards – he was still cash if a place took it. But I didn't know where he was – he just disappeared. How can I know anything now?' Grace reached across the table and placed her hand gently on Mrs Sumal's.

'Your girls said that Diana Parks came in after your husband was found and gave you a hand massage. Had you met her before?'

'I don't think so. She was kind, but a bit bossy. She asked me if I would like to go swimming with them. I might.' Her phone dinged and she took it out of her bag and smiled. 'The puppy! It will be ready soon.'

'Oh, that's lovely,' said Grace. 'That will really help you all through your grief. Lots of nice walks on the beach, lots of fun.'

'And when the beach is No Dogs, we'll go on the cliffs. The cliffs are lovely too.'

'Oh, do you like walking on the cliffs?' asked Grace.

'Very much. Ever since we first moved to Ottersea.'

'Picnics?' asked Grace.

'And sometimes just for peace. The town is so busy, so sometimes just for a few minutes. Now if we go, the girls can be near their daddy. Do you want to see a picture?'

'Yes, please,' said Grace.

'There,' said Mrs Sumal. 'She's a honey working cocker spaniel.'

'Oh, she's gorgeous,' said Grace, almost laughing – she'd been expecting a pic of Mr Sumal.

'At last, I can have a dog,' said Mrs Sumal. 'I always watch the people with dogs on the beach and on the cliffs and wish one was mine. Now, at last, I can have one.'

'Was your husband allergic to dogs?'

'He just didn't like any animals.'

As Grace drove away, she wondered if Mrs Sumal might be mad, or mad with grief. She seemed more fixated on getting a dog than anything else. And the way she had spoken about the cliffs and said that if they went there, the girls would be "near their daddy". Why would she think that? Did she know that he had jumped off the cliffs or been pushed off? Had she done the pushing?

Could Sukhi Sumal have picked him up from near the bookies on some pretext and they'd gone for a walk and then she'd pushed him off those cliffs? They had a van as well as Mr Sumal's car. Had the uniforms properly trawled through the CCTV for that? God, what if they'd missed that, missed what was staring them in the face all along?

Back at the station, Jim was peering morosely at a map of Ottersea again.

'I'm still sure we're missing something,' he said.

'I've been thinking that too. Just back from the Sumals'. You remember the mum saying about getting a dog at the appeal – well, she showed me a picture of the puppy she's got coming – that seemed the main thing she wanted to talk about. And she said that when they took it up on the cliffs, the girls would be closer to their dad. Why would she say that – I mean the cliffs?'

'Hmm. Family picnics? Likes walking after midnight?'

'Yeah, but she's mentioned the cliffs a few times. Said they used to like walking up there after the café was closed. Maybe what we're missing, is that she just pushed him off. She's never seemed that upset – always a bit detached. Just cos she's a polite Asian woman doesn't mean she's incapable of killing someone. Maybe he was having an affair. Maybe she heard about what he asked his tenants. Maybe he was a bully and she struck back – coercive control, then provocation.'

'Hmm,' said Jim. 'Have we looked in enough detail at her movements over the days he was missing?'

'The van. Have the uniforms looked properly for that?'

'We need to check,' said Jim. 'And this cliffs business. Let's go up there again – maybe we missed something. And maybe if we pull her in, she'll just fold.'

'I doubt it,' said Grace. 'I think she's cooler and tougher than people assume.'

'And Diana Parks,' said Jim.

'Yes, her,' said Grace. 'Apparently, she went round there soon after he was found and gave Mrs Sumal and the little one a hand massage and manicure. Said she was coming on behalf of the WI.'

'Hmm. Is that normal for the Ottersea WI?'

'You expect me to know that?'

'Rhetorical question.'

'Well, the Sumals thought it was a bit weird,' said Grace.

'Curious or a guilty conscience if she was banging the husband?' said Jim. Grace smiled.

'There have been less likely couples,' she said.

'Fancy another stroll on the cliffs? I wonder if we could have missed anything.'

'What she said about being nearer their dad up there – it does make you wonder.'

The nature reserve car park was busy. Jim and Grace got out of the car and stood beside it for a few minutes, just looking about.

'Last time we came,' said Grace, 'we took that path – straight to the cliff top, but there is another one – look.' She gestured towards the one that went through the woods. 'I guess someone might go that way, if they were worried about being seen.'

They set off in that direction, scanning around and looking at the ground as they went. Everything was very dry – there had been so little rain – but it was still worth looking for anything of possible interest. The path was well trodden and flat.

'You couldn't get a car along here, let alone a van,' said Jim. 'But maybe they came for a stroll and she just pushed him off. But then why not say it was an accident?'

They reached a point about halfway along. The path got wider and there was a fallen tree ideal for sitting on. There were cigarette butts near it and a few fresh-looking empty cans. They sat down for a minute.

'I don't think Mrs Sumal is a few cans of lager and some

fags in the woods kind of woman,' said Grace. Jim wandered off a little way into the woods where there was a sandy bank and some big holes.

'A badger sett,' he said, smiling. He looked around and then up at the ceiling of beech leaves, as though for inspiration. The wind was swishing through the trees, singing to the rhythm of the distant waves.

'Look' he said, 'there's some sort of trail camera. We'll have that.' He could reach it without climbing. He unstrapped it. On the back was a faded sticker: "Property of Ottersea Wildlife Society. Do Not Remove" and a landline phone number. 'No reason to suppose there's anything on it, but worth a look.' They went back to the path and carried on towards the clifftop. They came to a stump which was encrusted with bird droppings and surrounded by feathers.

'This looks like a killing stump,' said Jim. 'I think that's what they call them. Where birds of prey dismember things.' He went up to it and peered at the ground. 'Probably owl pellets, or whatever.'

'Wrong sort of forensics, Skip.' Grace folded her arms and waited for him. She knew Jim liked nature – he didn't seem to have much else in his life. Then she spotted it.

'Here's another camera,' said Grace, pointing right at the path. 'Might have something.'

They unstrapped that one too.

'We'll give them a ring when we get back,' said Jim. 'I wonder how long their footage goes back, assuming they've been functioning.'

'Still wanna follow the path to the end?' asked Grace.

'Always, Grace, always to the very end.'

Carrying one camera each, they followed the path – it was only a couple of minutes further.

They met some dogwalkers on the way and a couple of guys on bikes overtook them.

'Any tracks anyone made when he first went missing would be long gone by now,' said Grace.

The path led them to the edge of the woods and out onto the clifftop.

'So, someone coming along here would have good cover and get to the edge almost as quickly as if they took the path straight across the open clifftops,' said Grace. They looked east along to the spot where Jim had crawled under the fence – what now seemed liked ages ago.

'Still all signifies nothing,' said Jim morosely.

'Maybe there'll be something on these cameras,' said Grace.

'It would be just as easy to get under the fence, or shove someone under the fence here as along there,' said Jim.

'If you wanted to push someone off, you'd have to get them to go to the other side of the fence,' said Grace. 'But you could just accidentally drop your bag and ask them to get it.'

'The RNLI post pictures every year of people picnicking on the wrong side, sitting with their legs dangling over. Maybe they did that – then just one shove. He'd be gone and she walks home. But she has to get him up here after he's seen on the cameras at the bookies and left his car on the seafront. We have him doing that. Probably the same day – why would he leave his car there? She has to have intercepted him. Let's see what the uniforms have on the van and her movements and if these cameras have anything.'

'Maybe we're getting there, Boss.'

Back at the station, they took the SD cards out of the cameras and flicked through the images. There were plenty of cute badgers, rats, foxes, some birds of prey, plenty of dog-walkers and people out for strolls, and in pictures on five different days, Mrs Sumal was walking briskly past by herself, always coming back from the clifftop, never walking towards it, presumably doing a circuit. Each image had a date and time, but they were all from over a month after Mr Sumal's body had been found.

'She really likes it up on those cliffs,' said Grace. 'I think this woman has hidden depths.' Jim rang the number on the back of the camera and a woman picked up. The voice was familiar.

'Oh, hello,' she said brightly when he introduced himself. 'How are you?'

'Er, well, thank you. I was just ringing about the Ottersea Wildlife Society's cameras from the nature reserve.'

'Oh no!' cried the woman. 'They haven't been vandalised, have they? It is a risk having them out there so near the path, but we do get such good shots of the badgers.'

'It's not that, the cameras are fine. I've got them both right here. Can I ask who I'm talking to?'

'Katie. Katie Grayling. You were so kind when my poor husband fell down the stairs, if you remember.'

'Yes, of course,' said Jim. 'How are you doing?' He remembered her now, and from when he'd met them on top of the cliffs. They'd been counting birds and she'd been generous with her homemade flapjacks against her husband's wishes.

'Oh, not too bad,' said Katie. 'Mustn't grumble.' She sounded pretty jolly. And back we come to Ottersea WI, thought Jim. Forget the Lizard People, here was the real secret society running things.

'I'm interested in any images you have from your cameras earlier in the summer. Would you be able to share those with us?'

'Of course,' said Katie. 'I'm not very good at these things, but I'll try to send them.'

'I can help with that, if you aren't sure how,' said Jim. 'Shall I talk you through it?'

'No, I'll have a go first. But who am I meant to send them to?'

He gave her the email address.

'I just thought,' said Katie. 'I should have checked if you're a fraudster. But I recognise your voice, so I won't bother.'

'I can come round with a female colleague if you prefer,' said Jim.

'No, no, that's quite alright.'

'Do you think you could send the pictures now?'

'Well, I've got some cakes in the oven that need attention, but yes.'

Half an hour later, the email arrived:

'Dear Inspector Jim,

Here are the pictures from the last time we checked the cameras. Unless you are after some criminal badgers, I don't think they'll be much use! If you want pictures from before then, we have records of the sightings in the minutes. I do hope you aren't investigating something as unpleasant as wildlife crime. We would certainly have noticed something as terrible as that if it had been there in the pictures and we would have reported it straight away.

With best wishes,

Katie Grayling.'

Jim downloaded the pictures and began clicking through them. There were some interesting pictures of woodland animals and birds, but he soon realised that this was an edited collection as there were major gaps in time and each image was of something Wildlife Society members would find interesting. So where were all the outtakes?

'Katie, hello again. It's DI Jim Paddon. Thank you for sending the pictures, but I was wondering, these ones are all very good shots of wildlife. What about any of people who might have walked by? Have you got everything that the cameras captured?'

'Oh no, only those. I sent you all I have.'

'Ah, thanks. Did anyone help you with the cameras or get the pictures off before you saw them?'

'Oh yes, that was Arthur, one of our younger members. Graham always used to do it, but Arthur helped me after Graham died.'

'Arthur?'

'Arthur Parks. Such a sweet boy. He's our youngest member. He works at the aquarium.'

'Thank you. Yes, I know Arthur – he looks after the octopus. I'll see if he can help.' But it was a long shot and Jim had more pressing things to do first.

Gavin Poltree and Will Potterton walked in, laughing, with a big flat box of Krispy Kreme.

'Alright, Boss?' said PC Poltree.

'Fancy a doughnut, Sarge?' asked PC Potterton.

'No, thanks,' said Jim. 'But I want to check with you about the CCTV for the car park behind the high street – the small one with an alley to Cobble Lane. You have been through that?'

'Mostly, boss,' said PC Poltree.

'Mostly! For fuck's sake!' Jim yelled, bringing his fist down on the desk. 'This is a potential murder investigation and you have "mostly" been through the CCTV. God. Stop eating doughnuts and do it now. You remember what I wanted you to look for?'

'Mr Sumal, sir,' said PC Potterton.

'Not just him,' said Jim. 'His wife in particular, their van, his adult kids, anyone acting suspiciously on or soon after 4th July. Dear God.' He closed his eyes and sighed. 'I'm going out now, but I want it done straight away.'

'Right, sir,' they said. They at least had the decency to look sheepish, though he saw Poltree's eyes drifting back to the box of doughnuts.

Jim got up.

'Come on, Grace,' he said, 'we need to get back out there. We'll go and talk to Kayleigh Evans again,' said Jim. 'You'd think she'd have known if her boss, Diana, was having an affair with someone, even if she didn't know who it was.'

Brows!

When they got to Kayleigh's flat they found the door open. They went straight up the narrow stairs, being careful not to get the new wet paint on their sleeves.

The flat was transformed. Kayleigh and Georgia's things were gone. Everything had been painted a chalky white or was blue and white stripes, and standard seaside decorative items for West Country Airbnbs had been brought in – wooden seagulls, a mirror with a driftwood frame, some large shells that were clearly from some tropical beach, not a Devon one, a "Gone To The Beach" enamel sign, and there in the centre of it all stood Bal Sumal, talking on his phone. He nodded at them and indicated the new-looking sofa (bright blue corduroy with scatter cushions with puffins on) and they sat down, perching on the edge so as to not dent the puffins or the sofa's newness.

'Bal, how are you doing?' Jim asked when Bal had ended his call.

'Ah, you know. Any news?'

''Fraid not,' said Jim, 'but we're working on it. We wanted to talk to Kayleigh, the previous tenant again.'

'You think *she* did it?' asked Bal.

'Have you got a forwarding address for her? I take it these seagulls and puffins aren't for a local.'

'She's moved to Exeter with her mate. I've got her phone number, though.' He sat down in one of the new armchairs and began scrolling. 'Here you go.' He held up the phone to show them and Jim wrote it down.

'She say anything before she moved out?' asked Jim. 'Anything you remember about your dad? Did she mind moving out?'

'Don't think so.'

'Aren't young people pretty fed up with places being turned into holiday lets and Airbnbs?' said Grace.

'Maybe,' said Bal, 'but we have to go with the money.'

No, you don't, thought Jim.

'Did she say anything to you about it?' asked Grace.

'Nah, they worry they won't get their deposit back if they kick off about anything,' said Bal.

'Is she the type to kick off?' asked Jim.

'Only met her the once – my dad did the Ottersea lettings. Just seemed like the average tenant.'

'OK,' said Jim. 'If you think of anything – about her or any of the other tenants…'

'I know who to call,' said Bal.

Jim phoned Kayleigh later and she said they could chat at her work. He suspected she didn't want police in her flat again.

Jim drove to Exeter listening to Dwight Yoakam. He found a parking space not far from Brows! where Kayleigh was now working. He'd arrived just after 4.30 in the hope that Kayleigh wouldn't be that busy – he'd been wrong. Three young women and a man who looked to be in his mid-thirties sat waiting in some rattan chairs. There were four beauticians including Kayleigh at work and it seemed that they did a lot more than brows! He waited between the coat stand and the door, knowing he was doing his best impression of a copper as he stood there, having to bend his knees every so often so that they didn't seize up. *Evening, all.*

Kayleigh was doing something intricate with what looked like dental floss, working away at a woman's forehead and eyebrows. Being a woman involved so much extra maintenance. Thank God he didn't have to do any of that, although he suspected that he wouldn't bother, even if he was meant to. When he thought that the woman's eyebrows must, surely, be done, Kayleigh started work on the sides of the woman's face, which from where Jim was standing, looked to be completely hair-free anyway. Honestly – how pointless was this? It was, he supposed, an essential part of the post-Brexit economy, which ran on people selling coffee to each other and doing things to each other's hair, skin and nails. He wondered about interrupting but knew he would get a better response from Kayleigh if he didn't lose her money or clients.

The woman in the chair nearest to him was finished. She'd had her nails painted ('Oh, that "Mermaid's Tears" is lovely') and was moved to another station where she had to sit with her fingers under a hairdryer-type lamp affair. The now-free worker addressed the waiting crowd.

'Matt, would you like to come over and sit down?' The mid-thirties guy who'd been waiting did so and smiled up at the worker in the mirror.

'So, you've just come in for a consultation and a patch test. And you're interested in micro-needling?'

'Yeah, that's right.' The woman ran her hand through his hair in the way a mother might the untidy hair of one of her kids when there was no brush to hand. 'Yeah, I can see you've got a bit of thinning here, particularly around the crown.'

'I'm going to look like Milhouse's dad if I don't do something,' he said. She smiled at him in the mirror and put her head on one side appraisingly.

'You've a way to go yet, but it might speed up if you don't do something, so it's good you're looking at treatment now. You got any allergies?'

'Er, penicillin.'

'That don't matter. You had any hair-loss treatment before?'

'Nah,' he said. 'I'm mean I've been using Alpecin, but that's all.'

'The serum we use with the treatment contains much higher levels of caffeine as well as essential oils of nettle and chestnut, hyaluronic acid, panthenol and creatine, all to, you know, promote absorption of the active ingredients and faster regrowth.' She must have learnt that bit off by heart. She went to a shelf behind the counter and opened the transparent blue door of something space-age looking. She took out a strange roller device covered in tiny metal spikes and returned to her client, holding the implement up so that he could see it in the mirror. 'So, this is one of the micro-needlers we use. In a salon we can use *much* longer needles than if you were doing this at home, so we'll get much better results. It doesn't really hurt, but you may have some discomfort and redness, but that will mostly be hidden by the hair you've still got. This is straight out of the steriliser. Here, I'll just swab your arm so you can feel what it's like.' She wiped his forearm and then ran the roller along it. 'Not too bad, is it? I'll just get some of the special serum we use.'

She disappeared off-stage and came back with a glass bottle of some golden liquid – a supposed elixir of eternal youth, thought Jim. 'Now I'll just gentle apply some of this to where I did the needling to check that you don't have a reaction, and if after forty-eight hours, there's nothing, we can go ahead. OK?' It was fortunate that he didn't demur as she was already dabbing the oil onto his skin and rubbing it in with circular motions. Bloody hell, thought Jim, and he's happy to have this done in public? The guy stared down at his arm.

'There's red dots,' he said.

'That's normal, don't worry – you'll always get some of that with micro-needling. We're just checking for inflammation or an allergic reaction. So, if you can come back in a couple of days, we can go ahead. Shall I book you in? You'll need treatments every two weeks, for like six weeks, and there's special offers on the full course. You need the full course to see the improvement.'

'Does it work?'

'It's the needling that sends signals to the hair follicles, and the caffeine and essential oils will open them up too so all that lovely hair can get out again. It's all scientific. We do it in one of our treatment rooms – it's more relaxing – and you have a complimentary head massage and tea or coffee.' The man looked down at his arm again, somewhat dubiously.

'So, these dots are normal?' He stuck his arm out to better examine it.

'Absolutely.'

Bloody baby, thought Jim. If you want someone to roll that thing over your bonce, you're gonna get prickles.

'And, did I say, you mustn't have any henna tattoos during the treatment period – that can give you a reaction. Regular tattoos are fine, not on your scalp, obvs,' said the woman.

'Got it,' said the guy. 'No henna tattoos.'

'Come over to the desk and we'll get you booked in.' She put the roller thing on the shelf beneath the mirror. It looked pretty vicious. Jim stepped closer to the guy whilst the woman was doing something on the salon computer.

'I could go for some of that,' Jim said, running a hand through his own hair, which wasn't actually thinning, though his forehead was significantly higher than it had once been. 'Think you're getting a reaction?' The guy held his arm out.

'Don't think so, she said this is normal.' Jim peered at the man's forearm – there was general redness and loads of dots.

'It is normal,' said the woman, looking over from her screen. 'So how about Thursday?' The guy got his phone out to check.

Kayleigh's client was done now too. Jim stepped back so as not to be in the way whilst Kayleigh took her payment. She's in a newish job, he thought, she won't want them to think the cops are after her.

'Kayleigh, can we have a quick chat somewhere quiet?' he asked when she was free.

'Sure,' she said, pulling a face. 'That was my last lady.' She led Jim through to one of the treatment rooms out the back. It smelled strongly of lavender and something fruity – what was that – mango? There was nowhere to sit apart from the treatment couch. Kayleigh perched on that, swinging her legs. Jim stood.

'Thanks, for seeing me,' said Jim. 'We're still investigating the death of Raj Sumal.'

'I told you all I know,' said Kayleigh.

'Thanks, but one thing I've been wondering, were you aware of any relationship between Mr Sumal and your old boss, Diana Parks?'

'Diana? God, no!' Kayleigh pulled a face. 'Really? You think that?'

'Was Diana in a relationship with anyone while you were working for her?'

'She never said anything about anyone, but I never asked. I mean, she wasn't like, mates with me.'

'And you never saw him come into Marine Heaven?'

'No. I would have remembered – what with him being my landlord. I would've hid if he had. Specially when I knew the rent was late. I told you he was hassling me, what he said and everything.'

'Yes, thank you. I remember that. What about bookings? Did you ever see his name in the diary?'

'I dunno. I don't think so – I'd only bother looking at who I had each day.'

'So, when you worked at Marine Beauty, did you do treatments for men?' Jim asked.

'Mostly for ladies – all places are mostly ladies. We do get more men coming in here, but there weren't that many in Ottersea.'

'But there were some?'

'Sometimes, but you get more in a big place.'

'But never Mr Sumal, as far as you know?'

'I don't think so, but I was just part-time – just came in and did what she said.'

'Would you be able to check? Can you still get into the

bookings?' Jim asked, just in case Diana Parks had been doing something underhand when she had searched in front of him.

'Nah, Diana locked me out the day I left – worried about me stealing her ladies, but I would *never* have done that,' Kayleigh replied, as though he might be investigating her for industrial espionage. 'I only ever logged into it when I was at work. Diana did all the web-stuff – I was just doing whatever treatments she said and cleaning up and stuff. Mostly cleaning.'

'Did she ever talk to you about her life outside work? Was she dating anyone?'

'God, no. Well, if she was, she never told me. All I knew was she lived with her nerdy brother – I only met him a few times. She bossed him and everybody about. I didn't mind leaving when I moved to here. It's nice working somewhere busier with people my own age, and I've got more hours.'

'So, do you know if she did online dating, or Tinder or anything?'

'No! Can't imagine her swiping right on anyone, ever. She would be nice to her ladies, but she still just kind of looked down her nose and disapproved of the whole world. Why are you so interested in her?'

'We're just trying to trace Mr Sumal's last movements. So, what did she do outside work – did she ever talk about that?'

'Not really. I know she's in the WI cos she would have leaflets on the counter, and she didn't allow any other leaflets, apart from the salon ones. So, I guess she has friends there. She was really into the business, really interested in all the products and stuff. She was always on Cult Beauty looking at stuff. She's really fit – she would go swimming all the time and I know she did spin and stuff. Just all the usual things.'

'OK. And that guy who was having the hair treatment with that roller – is that something you did at Marine Beauty?'

'We did, but there weren't many takers, so Diana said we might as well take it off the list.'

'And when was that?'

'I dunno, not that long ago. She would put new things on the list sometimes and take others off. She would add them if they were really good and in magazines and stuff. And people go off things – like the treatment with fish that ate the hard skin off your feet – all the salons were doing that until there were infections – we did about it at college. It was really gross. Diana never minded if things were a bit gross though – like she loves all the snail gel products.'

'Snail products, really?' Jim always tried to look nonplussed when people divulged information. This time he failed.

'Yeah, snail trail is excellent for skin – it doesn't hurt the snails – people just collect it – it's all organic.'

'Hmm,' said Jim. Fish eating your hard skin, snail trail gel – it seemed there was plenty in this world he still didn't know about. 'And after you left, have you been in touch with Diana at all?'

'No, well, I still follow Marine Heaven on insta, but nothing else.'

'What about Mr Sumal or his family? Were they ever in touch again after you moved out?'

'Nah. His son was pretty good about the deposit – I mean you always lose a bit for stuff that wasn't your fault. But I got most of it back. Are we done?'

'Just one more thing,' said Jim (his favourite line). 'Could I have a look at one of those rollers with the needles?'

'Sure. You thinking about getting it done? I could do a test on you.'

'That would be helpful,' said Jim. He rolled up his sleeve and Kayleigh cleaned a patch of his forearm with a surgical wipe and fetched a roller. The sensation from the needles was only mildly unpleasant. He wondered how it would feel on a bald head. 'Are all the rollers the same?'

'The ones people use at home aren't as good – the needles aren't as long. Now this is the serum we use – it's really good – rich in caffeine and antioxidants.' And other crap, thought

Jim. 'I'll gently rub a little on – then you can see if you have a reaction.'

'And would Diana always do a test? Could someone come in off the street and have the whole treatment?'

'No – she'd always do a patch test – or they might get a toxic shock in the salon and it would be on the news, Google reviews, everything. You have to cover yourself.'

'Yes,' said Jim, looking down at his arm, which was now speckled red, 'you would have to cover yourself.'

The Car Park

The next morning Jim was gratified to see that PCs Poltree and Potterton were in before him. There was no box of doughnuts, just a few paper bags from the baker and some greasy flakes of sausage roll pastry in the bin. At least they'd supported somewhere local this time.

'We got something, Sarge,' said Potterton. 'Look at this. Mrs Sumal on the camera in that car park on the day he goes missing.'

'What time? Show me,' said Jim. PC Potterton got an image up on his screen.

'Here she is – July 4th.' The CCTV wasn't that great, but at least it had her arriving in the van at 4.10pm on July 4th and then walking out two minutes later at 4.12pm. At 4.33 she returned to the car park, and then the van was seen driving out at 4.38pm. You only saw the back view of the van when it left, though – there was only one camera and it didn't capture the whole car park. You could see the number plate on the Flakies van departing but not who was in it.

'Bloody hell!' said Jim. Grace walked in. 'Come and see this, Grace. Here's Mrs Sumal, she arrives while he's at the bookies and then the van leaves at 4.38pm. That's plenty of time for him to walk down Cobble Lane, along the alleyway and get into the van with her.'

'So where does the van go next?'

'We have it going out of Ottersea straight after that,' said PC Poltree, waking up his screen.

'OK. 16.45. But we can't see who's in there.' said Jim. 'Enlarge that, please.' The PC did, but it was no good – the van's windscreen was tinted and there were shadows from the trees by the road. In the next picture, the light was bouncing off the windscreen, obscuring who was inside.

'So where does it go?' asked Grace.

'Not far. We get it going up the hill out of town, and back the same way an hour later – but nothing between that. She must have stopped somewhere nearby for that time?

'Red Cliffs Nature Reserve,' said Jim. 'What about the pics coming back?'

'Here it is heading back towards Ottersea at 17.52, then we get the van on some cameras in town – the last time near where their café is, likely going home. Much better shots – you can see one figure in the car,' said PC Poltree and got that one up on his screen.

'Looks like her,' said Jim.

'It's her,' said Grace. 'It could have been Kiran driving, but it's not. It's her.'

'OK,' said Jim. 'I want you guys to keep going through that CCTV – check for other days she goes out of town in that direction. Look at the week up until 4th July until the week after his body is found. That was 18th July. I want to know if she keeps going up there.'

'We already know she does,' said Grace. 'She says she does. She's talked about the cliffs and walking there. But why would he abandon his car?' asked Grace. 'Why would he go back with her in the van and leave his own car by the seafront?'

'Good question,' said Jim. 'Maybe she said there was some emergency. Maybe she said he had to go somewhere with her – school meeting, or something. Maybe she said they had to talk, and then they went for a walk on the cliffs. Then she checks around – there's no one else there – she pushes him off. She drives home. Kiran discovers the car a few days later, reports him missing. Nobody else is in on it. Or if she does tell the older kids – one or both – they protect her. We've seen how they are with her. They must have known what he was like. They aren't dumb.'

'Hmm, maybe,' said Grace. 'And I guess he'd bought a ticket for 4th July, so it wasn't abandoned, so to speak until 5th July. Maybe he was planning on getting it back later that evening – it wasn't parked far from Flakies. I guess if he went with her, she must have said something had come up, or that he'd forgotten something. I guess they could have done spontaneous things, a walk on the cliffs, leaving Kiran in charge of the café…'

'Yeah,' said Jim. 'But we still haven't got a motive, unless she found out about something. If only we had his phone. All we have is the last ping. That's a real bugger. Carry on, guys. Follow that van.'

Jim's phone rang. It was Liam from digital forensics.

'Interesting stuff from that Fitbit for you, Jim. I'll email it over.'

'Can you talk me through it now?'

'Sure. The serial number matches the one on the box so must be your guy's. The last day of functioning is July 4th. He seems pretty chilled – we have his heart rate, pretty much normal. Some rises and falls – he's probably just walking, walking a bit faster, sitting about. Then he really starts to relax, like he's falling asleep, sunbathing or something, drifting off, he's really chilled. Then his pulse suddenly goes right up – then it stops. Unless the device was taken off at that moment and never put on again, we have a likely time of death here – 5.22pm.'

'And do you know where he was?'

'No built in GPS with this type of Fitbit.'

'Shame,' said Jim.

'What about swimming? Can you tell if he did any of that?'

'He didn't. We've got his steps, but no swimming that day or in the week before.'

'Extremely useful, Liam. Cheers.' Jim sat back in his chair. 'Right,' he said, 'I'll draw the timeline of everything we have. Then first thing tomorrow – Sukhi Sumal – we'll bring her in.'

Interview With Sukhi Sumal

'I'm starting the recording now,' said Jim. 'Interview with Sukhi Sumal. Present are DI Jim Paddon and DC Andrew Barns. Interview room at Ottersea Police Station.

'Mrs Sumal, you have been arrested on suspicion of the murder of your husband. You do not have to say anything, but, it may harm your defence if you do not mention when questioned something which you later rely on in court. Anything you do say may be given in evidence.'

Sukhi Sumal just kept staring at a spot in front of her on the table. She didn't reply.

'Are there things that you haven't told us, Mrs Sumal?' asked Jim. She shook her head.

'Subject shook her head,' said DC Barns.

'It would be helpful if you could answer out loud,' said Jim. 'I'm sure your children want to know what happened to their father. Don't you think?' She still said nothing. 'You can have a solicitor here,' said Jim after a while. 'You have a right to legal advice.'

'I want a solicitor,' she whispered.

'Do you have one you want to call, or one can be arranged for you?' said Jim.

'I don't have one,' she said, still looking down.

'OK,' said Jim. 'We'll carry on when one arrives. Interview

ended at 7.49am.' He and DC Barns got up and left the room, deliberately not telling her how long it might be.

Jim and Andy Barns had gone round to Flakies at 7am. Kiran had answered the door, looking expectant.

'Have you got someone?' she asked.

'No,' said Jim. 'We need to ask your mum some more questions.'

'Oh, OK,' she said, biting her lower lip. 'Come in, she's not up yet.' Upstairs, the Sumal's sitting room looked different. Jim noticed that there was more clutter about – nice feminine stuff making it look more homely. The brown leather sofa was now covered by bright pink throws. The curtains had changed – the dull beige ones had been replaced by much jollier ones with orange and red flowers on a pink background. On the coffee table was an Ikea catalogue with lots of Post-it notes sticking out. He and Andy stayed standing, wanting to indicate the seriousness of their visit. After a few minutes, Mrs Sumal came in looking very much as though she had just woken up. Her feet were bare. Her nails were a shiny coral, toes and fingers matching. She was wearing a black Flakies T-shirt, just like Kiran, but with more flowing trousers so that the ensemble was more elegant. She blinked when she saw them and swallowed.

'Would you like some tea?' Kiran asked, 'I'm making some for Mum anyway.'

'No thanks,' said Jim. 'Mrs Sumal, we have some questions we'd like you to answer, and we need to do that down at the station.'

'No way,' said Kiran. 'Ask her here. She doesn't need to go down to the station.'

'We need to video this interview,' said Jim.

'What?' cried Kiran. 'She hasn't done anything!'

'Sukhi Sumal,' said Jim, 'I'm arresting you on suspicion of the murder of your husband. You do not have to say anything, but it may harm your defence if you do not mention when questioned something which you later rely on in court. Anything you do say may be given in evidence.'

Andy Barns took a pair of cuffs out of his pocket.

'You're not bloody handcuffing her! She hasn't done anything!' Kiran stepped between her mother and the police.

'Kiran, shush, you'll wake Nindy,' said her mother.

'Oh my God, you can't just take her away!'

'I'll go quietly.' Sukhi bent and fished a pair of new pink running shoes out from under the sofa and put them on. 'Let me just kiss my daughters.' She left the room, but not for long. Jim imagined her going into her little girl's bedroom, smoothing the hair away from her sleeping face and gently kissing her on the forehead. When she returned, she had an expensive-looking pale blue leather bag with her. It had a picture of a dog in other colours of leather on it, plus trees and flowers. The dog was looking at a sign that pointed the way to Greenwich Market. The bag looked many steps up from the battered maroon one she'd brought to the press appeal. There were clearly some benefits to being without her husband. Kiran hugged her for a long time.

'I'll call Bal,' Kiran said.

'No, don't bother him yet. There's no need. I haven't done anything wrong.'

'Are you ready?' asked Andy Barns. There was no need for the cuffs.

'Let me go now, before anyone sees,' said Mrs Sumal and she led the way out of the flat, down the stairs, and out to the waiting car.

Now Jim was watching her through the one-way glass while they waited for the duty solicitor. Sukhi Sumal's fists were held in front of her mouth, like a boxer at the start of a bout. When the solicitor arrived, Jim was pleased to see that it was Mira Anand – he hoped that having an Asian woman would put Sukhi Sumal more at ease, plus he knew Mira Anand was good. He did want Sukhi Sumal to have sound advice, whatever she had done, and knowing what he did of Raj

Sumal, she would likely be able to plead coercive control. After they'd been in there alone for about ten minutes, Jim and Andy went back in, read her her rights, and started the recording again.

'So, Mrs Sumal, or can I call you Sukhi? We would like you to tell us everything you remember, everything you did, on the day your husband disappeared which was July 4th. What do you remember about that day?' asked Jim.

'You don't have to say anything,' said Mira Anand.

'I don't mind,' said Sukhi. 'I didn't do anything. But I don't really remember much. We didn't know he was missing.'

'You can just say "no comment",' said Mira.

'It will help us to find out what happened to your husband if you tell us as much as you can, Sukhi,' said Jim.

'What were you doing on that day, July 4th? It was a Monday,' asked Andy.

'I don't remember,' said Sukhi.

'It's not that long ago. Surely you can remember the last time you saw your husband alive?'

'I think it was just a normal day,' said Sukhi. The solicitor gently rested a hand on Sukhi's arm and said:

'You can say "no comment".'

'It may help us find out what happened to your husband if you can remember,' said Jim, gently. 'Did you go anywhere? Take your daughter to school?'

'Kiran usually does that. I'll be in the freezer room.'

'What about Monday 4th July?'

'I expect Kiran took her.'

'And what did you do for the rest of the day?' asked Andy.

'Just work, I expect.'

'Did you go anywhere else? To the shops, to pick up Nindy?' asked Jim.

'I don't know.'

'Say "no comment",' said her solicitor.

'So, when was the last time you saw your husband?' asked Jim.

'No comment.'

'Was he there in the morning that Monday, 4th July?'

'Yes, I think so.'

'Then what happened?'

'I don't know. It was just a normal day.'

'That seems strange,' said Andy. 'It might be the last time you saw your husband alive, but you don't remember?'

'Say "no comment",' said Mira.

'No comment,' Sukhi whispered.

'Please try to remember what you did that day, Sukhi,' said Jim.

'I didn't do anything. I was just at work, just at home.'

'Monday July 4th,' said Jim. 'What did your husband do or say to you that day?'

'Oh, I remember now,' said Sukhi. '4th July. We always do special offers on waffles. For the America thing.'

'And what else do you remember?' asked Jim.

'We sold lots of waffles and ice cream.'

'What about the last time you saw your husband?'

'I think he said he was going to Reading. That's why we didn't know he was missing. But I don't remember.'

'OK,' said Jim. 'Maybe if we show you some images of that day it will help.' He opened the folder he'd brought in with printouts of the CCTV images. 'Here is your husband when he's last seen on camera, he's leaving Freddy's Racing on the high street. It's 4.17pm. I'm showing Sukhi Sumal images from CCTV of her late husband leaving Freddy's Racing on July 4th at 4.17pm. Would you say that was your late husband?' She nodded. 'Please could you answer out loud for the recording?'

'You don't have to answer,' said Mira Anand.

'I don't mind. It's him,' she said. 'I have seen this picture before.'

'It seems as though your husband then went down Cobble Lane. Why do you think he would have done that? Do you think he was going to meet somebody?'

'I don't know.'

'Was he going to meet you?'

'No. I would have remembered.'

'And where were you whilst your husband was in Freddy's Racing?'

'You don't have to answer,' said Mira Anand.

'I don't remember,' said Sukhi. 'I'm always at Flakies unless I'm shopping or doing something with the kids, or sometimes I go for a little walk.'

'You like going for walks?' asked Jim. 'Where do you like to go?'

'Anywhere. The beach when it's quiet. Red Cliffs is nice,' said Suhki.

'Why do you like it there?' asked Jim, keeping his expression blank.

'There's a nice breeze, people take their dogs,'

'Say no comment,' said Mira.

'We think that you weren't at Flakies or at home when your husband was last seen on CCTV,' said Jim. 'It seems as though this is you driving into the short stay car park behind the high street at 4.10pm on July 4th.' He showed her the picture of the van driving in and then two more. 'And here you are, that's you, isn't it, walking out of the car park at 4.12pm? And here you are returning at 4.33pm where you wait for five minutes, maybe for your husband, or you're already having a row with him. Would you say that is you, Sukhi?'

'Um...'

'Say "no comment",' said Mira.

'No comment.'

'That was you, walking, wasn't it, Sukhi? And that's the Flakies van, isn't it, Sukhi? We can see that it says "Flakies" on the bonnet and we've checked the registration number. It is your family's van and you walked towards it. Then we see it being driven away. Was that you driving it, or might it have been Kiran? Was she there?'

'Would you like us to bring Kiran in for questioning too?' asked Jim.

'No, no,' said Sukhi. 'It's me. I park there if I just need to go to one shop.'

'So, it is you?' asked Jim.

'It must be, yes.'

'So, while your husband is at the last place he was seen alive, you are just a couple of minutes' walk away? Is that correct?'

'I don't remember. We didn't notice he was gone at first – we thought he had gone to Reading.'

'But you didn't try to contact him for days when he was missing,' said Jim. 'That seems very strange. Your husband disappeared and you say you didn't notice for several days until your daughter found his abandoned car and pointed it out to you?'

'He often went away. He didn't like me to bother him.'

'We'll be looking at your phone records,' said Jim. 'Your phone will tell us where you were as well as who you were communicating with, even if you have deleted messages.'

'I haven't done anything,' she said. 'He just disappeared.' Jim ignored her and went on:

'So, just to go over this again, your husband leaves Freddy's Racing at 4.17pm. Presumably he had a key to the van that was registered in his name and belongs to the family business. You return to the van at 4.33pm and the van drives out of the car park at 4.38pm. Is that correct?'

'I don't know.'

'I think it is,' said Jim.'

'Sukhi, you don't have to say anything,' said her solicitor. 'And, she isn't visible in the van driving out – it's a rear view – you can't see her or anybody else in that.'

'So, was that you driving the van out of the car park at 4.38pm on the day your husband went missing?'

'No comment.'

Jim turned to another picture.

'And then why is the van driven out of Ottersea up to, it seems, Red Cliffs Nature Reserve? Here we have it at 4.45pm on the road up to the cliffs. Why was that?'

'No comment.'

'Nobody is visible in there,' said Mira. Jim ignored her.

'But, you've already told us, Sukhi, that you like going to the cliffs, and that if you go there with your daughters,' Jim pulled out his notebook, '"they will be closer to their dad", that's what you said. Those cliffs are a particular destination for you, aren't they? We have other footage of you, walking back from the clifftop alone.' He turned a page in the folder to an image of her from the trail cam, ignoring the fact that the date was well after her husband's body had been found. 'Why do you keep going to the cliffs?'

'No comment.'

'We have more footage from the clifftops on the way, Sukhi, so you might as well tell us what happened. It must be awful keeping this all to yourself. We know that you came back from somewhere near the cliffs alone on the day your husband went missing.' He showed her the image of her driving back into town at 5.52pm. 'So, here you are, coming back by yourself. What happened to your husband in that time?'

'I don't know. He just disappeared.'

'Disappeared off the cliff when you pushed him?' asked Andy.

'No!'

'We know he was a bit of a bully, you can tell us what happened, Sukhi.' She sniffed. Jim could see that she was about to cry, and a tiny part of him wanted to let her off, but he couldn't.

'What happened?' he asked.

'Nothing happened. I don't know what happened.'

'Your husband's neck was broken and he had other fractures when he was found. The pathologist says this is consistent with a fall from the cliffs. Shall I show you the pictures from the report?' She began to cry properly now.

'My client needs a break,' said Mira.

'OK,' said Jim. 'I'm stopping the recording.'

'I think we've got her,' said Andy once they were outside the room. After ten minutes they went back in with a tray of tea. Jim thought of all the tea and coffee he'd been offered at the Sumals' and how their business, Flakies anyway, was about bringing people things to make them feel better – the comfort of ice cream and chocolate, treats on a washed-out summer's day, things to quench the thirst, swirls, sprinkles, and sweeties, chocolate-dipped cones, watermelon sorbet, and Oreo ice cream. Her husband had clearly been a nasty piece of work. If he threatened a young female tenant the way he had Kayleigh, what must have he been like to his wife? Despite these thoughts, Jim started the recording and carried on.

'So, your husband disappeared, but it wasn't you who reported him missing, it was your daughter, Kiran, is that correct?'

'We did it together.'

'But she made the phone call? We have it on tape.'

'Yes.'

And so it went on. Was she pleased that he hadn't come back? Had he bullied her? Was he ever threatening to her or the girls? Was he having an affair? Had she found out something about him? Did she know he'd be pressuring a female tenant for sex?

There was a sharp intake of breath at that. She looked horrified, but all she said was 'no comment'.

'Please,' she said. 'I need to go home. I need to be with my girls.'

'We can keep you here for much longer before we charge you,' said Andy. 'Think about that. Why not just tell us what happened.'

'Nothing happened.'

'You went to the cliffs, your husband had injuries consistent with a fall from the cliffs, but nothing happened?'

'No comment.' She was crying again.

'My client needs a break.'

'OK, that's enough for now,' said Jim. 'We're going to keep you here though.'

'No!'

'They can do that, Sukhi, for twenty-four hours, then they have to charge you or let you go,' said Mira Anand.

They locked her up.

'You gonna charge her, Boss?' Grace asked. She'd been watching through the glass. 'We got everything we need?'

'The Fitbit gives us a likely time of death after he's been walking and then relaxes,' said Jim. 'But there might be more pictures from the trail cams – maybe on the actual day. We've got circumstantial footage of her driving near there, but that's all. We might have them both going along the path through the woods, and only her coming back. That'll nail it. I'm gonna see about that now. Can you stay and do the paperwork, Andy?'

'OK, Skip.'

'You need me?' asked Grace.

'Maybe not. I hope those girls are OK. Can you check in on them?'

Jim needed some air. Maybe it was just the heat, but seeing Sukhi Sumal crying like that tugged at his achy breaky heart. Now all he could think of was her kids losing their mother as well as their dad. But he needed to make progress on the case. He decided to release a media update before he went to the aquarium to ask Arthur about the wildlife cam. He glanced down at the red dots that were still visible on his arm. What about those?

What Jane Knew

Diana was annoyed to see that she had forgotten her packed lunch. She'd had a busy morning of manicures and eyebrow tidies – lots of clients but none of them paying much and she had an equally busy evening planned, making chutney for the WI stall at the Extravaganza. It was getting on for three before she had time to nip out and get something. Leaving her newish assistant in charge, she took her purse, her black knitted-linen cardigan, and the straw basket she always carried in summer. The nearest place was an independent baker. She hoped they'd have something halfway edible. There was a queue of people all taking far too long to choose cakes which they would clearly be better off without. The shop's radio was tuned to a local station playing "Y Viva Espana". If only these bloody tourists had all gone to Spain instead of cluttering up Ottersea with their stupid buggies and sunburnt shoulders. The three o'clock news came on. She braced for the usual litany of warnings not to tombstone off the harbour wall or leave dogs in hot cars and updates about the heatwave and the pending hosepipe ban. But there was something else:

'Police in Ottersea say that a local woman is helping police with their enquiries into the death of Raj Sumal, local landlord and owner of the ice cream parlour, Flakies. The woman was known to Mr Sumal. No charges have yet been made but the police are holding her pending further investigations.'

My God, thought Diana, a local woman. She looked down at her feet to check that she was actually where she thought she was and not somehow arrested and in custody. Her feet were there in her black Fitflop clogs, firmly planted on the baker's tiled floor. And the police had got someone. She could be off the hook – home free.

'Miss, what can I get you? Miss?'

'Oh, sorry. Um...' and suddenly she was as bad as the tourists. 'Um, I don't know.' She saw the girl look to the heavens. 'Just a Diet Coke and one of those Belgian buns. No, not that, I mean, yes. Just those, a Belgian bun and a Diet Coke.'

Diana put them in her basket. The bun was gluing itself to the interior of its paper bag with its icing; that made it all the more appetising. She walked to the seafront and found an empty bench. When she'd devoured the bun, she tore the bag open, scraped off the stranded icing with her finger and licked it all up. She needed the Diet Coke to wash it down, and that was heaven too, especially drinking out of the can, which was something she hadn't done in years. When she'd finished, she saw that a herring gull was standing just inches away from her feet. Instead of telling it to bugger off, she just said:

'Bad luck, Beaky,' and gave it a superior smile. She sat back on the bench in the sun and closed her eyes. And then she thought – Arthur. Arthur and the images. What if he heard about the woman in custody? What if he saw injustice and was compelled to intervene? She knew what he was like. And what if he hadn't really deleted the pictures and they were somewhere else, in some file or backed up online? She realised that in her shock, she hadn't checked that. She had to stop him. She rang her assistant and asked her to do the last appointments and lock up.

Diana set off for the Oceanworld Centre. She had to get

to Arthur before he did anything rash. She hurried along the promenade, wondering about the best way to tackle him. She didn't *think* Arthur would betray her, but what if he'd told someone else? His best friend was an octopus, that much she knew, but what if he'd told that Lottie? She could invite Lottie to dinner and try to work out what she might know. She had to be careful and take time to think, so first she took a walk along the beach to do some foraging.

Grace couldn't stop worrying about Kiran and Nindy. When she got to Flakies, it was shut with a new "Closed Due To Family Emergency" sign on the door. She knocked and rang the bell for the flat upstairs. No reply. She wondered if they'd seen her from the upstairs window. She wouldn't blame them for not wanting to talk to her now. She stood there for a couple of minutes and then walked further along the seafront, hoping that they hadn't gone far. She soon spotted them, sitting on the seawall. Kiran had her arm around Nindy's shoulders and Nindy was tucked right into her, despite the heat. Those poor girls, thought Grace, unsure whether to approach. She carried on walking towards them, but more slowly. Something about the whole thing didn't sit right. As if sensing her presence, Nindy pulled away from Kiran and turned. Grace raised her arm and half-waved. She saw Kiran pull a face.

'Where's Mum?' Nindy asked.

'I'm sorry,' said Grace. 'She's still at the police station. I know it's really tough for you.' Kiran rolled her eyes.

'Right now,' said Kiran, glancing towards Nindy, 'I can't say aloud what I'm thinking.'

'Want to walk?' asked Grace. 'Can I buy you a coffee or an ice cream?'

'OK,' said Kiran. They walked on a bit and soon were at the Oceanworld Centre.

'Would you like to go in,' asked Grace, 'on me?'

'What do you think, Ninds?'

'I don't mind,' whispered Nindy.

'OK,' said Kiran, 'we might as well.'

'It might be nice and cool and peaceful in there,' said Grace.

It was. As it was now past 4pm, things were quietening down. They stopped to look at the jellyfish. Nindy went up close to the glass and Kiran and Grace stepped backwards.

'You know my mum didn't do it – she didn't do anything – she never would. I don't know how you could do this to us. You've seen what she's like,' hissed Kiran.

'It's on CCTV. She was near where your dad was last seen.'

'What? Together?' Kiran turned to Grace. 'Really?' Grace paused.

'I guess I can tell you, your mum will be able to. No. Not together. But she was very close to where he was last seen and at the same time.'

'So? Coincidence! It's a small town. That doesn't mean anything. Mum's always going into town – she likes to – and for little walks – it's what she does.'

'She was in the van. We don't have pictures of her with him yet, just near to where he was.'

'It's fucking ridiculous. You have to let her go.' Kiran stopped and lowered her voice then carried on: 'What happens? How does it work?'

'They can hold her for twenty-four hours without charging her. She has a solicitor, a woman, who's very good. She'll advise your mum. Maybe your mum has records of what she spent on those days to show where she was and what she was doing.'

'She was probably just at bloody Superdrug,' said Kiran. 'I thought you were on our side.'

'I am, Kiran, I'll do everything I can to help you through this.'

'But not my mum? Do you really think she did anything?'

Nindy was back beside them before Grace could answer. They wandered on. Lots of the exhibits seemed pretty morose.

They stood in the tunnel and watched the sharks and turtles swim above them.

'They're in fish prison,' said Nindy. 'When will Mum be home?'

'Soon,' said Grace. 'They just need to check some things with her.' Kiran took Nindy's hand and they walked on.

When they reached the room where Jane the Octopus was, they found that Lottie and Arthur were there, up behind the tank with the lid off.

'Hey Kiran, Nindy,' said Lottie. 'Look, Jane is just having her food for the night.'

'Can I give her some?' asked Nindy.

'Well,' said Arthur, 'it is only meant to be staff behind here…' But they looked so sad and it was all his sister's fault. He gulped, felt himself blushing. 'But, well, we're closing soon, there aren't many people about…'

'Please?' asked Nindy. Lottie looked at him and smiled.

'OK, wait there, I'll come round and get you.' He soon appeared through the 'staff only' door. Grace sat back on the bench by the wall, not wanting to interfere or to have to go too near an octopus. He led Kiran and Nindy round the back and showed them how to wash their hands and arms before they went near Jane.

'Thanks, Arthur. It's kind of you. We're having a pretty bad day,' said Kiran.

'My mum had to go to the police station,' said Nindy.

'You don't have to tell people, Nindy.' said Kiran. 'She's just helping the police find out what happened.'

'I'm sorry,' said Arthur; he didn't know what else to say. He led them up the couple of steps to the platform behind the tank where Lottie was waiting. He clenched his fists so they wouldn't see that his hands were shaking.

'She's friendly if she likes you,' said Lottie.

'Will she like me?' asked Nindy.

'I'm sure she will. She does sometimes squirt people if she doesn't like them, or for a joke,' said Lottie.

'Can I touch her?'

'Put your hands near the water and see what she does,' said Arthur. They stood in a row, Lottie, Kiran, Nindy, then Arthur.

'The police took my mum in for questioning, she actually was arrested,' Kiran whispered to Lottie.

'Oh my God,' she whispered back.

'The woman sitting over there is Grace Brown. She's a copper. She's *meant* to be helping us..'

'I'm so sorry,' whispered Lottie. 'They'll have to let her go soon. She must be innocent.'

'She would never have done anything,' whispered Kiran, 'she just wouldn't. But they found she was near where he disappeared from.' Lottie took Kiran's hand.

Arthur was showing Nindy what Jane was going to have for supper – some parts of a crab – Jane's favourite.

'You can drop some bits in,' he said.

'It's a bit yukky,' said Nindy, 'but I don't mind.' She dropped some claws and pieces in. 'It smells.'

Jane picked up some crab and examined it. They watched as she lifted it to her beak and most of it disappeared. Instead of taking the next bit, she moved slowly up to the surface.

'I think she's coming to see you,' said Arthur. 'She can tell that you're nice, good people.'

'Can I touch her?' asked Nindy.

'Yes, you can just gently stroke her if she lets you. Sometimes she will put one of her arms onto you, but she'll be quite gentle. If you don't like it, just gently move your hand away or I can take her off you.'

Jane let Nindy stroke her mantle and then extended an arm up the side of the tank towards her. Nindy reached out and touched the tip of it.

'That's like shaking hands,' said Arthur, 'she's saying hello.' Jane coiled the end of that arm around Nindy's little wrist. Nindy squealed.

'Will she pull me in?'

'No, and we wouldn't let her even if she wanted to,' said

Arthur. Kiran reached out too and Jane extended another arm to her and then faded to a pale shade of yellowy pink.

'The paler colours mean she's relaxed,' said Lottie. 'She really likes you both.'

'This is so weird,' said Kiran, but she was smiling.

'I love her,' said Nindy.

'So do we,' said Lottie.

'Grace,' said Kiran, addressing her over the top of the tank, 'can you take a picture or video?'

'Sure,' said Grace. 'No flash – I see the sign.'

'We can show Mum when she's home,' said Nindy, 'and send it to Bal.'

'He'll be home tonight,' said Kiran. 'And we should probably get back. Thanks, Arthur, Lottie.'

'But Jane doesn't want you to go,' said Lottie. And she didn't. She extended her arms a little further up theirs.

'I can feel her sucking, will she eat me?' said Nindy.

'No, she's just seeing what you feel like. She senses lots of things through her suckers and skin.' Kiran's phone dinged in her pocket. Jane slid away from them and glided down to where her supper waited.

'Sorry,' said Kiran. 'I guess she doesn't like phones.'

'Don't worry. She probably just wanted something to eat,' said Arthur.

'Come on, Ninds, we should go.' Kiran shook her hands dry, wiped them on her trousers, and got her phone out. 'Oh, that was Bal, he's arrived.' Lottie led them back to the public area and hugged them before they left. Grace walked out with them too. She felt like hugging them, but Kiran quickly led Nindy away.

Jim realised he was following Diana Parks into the Oceanworld Centre. She was carrying a straw basket containing a black garment on top of some sort of vegetable. She strode up to the admissions desk. He supposed she must want to see Arthur.

He did too, for the wildlife cam photos that might put the Sumals on the cliffs together. He hung back but could hear what she said to the lad selling tickets.

'Hello. I'm Diana Parks, Arthur's sister. I need to talk to him, but I don't want to buy a ticket. I really don't want to look at any of the creatures you have here.'

'Um, OK,' said the boy. 'I can page Arthur if you like, he's probably in the middle of something.'

'With something slimy or scaly, I expect. Thank you.' The lad picked up a radio from under the counter, pressed something and spoke into it: 'Arthur to reception, please. Arthur to reception. Someone here to see you.' The radio crackled and then Arthur's voice came back – it sounded as though he was wearing a diving helmet:

'Er, in the middle of something with Jane. Is it there a problem?'

'Nah, it's a lady who says she's your sister.'

'OK. Thanks, tell her I'll be about ten. Thanks.'

'He says he'll be about ten minutes,' said the boy.

'Yes, I heard that, but I can't wait. Could you just let me go through?'

'Er, OK, he says he's with the octopus. You go straight through the shark tunnel.'

'Thank you,' said Diana, and the shiny metal gate swung open to admit her. Jim waited a moment, pretending to read a poster about upcoming events and then approached the desk.

'Hi. I've got an annual pass. Cheers.' He showed it and followed Diana, who walked briskly, seemingly determined not to look at anything but the path ahead. What sort of person didn't even look at the illuminated jellyfish, the electric blue damsels, the lemon sharks, the seahorses or the sea dragons? Well, he thought, the kind of person who sprayed weedkiller on municipal plants and probably enjoyed going at somebody's bald head with a spiky roller. He smirked when she kept following the arrows and was taken to the dead-end room where the piranhas were. She huffed and didn't notice him lurking behind her. When she reached the room where Jane was, he hung back so he could see into it, still without being noticed.

'Hello, Arthur, Lottie,' she said, now all charming. Arthur and Lottie were behind Jane's tank with the lid off. Jane was up at the surface with two arms extended so she could hold their hands. 'So, this is the famous octopus,' Diana went on. 'She is very impressive.'

'Sis, what's up?' said Arthur.

'Oh, nothing, I just thought it would be nice if Lottie came to supper tonight. Would that work for you both?'

'Um, sure,' said Lottie. 'I want to go and see my friend Kiran, but before or after that would be nice.'

'Er, OK,' said Arthur. 'If Lottie's not busy.'

'Great. Why don't you come straight from work?'

'Thanks,' said Lottie, 'I usually go home and shower first…'

'Oh, don't worry about that,' said Diana. 'Come as soon as you can. So, now can I meet the famous Jean?'

'It's Jane,' said Arthur. 'Her name is Jane.' Diana walked forwards and tapped on the tank.

'Don't tap on the glass,' said Arthur.

'Hello Octopus Jane,' said Diana, 'I'm your keeper's sister, ha ha.' Jane uncoiled herself from Lottie and Arthur and slid down to the bottom of the tank. She walked across the sand towards where Diana was standing then stayed still, looking at her.

'She's interested. Do you want to come round and meet her properly?'

'Of course,' said Diana. Arthur disappeared and soon reappeared through the staff only door, got Diana to wash her arms and hands, and led her up to the platform. Jane stayed on the bottom, darkening to a sage green.

'Jane, this is my sister, Diana,' said Arthur. Jane returned to the surface. Diana extended a hand over the water. Jane reached out and put the end of one arm on Diana's wrist, as though she was taking her pulse. 'Stay still,' said Arthur.

'She's getting the measure of you, sensing you through her skin.'

'Euuch,' said Diana and she froze. Jane whooshed away – paused – sent a huge jet of water up out of the tank, straight into Diana's face.

'Fuck!' cried Diana, 'I'm soaked!' Arthur laughed. Lottie snorted. 'That creature – it's so primitive, disgusting!'

'No,' said Arthur, grinning. 'She's extremely intelligent with perceptions that we can't even imagine.'

'God,' said Diana.

'I'll get you a towel,' said Lottie, trying not to laugh. She led Diana off backstage. When Diana emerged a couple of minutes later, she was carrying her basket again. She still looked pretty wet. Jim stepped further back into the shadows.

'I was just shocked,' Diana told Lottie. 'Does she do that to everyone?'

'No,' said Lottie. 'It's unusual.'

'See you later for supper,' said Diana. When she and then Lottie and Arthur were gone, Jim stepped smiling into the room and stood where Diana had.

'Hello, Jane,' he said. 'Do you think she's a wrong 'un?' Jane crossed the tank floor and pressed a tentacle to the glass. He did the same. 'You don't need to reply,' he said. 'I think we both know the answer.' They stood for a little while until the message came over the speaker system saying that the centre was closing soon. 'So, I'd better exit via the giftshop, eh?' He glanced up and noticed that Jane's lid was still slightly open. ''Spect they'll be back in a minute to lock you up properly, eh Jane?' He remembered that he'd come to ask Arthur about the photos. 'Never mind, Jane,' he said, 'I'll pay them a visit.' On the way out, he stopped for a moment to look at the display of washed-up rubbish. God, he thought. Humans.

Back-Up Chutney

'I've got to go and see Kiran,' said Lottie, as she and Arthur walked along the seafront together at six o'clock after they'd locked up. 'It's nice of your sister to invite me, but I really have to see Kiran. You can come too – we'll go after supper if that's not rude.' Arthur slowed and then stopped and leant over the rail to look at the sea.

'There's something about my sister I haven't told anyone. I promised not to. She made me promise.'

'Is she ill?' asked Lottie. She stood beside him and gazed at his kind face, but he just looked out to sea. 'I know you've been worried about something.'

'Ill? Kind of.' He still didn't look at her.

'I'm so sorry,' said Lottie, resting her hand on his upper arm. 'Maybe Jane knew – maybe she can detect diseases, taste them through the skin, and that's why she reacted like that. I mean, it seemed funny but…'

'She could tell there's something wrong with Diana. She squirts Helen, but I'm sure that's just cos of the nicotine. She never does it that violently. That was different.'

'You can tell me,' said Lottie. 'I won't let Diana know I know, if you're sworn to secrecy.'

'It's awful,' said Arthur, and he turned to look at her. 'But please, don't say anything.'

'I promise,' said Lottie.

'You might not say that if you knew what I was going to say.' Now she slipped her hand into his.

'You can tell me.'

'You remember my laptop, when it got wet, and I was so freaked out? There were, are, photos on it, of Diana. And Kiran's dad.'

'Oh my God. Does Kiran know? Does her mum know?'

'It's not like that. I shouldn't have said anything.'

'You have to tell me now, tell the police if you know anything – they've got Kiran's mum. Did *she* do it?'

'It wasn't Kiran's mum. I know that.'

'Did Diana have something to do with it? Arthur, you should tell the police what you know.'

'I can't. She's my sister. I'm sorry. I shouldn't have put you in this position. You don't have to come now. I'll say you're ill. She won't know I told you.'

'I want to come,' said Lottie. 'I want to be with you. We'll just have supper and act normal. And then we'll talk. Come on.' Still holding his hand, she led him away from the sea.

'Lottie, come on in. Don't worry about your shoes,' said Diana. Lottie took her sandals off anyway. She knew it was a no-shoes house. Something smelled vinegary. 'I've started making some chutney,' said Diana, 'for the Ottersea Extravaganza. It's a kind that doesn't need to mature. We always have a stall – I expect Cass's told you all about it.' She led them into the kitchen. There was a large saucepan of soup and one of chutney on the stove and a line of sparkling jam jars stood waiting. The table was set with wine glasses and napkins and there were roses from the garden in a jug. 'Do sit down. White wine will go well with this.'

Lottie smiled and dared a glimpse at Arthur. Maybe Diana was trying to set them up. She must know the internship was nearly over and nothing had really happened between them.

There was a loaf of crusty bread with some slices already

on the table and a bowl of strawberries waiting on the side. 'There's some vegan cheese to go with it the soup. Arthur, do pour the wine.'

'This is so nice,' said Lottie. 'I wish I'd got changed. I feel awful in my work clothes.'

'Don't be silly,' said Diana. 'Arthur knows I never mind what people wear.' Arthur handed Lottie a glass of wine. She took a sip.

'Let me just go wash my hands,' said Lottie, going over to the sink. She washed and dried her hands, but stayed there, looking through the window. 'Your back garden is so pretty,' said Lottie. 'Can I have a look? I love seaside gardens. It's my dream to have one like Derek Jarman's, all pebbles and horned poppies and sea holly.'

'Ours is a bit more cottagey,' said Diana. 'Our mother loved that way of planting.'

Arthur and Lottie, still with bare feet, carried their glasses outside. Diana followed them out.

'Oh, it's lovely,' said Lottie. The garden was small and square with a high brick wall around it. There were old stone animals. All the plants looked long established – roses, lavender, salvias, many kinds of thyme, and pots with chillies and tomatoes in. 'Who looks after it?'

'I do most of it,' said Diana. 'Arthur does any heavy lifting.'

'I built the wormery, though,' said Arthur. 'And the hedgehog house and the bird and bat boxes.'

'I'd love a wormery, if I ever have my own garden,' said Lottie. 'I was going to make one for our student flat, but everyone else was so against it, worried the worms might escape.'

'I'll show you,' said Arthur. 'It's really cool. They're tiger worms.'

'No!' cried Diana. 'Er, you'll have to wash your hands again – don't lift the lid – it's—'

But Arthur already had.

'See,' he said, 'you can put anything organic in here and

they're happy.' He picked up some of the fresh leafy stuff on the top – the tops and tails of some white root vegetables.

'God! Don't touch that!' cried Lottie. She slapped at his hand and he dropped it. 'That looks like water parsnip – it's poisonous. Oh my God, wash your hands! Quick! Straight away!' She turned to Diana. 'Did you eat this? Is it in the soup, the chutney? Are you OK?'

'I do feel a little odd,' said Diana.

'You have to go to hospital. We need an ambulance. It's that stuff she showed us foraging.'

'I must have made a mistake,' said Diana.

'Arthur, it could kill her,' cried Lottie.

'Let's go inside,' said Arthur. They went back into the kitchen. He locked the back door behind them and put the key in his pocket. 'Don't touch the food, don't touch anything. Diana, did you know what it was? Did you actually eat any?'

Loud knocking at the front door.

Jim Paddon and another guy stood on the doorstep.

'Hello, Arthur,' said Jim, 'I have DC Andy Barns with me today too. Can we come in?' He turned to Lottie. 'I'm DI Jim Paddon,'

'Oh, thank God,' said Lottie. 'Arthur's sister might have just eaten something really poisonous. We need an ambulance!'

'I bet she didn't eat any of it,' said Arthur.

The detectives stared at him.

'Has your sister eaten poison? Is she trying to poison someone?' asked Jim.

'I don't know,' said Arthur.

'Where is she? Andy, radio an ambulance and assistance. We need backup.'

'It's water parsnip,' said Lottie, 'like water hemlock, dropwort, it grows by the beach. A lady showed us on a WI walk, but I already knew – it's been in the news.'

'Ottersea WI,' said Jim. 'An accident-prone lot this summer. Where's Ms Parks?'

'In the kitchen,' said Arthur.

Diana was tipping the chutney into a bin bag, but the saucepan was still coated in it.

'Smells nice,' said Andy Barns. 'You sure it's poisonous?'

'I'm sure,' said Arthur.

'Go and stand by the front door, Andy. Flag down the ambulance,' said Jim.

'Arthur – it was a genuine mistake,' said Diana, who was at the sink now, blasting the pan with cold water. 'It was only in the chutney, not the soup.'

'Leave that please, and sit down,' said Jim. She carried on. 'It seems like you're a danger to yourself and other people. The ambulance is on its way. Now sit down.' She did but left the tap running. Jim stood right in front of her.

'Turn off the tap please, Arthur.' He did.

'You should wash your hands, Arthur,' said Lottie. 'He touched the plants – there were bits in the compost.' Arthur turned to his sister.

'For God's sake, Diana, you're insane. You've been making jars of poison!'

'Don't be ridiculous, Arthur. It was a silly mistake.'

'You really should wash your hands, Arthur,' said Lottie.

'You seem to like poison, Ms Parks, for palm trees and now for people too. You two,' he jerked his head towards Arthur and Lottie, but didn't take his eyes off Diana, 'go wash your hands in another sink, then come straight back.'

In the bathroom upstairs they soaped their arms and hands together and ran them under the cold tap for ages.

'I'm sorry, Lottie,' said Arthur. 'I think she's gone mad. She always knows what she's doing.'

'It's so surreal,' said Lottie. 'I don't know what to think. How come the police are here?'

'I don't know. Maybe they know something. I mean, what if you hadn't looked in the wormery?'

'Can we hide up here?' said Lottie. But they heard the siren and then voices in the hall and went back down the stairs. Two paramedics were waiting.

'Diana Parks,' Jim said, 'I'm arresting you on suspicion of criminal damage, on suspicion of the murder of Raj Sumal, and on suspicion of planning another murder or murders. You do not have to say anything, but it may harm your defence if you do not mention, when questioned, something that you later rely on in court. Anything you do say may be given in evidence. Cuff her.'

'No way!' cried Diana. 'I will not be taken out in cuffs. I haven't done anything. You can't arrest me for picking the wrong vegetable.'

'Andy, can you go in the ambulance with her. Explain the situation. She might have eaten something poisonous, but it seems unlikely. I'll stay here.'

They took her away.

Lottie and Arthur sat down on the stairs together. Lottie took his hand. It was cold.

'I'm so sorry,' said Arthur. 'She could have killed you, killed lots of people. What if you'd tried it?' Tears were running down his cheeks. She put her arms around him and held him tight. When she looked up, she saw that they were alone. The front door was still open. She got up and closed it. Jim returned from the kitchen.

'It's Lottie, isn't it?' he said. 'I've seen you at the aquarium. Do you two want to get checked at the hospital?'

'We didn't eat any,' said Arthur. 'Lottie saved us.'

'I need to secure the scene here,' said Jim. 'Have you got somewhere you can stay tonight?'

'You can stay with me,' said Lottie. 'Cass won't mind.'

'Just collect what stuff you need, but don't touch anything in the kitchen.'

'But how come you arrived?' asked Lottie.

'Luck in terms of the pickle,' said Jim. 'I came to talk to you, Arthur.' Arthur gulped and wiped his face with his palms. 'Katie Grayling said you helped her with some wildlife cameras, that you downloaded the pictures for her. I need to see everything you downloaded. Where are the pictures?' Jim loomed over them. Arthur stared at his own knees and asked:

'What are you looking for? Kiran said her mum was arrested. Is it for that?'

'Can you just show me what you have?' said Jim. 'We can seize it, but it's simpler if you just give it to me.'

'They're in my downloads. I've still got them. It isn't Mrs Sumal in the pictures.'

'I was coming to that conclusion,' said Jim. 'I had a tip off from a mutual friend.'

'Really? Who?' asked Arthur.

'I was at the aquarium this afternoon. I saw how Jane reacted to your sister. And I think Raj Sumal had an appointment at her salon for hair loss treatment. The marks on his head I asked you about – we thought they were from sea anemones or something, but look at this from a beautician's tool.' He showed them his arm, still speckled red. 'Maybe he just saw your sister for that, maybe there was something between them. I think Marine Heaven was the last place he went.'

Arthur put his head in his hands.

'I need to see that laptop, Arthur.'

The Alarm

Lottie and Arthur lay in each other's arms in the attic bedroom where Lottie had slept alone all summer.

'I still can't believe it all,' said Lottie. 'I wish you'd told me.'

'I'm sorry,' whispered Arthur. 'And how can I ever face Kiran and her family?'

'You would never have let her mum go to jail. I know you wouldn't. You were in an impossible position.' Lottie hadn't been round to see Kiran, but she'd texted and had a message back: 'Mum home. Paddon and Grace drove her. Apologised. Ordered us pizza. They know it wasn't her.'

'I can't stay in Ottersea,' said Arthur. 'It's going to be awful – a trial – what Diana did. I'll have to find a new job, leave Jane, everything.'

'Do something you really want,' said Lottie. 'Run away to sea. Be a Sea Shepherd or Greenpeace volunteer. And you can always stay with me – I'd like that.'

'I'll sell the house, give them the money, but nothing will ever make amends.' His breathing slowed. Had he fallen asleep?

'Lottie,' he whispered, 'do you think water parsnips are toxic to tiger worms?'

'Don't worry. We can check tomorrow. They'll probably know to avoid them.'

One o'clock. Arthur's phone woke him. Oh God, he thought. Diana. Diana in a police cell. But it was the Centre's alarm company. They'd tried to get hold of Helen, but she wasn't answering. There'd been a break-in. The police had been called too. He had to go and check it out. Lottie went with him.

There was a panda car with its light flashing parked by the Oceanworld entrance. A pair of coppers stood beside it; they didn't look very concerned.

'You the boss?' said one of them.

'Deputy,' said Arthur.

'You've got a pair of lads trapped under your netting,' the policeman said, laughing. 'They aren't hurt, but they can't get out.'

'Oh, no, not the puffins!' said Lottie.

Arthur unlocked the door, put the alarm off, and led the policemen through the building to the outside area where he put the lights on. Two boys who Lottie recognised as the teenagers from Flakies stood by the puffins' pool looking queasy and smelling of weed. The puffins, Arthur was relieved to see, had remained oblivious to the invasion and were still asleep.

'What were you doing?' Arthur demanded. 'You could have been killed, or worse, hurt some of the creatures. You could have crushed a puffin or fallen into the otters or seals and been bitten.' The boys stared at their feet.

'Sorry,' said one.

'Yeah, sorry,' said the other.

'The netting's all ripped,' said Arthur. 'Loads of damage.'

'Criminal damage,' said one of the coppers. 'Let's get them out of here.' Arthur led them back through the centre and watched as they were put into the police car, but Lottie stayed in the enclosure, looking up at the stars through the hole in the netting.

'We can't fix this all tonight,' said Arthur when he returned.

'We can try,' said Lottie, 'with a ladder and wire or string or something.'

'It's too high up,' said Arthur. 'And I just feel like letting them all fly free. Let's leave it and go and see Jane. If some get out, they'll be fine. And if they want to come back after it's fixed, we can let them in.' They managed to hitch up the torn netting so the birds wouldn't get tangled in it in the morning. The was a big hole so they could leave when the sun came up if they chose. Lottie and Arthur went back inside and put the light on in the room with Jane.

'She must be in her den,' said Arthur when they couldn't spot her.

'I've always wanted to see her at night,' said Lottie. 'Wait, look, the lid's not on properly.'

'We'll check round the back. I must have been distracted by everything.'

Jane wasn't gone. She was on the platform where they usually stood to talk to her.

'You OK, Jane?' asked Lottie bending down. She seemed OK. She was still very wet. 'Thank God there's no cleaning fluid on the floor, they clean first thing, don't they? I wonder where she was going. Maybe she was going to get a snack from another tank.' As they watched, Jane began to walk down the steps from the platform and to an outlet cover on the ground.

'There's no way she can open that,' said Arthur. But she could. Jane lifted the lid by squeezing an arm underneath it and flipping it upwards. With her other arms she moved it aside revealing the water flowing beneath it.

'Where does that go?'

'Straight out to sea,' said Arthur.

'Should we put her back? What if she gets stuck or hurt?'

'I think she'll be OK, it's just a pipe on the way out, nothing to stop her. She's choosing freedom. The water temperature will be what she's used to. She's so clever. She started life in the sea.'

'We'll lose our jobs. Is there CCTV?'

'Not at night. Only when the public are in. I'm going to have to leave anyway.'

They knelt beside Jane, stroking her mantle.

'Good luck, Jane,' said Lottie.

'Goodbye, Jane. We love you,' whispered Arthur. Jane slipped down into the water and was gone. They knelt there in case she came back, but she didn't. After a while they put the cover halfway back over the outlet, turned out the lights and left.

'This will be my fault too,' said Arthur. 'I'm the one who should have checked the tank.' Lottie kissed him.

Any One of Us

Katie wanted to take some flapjacks to the prison where Diana was on remand, but Caroline thought they wouldn't be allowed.

'You could hide a file or a knife in them if they weren't cut up really small. Anyway, you know she doesn't eat sugar,' Caroline said.

'How about cheese straws?' said Katie. 'You couldn't hide much in a cheese straw.'

'Dairy,' said Caroline, 'white flour.' So Katie decided not to.

When they arrived, they were pleased to see that Diana wasn't dressed in a grey tracksuit.

'Oh, I can wear my own clothes,' she said. 'And I had make-up and toiletries packed for such sudden eventualities, though I had to remind Arthur to check my list of things he had to do. He'd forgotten about it, of course.'

'How are you doing? What's it like?'

'Oh, I'm very popular,' said Diana. 'I've been doing people's nails – you wouldn't believe the state of some women's. And I've written to head office about starting a branch of the WI. But Katie, your hair looks wonderful – *so* much better.'

'Thank you,' said Katie, smoothing her hands over the sleek bob that had replaced her long grey tresses. 'I do feel transformed.'

'It was very nice before too,' said Caroline.

'We're so sorry you ended up here, Diana,' said Katie. 'It must be awful.'

'I've no regrets, though I won't tell anyone else that. And I haven't been found guilty yet. We're planning on a red mist, diminished responsibility defence,' said Diana. 'And they aren't charging me about the chutney – they don't think that one would stick. *Such* an easy mistake to make.'

'Who was it intended for?' whispered Caroline.

'It was just a mistake,' said Diana, smiling. 'As if I would have given out cheese scones with my chutney to the more obnoxious members of Shanty Crew at the Extravaganza! I would never do something like that. Or given some to the police when they came round, though I didn't get a chance for that. Pesky kids, Arthur and that Lottie. I did consider going down in a blaze of glory. Chutney for everybody. It's the spirit of the WI, isn't it, having some chutney ready in the cupboard…'

'Arthur and Lottie told Cass what they knew, about Raj Sumal, the sex for rent thing, and what happened,' said Caroline, in a low voice. 'Cass told us.'

'I didn't exactly plan things,' said Diana, whispering from behind her hand. 'When I realised who he was, how he'd threatened Kayleigh, what he assumed I'd do… rage, I suppose. And clingfilm and a towel.'

'None of us planned things this summer,' said Caroline, 'with bath bombs or plastic bags, or clingfilm and towels. And who knows what other mishaps take place, up and down the country, the millions of angry, invisible women. Any one of us might have done it.' She reached across the table and squeezed Diana's hand.

'Yes,' whispered Katie, 'any one of us.'

She took Diana's other hand and the three of them sat there, linked, together, at least for a while.

Ottersea Extravaganza

August Bank Holiday weekend. Saturday, 6am. The WI's secret knitting and crochet team was ready for action. They met at the sea pool with everything they'd made, ropes, and two stepladders. It was already hot; it seemed the heatwave would never end. The evening before the garments had been stitched together with Katie directing proceedings. Now there were hooded ponchos and bathing gear for Ottersea's most exposed residents – the bronze *Wild Swimmers*. Katie had made a toy octopus and a toy shark for the children. They moved swiftly and efficiently to clothe the statues and soon, instead of them looking chilly and undignified, even given the incessant heat, they were ready for a perpetually jolly day at the beach.

'Well, Si Jacks should really approve,' said Cass. 'What we're doing is guerrilla art, or at least a community project.'

'His mum will definitely approve,' said Caroline. 'She told me she knew Si had modelled that poor one on the end with the dimpled thighs and all the rolls on her.'

Once *The Wild Swimmers* were properly clad, the WI friends shed most of their own clothes for a dip. Kiran, Sukhi and Nindy came past on their early morning walk with Flossie, their spaniel puppy. They stopped and laughed at the newly dressed statues. Cass got out of the pool to chat to them.

'It's very good,' said Sukhi.

'Would you like to start swimming with us?' asked Cass.

'I'll come tomorrow,' said Sukhi. 'Kiran, you should invite Grace. They've become such good friends,' Sukhi told Cass. 'She's very nice, for a police officer.'

Not long afterwards, Lottie and Arthur walked past on the way to open the Oceanworld Centre. They stood for a minute to admire the new-look sculpture, though they both knew the woollen garments wouldn't endure forever. It was Lottie's last weekend at the centre, and Arthur had only a few more weeks of his notice to work. He had an interview to become a Sea Shepherd volunteer and was waiting to hear back from The British Antarctic Survey, though Lottie was hoping he wouldn't go quite that far away. Diana's trial date was pending. It looked as though they weren't going to charge him with aiding and abetting. He suspected that Jim had something to do with that. But Arthur knew that whatever he did, he could never make amends to the Sumals. He was planning on giving them the house or the proceeds of its sale, even though Lottie said they already owned plenty of houses.

On Bank Holiday Monday, the Ottersea Shanty Crew gathered to perform beside *The Wild Swimmers*. They dedicated a song to their fallen members, Graham Grayling and Jeremy Todd, who had been taken so suddenly that summer. Nearby, the WI were doing brisk trade from their Pimm's lolly, strawberries and cream, and cake stalls. The only chutney for sale was runner bean and green tomato, not made by Diana, but there was plenty of jam.

DI Jim Paddon decided to walk down to the beach. Sitting outside The Blue Anchor were PCs Poltree and Potterton with their wives and kids.

'Hey, Sarge, join us for a pint?' called PC Poltree. Jim glanced at his watch. It was 12.30.

'OK,' he said, 'thanks. I guess it's five o'clock some-where.' He got a round in for everyone with J2Os for the little Poltrees and Pottertons. He drank his pint, but left rather than join them for pub grub.

Jim walked on to Flakies and bought an orange sorbet through the window.

'I always knew you were an orange sorbet guy,' Kiran told him.

'How are you all doing?' he asked.

'Oh, you know, not great, but not as bad as before.' He saw that Grace, on her day off, was there behind the counter, wearing a Flakies T-shirt, looking very at home.

He walked down to the beach to eat his ice cream. And then he couldn't resist. He took off his socks and shoes, rolled up his trousers, and went for a paddle. The first clouds he'd seen in what felt like months were rolling in from the Atlantic. The temperature dropped. The waves grew bigger. And finally, finally, it began to rain. Jim stood there, feet in the sea, as huge drops soaked his hair and shoulders through his shirt.

Senescence

Along the coast, in an undersea cave, Jane stood guard in her blue and green world. After the swishing and swirling of her escape, she'd built a garden of oyster shells beneath the waves. Another of her kind had appeared, coming to her through the kelp, dancing with her in the eel grass. She'd accepted his gift, then killed and consumed him. He would have died soon after anyway. It was the natural order of things. Females can do that, they don't always, but they can.

Now Jane had stopped eating and was getting paler; even if a crab walked right past her den, she ignored it. The garlands of her eggs hung around her and she tended them, blowing clean water across them and protecting them from hungry fish. The babies were developing inside. She understood this, of course.

Acknowledgments

I am very grateful to Lauren Wolff-Jones, Cari Rosen, Lucy Chamberlain, Ditte Loekkegaard, Olivia Le Maistre and their colleagues at Legend Press for their invaluable help and advice. I would also like to thank Rose Cooper for the gorgeous cover design, and Stephen, my beloved family and friends, and my dear colleagues at the University of Southampton for their help and encouragement. Robbie Robinson, the Aquarium Technician at the National Oceanography Centre, University of Southampton kindly answered my questions about being an aquarist. He advised against an aspect of this novel's ending. Dr Victoria L. Humphreys was immensely generous with her time and her knowledge of being a detective and matters of police procedure. Any mistakes are mine.